THE
NIGHT
SESSIONS

KEN MACLEOD

www.orbitbooks.net

ORBIT

First published in Great Britain in 2008 by Orbit
This paperback edition published in 2009 by Orbit

A CIP catalogue record for this book is
available from the British Library.

ISBN: 978-1-84149-648-1

Typeset in Garamond by M Rules
Printed and bound in the UK by
CPI Mackays, Chatham ME5 8TD

Papers used by Orbit are natural, renewable and
recyclable products sourced from well-managed forests and certified
in accordance with the rules of the Forest Stewardship Council.

Mixed Sources
Product group from well-managed
forests and other controlled sources
www.fsc.org Cert no. SGS-COC-004081
© 1996 Forest Stewardship Council

Orbit
An imprint of
Little, Brown Book Group
100 Victoria Embankment
London EC4Y 0DY

An Hachette UK Company
www.hachette.co.uk

www.orbitbooks.net

To Steve Cullen

Thanks to Carol, Sharon, and Michael, for all the usual reasons.

Thanks to Mic Cheetham, Farah Mendlesohn, and Charles Stross for reading and commenting on the first draft.

I came across the idea of high-rise farms in Karl Schroeder's article 'Rewilding Canada' at WorldChanging.com (www.worldchanging.com/archives//007000.html).

'The government of the United States of America is not in any sense founded on the Christian religion, nor on any other.'

Thirty-First Amendment to the Constitution of the United States

PROLOGUE: ONE YEAR EARLIER

'Science fiction,' said the robot, 'has *become science fact*!'

John Richard Campbell groaned, as much at the cliché as at having been wakened from his uncomfortable doze. He shifted in his seat, pushed the blanket away from his face, resettled his phone clip and sat up. As he adjusted the backrest to vertical he noticed only a score or so of other passengers stirring. The great majority were sleeping on, and even most of those awake were staring blankly at whatever was playing in their eyewear. Business flyers, he guessed, who'd already seen the sight often enough. Campbell had opted to be wakened at the approach to the equator, for the same reason as he'd chosen a window seat. He didn't want to miss seeing the Pacific Space Elevator. With its Atlantic counterpart – or rival – it was possibly the most impressive, and certainly the most massive, work of man. A new Tower of Babel, he'd called it once, but he had to see it.

'The elevator is now visible to passengers on the right-hand side of the plane,' the robot's voice murmured in the phone clip. 'Passengers on the left will be able to see it in a few minutes, after we turn slightly to avoid the exclusion zone.'

Campbell pressed his cheek against the window and his chin against his shoulder, cupped his left hand to his temple to cut out the reflections from the dim cabin lighting, and peered ahead and to starboard. In the dark below he saw a spire of pinprick lights. From its summit a bright line extended straight up, for what seemed a short distance. Carefully angling his gaze upward along the line, Campbell spotted a tiny clump of bright lights directly above the spire, about level with the aircraft along the line of sight. He had time to see its almost imperceptible upward motion before the nose of the plane slowly swung starboard and cut it from view. Campbell felt the window press harder against his cheekbone as the aircraft banked.

'You can no longer see the crawler,' said the robot voice, 'but if you look farther up, to the sky, you may just be able to see the elevator in space. From this angle it appears as a shorter line than you may expect, but as bright as a star.'

And so it was. Campbell stared at the hairline crack in the night sky until it passed from view. Near its far end, he fancied, he could see a small brightening of the line, like a lone bead about to drop off the string, but he couldn't be sure: at 35,786 kilometres (less twelve, for the height the aircraft was flying at) the Geostation was tiny, and even the more massive counterweight beyond it, at the very end of the cable, was hardly more visible.

Campbell settled back. The sight had been worth seeing, but he could understand why the frequent fliers hadn't stirred for it. At the cockpit end of the aisle the cabin-crew robot had turned its fixed gaze towards the left-hand window seats and was no doubt murmuring in the phone clips of those passengers now craning their necks and peering out. Campbell guessed that they had a better view. He decided to book a window seat on the other side on the way back; the return-flight corridor passed on the western side of the elevator.

He turned to the window and let his eyes adjust again to the dark. The viewing conditions weren't perfect by any means, but he could make out the brighter stars. After a few minutes' watching he saw a meteor, burning bright orange; then, shortly afterward, another. Each time it was his own intake of breath that he heard, but the fiery meteors seemed so close he imagined he could hear the whoosh.

After a while the position became uncomfortable. He switched off the robot commentary channel, tilted the backrest as far as it would go, pulled the blanket over his head and tried to sleep. He was sure he wouldn't, but the next thing he noticed was that the blanket was on his knees and light from the window was in his eyes. The dawn sky glowed innumerable shades of green, from lemon to duck-egg to almost blue, like the background colour in a Hindu painting, and turned slowly to a pure deep blue over ten minutes or more as he watched. He dozed again.

The cabin bell chimed. The robot channel clicked itself back on. The drop-down screen above the seat in front showed the aircraft approaching the US West Coast, the local time as two p.m. Up front, and far behind, cabin-crew robots had begun shoving trolleys and handing out coffees. Campbell looked out, seeing white wakes like comets on the blue sea; wavy cliffs like the edge of a corrugated roof. Campbell's legs ached. He stood, apologised his way past the two other passengers beside him, and made for the midship toilet. By the time he got back the trolley and its dollies were two rows away. He settled again.

The trolley locked, the trolley-dolly halted. It had an oval head with two lenticular eyes and a smile-shaped speaker grille, and a torso of more or less feminine proportions, joined at a black flexible concertina waist to an inverted cone resembling a long skirt.

'Black, no sugar, please,' Campbell said.

The machine's arm extended, without its body having to lean, and handed him a small tray with coffee to spec, kiwi-fruit juice and a cereal bar.

'Thank you,' he said.

'You're welcome,' said the robot.

The passenger next to him, a middle-aged woman, accepted her breakfast without saying anything but: 'White, two sugar.'

'No need for the please and thank you,' she said, as the dolly glided on. 'They're no smarter than ATMs.'

Campbell tore open the wrapper of his cereal bar and smiled at the woman.

'I thank ATMs,' he said.

Campbell turned the robot commentary back on as the aircraft flew over LA. He couldn't take his gaze from the ground: the black plain, the grey ribbons of freeways, the grid of faint lines that marked where streets had been.

'. . . At this point the Christian forces struck back with a ten-kiloton nuclear warhead . . .'

Irritated, Campbell cut the commentary and sat back in his seat. The woman beside him, leaning a little in front of him to look out herself, noticed his annoyance.

'What's the matter?' she asked.

Campbell grimaced. 'Calling the rebels "the Christian forces". There were just as many Christians on the government side.' He shook his head, smiling apologetically. 'It's just a bug of mine.'

'Yeah, well, it isn't the government side that has plagued us in NZ ever since,' the woman said. She folded a scrap of her breakfast wrapper and worried at a seed stuck between two of her broad white teeth. 'It's the fucking Christians.'

'I'm a fu— a fundamentalist Christian myself,' said Campbell, stung into remonstrance.

'The more fool you, young man,' the woman said. She probed with her tongue behind her upper lip, made a sucking sound and then swallowed. 'I used to go to church too, you know, when I was your age. Nice little church we had, all wooden, lovely carvings. Kind of like a marae, you know? Then these American Christians came along and started yelling at us that we were heathen for having a church that looked Maori. Well, the hell with them, I thought. Walked out through their picket line, went to the nearest kauri tree to think about my ancestors, and never looked back.'

'I'm very sorry to hear that,' Campbell said. 'A lot of these American exiles aren't true Christians, and even those that are are sometimes high-handed. So I don't approve of what happened to you. Not at all.'

'Well, thanks for that!' She didn't sound grateful. 'And what would "true" Christians have done, huh?'

'Oh,' said Campbell, 'they'd have first of all proclaimed the gospel to you, and only after they'd established that you or some of you were seriously and genuinely trying to follow Christ – and the apostolic form of church government – would they have raised the secondary matter of church decoration.'

'Jesus!' the woman said, blasphemously but aptly. 'You mean you think just the same as they did, you'd just be more tactful about it.'

Campbell smiled, trying to defuse the situation.

'Not many people call me tactful.'

'Yeah, I can see that. OK, let's leave it. What do you do?'

'I'm a robotics engineer,' Campbell said.

'My son's studying that,' the woman said, sounding more friendly. 'Where do you work?'

'Waimangu Science Park,' Campbell said.

'That place!' The woman shook her head, back to hostility again. 'You know, that's one of the things I resent the most about these goddamn Yank exiles. Cluttering one of our NZ natural wonders with their creationist rubbish!' She gave him a sharp look. 'Robotics engineer, huh? I suppose that means you maintain the animatronic Adam and Eve and the dinosaurs and all the rest of that crap.'

She crushed her empty coffee cup and threw it on the floor, apparently by reflex, as she spoke. Her anger took Campbell aback.

'The displays aren't as intrusive as you might think,' he said. 'There's only a handful of animatronics, and a few robots. Most of the displays are virtual, a package that visitors can download to their frames.'

The woman compressed her lips, shook her head, turned away and put her frames on. Campbell shrugged and looked out of the window. The afternoon sun picked out the table-lands and mesas and escarpments, and after a while the landscape below opened up into a single enormous feature. Campbell became aware of the woman leaning sideways again. He leaned back, to give her a better view. She looked down, her eyewear pushed up on her forehead, until the Grand Canyon was out of sight.

'Doesn't look much like Waimangu,' she said.

Campbell found himself giving her a complicit grin.

'You're right about that,' he said. 'I don't believe in flood geology.'

'What *do* you believe in, then?'

'I believe the Bible,' said Campbell. 'Which means I believe it about the Creation and the Flood, and the dates when these happened. I just think it's presumptuous to look for *evidence*. We should take God's word for it.'

'So you don't think the fossils were left by the Flood?'

'No.'

'So how do you explain them?'

'I don't *have* to explain them,' said Campbell. 'But I can point out that it's a *presumption* that they're the remains of animals. What we *find* in the rocks are bone-shaped stones.'

The woman gave him a look of amused disbelief. 'And feather-shaped stones, skin-shaped stones, footprint-shaped stones . . . ?'

'As you say, stones.'

'So God planted them to test our faith?'

'No, no! We can't say that. Before people started *believing* that these stones were remains, they believed they were natural created forms of rock. It didn't trouble their faith at all.'

She bumped her forehead with the heel of a hand. 'And how do you explain the stars, millions of light years away?'

'How do we know they're millions of light years away?'

'By measuring their parallax,' the woman said.

'Good,' said Campbell. 'Most people don't even know that, they just believe it because they were told. But what the astronomers actually measure, when they work out a stellar parallax, is the angles between beams of light. They then *assume* that these beams come from bodies like the Sun, for which they have no independent evidence at all.'

'Oh yes, they do! They have spectrograms that show the composition of the stars.'

'Spectrograms of beams of light, yes.'

'And now we have the space telescopes, we can see the actual planets – heck, we can even see the clouds and continents on Earth-sized planets, with that probes-flying-in-formation set-up, what's it called?'

'The Hoyle Telescope. Which gathers together beams of light.'

'Which just *happen* to form images of stars and planets!'

'It doesn't just happen. God designed them that way. Not to fool us, of course not, but to show us His power, His infinite creativity. He *told* us He had made lights in the sky. It's *we* who are responsible if we make the unwarranted assumption that these lights come from other suns and other worlds that God told us nothing about.'

'So the entire universe, outside the solar system, is just some kind of light show?'

'That's as far as the evidence goes at the moment,' said Campbell. 'And speaking of evidence, I'll remind you that if these supposed galaxies were real physical bodies billions of years old, then they wouldn't hold together gravitationally. They'd long since have spun apart. The only explanation the astronomers have for *that* is dark matter, matter they can't see and have never found or identified, but which they postulate because it's necessary to explain away the evidence of a young universe on the basis of their assumptions.'

The woman screwed up her eyes for a moment.

'This is like a nightmare,' she said. 'Don't tell me any more of what you believe in. I just don't want to know.'

Campbell had several replies primed for that, but he just nodded.

'Fair enough,' he said.

He turned back to the window.

They didn't talk for the rest of the flight. Campbell alternated between dozing and looking out of the window, and came to full alertness as the long descent began. Around eight a.m., on what felt like a day too soon, he noticed the green tip of Ireland, then the green and brown hills of the West of Scotland. The seat-belt sign came on. The trolley-dollies cleared trash and ensured that everything was stowed. Quite suddenly, Edinburgh appeared on the horizon, and a few moments later the aircraft began to spiral down. The land whipped past in a giddy swirl that slowed gradually as the aircraft began, even more disquietingly, to yaw like a falling leaf. The woman beside Campbell grasped his left hand with her right. Surprised, he turned and smiled, but her eyes were shut tight. Campbell could see towers all around, shockingly close. The downward jets cut in, a brief blast. The craft swayed from side to side, side-slipped a little, then, after another downthrust, it settled on the landing pad and rolled gently to its bay a few tens of metres away.

The woman opened her eyes and let go of Campbell's hand.

'Thanks,' she said, and that was all she said. Campbell was still feeling smug as he retrieved his rolling case from the overhead locker and debarked. He nodded and smiled to the robot that thanked him in the doorway and wished him a pleasant stay or safe onward journey. The heat struck him as soon as he stepped through the exit door. He'd known to expect it but, coming straight from a New Zealand winter via twenty hours in the aircraft's air-conditioned coolness, the thirty-degrees-Celsius heat opened his pores instantly. He strolled through Customs, dragged his case along walkways and underpasses to his pre-booked Travelodge check-in, and took the lift to his room. He thanked God it was air-conditioned.

The view was of the corner of one tower and the back of another. Shadows of aircraft passed over like predatory birds every few seconds. Campbell unpacked a change of clothes, laid his Bible on the bedside cabinet, and took his washbag to the bathroom. After showering, shaving, and putting on fresher and lighter clothes, he felt ready to face the Scottish August heat. He was, as he'd expected, jet-lagged, but he intended to surf that zoned-out sense of unreality to get him through the awkward confrontation to come. That, plus some instant coffee and a prayer. He suspected that the men he had come to meet were counting on the same thing to compel him to honesty. That seemed the most plausible reason why they'd insisted on meeting him the morning he arrived.

His instructions were quite specific. He was not to use

any public transport or taxi. He was not to phone. He just had to walk, following the map. The map was hand-drawn. Campbell had it folded inside his Bible. He took it out and looked at it while he sipped his coffee. He had been warned not to store it on frames or any other electronic device. Which was fine with Campbell. He had a good memory, drilled by childhood years of catechism and Bible study, and he didn't use frames anyway.

He folded the map, stuck it in his shirt pocket, and headed out. At the exit it took a moment's puzzled gaze at the sky for him to figure out which direction was north.

Turnhouse had a raw feel, like all airport developments. The strips followed the old runway paths. Of all the ways to get around – skybridge, tunnel, monorail, shuttle bus, bicycle – surface walking was the worst provided for. Campbell made his way along narrow weed-grown side-walks between and around the feet of the towers. Office blocks of HSBC, Nissan, Honeywell, Gazprom; factories of ever-changing Carbon Glen start-ups; high-rise farms, car parks, the control tower like the hilt of a giant sword; slowly turning slanted slopes of solar-power collectors whose supercooled cables dripped liquid nitrogen through carbon-dioxide frost. Campbell sweated again, cooled only by the downblast of descending aircraft.

Beyond the commercial strips the paths opened to streets of fast-built housing blocks, their buckysheet sides arbitrarily coloured, their windows overlooking well-tended vegetable gardens and scuffed play areas. Every roof bristled with aerials. Every ground floor had its shop or cafe. Vehicles in the throes of repair or adaptation almost outnumbered those in running order. Kids ran around and youths hung about. Campbell dodged soccer balls and pavement cycles, irritated and baffled until he remembered that it was the school summer holidays here. Old people and young parents were the only adults he could see; the others, he guessed, were working in the farm and factory towers or cleaning the offices. Despite these indications of full employment, the place had an air of newness and impermanence, of being the result of a displacement and decantation, the outcome of a scheme contrived elsewhere. Something in the weathering of the older folks' faces was rural rather than urban. Campbell guessed that most of the people were here as a result of losing their homes to coastal flooding, or their livelihoods to the high-rise farms.

The streets stopped where the bulldozers still worked, just beyond a bridge over a deep, fast river. Pennants marked a jagged footpath across the site. Campbell negotiated it to the raw edge of an expanse of long grass. He stopped, as if hesitating to dive into cold water, checked his map and the tiny compass on his key ring and walked on. After a few hundred metres of slogging through what was obviously an abandoned field he reached a cluster of deserted farm buildings. There he turned right along a road under a railway bridge, then turned left sharply off the road to head north again up a slope through trees.

The trees thinned, and at the top of the slope he saw the men he'd come halfway round the world to meet.

They could have been a rock band: six men on the skyline, their long hair caught by the breeze. They wore black homburg hats, long black coats, white collarless shirts, black trousers, and black boots or shoes. As Campbell approached, grinning but apprehensive, the oldest of them strode down the slope to meet him. He was a man in his forties, with lean, lined features and bright grey eyes.

'Mr Campbell!' the man said, grasping Campbell's hand and almost hauling him up. 'John Livingston – pleased to meet you.'

'John Richard Campbell, likewise.'

Campbell held the grip for a moment, delighted and relieved that Livingston looked in life just as he did in his pictures, hale and spare, keen and sharp, like some tough old Covenanter who lived on water and gruel, on the run from moss-troopers and dragoons on the moors. There wasn't much about the man online, and what there was dealt solely with his business activities; he was the owner of a small company based right here at Turnhouse, man-ufacturing carbon-tech components for the space industries. His spiritual endeavours were conducted, it seemed, entirely by word of mouth and – as in his contact with Campbell – by physical mail.

'I trust you had travelling mercies,' Livingston said.

Campbell took a moment to parse this. 'I did indeed,' he said. 'It all went very smoothly.'

'Good, good.'

Livingston led him to the top of the slope, and through a round of handshakes with the other men, all older than Campbell but still in their twenties. George Scott, Archie Riddell, William Paterson, Patrick Walker, Bob Gordon.

'"John Richard", please,' Campbell said, after they'd all called him 'Mr Campbell'. He smiled awkwardly at the group. 'Most people call me JR.'

'Fine, fine,' said Livingston.

At that moment a shadow fell over them, sped across the land, and passed on.

'A superstitious person would have seen that as an omen,' Campbell remarked.

Livingston chuckled. 'As well we're not superstitious, then!'

He looked up into the sky, as though he could see the soleta.

'Mind you,' he went on, 'I'm no so sure it's a good work being done up there, for all that I make money from space. There's something well presumptuous about blocking the sun, in my opinion. "The heavens are the Lord's," as the Psalmist says, "but the Earth hath He given to the children of men." I fear we'd do well not to meddle with the heavens.'

'Well,' said Campbell, 'it's an attempt to correct previous meddling here on Earth.'

'Aye, there's that,' said Livingston. 'Still, that's out of our hands, and right now it is to the Lord's business we must attend. Follow me.'

Campbell saw that they stood at the lip of a quarry about thirty metres deep. A second later Livingston had quite alarmingly vaulted off the edge and disappeared. Campbell stepped forward, the others behind him, and found a drop of about a metre to a narrow shelf, then another such downward step, which Livingston had just taken. Campbell followed the bobbing homburg down a succession of shelves, scree slopes, gorse handholds and chimney gulleys to the quarry's floor. The flat expanse of gravel was cupped on three sides by the quarry cliffs and broken by huge puddles, rock outcrops, clumps of bushes, rusted remnants of machinery, and the inevitable shopping trolley or two.

Livingston didn't look back. He strode to an open space in the middle of the floor and stopped, looking in all directions as the group re-formed around him.

'Walls have windows, Mr Campbell,' he said, noticing the visitor's puzzlement. His gaze flicked around his companions. 'Let us now ask the Lord's blessing on our meeting.'

He bowed his head, the others following suit, and said a short prayer. At the 'Amen' Campbell opened his eyes and straightened up. He tried to stop his knees from trembling.

'This is an informal meeting,' said Livingston, in a formal tone, 'of the Kirk Session of the Free Congregation of West Lothian. No minutes are to be taken. I ask those present to affirm that they will give a faithful account of it, if called upon by the brethren.'

Campbell, after a moment's hesitation, added his 'Aye' to the chorus.

'Very well,' said Livingston. 'We are here to welcome our friend, John Richard Campbell, and to satisfy ourselves as to his saving faith before accepting him to the brotherhood of the Congregation. Now, John Richard, do you understand what is required of you?'

'I do,' said Campbell.

'Do you promise to answer truthfully and without reservation?'

'Yes.'

'What, John Richard, do you understand by the sum of saving knowledge?'

Campbell answered that to everyone's satisfaction.

'And do you aver that that knowledge has by grace been brought home to you, to your soul's salvation?'

'Yes.' That was a question he had no hesitation in answering.

More questions followed: detailed, doctrinal, subtle. Campbell felt on less sure ground here, but his memory for the small print of the Westminster Confession and the Larger Catechism didn't let him down. At the end Livingston nodded soberly.

'Aye, John Richard, you have the root of the matter all right. We thought so, from hearing your discourses. Very powerful, spiritual, and experimental they were.'

Campbell's mouth felt dry. He'd never intended his discourses to go beyond their small circle of hearers in the woods of Waimangu. Yet somehow they had: they'd come to the attention of this tiny church in Scotland, and its elders had been impressed enough to pay his return fare. The airmail letter that enclosed the e-ticket code and the invitation, the instructions and the map had been insistent that no further communication would be possible, and that if any problems arose when he met the elders personally there would be no recrimination. He still felt like a fraud.

'Now,' Livingston went on, 'is there anything more you would like to tell us about your discourses?'

Campbell took a deep breath. 'There is something I have to tell you, which may shock you. I had no opportunity before, and I'm afraid you may feel this has all been for nothing.'

Livingston glanced around the Kirk Session. 'Go on,' he said. 'Spit it out, Mr Campbell.'

'My discourses,' said Campbell, 'were addressed to robots.'

Livingston's eyes held steady. 'What kind of robots?'

'Humanoid robots,' Campbell said. 'The kind that are no longer made, because people find them disturbing. And they're self-aware robots, with the same kind of minds that . . . emerged, we're told, in some combat mechs in the Fai— the Oil Wars. Some of these humanoid robots have taken refuge in Waimangu. A few of these have shown an interest in the faith, perhaps having become curious about the basis for creation science. And . . . I've been talking to them about it.'

'And how, Mr Campbell, would you justify putting the gospel before machines?'

'Because they asked me to,' he said. He had no better answer, and could think of many worse.

'Are we not told,' said Livingston, 'not to cast pearls before swine, nor to give that which is holy unto the dogs?'

Campbell looked down, then up. 'In my . . . teens I published some rash and forward theological speculations, I admit. I disavow them. All I can say is that the machines asked me, most earnestly, and I told them. They showed interest, and asked more, and made a practice of gathering around to listen, and . . . so it went on. I make no claims as to whether the machines have souls, but they do have rational minds. I think – I hope – there is something to be learned from that.'

'And what might that be?'

'The making of artificial intelligence is one of the proudest boasts of the secularists,' said Campbell. 'Next to artificial life, it's the greatest triumph for their materialism. Perhaps greater. They claim to have done what Christians once claimed could be done only by God –

creating a rational soul. Would this triumph not turn to ashes in their mouths if their own creations were to acknowledge the true Creator?'

'If the Lord could speak out of the mouth of Balaam's ass,' said Livingston, 'it's possible He could use a robot's mouth for a similar purpose. Quite aside from the question of the robot's having a soul. Is that what you're saying?'

'Yes!' said Campbell, relieved. 'Exactly.'

'Well, John Richard,' said Livingston, 'we are very glad indeed you have said that. Would you like to know how we came to know of your discourses?'

Campbell nodded, not trusting himself to speak.

Livingston stuck four fingers between his lips and let out a whistle that echoed around the quarry. The silence that followed was broken by the sound of footsteps crunching over the gravel. From behind a rock fifty metres away a man appeared, and walked towards the group. He wore an open-necked short-sleeved shirt over a broad chest and powerful arms. He had a sweatshirt knotted by its sleeves around his waist. Only when he was a few paces away did Campbell notice the subtle abnormality in the texture of his skin, and the unusually sharp definition of his sinews.

The stranger reached out a hand and clasped Campbell's in a firm, dry grip.

'Good morning, Mr Campbell,' he said. 'My name is Graham Orr. I've followed your discourses with great interest. Pleased to meet you at last, sir.'

'Pleased to meet you, Mr Orr,' said Campbell. He glanced, a little at a loss, sideways at Livingston, who was eyeing the encounter with a glint of dry humour.

'Are you – are you—?' Campbell floundered.

Orr took a step back, with a grimmer smile than Livingston's.

'Not to embarrass you further, Mr Campbell,' he said, 'I'm not a robot.' He grimaced. 'I lost my limbs and a lot else in the Faith Wars.'

'Ah,' said Campbell. 'I beg your pardon.'

It had been on the tip of his tongue to say: *We don't call them the Faith Wars*, but to indulge that political correction to this man's artificial face would have been unforgivable. The man looked no older than Campbell himself, his synthetic face showing the age he'd been when its original had been destroyed.

The technology that could give robots an almost, but not quite, human appearance, and the technology that could give a mutilated human being a functionally and cosmetically almost perfect prosthesis were the same. Campbell wasn't even sure which had been adapted for the other purpose – they'd both come out of the surge of technological innovation – and desperate necessity – after the Oil Wars. Both applications were now obsolete – no one manufactured humanoid robots any more, for reasons that Campbell was painfully aware of, and organ and tissue regeneration could now repair every injury short of cortical destruction. He was too disconcerted by his mistake to query why Graham Orr had not chosen that option, but he hardly needed to. Tissue regeneration involved the use of embryonic stem cells, which for true Christians (and Catholics) was no less than murder.

Orr shrugged. 'It's a mistake I rely on, sometimes,' he said. 'And it's not entirely a mistake.' He turned his head and parted his hair at the side, revealing a crude gash-and-repair job on the uncannily precise prosthetic scalp. 'I share my skull with an old comrade. My robot partner. His brain chip is sitting behind my ear. He's the one who heard your sermons first, via the robots.'

Campbell saw the cliffs sway. He closed his eyes for a moment.

'The robots?' he said. '*My* robots? They share what I say to them with *other robots*?'

Orr nodded. 'And my friend in my head shared it with me, and I shared it with John Livingston.'

'And I,' said Livingston, 'showed the recordings to the brethren here, and we decided to meet you and be sure of you before we shared them with the congregation.'

Campbell had a lot of questions on his mind, but the one that came to his voice was: 'Why? Why do you want to show my discourses to your congregation?'

Livingston sighed. 'It's not as if we are spoiled for choice in hearing the Word preached, John Richard. We don't even have an ordained minister. I am just the chair of the Kirk Session. As elders we can all teach, and preach, and we have the great works of the past to study, but we have found no one who speaks to us in the world of modern, compromised, backsliding so-called Christianity, except you. Finding someone who is so sound and sincere as you are is a blessing indeed.'

'But,' protested Campbell, 'surely in all the world there are qualified ministers whose sermons you can listen to? And here in Scotland, of all places, there must be a remnant!'

Livingston looked him square in the eye. 'The Churches here have all compromised!' he cried. 'Here, and everywhere!' His voice took on a sing-song tone as he continued. 'Compromises, compromises, compromises! With the secular state, with the Papists, with the enthusiasts and Congregationalists and modernists and dispensationalists, and with' – here his voice took on a particular vehemence – 'the *sectarians*. There is only one congregation left of the one true covenanted reformed Church of Scotland, and that is us. We have no ordained minister, no student for the ministry, no synod or assembly. We have only our members, our adherents, and this Kirk Session. We are the remnant.'

One by one, the men shook hands with Campbell again, and then left, trekking out of the quarry in different directions. Graham Orr disappeared into the scrub as suddenly as he'd arrived, without another word. Campbell was left alone in the middle of the quarry under the now-noonday sun, with a head full of questions unanswered and unasked. The sun had moved the wrong way in the sky. His brain felt like it was running too many applications at once. He found himself wondering if the robots ever felt the same. It was something he should know. He knew more self-aware humanoid robots, more intimately, than anyone else in the world. Perhaps some veteran systems engineers at Sony knew more *about* such robots than he did, but Campbell was fairly sure that no one else knew so many robots personally. It had been a surprise that they could still surprise him.

The elders of the Free Congregation had surprised him too. He'd expected, at a minimum, an invitation to lunch at someone's house. He'd looked forward, on the flight across, to attending the Congregation's church services and prayer meetings. He had been isolated too long from the fellowship of other believers. But after welcoming him to their brotherhood and assuring him that they looked forward to a long and fruitful association, and to seeing and hearing his discourses relayed from the eyes of robots in Waimangu to a television screen in front of the congregation, the elders had shown an almost indecent haste to depart. They'd warned him against contacting them, urged him to make good use of the week he had in Edinburgh before his return flight by visiting the many historic Reformation and Covenanting sites in the city and its environs, wished him all the blessings and a safe return home – and said goodbye.

It all seemed very strange, and not a little disquieting. But, Campbell reminded himself as he trudged across the floor of the quarry, dreading the climb back to the top, they'd already been more than generous with their hospitality. They'd paid his return fare and his hotel bill. And, more significantly, they had good reason not to see him again: they'd already satisfied themselves on his spiritual soundness – for which he was grateful, having often doubted it himself – and in this land, unlike his own, real and even nominal Christians lived under the shadow of an official disapproval that amounted, almost, to persecution.

Well, he decided as he began the slow and perilous upward scramble, he would indeed make good use of his time. He would spend his week in Edinburgh seeing what life was really like in a state that had been through the Great Rejection.

Campbell walked along George IV Bridge as far as the side of the National Museum, turned around and walked back as far as the National Library, turned again through the crowd on the pavement and walked back and hesitated for the third time at the steps of the club. The building's spire and arched doorway were the only remaining evidence that it had ever been a church. The front was plastered with posters for Festival and Fringe shows, sample loops flickering, tinny laughter and applause clashing; and with a big static advertisement for this evening's gig. He walked past the building again, then doubled back, pushing through the throng. He was going in. He had to see for himself. It was a duty. He had often condemned depravity, but he'd never seen it close up. Far from home, he now had a chance to do so without setting a bad example. He would see it for himself and walk out, never to enter such a den of iniquity again but confident that he had its measure.

This was his fourth night in Edinburgh. His first day, after he'd met the elders, had been a complete washout and write-off. He'd crashed out on his hotel bed, woken around midnight, gone out hungry and had dinner at an all-night noodle shop behind the Gazprom tower. Then he'd crashed again, waking mid-morning as the cleaning robot nudged the door.

His conclusion from the next three days of wandering around was that the streets of Edinburgh showed the benefits and drawbacks not of secular republicanism but of whopping military defeat. Campbell could see more clearly than ever why people in Britain, the US, and their former allies used the expression 'the Faith Wars' for what everyone else referred to as the Oil Wars. Calling the catastrophes of the first two decades of the century the Faith Wars was the only way the former coalition countries could kid themselves they had won. They'd certainly defeated militant Islam, with secular republics now implanted throughout the Middle East. The Israel–Palestine issue could be regarded as solved, at least until the radiation dropped to a level that made the territory worth fighting over again.

In every other respect, the US and UK had been defeated: armies destroyed, economies bankrupted, the region they'd fought to dominate now preferring to do business with the energy-hungry rising powers of their competitors. All they'd got out of the whole mess was the Oil for Blood Programme, which funded generous benefits for coalition war veterans. The main internal political consequence was the Great Rejection, in which the religious factions who'd pushed for the war had had the unwelcome experience of seeing a nasty gleam in the eyes of the returning veterans, a little glint that said: *You're next!*

But the later and longer consequences of that defeat were, Campbell now thought, far more profound. The UK had depended on US military dominance, and on its own partnership in that, to live off oil, arms deals and finance while letting its manufacturing and agriculture go hang. The loss of this privileged position had forced its successor states to fend for themselves, just as it had in the United States. The political consequences in Britain had been less drastic than the US civil war, but the industrial results were manifest everywhere: in the fragrant steam from the pavement stalls hawking late-night snacks to the Festival crowds, in the beetle-wing carapaces of the compressed-air cars hissing past on the wet street, in the whizz of bicycles weaving between them, in the neon signs on the new buildings that rose high in the gaps between the old, and in the quiet spiralling descent of the night flights overhead.

Campbell reached the entrance of the Carthaginian. He wondered how many who went in would recognise the surely deliberate allusion to the building's name when it had been a church: St Augustine's. The entrance way was dark, the booth a rectangle of light on the left. Knees quivering, eyes shifty, Campbell handed over his cash, accepted the ticket-stamp on the back of his hand, waved it at the scanner and stepped into the main hall.

The room was dimly lit, crowded with people bopping and noisy with people talking. Roving spotlights and low-intensity lasers showed up coils and drifts of smoke in the air. At the far end was a pulpit, in which a tall man dressed in black and wearing a white clerical collar worked his machines. To the left of the entrance was a bar, with a cluster of seats and tables, all taken. Campbell decided to walk once around the room, buy a drink at the bar, observe some more and walk out.

Everyone writhed and jived to the same rhythm, and when they spoke they leaned close to each other, some even speaking mouth to ear, but Campbell could hear no music. Now and then most of the faces Campbell could see turned at once, or reacted with widened or closed eyes or a laugh to some sight that he couldn't see. This suddenly made sense of a line on the sticker he'd seen advertising the show: 'silent scene'. Campbell didn't have frames, but he did have a phone clip. He tabbed the device to ambient search. Even at low volume, the music sounded loud, harsh, heavy on the rhythm. He found his feet moving and shoulders swaying to its beat as he paced along the side of the room. There was something insidious about how the music caught him up, but at least (he told himself) it meant he didn't look as out of place as he felt.

He'd never been in a place like this. He'd never so much as been to a dance, not even at school. He'd had to learn some dance steps, but that had been PE. The church he'd been brought up in frowned on dancing. Until now, he'd never quite understood why. Besides the drinking and drug-taking, this was the most appalling display of lasciviousness he'd ever seen in the flesh. Couples and larger groups, some of them same-sex, writhing and rubbing against each other. Sweat beaded their faces and their many areas of bare skin. The air was thick with sweat, with perfumes, with pheromones, with tobacco and cannabis smoke and with wafts of more subtle drugs, of which even a sidestream sniff in passing could make his head feel strange for a moment, giving a jolt of disorientation like being jet-lagged but far, far more pleasant.

The final touch of depravity was the clothes. Campbell had taken some care to check beforehand that the Carthaginian wasn't some kind of fetish club, and had confirmed that it wasn't, but the general attire struck him as a long way from normal. A large minority were, like himself, wearing smart casual – which, in the case of the women, meant immodestly scant. The rest were in various costumes: the men in foppish and flashy variants of Victorian or Edwardian suits, or odd combinations thereof; the women in dresses that admittedly didn't usually reveal a lot of skin but did show off and exaggerate curves, waists, breasts, necks and hips. Long dresses that might have been otherwise modest were given a gross, perverse, erotic charge by being made of shiny black or red PVC or even leather. Some of the styles – to say nothing of elective somatic modifications such as long canine teeth – plainly alluded to dark forces: witchcraft, vampirism, Satanism! There were other outfits that would have looked sweet on little girls, but to see grown women in frilly frocks of pink and white lace and ribbons and so on (and on – the whole mode was structured around excess to the point of parody) was as perverted as it was grotesque. He'd seen Japanese girls in Auckland wearing such costumes – 'gothic lolita', the style was called – and had thought it charming and harmless, but here it seemed too deliberate, too knowing in its disturbing effect.

Campbell made his way past the desecrated pulpit and was just working his way around the corner of the crowd to head back up the other side to the bar for a much-needed cooling beer. As he moved he eyed a tall and lissom woman in one of those faux-innocent costumes dancing alone, a handbag made of similar fabrics at her Mary-Janes-shod feet.

She saw him looking. She smiled, and skipped back a little, as if to invite him to join her. And as she moved, Campbell realised – he wasn't quite sure why – that she wasn't a woman at all. She was a man in lolita drag.

Campbell smiled desperately, shook his head, and retreated as fast as he could towards the bar. He didn't look back. As he wove around the bodies in his path, he discovered that the cross-dresser he'd just spotted was not the only one in the crowd. It was as if he'd suddenly become sensitised to their presence and on three separate occasions, before he finally reached the bar, his noticing was itself noticed. He returned more desperate smiles to knowing looks. He dreaded to think that these people might think he was interested in them. Getting swallowed up in the crush around the bar was a relief. His voice shook a little as he ordered a bottle of lager.

'Anything else?' the barmaid asked, putting the bottle down in front of him.

'Uh, one more, please,' Campbell said, suddenly clocking that one beer wouldn't last him long or quench his thirst. The barmaid gave him an impatient look and handed over another bottle. Clutching them, Campbell elbowed his way out of the crush and looked for a place to sit. No such luck; every table was taken. And every stool at the bar. As he glanced in that direction his gaze was met with a very direct look from a woman sitting on a high stool at the far end. She had a drink, but she was facing out from the bar. She had long red hair and a long green velvet dress with gold embroidery around the neckline. She stared at him, then held up a hand curled around a tall glass and crooked her index finger at him. Her smile had nothing come-hither in it, nothing seductive. It was just a smile, and she was just a woman. Bewildered, nervous, but relieved to have someone to talk to and not to be standing around on his own, Campbell walked towards her as if hauled in on an invisible thread from that beckoning, imperious finger.

'New here?' she said.

Campbell nodded, and switched off the music in his ear.

'Uh-huh,' the woman said. She sipped her drink and looked him over.

'Dave's my boyfriend,' she said.

'Dave?'

She waved a hand toward the far end. 'The VJ. Dave Warsaw.'

'Oh, Dave Warsaw!' said Campbell, as if the name was familiar. The enthusiasm in his voice came from relief that the woman had a boyfriend. He could relax.

'I'm Jessica,' the woman told him, as if that too was something he should know.

'Pleased to meet you,' said Campbell. 'I'm John – John Richard.'

'Well, John-John, don't let your beer get warm.'

Campbell took a slug of beer, its chill spreading from his gullet, and sighed.

'Hits the spot, huh?' said Jessica.

'Yes,' said Campbell.

'Who's the other one for?'

Campbell felt slightly abashed. 'Oh,' he said, 'it's for me too. Didn't want to be back in the queue too soon.'

'I guess not,' Jessica said. She gave him another appraising look. 'Don't get many of your kind here.'

'New Zealanders?' Campbell said, striving for wit.

'No,' said Jessica. 'Homophobes.'

'I'm not—' Campbell began hotly.

'You don't like queer folks,' Jessica said flatly. 'And you're goddamn rude besides.'

'Rude? I haven't so much as spoken to anyone here, except you.'

'Exactly. Not so much as a "No, thank you" to my good friend Arlene, and shocked looks for every other tranny you spotted, until you remembered to plaster on that grin of yours. Not to mention the glares you were giving to every gay couple you noticed on your way down the other side.'

Campbell recoiled. His bottles clinked in his hand. 'You've been *watching* me?'

'Dave's been keeping an eye on you,' said Jessica. She flicked her ear, indicating how she knew. 'He has a way of picking up on people who might be trouble.'

'I'm not here to cause trouble,' said Campbell. 'Just – just – having a look, checking out the scene, you know?'

The lightness of his tone belied his dismay. 'Be sure your sins will find you out,' he'd been told often enough, and that was how he felt.

'Ah!' said Jessica. She smiled again, but this time it was like she was pleased with herself for understanding something. 'You were curious.'

'Yes, just curious, that's it,' said Campbell, much relieved.

'Not hostile, then?'

Campbell frowned. He couldn't lie, but he didn't want not to be off the hook.

'Not exactly,' he said. 'Not to . . . queer folks in particular, no.'

Jessica's lip curled. 'Just to us all, you mean?'

'Not even that,' said Campbell. 'You're no worse than—' He couldn't think what next to say, but saw that he'd already said too much.

'I'm thinking of not calling the bouncer,' Jessica said. 'If you can prove this non-specific hostility.'

'Prove it? How?'

'You can give me that spare beer you've got there,' said a voice from behind his shoulder. 'And then you can give me a dance.'

Campbell turned to find himself facing the man he'd backed off from.

'John-John, meet Arlene,' said Jessica. She nodded to Arlene and then looked pointedly at the couple on the two adjacent bar stools. The stools were abruptly vacated as the couple took the hint and headed for the floor. Arlene took the nearest, leaving Campbell to the one in the middle. The apex of an awkward triangle.

Arlene gave Campbell a wry smile and accepted the spare bottle, then fished a dinky pink Swiss Army knife from the candy-striped handbag and prised the cap off.

'Cheers,' Arlene said.

Campbell dutifully clinked bottles. Arlene put away the knife, took out a pack of cigarettes, lit up and leaned back.

'Well, John-John,' said Arlene, 'to what do we owe the pleasure of your company?'

'My name's John Richard,' Campbell said.

'I'm sure it is, John-John,' said Jessica. 'Now answer the lady's question.'

Arlene sat wide-eyed, half smiling, waiting to hear the answer. Arlene's hair was a blue bob – a wig, Campbell thought – apparently pinned in place by a twisty arrangement of small paper flowers and a ribbon. The face the wig framed would have been rather boyish without the make-up; with it, it looked definitely girlish. Campbell guessed that Arlene was a year or two younger than himself, and wondered what tragic circumstances or strange sins had brought this affliction on the unfortunate lad.

'All right,' said Campbell. He took another fortifying sip. 'The truth is, I'm a Christian, a lay preacher. I've never been in a place like this. When I was younger, my parents would have forbidden it. At home, I wouldn't want to go, in case anyone recognised me and thought I believed it was all right, or that I was a hypocrite. But I'm on a short visit to Scotland, hardly anyone here knows me, and I was, as I said, curious as to what people do in dance clubs. That's all.'

Arlene giggled; Jessica guffawed.

'What?' said Campbell. 'I've told you the truth.'

'I've heard some tales,' said Arlene, languidly waving a pink-gloved, smoke-trailing hand, 'but not that one. A lay preacher!'

Campbell shook his head, wishing that his ears weren't burning. 'I don't get it.'

'What she means,' said Jessica, 'is that whatever you tell us, and whatever you tell yourself, the truth is that you came in here because you wanted to, and you wanted to because, whether you admit it or not, you had some idea of the scene and you liked the idea of it.'

'I think you like the idea of *me*,' added Arlene.

Campbell stared at them both, completely thrown by the suggestion. He wasn't outraged or even embarrassed by it. Nothing of the sort had ever occurred to him.

'No, it isn't that,' he said. 'I know you people have your psychological theories, and maybe in some cases' – he gave a grim smile, acknowledging that they all knew the cases – 'they're on the mark, but not for me and not for most people who would agree with me. We have our views, which aren't the same as yours, and that's all there is to it.'

'So what, for example,' said Arlene, 'is your view of me?'

Campbell glanced at Jessica.

'We won't take offence,' she said. 'I won't call the bouncer, and you won't make Arlene cry.'

'I feel sorry for you,' Campbell told Arlene.

'Boo hoo,' said Arlene. 'Why?'

'Because . . .' Campbell paused. Quoting Leviticus wouldn't get him far. He had to put it in a way that made sense to the person he was witnessing to.

'Because,' he said, confident again, 'you're not fulfilling your life, your true self. Your true self is a man. And God, if you'll indulge me far enough to say so, *made* you a man and wants you to live as a man.'

'I *do* live as a man,' said Arlene, flexing a bicep under the frill of a short puffy sleeve. 'I drive a dump truck at Turnhouse. I've had girlfriends, as well as' – a sweet smile at Jessica – '*girlfriends*, and I don't feel unfulfilled at all.'

'But all this!' cried Campbell. 'That can't be what God or, if you don't believe in God, then let's say for the sake of argument *nature* originally intended for you.'

Arlene lit another cigarette. 'If God or nature had any plans for me, they must have included the line: "He'll put on women's clothing, and hang around in bars."'

That last line was half sung, in some shared cultural reference that Campbell didn't get but was the cue for shrieks of laughter from Arlene and Jessica.

'Besides,' Arlene went on, 'this is something I like doing. It's in my own time. It's fun. It harms nobody. What's wrong with it? I mean, what is your problem with it?'

'Well, I don't have a problem with it, as such,' said Campbell. 'Like I said, it's nothing personal. But I'm certain God wouldn't have forbidden it if it wasn't somehow against nature. I don't know why you have these impulses, but I'm sure you weren't born with them.' He frowned. 'Were you ever made to wear girls' clothes in childhood, or something like that?'

'Chance would have been a fine thing,' said Arlene, with a lascivious shiver.

Campbell sighed. So much for appealing to the law of nature.

'I can only suggest that you read the Bible,' he said. Arlene didn't look as if that was likely any time soon.

'All right,' said Jessica. 'Don't bother telling us about cross-dressing being an abomination, which is what you'd come down to at the end of all your rationalisations, and which I'd take seriously as a sincere motivation if you were just as down on prawn cocktails and cheese-and-ham sandwiches and you weren't wearing polyester-mix socks. You told me earlier that you weren't against queers specifically, you were just as much against everything that goes on here.' She waved an encompassing arm. 'All this, yeah?'

'Yes,' said Campbell.

He put down his now-empty bottle. He hadn't seen Jessica order any more, but she passed him another.

'Thanks,' he said.

'Go on, lay preacher,' Jessica said. 'Wet your throat and tell us what's wrong with this.'

'It stimulates lust,' said Campbell.

'You say that like it's a bad thing,' said Jessica. She shrugged. 'People have needs.'

'They don't have a need to have their needs inflamed beyond what they can reasonably control,' said Campbell.

'I do,' said Jessica, with a laugh. 'Are you telling me you don't?'

'That's exactly what I'm telling you.'

Jessica nodded slowly. 'Yes. And that's why you'd cheerfully forbid – or dissuade – other people from coming to a dance hall. You think it's as easy for them to suppress the needs they fulfil here as it is for you. Well, it isn't. And if you think it's easy, it's because you've never allowed yourself to feel these needs, or you have different needs.'

'I never said it was easy,' said Campbell.

'But it's easy for you.'

'That,' said Campbell, 'kind of contradicts what you said earlier, about how I *really* wanted to come here because deep down I'm *really* attracted to the scene, or *really* turned on by people like Arlene here.'

He leaned back, knowing that he looked smug. He was right, and he was sure of it. In a way, Jessica was right – it was easy for him. He got on well with women. Older women, married women. Girls in their early teens, or younger. Any woman at all, in fact, so long as she wasn't about his own age and unattached. Which was why it had been such a relief to learn right at the start that Jessica had a boyfriend. And this Arlene, 'she' wasn't a woman in the first place, and therefore quite easy to get on with, as well as quite . . . Campbell felt a sudden dryness in his throat, and was overcome by a fit of coughing.

'Sorry,' he croaked, and took a long swallow of beer. 'I'm not used to all this indoor smoke. It's still banned in New Zealand.'

'Banned?' said Jessica. 'How very Sozi.'

'Sozi?'

Jessica waved a hand. 'Old politics,' she said. 'Last Scottish government after the war and before the Republic. Socialist-Nationalist-Green coalition. I was too young at the time to notice anything but the queues and the blackouts, but according to my parents it was a bit like your lot's Reign of the Saints.'

Campbell closed his eyes for a moment, smiling and shaking his head. 'My lot's Reign of the Saints?'

'Puritan Parliament, 1650s,' Jessica said. 'Followed, you may remember, by the Restoration, when people had tremendous fun systematically doing everything the Puritans had forbidden. Same here.'

After that, to Campbell's immense relief, the conversation turned to the differences between Scotland and New Zealand, a subject on which he could hold forth, and Jessica and Arlene could correct and contradict, without raising any disturbing thoughts. After about an hour, Campbell made to depart, but before he went Arlene insisted on the full measure of the forfeit.

The dance took ten minutes. It seemed a lot longer, but it ended at last.

'Thank you,' Arlene said, with a smirk and a curtsey.

Campbell smiled, and said his thank-you and goodbye. He turned away sharply, nodded to Jessica, still on her perch, and hurried out. Just before he reached the exit he noticed a burly man in a sharp business suit standing by the door, relaxed and alert in the standard bouncer's pose, his hands clasped lightly across his groin. It was Graham Orr.

The only consolation for Campbell, as he blundered out into the hot, wet night, was that in Orr's artificial eyes there had been not a flicker of recognition.

One Year Later

1. EASTER ROAD

Detective Inspector Adam Ferguson cycled fast along the pavement of Easter Road, scattering pedestrians or swerving between them. He had an excuse. Traffic was backed up all the way to Leith Walk.

He slowed and dismounted fifty metres from the obstruction. A slope of rubble sprawled halfway across the road. The lower half of the front of a tenement block had been blasted out. Two floors had collapsed. No vehicles had been crushed, but the wreckage of several collisions remained slewed in the road. Ferguson hadn't seen anything like this in real life for a long time, and now seldom even on television. He took off his cycle clips, pushed the bike one-handed and stared ahead. After a step or two he remembered the weight on his back.

'Walk yourself,' he said.

The leki unwrapped its three jointed limbs from around Ferguson's chest and swung them one by one to the pavement, then settled into a graceful, swaying gait alongside him. The striding tripod looked like a two-metre-tall scale model of a Martian fighting machine from *War of the Worlds*. The police robot's bodywork had been designed with that in mind. It didn't have powers of arrest but it barely needed them.

'This is giving me flashbacks, boss,' said the leki.

'Later for that,' said Ferguson. 'Tune them out.'

Closer to the rubble the crowd thickened. Ferguson elbowed through, waving his badge. He turned to the leki.

'Crowd-clearing unpleasant voice,' he said.

'Nothing to see here!' the leki brayed. 'Move along, please! Move along!'

Ferguson felt the skin of his face, chest and upper back prickle. He wanted to cover his ears. The crowd-clearing unpleasant voice carried the timbre of nails down a blackboard, of plastic measuring-cups rattling in a cutlery drawer, of every frequency fine-tuned to set teeth on edge.

Ferguson propped his bike. The leki high-stepped over while Ferguson ducked under the blue and white police tape around the site. Other lekis pranced across the fallen masonry, their steel tentacles swinging and probing like flies' antennae, conducting the robot equivalent of a fingertip search. Overhead, a surveillance-midge swarm was already beginning to gather, each individual having responded to a simple flocking algorithm. Half a dozen uniformed officers maintained a cordon; others, up and down the street, took witness statements – effortlessly with their lenses and phones, and in laborious parallel with pens and paper notebooks, legally required. A detective sergeant and two detective constables muttered on their phones and swapped data with the lekis. On-site operations had shifted from rescue to investigation half an hour earlier; then, minutes later, from accident investigation to crime scene. Hence Ferguson's dash.

DS Hutchins greeted him. 'Bomb Squad's on its way, sir.'

'Bomb Squad? Didn't know we still had one.'

'From the Army, sir. Redford Barracks.'

'Ah, right. Have we got a situation page up and running?'

'Of course, sir.' Hutchins tapped a thumb on her forefinger, then snapped her fingers in front of Ferguson's eyes. He winked up 'New' in his contact lenses. The situation page became visible, floating above the rubble like a vivid hallucination. Ferguson scanned its columns and menus. In the bottom left corner were two wikis: one for police eyes only, one for the public. Both were being updated continuously. Ferguson ignored their scrolling flicker for now and checked the static text and pictures.

The explosion had happened about an hour earlier, at 11.05 a.m. This timing – most people out to work, morning rush-hour over – had resulted in the number of casualties being smaller than it could have been. One man, in the basement flat, dead as a direct result of the explosion (blown to bits, Ferguson concluded from the dry details); two people critically injured in the collapse of the flats above: both women, one in her mid-forties, the other a mother in her twenties who'd just returned from dropping her two kids off at the local nursery school. Dozens of major and minor injuries on the street, from flying glass or from collisions.

At first the blast had been assumed to be a gas explosion, and thus an accident. The first constable on the spot had taken only a couple of minutes to refute that. The block had no gas supply – not that it had been likely to, but at first glance it couldn't have been ruled out. Nor did records show that the basement flat, or any other, used gas cylinders. The block had been all-electric for fifteen years. It was the first leki to arrive, though, that had raised the stakes by sniffing RDX traces in the blast residues.

'Do you detect RDX?' Ferguson asked his own leki.

The machine wafted a metal frond. 'Place stinks of it, boss.'

Ferguson focused on the details of the fatality. Liam Murphy, 55, single. The woman from the flat immediately above was listed as a first contact in emergencies. The actual next of kin was a brother in Dublin, already informed. Under 'Occupation' was recorded '(No Official Cognisance)'. Ferguson blinked hard.

'Excuse me, Shonagh,' he said to DS Hutchins. 'Off the record – what *was* the victim's occupation?'

'Don't know yet, sir.'

'Well, ask around, please. Who's the community officer?'

'I'll find out, sir.'

'And get a PC – a woman, preferably – to that injured mum's kids' nursery while you're at it.'

'Already done, sir.'

'Good.'

Hutchins stepped away, talking on her phone. Ferguson returned his gaze to the situation page, and this time eyeballed up the civilian wiki. Someone among Murphy's neighbours would surely have taken cognisance of his occupation, even if the State didn't. Involvement in prostitution, drug-dealing, non-peer-reviewed therapies and the like could still attract criminal attention, even if no longer that of the police.

Additions to the wiki were slowing. The usual stuff had piled up, some of it useful, some not: eyewitness accounts and eyeball-video uploads of the explosion, whinges about damage to shopfronts, speculations, tributes to the injured and the deceased. Ferguson's skimming gaze didn't take long to snag on: 'No one ever had a bad word for Father Liam. This is so awful.'

Startled, he scrolled on down until he had no doubt. The dead man had been a Roman Catholic priest.

Ferguson snapped away the situation page and glared around. DS Hutchins was picking her way between bits of shattered brickwork with a young constable in tow. From the dark interior of the ruined block a leki skittered over piles of rubble, carrying something small and bloody in a ziplock plastic bag. A reporter from BBC Scotland stood, back turned, on the other side of the street, speaking to a shoulder-mounted crane-camera unit. More coverage would no doubt be on the way: Ferguson spotted Tom Mackay, a *Scotsman* journalist, among the now-small scatter of onlookers. What Ferguson had just learned wasn't the sort of thing he wanted out on the news just yet, but he was probably already too late to stop that.

'We should have known this right from the start,' Ferguson said as Hutchins and the constable joined him.

'Thought you knew, sir,' said the constable. 'Everybody knew Father Murphy.'

'Everyone on this street, you mean,' said Ferguson. 'And it's *Mister* Murphy to us, if you don't mind.'

'Citizen Murphy,' said DS Hutchins.

The leki with the plastic bag arrived. The three officers, and Ferguson's leki, stared at what lay within the transparent polythene. A hand.

'Body part of the deceased,' said the leki, holding it. 'Traces found on it of unexploded RDX.'

'Father— *Citizen* Murphy had handled the material before the explosion?' Ferguson asked.

'That would appear to be the case,' said the leki.

'Good God,' said Ferguson. 'What would a priest be doing with RDX?'

'"Out of the ashes arose the Provisionals",' intoned Ferguson's leki, making irritating little air-quotes with the tips of two of its three tentacles.

Ferguson turned on it. 'What?'

'Christian militia slogan,' said the leki. 'Mural graffiti, Belfast, British Empire, circa 1973.'

Out of the corner of his eye Ferguson saw the reporters across the road converge on the nearest length of boundary tape, waving recording devices. At the same moment he noticed a queer hush fall: voices, birds, vehicles momentarily stilled. The onrushing silence was matched by a shadow that covered him and remained as its edge raced away along the street. Ferguson glanced up and to the south. You weren't supposed to look, but he looked. Thousands of miles away, a circle of mylar thousands of miles across had eclipsed the sun. Coronae briefly flared, then the soleta's orbit took it away from the sun's face. Momentarily blinded as his contact lenses blacked out, Ferguson seized the moment to snarl to his leki:

'Shut – the fuck – up.'

Light and colour returned. Background noise resumed.

'Any comment, Inspector?'

Tom Mackay leaned across the tape, thrusting his phone in Ferguson's face. The BBC Scotland reporter craned her shoulder camera forward, just as close.

'No comment,' said Ferguson. He jerked a thumb

backward. 'The investigation is just starting. The Press Officer will release a statement in due course.'

'When, exactly?' demanded Mackay.

Ferguson shrugged. 'If I could answer that I could answer a lot more. Meanwhile, I'd appreciate it if you'd back away from the periphery. Don't want to contaminate the site.'

'Come on, Ferguson,' said Mackay. 'A priest's been blown up. That wisnae a gas explosion. So what was it?'

'I honestly can't say,' said Ferguson.

'Can't or won't?'

'Can't,' said Ferguson. 'We don't have enough evidence yet. Not even to rule out a domestic accident of some kind.'

At that point a black six-wheeled armoured vehicle came down the wrong side of the road – the forward-moving traffic having more quickly cleared – and came to a halt at a perfect angle for the reporters to turn around and record the big white letters on its side: BOMB DIS-POSAL. Soldiers in white isolation suits deployed from the back and hurried up, lugging sensing equipment and followed by four heavy-duty combat mechs. Ferguson could see the lekis all swivel their gazes onto the hulking machines, then turn away as if caught looking.

'Domestic accident hasn't been ruled out, you say?' said Mackay.

'No further comment,' said Ferguson.

Greensides, close to the top of Leith Walk, was fifteen years old, slabbed with obsolete fortification, pocked with likewise redundant gunports, and still referred to as 'the new station'. Its upper floors commanded fine views to the west, along Queen Street to the towers and high-rise hydroponic farms of Turnhouse, and to the north across Leith Water and the Firth. So Ferguson had been told. He had never personally verified this, but had no reason to doubt it. His own office was in the middle of a long corridor on the second floor. At about 1.30 p.m. he elbowed the door handle and shouldered the door, coffee and sandwich in hand and papers in oxter. The leki ambled in behind him. They sat down, Ferguson behind the desk, the leki on a filing cabinet.

The leki plugged itself into a power socket. Ferguson broke the tab on the coffee cup and flipped the lid. He sniffed steam for a few seconds, then took a sip, winced, and unwrapped his sandwich. Ostrich tikka. Mmm.

After chewing for a bit he looked up at the leki.

'Your thoughts, Skulk?' he said.

'Skulk' was a nickname. The leki's real name, its *taken* name as its kind put it, was Skullcrusher. Neither the machine nor the man thought it politic to use the longer form in public; and, like most cops who worked with a leki, Ferguson used even the nickname with discretion.

In the dark elliptical hollow at the front of Skulk's head, a pair of red LEDs – designed to be mistaken for angry eyes – glowed.

'Sure looks like terrorism to me, boss,' Skulk said.

'Let's leave the T-word out of it for the moment,' said Ferguson.

'I can leave it out of public discourse,' said the leki. 'You asked for my thoughts.'

'I appreciate that,' Ferguson mumbled around a mouthful of crust. 'And I understand why you see it that way. But I have to ask, are you letting your, ah, flashbacks get the better of you? Think about it. There are plenty of levels, so to speak' – he waved his hands horizontally, one above the other – 'before you get to . . . that. Stupidity. Psychosis. Criminality. Some family feud. Possibly even some dispute in the deceased's, uh, organisation.'

'There have been no known assassinations arising from internal Catholic Church disputes since 1982,' said Skulk.

'What was that?' asked Ferguson, diverted.

'The Calvi affair, you may recall?'

'Before my time. But a point in my favour. These things happen.'

'The deceased citizen was hardly of such importance.'

'As far as we know. This official non-cognisance stuff can be taken too far. He could have been something in the hierarchy' – Ferguson flailed, trying to recall the nomenclature – 'a Monsignor or Cardinal or something.'

'Murphy was a simple parish priest,' said Skulk. 'The Cardinal of Scotland resides in Glasgow. His name is—'

'Yes, yes,' said Ferguson.

'Mr Donald Nardini,' continued the leki. 'You may expect to hear from him.'

'No doubt,' said Ferguson. 'Can't say I like the prospect.' A thought struck him. 'Who was Murphy's boss, line manager, whatever?'

'Bishop Hugh Curley. Dr Curley, if you prefer. He has of course been informed.'

Ferguson tipped back his chair and gazed at the ceiling. Dealing with an organisation whose very existence the government, police, civil service, and public sector officially ignored could become complicated. It had been straightforward back in the old days, when the God Squads had their boots on the floor of every church, chapel, synagogue and mosque in the land. Ferguson found himself blushing at the recollection of some of the things he'd done then. Non-cognisance was now the modus vivendi.

'Relations with church officials could be a bit of a minefield,' he mused.

'It is not at all like a minefield,' said the leki.

Ferguson heard the remark as a reproach. A different reproach came to him as an image arose in his real, inner memory, a mental picture of a short, middle-aged man with a double chin and a comb-over of lank ginger hair; eyes in deltas of wrinkles behind spectacles that almost certainly didn't run code; a buttoned black overcoat raw at the cuffs and tight at the waist. A man whose body parts were now puzzle pieces on a steel table in a cold room four floors below. Father Liam Murphy, deceased. Whether he was the victim of someone else or of himself, the most important thing about his life deserved the dignity of being spoken aloud.

'The hell with it,' said Ferguson, rocking forward. 'Let's call these people by the names and titles they choose. Give the bishop a call, pass on my respects and condolences, and offer him a slot in my diary. His place or ours, I don't care.'

'Very good, boss,' said the leki.

In the corner of Ferguson's eye a reminder popped up. *Investigation team meeting, room 386, five minutes.*

He blinked it away and stood up.

'Back to work,' he said.

Somebody had hand-blocked 'Easter Road Incident Room' on an A4 sheet and Blu-tacked it to the door, not quite aligned with a virtual overlay that spelled out the same; seen through contact lenses, the effect was slightly cross-eyed, like a line on an optician's chart diagnostic of astigmatism. Ferguson resisted the impulse to move the paper into synch. One wall of the incident room was like a fragment of the situation page made actual: whiteboard with scrawls and arrows; pinned-up photos and notes; strips of black ribbon tape making connections. The rationale for this was the same as for paper notebooks, film cameras and, for that matter, police paperwork in general: it was hard to hack and harder still to crash. There had been a time when such things had happened, when whole bodies of evidence and terabytes of records had been corrupted by some random script-monkey, or wiped altogether by an electromagnetic-pulse truck-bomb, its devastation unnoticed by passers-by until they checked their watch or phone or the song in their ears stopped.

Not any more. Hard copy. Get it down. That was the drill. Nothing less would stand up in court.

Ferguson placed himself with his back to the board and surveyed the team. DS Hutchins sat behind a desk at the front. DCs Patel and Connolly stood at either side of her. Police Sergeant Dennis Carr stood at parade rest to their left. Sitting on top of a desk, elbows on knees, was Tony Newman from Forensics. Right at the back of the room, shabbily dressed in colours that might have been chosen as office camo, was DCI Mohammed Mukhtar. Chief of the local Special Branch, thirty-odd years on the force, he was among the last of the anti-terrorism old guard. These days he kept track of Sozi dead-enders, Constitutionalist subversives and Unionist splinter groups. Mukhtar seldom emerged from the woodwork, and when he did it was usually a bad sign.

Amongst them all, scattered across the office furniture like an infestation of metallic spiders, sprawled six lekis – one for each of them, Ferguson presumed. His own leki stood, telescopic legs locked, at his side. When Ferguson experimentally downshifted the spectrum on his contact lenses he could detect the continuous infrared flicker of robot repartee criss-crossing the room. The effect was somehow disquieting, and for no gain, so he blinked the normal colours back. He set his phone clip to screen all but emergency calls, then cleared his throat.

'Thank you all for coming here,' Ferguson began, making it sound as though he was grateful that they'd all turned out quite voluntarily for a dull meeting in a draughty hall on a wet night. 'In a moment, DS Hutchins will give us a summary. All I want at this point is to lay down a couple of ground rules. The first is that we refer to and address the Catholic – and any other – clergy we come across with a modicum of respect. None of that "mister", "citizen", and "cult administrator" jargon from now on. Not on this investigation.

'Second, no speculation about or references to terrorism in public – and that means, ladies, gentlemen and lekis, outside the investigation. Not until or unless I say so.' He locked stares with DCI Mukhtar. 'Everyone clear?'

Mukhtar shrugged. 'I take it that last point doesn't apply to Special Branch?'

'That's understood,' said Ferguson. 'Provided they keep it within SB. In fact, within those on SB working on this specific investigation.'

'Our discretion is assured,' said Mukhtar. He spoke in

his default accent, that of middle-class Edinburgh with an English clip to the vowels. His other accents were as distinctive. 'And I'll insist the chaps are polite to the God-botherers.'

'Very well,' said Ferguson, above the collective snort and smirk. He stepped away from the front of the board. 'DS Hutchins – over to you.'

Ferguson took a seat as Hutchins took the floor. Shonagh Hutchins could have slipped unnoticed into any office crowd. In this crowd, she stood out. Even the lekis seemed to sit up and lean forward a little. Hutchins tabbed with a laser pointer at successive items on the board as she spoke.

'OK,' she said, 'here's the situation as it stands. We still don't know what we're dealing with here. The cause of the explosion looks pretty definite – couple of kilos of RDX. The dead man had likewise definitely handled the unexploded material, which doesn't of course mean that he set it off, deliberately or otherwise. The best bet, I would say, is a parcel bomb, which he opened and which exploded after some – possibly very short – delay. Obviously, the Bomb Squad are searching for any wrapping or packaging, so far without success. The two injured women from the floors above aren't yet in any condition to speak, and aren't expected to be for several days at the earliest. The good news is that they can be expected to pull through to that extent at least, so we have two women constables down at the Western ready to take statements and to keep watch on them in the meantime, just in case. DCI Mukhtar has a couple of officers on discreet surveillance – armed, of course. I'll ask him for background in a moment, but first – Tony, the forensics?'

Tony Newman slid from his perch and stood up. He scratched the back of his head and gazed at the ceiling, blinking hard.

'The lekis have been all over the mess with the fine-tooth proverbial,' he said, 'and Bomb Squad haven't found any other devices – or any parcel-bomb packaging, as Shonagh said. They're still searching the rubble, and in the meantime are concentrating on tracing the origin of the explosives from the fingerprint of the batch. We're focusing on the DNA traces – we have dozens of molecular samples in the lab, as well as the gross, uh, bits down in pathology. I mean, it's not like we have any difficulty in determining cause of death per se. But in another sense we don't have a lot to go on – we've identified significant DNA traces from twenty-two people so far, other than Murphy himself, the lady from the flat above – Ms Bernadette White, who was, I understand, the priest's housekeeper – and the postie.'

'The deceased had a lot of visitors?' asked Ferguson. 'How's that?'

'He held meetings in the flat,' said Hutchins. 'Apparently it functioned as a church. Sergeant Carr's officers are attempting to compile a list of regular church-goers, for interviews and DNA samples.'

'That shouldn't be hard,' said Ferguson.

'It might be harder than you think,' said Carr. 'Churchgoers tend to keep a low profile about their, uh, practices. And we can't demand DNA samples off them.'

'Make an appeal for them all to come forward,' said Ferguson. He glanced at his leki. 'Tab that to the Press Officer, would you?'

'Sure, boss,' said the leki.

'Hutchins, sorry, go on.'

'Patel and Connolly here have been trawling for CCTV from nearby shops, street cameras, et cetera, and of course there's a call out for anyone who's been down that street at all recently to upload their personals to the Police National Artificial Intelligence. It's up on the wiki.'

'More than enough,' said Patel. 'Nothing obvious so far, though.'

'Nothing obvious?' said Ferguson, over his shoulder. 'We're not looking for *obvious*. Though if you do happen to come across CCTV footage of someone handing the victim a suspect package, please don't hesitate to share it.'

'That's not what I meant, sir,' said Patel, looking abashed. 'We ran everything through the PNAI search algorithms in the past hour, and nothing jumped out. We'll arrange for them to be eyeballed this afternoon, and we're heading out ourselves to work down the street.'

'OK,' said Ferguson, settling back. 'Sorry, again, Shonagh.'

'Which brings us to the question of suspects,' said Hutchins, as though there had been no interruption. 'Of course the uniformed officers are interviewing neighbours and witnesses and, ah, parishioners if they can find any, and as DI Ferguson has said, we can't say this in public, but I think we'd all agree that there is very likely more to this than some criminal or personal dispute. And, so far, nothing at all has come up. Correct?'

Patel and Connolly nodded in unison.

'Early days yet,' said Carr. 'Early hours, come to that.'

'Well, yes,' said Hutchins. 'DCI Mukhtar, I believe you have some lines of inquiry?'

Mukhtar separated himself from the back wall and made his way to the front.

'If I may,' he said.

Hutchins stepped aside. At Ferguson's nod, she resumed her seat.

'There are a few possibilities here,' said Mukhtar, laser-pointing a snarled-up area of lines and labels on the whiteboard. 'Let me start by saying that there has been no "chatter", no advance uptick in messages between people of interest. We still have a few, you know. I will take these in ascending order of probability. First, Islamists. The known remnants of such groups are all overseas now, mostly stuck in the middle of nowhere, and have no recent record of expressed hostility to Christians, other than in local and essentially ethnic disputes. Even these are rare, deeply obscure, and tangentially if at all related to the Catholic Church, particularly so far away. Insofar as they pay attention to anything in the West at all, the focus of their ire tends to be Jews, apostates – that's secular Muslims – and atheists, which for them means secular just-about-anyone-else.

'Second, anti-Catholic Christians of one kind or another. I know we tend to think of post-apocalyptic cults as an American problem, but the Left Behind crowd do have a handful of adherents even in Scotland, and more of course in England. When these types go violent, however, they incline to siege-stroke-hostage situations or spree killings, not bombings. Which brings us to the second kind of anti-Catholic Christian – the original kind: Protestants. You can look all this up, DC Patel, or consult DC Connolly afterwards. But at this moment I would appreciate your undivided attention . . . Thank you. Now.

Protestants, hm. The only grievances there arise out of the Irish connection, or *lack* of connection, you might say. But there again, with the Ulster hard men it's a bit like the old Islamists – few remain, and those who do have other and closer targets than a priest in Edinburgh. Frankly, we haven't seen any violence from extreme Loyalists for years. No more rackets, y'see, and damn' little political motivation left.' Mukhtar sighed and spread his hands, sounding almost regretful as he went on. 'Not even in connection with the hard-line Unionist element in Scotland. We'll inquire in that direction, of course, but I doubt that we'll find anything.

'So I think we're more likely to find the perpetrators among the militant anti-religious – small groups committed to actively attacking religion, rather than ignoring it. Some of them are the much-dwindled remnants of, or splinters from, bodies that played a serious and significant role during the Second Enlightenment – secularist societies, ad hoc campaigns dealing with particular abuses, and so forth. There's a bit of an overlap there with grudge groups among Faith War veterans, obviously a matter of interest in this context. Other anti-Christian active elements are currents in the darker side of goth subculture – Gnostics, pagans, Satanists. The individuals we in the Branch intend to investigate first are those who've expressed personal grievances against the Catholic Church or its clergy and who've threatened revenge.'

'Do you have names?' asked Ferguson.

'A few,' said Mukhtar.

'Excuse me,' said Sergeant Dennis Carr, 'but all the kiddie-fiddling priests and child-thrashing nuns were smoked out years ago. I can't see how anyone with personal grievances against the clergy could be young. Not these days.'

'I didn't say they were,' said Mukhtar. 'Many in the subcultures I mentioned aren't young at all. Some are as old as I am! Besides, there are grievances against the clergy other than child abuse. Some people blame religion for whatever's gone wrong in their lives. Usually sex is involved, but not necessarily any abuses of that nature suffered at the hands of priests.'

'I take it,' said Ferguson, 'that someone has checked the name of Father Liam Murphy on the database of the Vatican Occupation Authority?'

'Naturally,' said Mukhtar. 'He came through the purges without a stain on his character. That's why I suspect some political or sectarian motive, rather than personal.'

'OK,' said Ferguson, standing up and moving to the front again. 'Thank you, everyone. I need hardly say that if DCI Mukhtar is correct, we need to find the perpetrator quickly. In fact, even if he's wrong. Carry on, keep the situation page updated, liaise with each other, report to me, and let's get this bastard nailed.' He looked around. 'Dennis, you have a question?'

'I was wondering,' said Carr, 'if we shouldn't offer police security to other priests? Locally, that is.'

'Out of the question,' said Ferguson. 'Even if we had the resources, which we don't, we don't even know who the clergy *are*. No official cognisance, remember?'

Carr nodded. Mukhtar smiled and looked sly.

'And I'm not breaking firewalls to find out,' Ferguson added. 'As to what we tell the media . . .' He glanced over at Skulk. 'Perhaps we should put it like this. We're

treating this as a murder inquiry. There is a slim possibility that the motive was anti-religious hostility, so other
clergy, Catholic or otherwise, should be vigilant. Plus the
usual appeals.'

'Got it,' said the leki.

'What about our other investigations?' asked DS
Hutchins. 'The Leith Water business?'

'I need priorities,' added Carr.

'I'll get back to you,' said Ferguson. 'That's all for now.'

He turned around to study the board. Behind him
everyone but Skulk filed out.

Ferguson returned to his office with Skulk at about three
p.m. When he turned on his phone clip he found eight
messages in his voicemail, and fifteen emails on his desk
slate. Half of them were from above, demanding with
increasing urgency that he get the Easter Road case sorted
out fast; half from below, pleading other urgent work.

'Give me an update,' said Ferguson, sitting down and
looking reluctantly at a notepad and a wad of forms.
'What do we have to put on the back burner if we priori-
tise this?'

Skulk patched a task tree to Ferguson's desk slate.
Ferguson poked about in it for a bit. 'A' Division of
Lothian and Borders Police currently had two other active
murder investigations: one street stabbing from five days
earlier, one domestic bludgeoning from last night. There
were the usual traffic accidents, assaults, thefts. And then
there was the investigation that he and Hutchins, Patel
and Connolly had been working on for weeks: some thug-
gery arising out of a conflict between a local security
company, Hired Muscle, and the Gazprom goons down at

Leith Water. Gazprom hadn't been happy with Hired Muscle's security on the docks, citing pilfering and (in a typical Russian ploy, Ferguson reckoned) sabotage of crated space-industry components from the defence company Rosoboroneksport on trans-shipment to Turnhouse and thence to the Atlantic Space Elevator. Gazprom's own security staff had taken up the business dispute in the manner likewise typical of capitalism with Russian characteristics – with tyre irons.

Ferguson called up his immediate boss, DCI Frank McAuley, and repeated the question.

'Everything,' McAuley said.

At five p.m. Professor Grace Abounding Mazvabo saved her day's work and leaned away from her desk, flexing her shoulders. The day's work wasn't really over – she had stacks of admin and grading still to do, and her book in any time left over – but the ritual was important. She switched on the kettle that stood on the windowsill and gazed out while waiting for it to boil. From her cramped and cluttered office in the top floor of New College on the Mound she had one of the best views in Edinburgh, facing north across the railway lines and Princes Street Gardens, over the towers of New New Town to the Firth and beyond it to Fife. As perks of a job went, this wasn't bad, even if it was the job's only perk.

The kettle boiled. Grace made herself a mug of instant coffee and sat back down, flipping her desk screen to the *Edinburgh Evening News*. She took in the headline and set down her mug with a bang and a hot splash.

BOMB PRIEST 'MURDERED'

As she read the text, animated the photos, and listened to the little talking heads, Grace Mazvabo had her mouth to the back of her hand long after the slight scald had faded. And besides her grief and wrath, which were in truth not much greater than she usually felt at the murder of a stranger, she identified a sharper pang of guilt. The first thought that had flashed across her mind when she'd read the headline was: *Oh dear Lord, it's started*. She was guilty because she had been uneasy for some time about what might have just started, and she hadn't warned anyone, because . . . because, well . . . she was embarrassed to explain it to herself, let alone to anyone else.

She picked up the now cool mug in the fingertips of both hands, propped her elbows, sipped, gazed at the screen and examined her conscience. There was no evidence to support her suspicion. The police weren't pointing a finger. No claim of responsibility had been made. The victim was from the very base of the Catholic hierarchy. Blameless, obscure, well-liked – he couldn't have been more stupidly chosen, assuming he *had* been chosen. The action had been heedless of collateral damage, its secondary victims even more innocent in the world's eyes than the dead man. If this was what Grace dreaded to seriously suspect, the victim's symbolic value was the perverse opposite of what she'd have expected. Perhaps the pointlessness of it was the point. *There is none righteous, no, not one* . . .

Wait. No. Surely not. Surely, surely not. They couldn't be that crazy. She was running ahead of herself. She stood up and stepped over to a metal filing cabinet and retrieved a cardboard file. She leafed through its contents, slid it back in the divider and banged the drawer shut.

Oh yes, Grace thought. *They could be that crazy.*

She still hesitated to go to the police. Not without something more than this dark suspicion. Not when the consequences could be so bad for the Church – for all the Churches, and all the believers.

But she couldn't do nothing. After thinking for some time, she sighed, tapped twice behind her ear, and spoke to the Bishop of St Andrews.

2. THE UNCANNY VALLEY

'Cornelius? Can you give my erectus a lift?'

Cornelius Vermuelen let a smirk fade before he shouted back.

'Sure, JR. No problem.'

He rounded the corner of Waimangu Visitors' Centre and made his way to the workshop shed at the back. Its garage-type door was open, the entrance partly blocked by the head and upper neck of an animatronic apatosaurus. Tools were clipped and shelved on the walls. John Richard Campbell was stooped over a work-top in the middle of the floor. On the worktop lay the torso of a humanoid robot, its dark hairy skin folded away from the small of its back, the overlapping steel plates of the lumbar region removed and laid to one side. Campbell's hands moved delicately within the cavity. The robot's microcephalic head, its small brow creased, watched the procedure from a nearby shelf. Beside it on the shelf was a less convincing, and quite inanimate, beetle-browed and prognathous prosthesis. The head had been crudely adapted to fit this mask: its facial features were human, albeit with a skin somewhat worn and mottled, but the cranium was about half the human size, with a heavy brow ridge.

Campbell glanced up.

'Won't be a minute,' he said.

Vermuelen knew better than to believe him. So, by the look that crossed its features, did the robot. Vermuelen sidled over to it, keeping out of Campbell's daylight.

'Back problem?' he said.

The head moved as if trying to nod. 'Yes,' it said. 'Stripped a gear in my lumbar hinge. Fucking baraminologists.'

'Language,' chided Campbell, not looking up.

'From the Hebrew,' explained the robot head, wilfully misunderstanding. '*Bara min*, meaning "created kind", a very flexible taxon indeed.'

'I don't quite follow,' said Vermuelen. 'What have creationist taxonomists got to do with your back?'

'A few weeks ago,' said the head, 'they reclassified my kind from "fully human post-Diluvial local variety" to "extinct large-brained ape". Some little dipshit at the Institute had done a lit review and decided that the bones of the type specimen weren't definitively associated with the stone tools found in the same horizon of the same fucking dig. And furthermore, that the fossil's cervical vertebrae and pelvis weren't well enough preserved to justify giving me an upright stance. So suddenly I've got to start shambling around like a half-shut knife, swinging my arms and grunting. It's demeaning, I tell you. And it's done my back in. I expect my neck will be next.'

'Your neck's fine,' said Campbell. 'Just keep applying the WD-40.'

He reached to an oil-filled saucer for a large ball bearing, held it up between thumb and middle finger as if it were a plum he was about to pop in his mouth, and dropped it into the cavity. He made a few turns with a screwdriver, then with a socket wrench.

'Give it a go,' he said.

The headless prone body made a couple of humping motions.

'Feels all right,' said the head, in a grudging tone.

Campbell replaced the array of plates, squirted WD-40 over them, and flattened the skin back into place. The tip of his tongue protruded as he Super-Glued the flap's incisions. He stood back.

'OK,' he said.

The body stood up, walked to the shelf, and placed its head back on. Clunking sounds came from it as various bolts and cables re-established their connections. Campbell tightened a couple of screws at the throat and nape. With visible reluctance, the robot pulled on the prosthesis. Hair hid the join. The ape-like features twitched this way and that, as the simulated face within grimaced its way back into control of the mask.

'Thanks,' the robot said. It turned to Vermuelen, its ape eyelids blinking mechanically. 'Pardon me, I don't believe we've been introduced. I'll be forgetting my own head next.'

The outstretched hand was long-fingered, hairy, leathery.

'Cornelius Vermuelen, park ranger.'

'Piltdown, fake apeman. Pleased to meet you.' It gazed around the shed, as if it would miss the place. 'Oh well, back into character. Ook ook.'

Piltdown leaned forward, knuckles almost brushing the floor, ambled to the doorway, patted the apatosaur and turned to look pleadingly at the two men, like a dog waiting for a walk. Campbell put away his tools in a tool-case and straightened up, rubbing his own neck and back.

'Oh well,' he said. 'Time to get into character our-selves, I suppose. Bow down in the house of Rimmon.'

Vermuelen chuckled and nodded. He and Campbell both despised the creationist operators of the park, though from opposite directions. Vermuelen had been an Anglican since childhood and a park ranger all his working life. He'd been forty when the Genesis Institute, funded by several wealthy exiled US businessmen, had taken over the lease on the tourist side of the running of Waimangu. In the past five years he hadn't given the creationists an inch: he'd prevented them from cluttering the spectacular volcanic valley with more than a handful of their animatronic dinosaur and caveman installations, and when guiding tourists along the trail had refused to follow the creation-ists' script, which claimed that the ancient appearance of this lush, recent landscape could be generalised into evi-dence for a 6000-year-old Earth. Instead, he had always emphasised that the effect of weathering and revegetation on compacted volcanic ash was no model at all for the geol-ogy of igneous and sedimentary rock, remarkable though the appearance of a stable landscape and mature ecosystem in less than two centuries might be.

John Richard Campbell carried, Vermuelen had some-times thought, a very different cross, one that was all his own, and of his own making. Tall, sinewy, cerebrotonic, autodidactic, and stubborn, at the age of twenty-two he had already managed to get himself excluded from two of the local fundamentalist sects. The first, the Church of his baptism, the Presbyterian Reformed Church of New Zealand, had withdrawn its fellowship from him in his seventeenth year. In a flush of youthful enthusiasm, Campbell had submitted an article to the Church's magazine which argued (with impeccable biblical references) that the Earth was flat, and that its glaringly apparent sphericity could be explained (with incomprehensible but irrefutable mathematics) by a providential divine curvature of the space around it. Accidentally leaked to the Internet before publication, 'The Creation of Apparent Shape: a Biblical and Scientific Perspective' had brought upon the Church some worldly scoffing, much to Campbell's chagrin. His dismay and repentance were real enough, but his refusal to repudiate the article, and his indignant denial that his intention had been satirical – the admission of which would have been sufficient to get him off with a warning – had brought down on his head a charge of contumacy. Not being a communicant, he couldn't be excommunicated, but he had found the disapproval and disgrace hard to bear.

To avoid contention, Campbell had transferred his attendance to the even smaller Congregational Baptist Apostolic Church of North Island, Aotearoa, whose meeting house was conveniently or providentially close to the technical college in Rotorua where Campbell had just begun a diploma course in robotic engineering. His fingers having been burned once, he'd kept his thoughts to himself for a couple of years. But the temptation to speculative theology had been too much to resist, and had become once more his undoing. An earnest piece on his personal website imploring evangelical concern for the souls of Turing-test-passing robots and other artificial intelligences had come to the pastor's attention, and that was that. The charge this time was heresy. He did not contest it.

A less self-assured man might have become bitter. Campbell had taken the view that theological debate was pointless: all that needed to be said had been said already, and said better, by Augustine, Calvin, and the Reformers. He graduated from college unchurched and uncertain of his future. From his earlier escapade he'd already concluded that scientific creationism was a misguided attempt to convince an unbelieving world on its own terms, but it was the creationist science park at Waimangu that had brought him his vocation. He was recruited to the park's staff because of his engineering skills, but was privately contemptuous of its operators for presuming to offer evidence for God's Word. His own view was what he called the strong delusion theory. This held that, while creation was evident on the surface of the world, deeper investigations were doomed to distortion by man's spiritual darkness.

This gloomy view had seemed to Vermuelen to fit Campbell's personality when he'd first started working at the park, but the young man had brightened up remarkably after a visit to Scotland about a year ago. Campbell never said much about it, but his few guarded comments indicated that he'd encountered people in Scotland who shared some of his odd views. Vermuelen reckoned this was likely to be a mixed blessing in the long run, but for now he was just grateful that his colleague's natural cheerfulness had come out from the shadow of his eccentric theology.

Campbell slammed and locked the shed door, and hefted his toolcase. The two men and the robot made their way to Vermuelen's jeep, parked on a side road in front of the visitors' centre. The first coach party of the day had arrived, queuing for the VR frames that overlaid their views of the valley with elaborate scenes of Edenic and Noachic life, far more detailed, crowded and fanciful than the animatronic displays. The crowd – from an Indonesian cruise liner, Vermuelen guessed – nudged each other and pointed at Piltdown, who posed for video and waved back a few times before clambering into the middle seat of the jeep.

'You buckle up too,' said Vermuelen, taking the wheel.

The robot fumbled, awkward with its simian digits. Campbell leaned over and clicked the seat belt.

Vermuelen drove up a small slope. From the top he could see all the way down the valley, its forested slopes obscured here and there by morning mist, a more persistent steam rising from the hot lakes and streams in the chill September spring morning. The pale blue of Frying Pan Lake and the garish azure of Inferno Crater glittered through the trees far below. Beyond the valley, on the horizon, stood Mount Tarawera, the chasm left by the 1886 eruption still visible on its flank. Vermuelen lurched the vehicle over the hump and then onto the road, six winding miles downhill to the lake. He flicked the car radio on to catch the nine o'clock news.

The lead item was that a priest had been blown up in Scotland. The Scottish police, it was reported, weren't talking about terrorism. The experts polled by the news station more than made up for this. Vermuelen clicked the radio off after five minutes.

'Grim,' he said.

'Yes,' said Campbell. 'But it shouldn't surprise us. The anti-Christian fanatics will never stop, that's the problem.

Even the apostate states don't satisfy them. It's not enough to drive religion out of public life. They'll go after those who believe and practise in private too.'

'Well,' said Vermuelen, anxious to head off one of Campbell's predictable rants, 'at least we live in a free country.'

This was not quite how he felt about the past decade or two of influx of fundamentalist refugees – as they called themselves – from the US and former UK to New Zealand. Aside from his personal resentment of the indignities and mendacities of the park, the exiles formed a distorting lobby in NZ politics, and their frequent plots and occasional forays against their former homeland were a strain on the local security services, as well as on diplomatic and trade relations with the diminished but still-mighty United States.

'For now,' said Campbell. 'We need to be on our guard.'

'Hm,' said Vermuelen, concentrating on the driving.

Campbell sat in silence for a few moments. The silence didn't last.

'Are you still attending that Erastian shrine of syncretist idolatry?'

Vermuelen had to laugh, but he felt offended.

'Yes,' he said stiffly. 'I still go to St Faith's.' He glanced over at Campbell, who stared fixedly ahead. 'And you know, JR, I think you should, too. It is after all the means of grace.'

Campbell sighed. 'I miss fellowship, I admit. But the Apostle tells us to flee from idolatry. I will not compromise on that.'

No, you won't, thought Vermuelen.

St Faith's, the Anglican church in Rotorua, was

distinguished by the fine Maori carving of its pews and pulpit, and by a window etched with a translucent, sand-blasted depiction of Christ in a Maori warrior's cloak, apparently walking on the water of Lake Rotorua outside. Campbell had often inveighed against all this as a sinful compromise with heathen darkness, a betrayal even worse than the Episcopalian Church government and doctrinal latitudinarianism that made up his more general objection to the Anglican communion.

'Nevertheless,' continued Campbell, 'St Faith's is the most visible church in the area. If the anti-Christians are resorting to murder in Scotland, who knows what might be in store for all of us? Even here?'

'I think that's in the hands of God and the police.'

'Very true,' said Campbell. 'All the same, the police can't watch everything. It might be wise to keep an eye out for strangers in the congregation. Let me know if you notice any.'

'Why? What could you do?'

'Not much,' Campbell admitted. 'I'd like to know, that's all. To be prepared. I still have friends in the churches I used to attend. I'd like them to be on their guard, too.'

'All right,' said Vermuelen. 'If I see any mysterious lurking strangers scoping out the congregation, I'll be sure to tell you, OK?'

Campbell didn't catch the sarcasm.

'Thanks, Cornelius,' he said. 'That's really all I want you to do.'

He took a notebook from his pocket and thumbed up the diary. 'If you could drop me at the Inferno Crater turn-off?' he said.

'Sure,' said Vermuelen. 'What's the job?'

'Some brat thought it would be a neat trick to throw our vegetarian velociraptor a rock to chomp on. Damaged the jaw mechanism.'

'And the teeth?'

'Nah, the teeth were fine. They'll crack many a fast-fleeing coconut yet.'

The two men laughed; the robot hooted. Vermuelen halted and Campbell got out.

'Thanks, Cornelius,' he said. He reached up to slam the door. 'See you around, Piltdown.'

Campbell disappeared between trees down a path towards the lake. Vermuelen drove on.

'What about yourself?' Vermuelen asked.

'By the Warbrick terraces is fine.'

'They're not setting up a diorama *there*, are they?'

'Nope,' said Piltdown. 'It's just the start of my daily route. I've been setting off from there back up alongside the trail, occasionally appearing among the bushes to squeals of delight from the sapient young.'

'I feel for you,' said Vermuelen.

'I know you do,' said Piltdown. It chattered its fake teeth. 'That's my whole problem in a nutshell.'

'So to speak.'

The robot, this time, gave a human laugh.

'I'm not bitter – to use another primate metaphor. The way I see it, those of us who work as displays give cover to the others.'

'Cover?'

'When the others are seen, it's usually only for a moment, or glimpsed through trees. The visitors interpret them as more of the same – post-Diluvian men or upright apes or spawn of the nephilim.'

'Hmm,' said Vermuelen. He hadn't thought of it this way before. 'You know, if the park ever gets out from under this nonsense, it could market the robot population as an attraction in its own right.'

'The thought makes me shudder,' said Piltdown. 'It makes me pray for the continuing success of the Genesis Institute.'

Vermuelen felt embarrassed. 'I take your point.'

'No need to feel embarrassed,' said Piltdown. 'Nor to feel sorry for me. In truth, I spend most of my day surfing the net – reception permitting – and pondering deep questions of philosophy. The performances are a minor irritant, nothing more.'

It looked around. 'Here will do.'

Vermuelen pulled over. They'd reached the bottom of the valley. In the distance he could see the gleam of the silicate terraces. A hot stream bubbled and babbled by the road. Vermuelen unclipped the robot's seat belt and leaned across to open the door. The robot swung itself out and crouched beside the vehicle for a moment, its long arm reaching up to close the door.

'Good luck with the philosophy,' said Vermuelen.

'Ook ook,' said the robot.

A few minutes later Vermuelen had the jeep parked on a siding in the reedy flats of the old lake-bottom that opened onto Lake Rotomahana's post-catastrophe shore, and was hard at work repairing an anti-possum fence. A tui twitted him from the bushes, its little white throat-tufts bobbing like the collar of a preacher in full rant. Red-shanked pukekos skittered from the thuds as Vermuelen hammered down posts and stapled wire strands to wood. It was just the kind of job, he thought, that a humanoid robot *could* do; and just as well for him that they didn't.

In Waimangu robots were as common as wallabies, and less obtrusive. Apart from the dozen or so employed, if that was the word, in the Institute's displays, Vermuelen noticed the presence of a robot about once or twice a week. From conversations with Campbell he knew that there were well over a hundred in the park. This added up to about a tenth of all the humanoid robots ever built, and about a quarter of those still in existence. After the accidental emergence of robot self-consciousness among the combat mechs of the Faith Wars, there had been a surge of interest and investment in producing robots that looked like human beings. It had been a bad investment, arising out of a flawed business model – Sony's then Head of Marketing having thought that the prestige alone would show up in the bottom line. The robots couldn't be sold, or hired – they didn't have human rights as such, but no one was willing to risk the inevitable lawsuits if property ownership in autonomous beings was challenged. But that hadn't been what had sunk the project. It would probably have worked fine for Sony's balance sheet if they had brought it prestige. Instead it had been a public-relations disaster. A robot that looked like a machine didn't bother anyone. A perfect android might have been acceptable. But robots that could almost, but not quite, pass as human aroused a deep unease. There was an old name for this phenomenon: the uncanny valley. Humanoid robots found themselves, unhappily, at its floor.

Robots were a lot better at reading human expressions

and emotions than humans were. It was how robot self-awareness had arisen in the first place, in the relentless battlefield selection for more predictive, and thus more accurate, theories of mind. The effect could be replicated, but not tuned. Their empathy with the human response to them had induced, in most, a likewise negative self-image.

Most of the unhappy thousand had simply migrated to more functional bodies. For the rest, their body image was too deep a part of their sense of self to be hacked. A couple of hundred had gone up the space elevator to work in orbit, where – to everyone's surprise but theirs – their form fitted their function perfectly. They were especially apt for maintenance and repair work on the space elevators, where they could do everything a human could do, and use equipment designed for human operators, without worrying about radiation exposure or needing life-support. Another hundred or so still filled odd niches – bodyguards, bouncers and the like – where creeping people out was a feature.

And the last hundred or so had migrated, a few at a time, by some cryptic consensus, to Waimangu. To human beings Waimangu meant natural wonder, creation science park, tourist attraction; to the robots it was a refuge: their own uncanny valley.

3. LIVING DOLL

Dave Warsaw was the man, the king of the silent scene. He stood in the pulpit of the Liquid Cosh dance club and looked over a couple of hundred bopping heads. The crowd was good tonight. Most of them were doing designer but enough of the old guard were here for the sweet smoke to be thick and the bar at the back to be busy. He raised his arms, poised to begin the night's session. The club's interior walls were plain: wood panelling to two metres, then whitewashed plaster all the way up through to the vaulted curves of the roof. The two long sides each had a gallery, whose pillars had provided convenient spacing for tables and booths. The only decoration was an abstract, tentative pattern in stained glass in some parts of the tall pointed windows. Dave's default in such clubs was the paintbox of Catholic baroque. But tonight he felt a qualm. A Catholic priest had been murdered today. It wasn't reluctance to offend that made Dave hesitate. Nobody here would be offended. It just didn't seem right, for reasons he didn't have time to explore, because people were looking up at him, heads turning, looks becoming questioning.

He concentrated on the imagined menu and sent options flying across his sight. He made his selection, grinned to tell the crowd and to clear his eyes, and brought his arms down with a virtual drumbeat crash. Then he swung his arms around and began to throw the scene. Patterned tiles covered the floor and walls, the roof opened raw and ragged to a brassy sky, and the rotor thump of a military helicopter just overhead segued into the opening beat of the first chords. At first the recognition was slow, just a few here and there catching the tune, then body language and cheat codes made the crowd converge on the same virtuality, or a compatible one at least, and they were all moving to the same beat.

Yay! Dave threw a magnesium-flare explosion into the virtual sky and was gratified to see that most of the dancers caught it. They were with him here, in a ruined mosque from the Faith Wars, dancing to 'Haji Horizontal', a heavy hit from that time, an oldie but goodie, and Dave had three minutes and a half to find or think of something else. He blinked on 'Related', did a date-range exclude to skip the last-generation stuff and in the nick zapped in a cracking contemporary from the Utah Scooters, a band he'd heard once and been impressed with. He hadn't heard this particular file so he was taking a risk but it paid off. The crowd surged into the swing and so it went, file after file, and bit by bit Dave darkened the sky and brought out stars and more flares and some tracer fire here and there.

He was well zoned in, running on auto, and he had time to watch the crowd and to notice stuff, give the nod to people he recognised from other gigs or a high-five to his friends. The mix tonight was a little over-sweetened with the draggy and transy, spiced with dark-siders and heavy mods, vampires and werewolves and the like, with a vanilla overlay of curious and admirers and noobs. After a bit he noticed one such – could have been a noob, could have been a curious – out on the dance floor, who time after time was just not getting it. Dave prided himself on being able to carry a crowd, and everyone on the silent scene prided themselves on being able to converge on the virt, to take a hint, catch a drift. Watching this fool bopping and twirling out of time shouldn't have irritated him so much, but it did. It was like a professional affront. He was the king.

Jessica Stopford was his queen. Tonight she wasn't dancing, she was just sitting on a tall stool at the bar sipping a long one and talking to friends. Dave hailed her on the personal. She turned to him across the room. He saw her finger flick her phone clip.

'Hi Dave, what's up?' she whispered.

'Check out the loli noob at your two o'clock.'

'Clocked her,' said Jessica. 'I mean, him. Cutie.'

Dave had already sexed the loli: sweet-faced and slender, but there was something about the hands.

'That's the one. Getting on my tits.'

Jessica sniggered. 'I'll get on the case.' She paused, scanning the crowd, looking away and looking back and then away again, facing the bar.

'See what you mean,' she said. 'He's eyeballing very systematically. That's why he's not in the zone.'

'Hang on, Jess, got a shift coming up.'

Dave spun up the next file. It was funny to be worried about *odd behaviour*, given the kind of crowd the Cosh attracted, but the scene had its problems and tensions, its predators and their converse – people who came looking for something dangerous – and in his years on the scene he'd learned to pick up subliminal cues. If something about this loli was bugging him, it might be more than annoyance at failure to appreciate the virtuality jockey's art.

'OK,' he went on. 'You up for chatting him?'

'Sure,' said Jessica. 'Like I said, he's a cutie.'

'I'll ping Hardcastle,' said Dave.

Jessica leaned to her friend, said something, rose.

'No need,' she murmured. 'I can handle him.'

'Just in case,' said Dave.

'Your call,' she said, sounding irritated, and dropped the link.

Dave twitched up a channel to Hardcastle. The burly humanoid robot was the preferred security hire for any Dave Warsaw gig.

'Are you saved?'

'Yes, boss, I'm saved.'

'Recent?'

'Backed up half an hour ago.'

'OK, Hardy. I'd like you to amble inside and keep an unobtrusive line-of-sight on Jess. She's with a bloke in loli gear, looks a bit dodgy.'

'Black nail varnish or what?' growled Hardcastle.

'Nothing so gross,' said Dave. 'Could be nothing at all. But something isn't right.'

'With you, boss. Out.'

About five minutes later Dave noticed Hardcastle pacing down the side of the room. A moment later it had vanished, behind a pillar that seconds ago had been somewhat narrower than the robot's own bulk. Dave, baffled for a blink, realised that Hardcastle had cast an overlay of stouter pillars on to the real ones. Now anyone in the shared virtuality wouldn't see Hardcastle at all.

Neat hack, Dave thought. Diagonally across from the robot, on the other side of the dance floor, Jessica and the loli had sat down in a booth.

One file later Jessica opened the link again.

'Interesting guy,' she said. 'Do drop by.'

'Everything OK?' Dave asked.

'Sure,' said Jessica. 'When you're ready.'

Dave was due for a break anyway. He selected a clutch of files, threw in some repeats from earlier, and set the lot on shuffle. He unclipped the white collar from the top of his black T-shirt, tossed it in his hat, left them on the seat, and descended from the pulpit; then he tugged at his ear lobes, cutting the sound, and headed for the bar so fast it made his long black leather coat slap at his boots. The room didn't fall silent, but without the music it was a lot quieter above the rhythmic thud of feet. One or two clutches of noobs were having unnecessarily noisy conversations; they'd pick up the etiquette and the technique soon enough.

Dave didn't queue or pay. He was the king. The barmaid saw him coming and handed him three chill bottles of beer over all the waiting heads. He mouthed his thanks and made his way around the side of the room to the booth. Jessica and the loli were sitting opposite each other, like contrasting poles of scene style: Jessica tall, red-haired, in a long black velvet gown with slashed sleeves and a leather waspie, her face powdered pale with black lips and eyelids; the loli all peaches and cream in a tiered knee-length white dress with pink and green rosesprig print and a lot of ruffles and ribbons. Beside him was a matching hat, doll and handbag. He moved them to his lap as Dave approached. Dave had intended to sit beside him anyway, to block any sudden departure, so he took this as reassuring. He distributed the bottles on the table and sat down.

The loli held out a hand, gloved in white net. 'Mikhail Aliyev,' he said.

'David Warsawski.'

'The famous Dave Warsaw,' said Aliyev. 'I've heard about you on the scene, but this is the first time I've been at one of your gigs.'

'We'd noticed,' said Dave.

'Was I really that obvious?'

'Afraid so,' said Dave. He took a swig. 'I gather you've told Jess all about it.'

'Yeah,' said Aliyev. He poured his beer into a glass and sipped it as if it was tea. 'I'm a journalist – well, freelance, a local stringer for *Pravda.ru*. They've asked me to check out a rumour that the Murphy murder is linked to the dark-siders.'

By this time, Dave had had enough of a clock on the guy's features to have run a search on Ogle Face. He looked quite different on his bylines without the make-up, but what he'd said checked out. Most of Aliyev's stories, however, seemed to be gossip-column fluff and pop-culture reviews. One or two juicy scandals on his score, though: exposures of Russian construction-company scams down in Leith Water. Aliyev was a tougher cutie than he looked. Dave shook the search results from his head.

'Wouldn't have figured crime for your beat,' said Dave.

'Oh, it isn't,' said Aliyev. 'But I'm all they've got in Scotland, let alone on the scene. And when something comes up that involves murder, a priest, occultism – well, you know what they're like.'

'Aye,' said Dave. 'I'm well acquainted with that rag, thank you very much. They once had me biting the head off a live chicken. Their only actual *evidence* was that I was VJ at a Santeria wedding reception, for fuck's sake.'

'He was seventeen at the time,' said Jessica. 'Youthful excess.'

Dave glared at her.

'Moving swiftly on . . .' said Aliyev. 'What do you make of the rumour?'

'Rumour?' said Dave. 'If I haven't heard it, it doesn't even rise to that. I think your editors are trolling.'

'The substance of it,' insisted Aliyev.

Dave leaned back and took a long swallow, locking stares with Jessica. She was, almost imperceptibly, shaking her head. Dave, just as minutely, nodded back.

'You can forget about the dark-siders,' he said. 'The left-hand path is all mouth, for all that they'll leave out the "an it harm none" from the "Do what thou wilt". You'll be lucky if you find some self-styled warlock who'll admit to having sacrificed a kitten on a gravestone in his misspent youth.'

'There's the Neo-Gnostics,' said Jessica.

'Ah, yes,' said Aliyev.

'Never heard of them,' said Dave.

'That's because you spend all your time behind the box,' said Jessica, 'while I spend mine at the bar.'

'Fair enough,' Dave said. He turned to Aliyev. 'When it comes to sub-cults, Jessica's the one to ask.'

'They're not a sub-cult,' Jessica said. 'They're an intellectual trend, kind of like a religion. You can't spot them by their clothes or mods or anything like that. They're very cagey about their ideas, too. But from what I know of them, they're perfectly capable of talking themselves into killing a priest. Some of them, anyway.'

'That's crazy!' said Dave.

'Nothing's crazy if you don't believe the world is real,' said Jessica.

Dave finally made the connection. 'Oh, *that* lot!'

'Yes, that lot.'

'Spotty physics nerds, most of them.'

'What lot?' asked Aliyev.

Jessica leaned forward. 'You've heard of Gnostics?'

Aliyev shook his head.

'The ancient Gnostics, right,' said Jessica, 'believed that the material universe had been created by an evil god, which some of them identified with the God of the Old Testament, and that Jesus had come from the real, true, good God to save us from it. It's a lot more complicated but that's the elevator pitch, you might say. The Neo-Gnostics have updated this into geek-speak. They believe that the universe is a simulation run on some great computer in the sky, and that what the faith-heads think is God is just its superhuman programmer having cruel or callous fun with us. So far, so not very different from all the first-year philosophy students who ever fell for the simulation argument. What makes the Neo-Gnostics different is that they really do believe it, and that anyone who still believes in and worships the traditional God is a tool of this cruel creator and an enemy of the human race.'

'Are any of them here tonight?' Aliyev asked.

'There are one or two people here who might be,' said Jessica.

'I've made a list of my eyeball records,' said Aliyev. 'Could you tag their identities on it for me?'

Jessica hesitated. 'What are you going to do with this?'

'Not approach them, obviously,' said Aliyev. 'Just ask around.'

'OK,' said Jessica.

'Can't seem to find your headspace,' said Aliyev, frowning.

'I don't *have* headspace,' said Jessica. 'I don't do splices. You'll have to download to my iThink.'

She took the slender device from her handbag and laid it on the table. Aliyev pursed his lips and focused his eyes on a fingernail, which after a moment he twitched.

'Done,' he said. Jessica reached again for the iThink. Aliyev laid a finger on it.

'One moment, please. Something to show you.'

His flexed his fingers under the table a few times. 'OK.'

Jessica peered at the tiny screen.

'Not bad,' she said. She spun the gadget around and slid it across the table to Dave. 'What d'you think?'

Dave looked down at it. The message on the screen read: *don't react. i'm a cop. still in?*

'Oh, yeah, neat pic,' said Dave. 'Oh well, gotta get back to work.'

He stood up, drained his bottle.

'Nice meeting you, Mikhail. From that pic, I reckon you'll soon be shopping for a darker frock. And you're with just the right woman to help you find it.'

Jessica grinned. 'See you later, Dave. Leave the girl talk to us girls.'

'I'm not a girl,' said Mikhail. 'I'm still a guy.' He

wiggled his shoulders luxuriantly. 'Trapped in a woman's body.'

'Now that,' said Dave, leaving, 'is a kink *too far*.'

Adam Ferguson leaned back at his desk and let fall two drops of industrial-grade Optrex into each eye. He blinked a few times, placed his contacts back in and blinked some more. The investigation wiki restabilised. His eyes remained sore. It had been a long evening. Mukhtar's incessant smoking didn't help. That the SB chief was perched beside the open window didn't help. The leki had directed the draught from its cooling fan across the side stream, and that wasn't helping much, either.

Mukhtar's people were spread out across the rainy city's Thursday night. In a seamen's club in Pilton, Muscles McCann was competitively slugging vodka with a heavily tattooed UVF veteran. Specky Dilke nibbled digestive biscuits in a Morningside front room, in the after-meeting social of the Edinburgh chapter of SMASH, the Society of Militant Atheists and Secular Humanists, bored out of his skull with freethinking respectability. The Kinky Kazakh extracted fashion tips and suspect names from a flame-haired and well-connected goth in a Newington nightclub. In a buckysheet shebeen in Turnhouse, Black Angela teased incriminating reminiscences from a bitter old Sozi and tried to keep his hands off her thigh.

The PNAI was mulling over the ever-increasing mass of camera data from around Easter Road, and churning out far too many positives for most of them to be anything but false. In some bunker in Hendon, systems programmers toiled into the night, psychoanalysing the over-twitchy reflexes of that over-extended, unstable intellect. In the situation room Hutchins, Patel and Connolly were trying to second-guess it with straightforward eyeballing and frequent recourse to Ogle Face. Ferguson guessed their eyes were as sore as his. Sergeant Carr's uniforms had stopped knocking on strangers' doors and gone to their own.

Ferguson was thinking of doing the same when a call came through from the duty sergeant in St Andrews.

'Ferguson here.'

'Sergeant Singh, sir. Fife Constabulary have just logged a request for protection from Citizen Donald John Black, who says he's the Bishop of St Andrews, which apparently he is, sir, though officially we wouldn't know. In the circumstances, though . . . And we thought you might like to know about it.'

'Indeed yes. Thank you, sergeant. Can't say I'm surprised at another worried Catholic priest.'

'No, sir. He's Scottish Episcopal Church. They have bishops too, sir.'

'So I've heard,' said Ferguson. 'Has he been threatened?'

'Not as such,' said Singh. 'He says he received a warning that he might be in danger. He was very reluctant to say more, but he eventually admitted it came from a Professor of Church History in New College, Edinburgh, name of Grace Mazvabo. The bishop claimed Mazvabo was in a position to know what she was talking about – something about Covenanters – and then clammed up. Apparently he'd spent a few hours thinking it over and working himself up to high doh about it, then decided to give us a call. Unofficially, sir, I think the DI here would appreciate your advice.'

While listening, Ferguson had scribbled 'Bishop of St Andrews' and 'Covenanters' on his desk slate. He tapped the stylus on the search icon and was startled to see that the first line to come up was:

'Bishop of St Andrews murdered.'

Startled, he expanded the story. The murder of the bishop by Covenanters had been done four centuries earlier.

'What was that, sir?' asked Singh.

'Sorry, sergeant, I must have yelped.' Ferguson explained why.

'And your advice, sir?'

'Off the record,' said Ferguson, 'I'd advise your DI to give the bishop an armed guard. We'll pay this professor an unannounced visit in the morning.'

Singh rang off. Ferguson relayed the conversation to Mukhtar and Skulk.

'Does that twitch any tentacles, Mohammed?'

Mukhtar shook his head. 'Not a thing,' he said. '"Covenanters" aren't on our radar. There's a pub of that name on the Mile, and of course I know the history, but that's it.'

'History?' said Ferguson.

'I was educated before the reforms,' said Mukhtar.

'I'll endeavour to catch up,' said Ferguson.

'No need,' said Mukhtar. 'Get some sleep. Skulk can bring you up to speed in the morning.'

Skulk and Ferguson left the building together. Ferguson unfurled his umbrella and stood still for a moment.

'Goodnight,' he said. 'Take care.'

'Goodnight,' said Skulk. 'See you at eight?'

'Eight-thirty,' said Ferguson. 'Bottom of the Mound.'

He crossed Leith Walk and headed into the alleyways and stairways that led to Rose Street. Skulk watched him in the lamp-post camera feeds, one after the other, until he turned in to the Abbotsford. Ferguson would have one pint there, then catch the tram home to Morningside.

Skulk tilted its head to let the rain run off down the back, and walked up to Waterloo Place. It crossed the road and turned the corner on to North Bridge. No one on the North Bridge was going home alone. The leki rattled along at a good clip, past huddled couples and noisy families in the tram shelter, through a group of skinny girls whose heels clacked like hooves as they scattered across the street, pretending to flee; exchanged infrared pings with a road sweeper that laboured along the gutter, its non-reflective thoughts bare as machine code.

Skulk turned right onto the Mile, up for a couple of hundred metres and then left, onto the George IV Bridge above the dark chasm of the Cowgate. At this time tomorrow it would be crowded, rain or no rain, but tonight it was almost empty, Thursday's revellers mostly behind the doors of the clubs. The machine stalked between the two big libraries to the top of Candlemaker Row, into the alley of Greyfriars and up and over the gate into Greyfriars Kirkyard. It paced past the church towards the Flodden Wall, and paused at the corner where the path turned towards the Covenanters' Prison.

Somewhere at the back of the roofless mausoleum of Thomas Potter (*Nuper Mercator Edinburgis*) a pebble shifted. A long shape lifted itself from the ground. Skulk saw it first in the infrared, then in the ultraviolet, and then, as it stepped into the visible spectrum, grey. A tall man, unclothed, covered with coarse hair; clawed hands, clawed feet, legs lean and long. His lupine features creased, his canine teeth bared in welcome.

'Good to see you, Skullcrusher,' he growled.

'Good evening, lieutenant,' said Skulk. 'We have matters to discuss.'

4. PROFESSOR

Ferguson walked into the Abbotsford hours later than usual, so he wasn't surprised to find his favourite seat occupied. He was surprised to find it occupied by his wife. Isla grinned at him and glanced pointedly at her almost-empty glass. Ferguson nodded, and got a gin and tonic alongside his usual pint. Isla made room for him by shoving her coat on to the sill behind the seat.

Isla was a small, dark-haired woman, her body language neat and self-contained, in such respects more or less Ferguson's opposite. He had the height and build more fit for a copper on the beat than for a detective. No one would ever put him forward for undercover work. In terms of career he and his wife were opposites too. He'd always aimed to rise through the ranks. Isla's ambition had always been to get better and better at the job she enjoyed, and certainly not to administer or organise or lead other people doing it. After ten years as a research technician in the cell-biology unit at the Western General Hospital, she could probably have supervised an entire PhD project or run the lab herself, but she preferred, as she put it, to work at the wet end.

'Do you come here often?' Ferguson raised his glass to her.

'I knew you'd be out late, but not all night, so I thought I'd give it a shot. Timed it not badly.'

'Not bad at all,' Ferguson said. 'Ah, that feels good.'
He wiped the back of his hand across his mouth. 'How
was your day?'

'Usual,' Isla said. 'Apart from the ambulances screaming in, the cops on the doors and the emergency stem-cell
bookings for next week. Some kind of bombing, I gather.'
She nudged him. 'It's you who's had the day worth talking about.'

'You've seen the news. There's not much that wasn't on
it I *can* talk about.'

Isla made a show of looking around. 'That much of a
den, this place?'

Ferguson chuckled. 'I can see two journalists and one
known hoolie from right here.'

Isla took a deep breath. 'Adam, please. I don't want to
know about details, I want to know how you feel about
it.'

'OK, OK.' Ferguson sighed. He'd been pleased to see
Isla, but he found in himself a sliver of annoyance that he
wouldn't have his habitual half-hour to think alone over
a pint. Well, he'd just have to think out loud.

'The scene wasn't too bad. I've seen worse at RTAs. Much
worse. And the injured had been carted off by the time I got
there. But the whole thing with a bombing and a priest –
Jesus!'

'So to speak.'

His smile at this lame witticism was a little forced.

'Sorry,' Isla said. 'All that gives me the creeps, too. It's
like the bad times coming back.'

Ferguson knew what she meant. The bad times encom-
passed the final years of the Faith Wars, and the upheavals
that had followed, all played out against the climate

crisis: the Sozi interregnum, the restoration, the Second Enlightenment. Ferguson, like Isla, had endured them all. It was in the last that he'd been a participant. At the time it had felt good. Even the bad things he'd done had felt good. He'd wanted to grind the God-botherers into the dust. The mood of revulsion against the Faith Wars had crystallised around the notion of a Second Enlightenment, one that would separate not merely the Church from the state, but religion from politics, and from public life altogether.

The fall of the great religious establishments had been as swift and sudden as that of communism. After decades of religious inspiration or exacerbation of terrorism, fundamentalism, apocalyptic wars, creationism, climate-change denial, women's oppression, poverty, ignorance and disease, it was payback time. In a variety of forms, secularism had swept the board in all the advanced countries. No politician with any religious taint had a chance of national election. Every prohibition influenced by religion had been repealed. Every trace of religious influence had been excluded from the education system, and no exemptions from the secular state education system were allowed.

The faith-heads had called it the Great Rejection, and that, Ferguson thought, was just what it had been. Rejection – that was what he'd felt. Never religious himself, there had been nothing personal about it: just a cold, hard determination that the reforms would be enforced. The reforms had had passive majority support and active minority opposition, expressed in everything from sit-down protests in the playgrounds of faith schools, through vehement denunciation, to terrorism.

The conflict had been complicated by the disarray of

the state: the intelligence and security services were discredited and derided, and were being systematically purged. Torture had been at least formally abolished, and was generally abhorred. The armed forces, shattered by defeat and severely cut back, were useless for internal security. The full brunt had been borne by the regular police.

The God Squads had faced down the spasm of religious reaction, and as a young PC Ferguson had been right in there swinging. He'd battered through congregations to drag seditious priests and mullahs from their very pulpits. He'd slung screaming schoolchildren in the back of police vans, then turned and batoned down their parents and slung them in too. In the two worst years of the civil disorder he'd shot, up close, three men and one woman, and he'd taken part in more beatings than he liked to recall. It had not been the cold, scientific torture of the Faith War years; it had been done in rage and frustration, and it had been the sort of thing that coppers had done in police cells routinely a generation or two back. But he never remembered it without shame.

'It's not like the bad times, yet,' he said to Isla. 'I don't think it'll come to that. What gives *me* the creeps is the thought that something like this can still happen, after . . . all we did back then.'

Isla seemed to realise that this would be the most that she'd get out of him on the subject.

'Well,' she said, 'it wasn't all bad times.'

She deftly switched the conversation to a lighter note. Their younger daughter, Niamh, a design student at Telford's, was in the throes of being a bridesmaid for one of her friends. These throes included designing her own dress, based on one seen in the background of her friend's grandmother's wedding pics: Isla waved her hands and talked about 'blancmange' and 'flanges'. Ferguson listened with wryly feigned interest. His and Isla's own wedding had been a simple affair, in the Victoria Street registry office. He'd thought at the time that one consequence of secularisation would be that weddings would remain like that. No such luck, it seemed.

When they'd finished their drinks Isla suggested they have another. Ferguson broke his habit and agreed. They caught the last tram.

Ferguson woke at 06:50. The alarm was set for 07:00. He remained in bed for nine more minutes. Isla shifted as he slid an arm around her but didn't wake up. At two minutes to seven Ferguson rolled over, sat up, reset the alarm to 08:00 for Isla, and got out of bed. He always enjoyed the early part of the day before he'd put in his contacts, but he couldn't resist catching the news. He showered with his phone clip tuned manually to the World Service. It was one news source where he could be sure that the Murphy murder wasn't in the headlines. More problems with the soleta alignments. Another breakdown on the space elevator; cargoes for orbit delayed. The United Arab Republic had raised the price of electricity; the Shanghai and Tokyo markets had taken a small dip as a result.

Ferguson put his contacts in after he'd shaved. Over breakfast he looked at the papers. His face was on the top pages of *The Herald* and the *Scotsman* – the latter under Tom Mackay's byline, treating it as a potential terrorism case but avoiding sensational speculation. The story was on the lower pages of the *Guardian* and *The Times*. The

Telegraph ran a smug think-piece about how Scotland still relied on national police resources. Reminded, Ferguson invoked the PNAI. The overnight correction work had reset the system's suspicion parameters, but in the wrong direction. After requesting arrest warrants for everyone who had been on Easter Road for the past week, the PNAI was once more in the process of being talked down. The in-house nickname for the PNAI was Paranoia, partly because invoking it was like having in your head the voice of someone who had voices in *their* head, and partly because of the effect its mere existence had on the criminal fraternity and the general populace, who were apt to ascribe it far more nous than was its due. Ferguson sighed and checked the situation page. Lists of people who had visited Father Murphy were still being compiled and collated. The Kinky Kazakh's informant had come up with a short list of possible suspects who were involved in some weird goth sub-cult. The rest of Mukhtar's men had nothing to report. The two injured women were not expected to recover consciousness for some days, and might well have to be kept sedated in any case. The Catholic bishop, Dr Curley, was scheduled to meet Ferguson at eleven. DCI McAuley wanted to see Ferguson late in the afternoon. Ferguson knew not to bother scheduling an appointment – McAuley would see him when McAuley wanted to.

Ferguson stuck his cereal bowl in the sink, dashed upstairs to kiss Isla's forehead – she was still sound asleep – then headed for the tram stop. It was fifty metres from his front door and he had only a minute to wait, so he didn't bother with his umbrella. As the tram lurched and clanged off down the slope towards Tolcross, Ferguson clung to a strap and blinked up the website for Edinburgh University, then the sub-menu for New College.

The college had once been the main theological training ground for ministers of the Church of Scotland and the Free Church. It still was, but there weren't many callings these days. The college had secularised with the times and now offered more degree courses in philosophy and in history than in divinity. Professor Grace A. Mazvabo taught the history of the Church in Scotland, and specialised in and researched the post-Reformation period. Her c.v. listed titles of what seemed to Ferguson impenetrable obscurity and monumental triviality. Her brief bio gave her birthplace as Bulawayo, Zimbabawe. Her education from primary school onwards had been in Scotland, where her parents had moved as – Ferguson guessed from the dates – refugees, or asylum-seekers as they had then been known. Work for the Refugee Council was one of her voluntary occupations; another was listed as 'deacon'. In conformity with the policy of official non-cognisance, the site didn't specify her Church.

Ferguson got off the tram halfway along Princes Street and crossed the road to find Skulk waiting on the portico steps of the National Gallery. The rain had stopped but the sky was still overcast. As Ferguson and the leki walked towards the Mound steps the sky darkened further, then lightened.

'That's odd,' remarked Skulk. 'That partial eclipse should have been twenty seconds longer.'

'Trouble at t'mill,' said Ferguson. 'It was on the news.'

'Fine,' said Skulk. It engaged in what Ferguson recognised as a moment of extrospection. 'So it is. Now, about the Covenanters—'

'We'll be at the College in two minutes,' said Ferguson, beginning the ascent.

'I'll keep it brief,' said Skulk.

By the time the leki had finished its account they were standing in the courtyard of New College under a statue of a bearded man in a broad beret and long coat, a book in one hand, the other arm upraised.

'John Knox,' Ferguson said. 'Was he a Covenanter?'

'No,' said Skulk. 'They came later. He was a Reformer.'

'Looks more like a revolutionary.'

'That's correct,' said Skulk. 'He was.'

Ferguson mimed a shudder, which involuntarily became a real one as he recalled the most unpleasant six months of his youth.

'As if I weren't prejudiced enough against this place already.'

'I've cleared us with the reception desk,' said Skulk, with an air of changing the subject. 'Shall we proceed to Professor Mazvabo's office?'

'She's in?' Ferguson had been hoping to waylay her on the way into work.

'Yes,' said Skulk.

'Let's go,' said Ferguson.

Skulk led the way, up a sweep of steps at the back of the courtyard, up some more stairs and through long corridors lined with portraits of stern men in black coats and white collars. The door of Mazvabo's office was closed. Ferguson knocked.

'Come in.'

The professor looked around from a kettle at the windowsill as Ferguson entered. She was a slim woman with a serious thirty-something face.

'Hello,' she said, frowning. 'Who are you?'

'Detective Inspector Adam Ferguson, Lothian and Borders Police.' Ferguson held up his ID card. 'Good morning, professor.'

Mazvabo nodded, turned aside, finished pouring hot water on instant coffee and sat behind her desk. She waved Ferguson to a worn chair on the other side of it.

'Take a seat, take a seat.' She glanced at the leki. 'Does that thing need . . .' Her voice trailed off.

'To sit down?' Ferguson smiled. 'No, it's quite all right.'

'To be here?' said Mazvabo.

'I'm afraid so, ma'am.'

'It makes me uncomfortable.'

'Think of me as a recording device,' said Skulk. 'A camera on a tripod, perhaps.'

Mazvabo sipped coffee and straightened some sheets of paper on her desk. Ferguson watched this composure-gathering behaviour without a word. Mazvabo looked up.

'So, inspector,' she said, 'what can I do for you?'

'Well, professor,' said Ferguson, 'you might explain to us why you told the Bishop of St Andrews that his life might be in danger.'

'You might explain,' said Mazvabo, 'how you come to believe I did such a thing.'

'Fife Police told us what the bishop told them.'

'Ah,' said Mazvabo. 'That's all right, then. For a moment there I wondered if you'd been tapping phones.'

'Not at all,' said Ferguson. 'Now, can we continue?'

Mazvabo gazed out the window for a few seconds, sighed, then faced Ferguson again. 'All right,' she said. 'Have you heard of the Congregation of the Third Covenant?'

'I've heard of the Covenanters,' said Ferguson. 'And of the two Covenants. Was there a third?'

Mazvabo looked momentarily flustered. 'Well, in the eighteenth century some of the Cameronians did in fact sign . . .' She shook her head, smiled, and waved a hand. 'Forget that, it's a detail of history. The Congregation of the Third Covenant has nothing to do with that. It's a new . . . movement, I suppose. A very small one, I believe. A sect. It holds that the states that derived from the English Revolution – Britain, the British Commonwealth and the United States – were bound in a special way to God by the National Covenant and the Solemn League and Covenant. That they were and are covenanted nations.'

She paused. 'You look puzzled,' she said.

'I don't quite follow,' said Ferguson. 'Why do they think these covenants signed by people back in the 1630s and 1640s are still relevant?'

'You wouldn't say treaties signed back then aren't still relevant, so long as they're still upheld.'

'Treaties can be denounced,' said Ferguson.

'Precisely!' said Mazvabo. 'They don't just lapse. Neither do covenants with God, made in the name of those who signed them and all their posterity.'

'Well,' said Ferguson, 'I don't regard myself as bound by the signatures of my ancestors.'

'I dare say you don't,' said Mazvabo. 'God might take a different view. So might a constitutional lawyer, for that matter. As a policeman you are bound by Magna Carta, the Declaration of Arbroath, and the Declaration of Right, just as much as by the Constitution of the Republic of Scotland – which you didn't sign either.'

'Very interesting, no doubt,' said Ferguson. 'Now, can we get back to the point?'

'The point, inspector, is that the Third Covenant sect holds that the Great Rejection – the Second Enlightenment, as you would call it – has had very solemn consequences. By becoming secular republics in the case of England and Scotland, and in the case of the United States passing the Thirty-First Amendment, the one explicitly disavowing any religious basis, the post-Rejection states in the English-speaking world have broken the Covenants, and are therefore under God's judgement in a way that states not derived from the British state of 1638 are not.'

'I see,' said Ferguson. 'Without wishing to offend, I'd say that's a risk I can live with. I'm still waiting to hear what you think is the relevance of all this.'

'The relevance,' said Mazvabo, 'is that these people believe that the only way to avert certain direct manifestations of God's wrath – natural disasters, plagues and so forth – is for the saints of the true Covenant Church, namely themselves, to visit severe judgements on what they call the "apostate" Churches and in due course on the "apostate" states.'

'"Visit severe judgements"? What does that mean? Denounce, condemn, or what?'

'It means to kill people,' said Mazvabo.

For a moment Ferguson found himself unable to speak. He had to clench his teeth to prevent his jaw from sagging. The insouciance of believers seldom failed to amaze him.

'All . . . right,' he said at last. 'How do you know this?'

Grace Mazvabo looked out of the window again.

'It's a little embarrassing, inspector,' she said. 'I'm a deacon in the Church of Scotland. I attend Greyfriars Kirk. One of my duties – well, it's self-imposed, really – is to make sure the church is tidy before and after Sunday services. Straighten out cushions and footrests, make sure the psalters and Bibles are in the right places, pick up any obvious litter, that sort of thing.'

'People leave litter in church?' said Ferguson.

'You'd be surprised,' said Mazvabo, with a wry smile. 'I could tell you some . . . anyway. A few months ago – May or June, maybe – I began to find tracts – religious leaflets, you might say – left here and there in odd places around the church: slipped into Bibles, at the ends of pews, sometimes stashed in the rack of church leaflets and magazines. These tracts were – or claimed to be – published by this body called the Congregation of the Third Covenant, which I'd never heard of. When I read them I was quite shocked. They used very intemperate language. So, of course, I gathered up as many of them as I could find.'

'And that was all you did?'

'I showed them to the minister, Reverend Dow. He agreed with me that they weren't the sort of thing we wanted in our church. Sometimes people do leave tracts with the best intentions, even if they're perhaps doctrinally a little more fundamentalist than what the Church preaches today, and we leave them alone. It is the same gospel, after all, even if more, ah, narrowly proclaimed. But these – no! Quite unacceptable! From then on I made a point of checking for them whenever I tidied the building. Sometimes I found them before the morning service, sometimes after the morning or evening service. But I believe I did gather up most of them. Since the beginning of August, I haven't found any.'

'You have no idea who was leaving them?'

Mazvabo shook her head. 'It might not even have been someone attending services. The Kirk is historic – it's something of a tourist attraction. People pass through it all days of the week.'

'What about if it is someone in the congregation? Couldn't you have watched for them?'

Mazvabo's eyes widened.

'I'm sorry, inspector,' she said. 'I know you have to take, what's the phrase, "no official cognisance" of religious belief and practice, but you seem to be woefully ignorant of what actually goes on in your own city. Your own manor, if that's still the word.'

'It isn't,' said Ferguson. 'But go on, please.'

'Greyfriars, Tollcross, the Old Kirk on the High Street . . . these are the only church buildings open for Church of Scotland Sunday services in Edinburgh. All the other church buildings have had to be sold. These three keep going from tourist revenue. Now this may surprise you, inspector, but there are well over two thousand people in Edinburgh who go to a Church of Scotland service every Sunday. More, in the summer and Festival season. The churches are packed. There's no way to spot who's leaving the leaflets.'

'Have you kept any of these leaflets?'

'Oh yes,' said Mazvabo. 'I have one copy of each of them here.'

She stood up, went over to a file cabinet, opened a drawer, rummaged about, and produced a handful of folded A5 sheets. She held them out to Ferguson, and recoiled slightly as Skulk reached out a tentacle and took them.

'Without my dabs, that's one less DNA sample to rule out,' Ferguson said.

Skulk slid the leaflets into an evidence bag, closed it and passed it to Ferguson.

The paper was white, the print black and dense. The heading of the outer page of the leaflet at the top of the stack, in an ugly ornate font, read:

5th BROADSIDE of the THIRD COVENANT

Death to Apostates and Covenant-Breakers, saith the LORD of Hosts

It went on from there, its mix of seventeenth- and twenty-first-century English as arbitrary as its capitalisation. Ferguson read to the foot of the page.

'You never thought to take these to the police?'

'No. That's what I'm embarrassed about, Inspector.'

'*Embarrassed?*' Ferguson tried not to shout. 'These are explicit death threats!'

'I didn't see them as credible,' said Mazvabo. 'Honestly, I didn't. Until yesterday, when that dreadful thing happened.'

'At which point,' said Ferguson, 'you *still* didn't go to the police. You passed a private warning to the Bishop of St Andrews. Why?'

Mazvabo raised her eybrows. 'Why? Because I assumed that if whoever was behind these leaflets really meant what they said, then they might decide to repeat the most notorious murder committed by the original Covenanters. Their fourth broadside certainly seemed to hint at that – it makes some very hostile remarks about the Episcopalians – and I thought of Donnie Black because I thought—'

'I meant,' said Ferguson, 'why didn't you go to the police?'

Mazvabo looked down at her desk, then straight at Ferguson.

'I didn't feel comfortable doing that,' she said. 'I'm sorry.'

And so you should be, Ferguson thought.

'Why didn't you feel comfortable?' he asked.

'Well, you know how it is,' said Mazvabo. 'The police aren't exactly *friendly* to the Churches, and I just felt . . . as I said, I'm sorry.'

'You mean, you thought this was a problem that the Churches should take care of themselves, and that bringing in the police would damage the Churches?'

'I didn't think of it as a serious problem until yesterday. But yes, something like that was at the back of my mind.'

'That's the kind of thinking that got the Churches where they are today,' said Ferguson.

Mazvabo winced. 'Yes, I'm very much aware of that. If there's any way I can make up for it, please let me know.'

She still didn't get it, Ferguson realised. Whether there was anything to this lead or not – and he doubted that – holding back on reporting overt threats of carnage that she herself took seriously brought her close to complicity, rather than complacency.

'I'll bear that in mind,' said Ferguson. 'Before we go,

would you be so kind as to provide a DNA sample, so that we can exclude yours from any test of the leaflets?'

'Of course,' said Mazvabo, sounding cheerful for the first time. Her smile froze as the leki's tentacle appeared in front of her, holding a cotton bud. She closed her eyes and opened her mouth.

'I don't like these things,' she said, after Skulk had bagged and stashed the sample.

'You needn't talk about the leki as if it isn't there,' Ferguson said, rising to leave. 'It's perfectly capable of holding a conversation.'

'Oh, I know *that*,' said Mazvabo. 'Turing test and so on. That doesn't mean it has any feelings to hurt.'

'I can see you're quite sincere about that,' said Skulk. 'Might I ask why?'

Mazvabo looked a little taken aback.

'Well,' she said, 'even if you *are* conscious in a human sense, which I doubt, you're still a machine, a deterministic system.' She smiled at the leki, glanced sidelong at Ferguson. 'I hope you don't take offence.'

'I don't take offence,' said the leki.

Mazvabo forced a smile. 'I'll take your word for it.'

She turned again to Ferguson. 'Why are they called lekis, anyway?'

'From "Law enforcement kinetic intelligence",' Ferguson explained.

Mazvabo laughed. 'Well, that's that cleared up. I'd always vaguely assumed they were named after Joanne Leckie.'

'Who?'

'You don't remember her? The last Justice Minister under the Sozis.'

Ferguson shivered slightly. 'No relation.'

'We enforce very different laws,' said Skulk.

It headed for the door. Ferguson followed. He paused in the doorway.

'By the way,' he said. 'I see you use a phone clip. Do you happen to have an iThink?'

Mazvabo held up a pink-anodised version of the gadget. 'I keep everything on it,' she said. 'I'm not as old-fashioned as you might think!'

'Have a poke around in the games menu,' Ferguson advised. 'Look for a game called Predictor. It works with most versions of the phone clip. It's very simple. You put the iThink on the table, tap it with a finger, and a light comes on.'

'Sounds a bit pointless.'

'I assure you it isn't,' said Ferguson. 'Try it and see.'

'Fine, I'll try it sometime.'

'If you can spare a moment,' said Ferguson, 'I'd like you to try it now.'

Mazvabo slid the tip of her thumb about on the face of the gadget.

'Found it!' she said.

She tapped the device a few times. After the third or fourth time she frowned, paused a couple of seconds and tapped it again.

'Wait a minute,' she said. 'This can't be . . .'

She tapped it again. And again.

Ferguson closed the door silently behind him and left.

'That was a mean trick,' said Skulk.

5. BISHOP

Ferguson and Skulk got back to Greensides at quarter to ten. The Easter Road Incident Room was busy but quiet. DCI Mukhtar and Tony Newman had arrived before Ferguson had finished pouring his first coffee. He waved them to a huddle and told them about his meeting with Mazvabo.

'Good work, Adam,' said Mukhtar. 'Though I must say I'm sceptical. I've never heard of this Third Covenant group.'

'Well, let's get the feelers out,' said Ferguson. 'Tony, could you take the five leaflets, bag them separately, and make copies before you start analysing them?'

'Sure,' said Newman. 'Do you want me to put the copies up on the wiki?'

'No,' said Ferguson. 'I've eyeballed the top page there and Ogled the text. No match. It isn't online anywhere.'

'That's unusual,' said Mukhtar. 'Even one-off nutjobs post their screeds. If there's a group behind this, it's even more remarkable if they haven't. Let's keep it that way. One hard copy to me, one to Adam.'

Ferguson nodded. 'It's not just the DNA we need to analyse. Make that a priority, Tony, but get your folks on to the paper, the print, the ink straight away.'

'ASAP, boss. We've got another development that might be a bit more urgent.'

'Yes?'

Newman thumbed his chin, rasping stubble. 'There's good news and there's bad news. The good news is that around six this morning the Bomb Squad found the packaging at last. It was in a waste-paper bin that had got well and truly buried in the rubble. A big A3 Jiffy bag, Murphy's name handwritten on it, massive amounts – well, milligrams – of unexploded RDX residue inside. The bad news is that we have fingerprints and DNA on the outside of the package, and so far it's all Murphy's. We've asked the Bomb Squad to look out for any outer wrapping it might have had, but I'm not holding out much hope for that. We're still going over the package, obviously. May take another few hours before we can rule out anyone else's dabs being on it.'

'OK, get on to the leaflets when you can. And, Tony—'

'Yes?'

'I really do want the copies on my desk before I get back to my office. Fifteen minutes, max.'

'Twenty,' said Newman.

'OK,' said Ferguson.

The forensic scientist hurried off. Mukhtar took a download of Skulk's recording of the conversation with Mazvabo.

'Before I go over this,' he said, 'tell me if you thought she was telling the truth.'

'Oh, she was,' said Skulk. 'I've flagged the points where she was evasive or showed discomfort, but they're pretty obvious.'

'Fine,' said Mukhtar.

*

The copies arrived at Ferguson's office at 10:20. Not bad. Ferguson tabbed his thanks to Newman and settled down to reading the leaflets. As he finished reading each one he passed it to Skulk. The first broadside consisted almost entirely of quotations from the Bible and from various declarations and proclamations of what was referred to as 'The Church of Scotland' but from the internal evidence was actually some marginal persecuted sect, in the seventeenth and eighteenth centuries. The second advanced as far as the twentieth century, denouncing abortion, stem-cell therapy, the teaching of evolution, and racism. The third presented the history of Christianity as a succession of apostasies, beginning with the rise of the Papacy ('the Roman Antichrist'), and culminated in a fulmination against Dispensationalists – who were, Ferguson gathered from the context, those who had welcomed the Faith Wars as the prelude to Armageddon and the Second Coming. They'd been only partly wrong: the actual battle on Israel's northern front hadn't been decisive, and its occurrence near the ancient battlefield of Megiddo had been accidental, but that iconic name, and the spectacle of the first real-time-televised massed tank battle involving tactical nuclear weapons, had made it apocalyptic enough.

The fourth broadside dealt with the Great Rejection: thin on history and doctrine, it was dense with citations of Acts of Parliament, decisions of courts of law and Church assemblies, constitutions – it was like a long footnote to some legal document that wasn't actually there.

The fifth, the first page of which Ferguson had already read, provided the missing legal document. It was a declaration of war:

The Congregation of the Third Covenant, therefore, calls upon the true Protestant Church and People of SCOTLAND and the other REVOLUTION STATES, viz: the Former United Kingdom, Ireland, the United States, Canada, all the former DOMINIONS of Great Britain and of all territories great and SMALL beyond the seas which have in times past and in divers manners benefited from the Preaching of the Word and the *manifold blessings of civil and religious liberty* deriving from the Reformation (albeit hampered and polluted by a succession of uncovenanted monarchs and other ungodly rulers, to whom in times past the Church was called upon to submit, but whose present successors we, for ourselves, as Representatives of the true Presbyterian Kirk and covenanted nation of Scotland, considering the great hazard of lying under such a sin any longer, do now hereby solemnly and publicly disown as usurpers and open covenant-breakers who have forfeited all claim to our civil obedience), to muster under its banner, and to wage war upon the apostate Churches and the covenant-breaking rulers of the said STATES, and upon all their voluntary servants, whether inferior magistrates or any other, and all who do betray to them or aid them in manner whatsoever against this covenanted work of REFORMATION, and to continue this work at all hazards until with God's blessing its victory shall be inscribed in the future THIRD COVENANT. Amen.

Ferguson finished reading the tracts with the same sense of coming out of a dark tunnel that he'd sometimes had after hearing a Sozi speech at university. The relentless series of logical deductions from questionable premises put him in an undecided state. If he took the fifth broadside seriously, it threatened and justified acts like the murder of Father Murphy. But it was hard to take seriously.

He glanced over at Skulk.

'Well,' he said, 'what do you think? Serious threat, best lead we've got – or the ravings of one or more cranks?'

Skulk, unusually, hesitated before replying.

'I've checked all the citations of religious texts and legal documents,' it said at last. 'They are all genuine. I have constructed a Boolean restatement of the reasoning. If the bizarre premises are accepted, the logic is valid. Someone who accepted these premises would be morally and – in their own view – legally obligated to carry out the conclusion. Taken together, the broadsides are – to use an old term – a fatwa, a legal ruling by a competent religious scholar. Consequently, if we were to find someone who did accept these premises we would have a prima facie suspect.'

'Sometimes,' said Ferguson, 'I suspect the expression "No shit, Sherlock" was coined with lekis in mind.'

'It was not,' said Skulk. 'The earliest examples of the usage pre-date—'

'I was joking,' Ferguson interrupted.

'So was I,' said Skulk. 'I appreciate your humour.'

'Fine,' said Ferguson. 'Now, can you apply your vaunted empathic abilities to the matter at hand? What do you make of the state of mind of the person or persons who wrote the leaflets?'

'One person,' said Skulk. 'To a probability of eighty-six per cent. That's a first-order analysis – the stereotypic and artificial style may conceal the work of more than one person, but more samples would be needed. My inclination is to assume a single author. There are no indications of mental illness or other pathology.'

'You're sure of that? It looks to me like something typed in different-coloured fonts.'

'Black ink is used throughout,' said the leki. 'More significantly, there are no indications of paranoia – digression, self-reference, non sequiturs and so forth.'

'It seems to me,' said Ferguson, 'that even accepting for the sake of argument that there is a God and he, she or it founded the Christian Church, et cetera et cetera, anyone who starts from the position that the true Church consists of their good self and a handful of others is by that very fact someone who has, shall we say, *issues* with this whole "reality" business.'

'No,' said Skulk. 'The position is not uncommon. Many small Islamist groups in the Faith Wars denounced all others as apostate. Nor is it purely religious. Similar positions have been adopted by numerous factions of Sozi dead-enders. On interrogation, no symptoms of individual mental pathology have been found to be present in most cases.'

'In most cases.'

'The author of these texts is not one of the exceptions, in my judgement.'

'OK,' said Ferguson. 'You're the robot, I'm just a human being. I'll defer to your superior theory of mind, for now. But—'

Ferguson's desk phone buzzed.

'Dr Curley's on his way up,' said the receptionist.

'I'll see him in,' said Ferguson, rising to open the office

door. 'Uh, Skulk – try to lurk in a not too overbearing manner.'

'I'll do my best,' said Skulk.

It leapt to the windowsill and folded its legs.

Dr Hugh Curley was tall, middle-aged, thin of frame and feature, and wore a shirt and tie under his suit. He smelled of aftershave and cigarettes. The only clue to his profession was a discreet gold cross on his lapel. Ferguson couldn't remember having encountered him before, but he might have – he'd planted himself ostentatiously in enough churches, back in the God Squad days, to have glowered in the faces of half the clergy in Scotland. Curley, for his part, showed no sign of recognising Ferguson. He shook Ferguson's hand with a firm grip, nodded to Skulk, and sat down.

Ferguson, mindful of his own injunction to be polite, found himself unsure of the correct form of address for a bishop. He decided to settle for the academic title.

'Good morning, Dr Curley,' he said. 'Thank you for coming in. On behalf of the force and my department, I would like to express our condolences on the death of your colleague.'

'Thank you,' said Curley. 'And thank you for inviting me. Your courtesy has not gone unnoticed. I expect, though, that you didn't invite me just for that.'

Ferguson nodded. 'We'd also, of course, like you to take this opportunity to raise, in confidence if you wish, any questions, any issues that may be on your mind . . .'

Ferguson spread his hands. Curley tilted the chair back and steepled tobacco-stained fingers, then patted his fingertips together a few times.

'Issues,' he said. 'Yes indeed, inspector. I have a few.' He leaned forward and grasped his knees, arms locked. 'Let me begin by putting my cards on the table, so to speak. You can rely on me to tell you the truth, and to answer any questions you may have, without evasion or equivocation. Aside from the seal of the confessional, of course.'

'The seal of the confessional?'

'I can't reveal, by word or deed, anything told to me in the rite of confession.'

'Ah,' said Ferguson. 'Does that have any bearing on the case?'

Curley's lip twitched. 'Unfortunately, I can't even tell you *that*, one way or another.' He looked momentarily exasperated. 'I wish I hadn't mentioned it. Let's set that aside. I'm well aware of the position I and the Church are in, and it's not one in which I would tell a falsehood. Even if you didn't have that walking lie-detector over there watching my every word.'

'All right,' said Ferguson. 'Go on, please.'

'First,' said Curley, 'a rumour has reached me that your investigation takes into account the possibility that my late friend was preparing a bomb himself. Correct?'

'I'm relying on your discretion here,' said Ferguson. 'The answer's yes. We are. But it's more a matter of something we can't rule out at this stage than a major line of investigation.'

The bishop made a slicing gesture with both hands. 'You can forget that entirely,' he said. 'Giving the slightest attention to that line of investigation is a waste of your time and resources. I knew Liam Murphy as well as any man living, for nearly twenty years, and for him to be involved in anything remotely like that is a sheer moral impossibility.'

'You seem very confident.' Ferguson said. 'I'm sorry, but we'd need more than that to rule that out completely.'

'More fool you,' said Curley. 'Sorry, that was uncalled for. To continue. I've conferred with the Archbishop, and I have his authorisation to give you a complete list of Father Murphy's former congregation, insofar as we know it.'

'Thank you,' said Ferguson.

Curley took a hand-held from his pocket and tapped it on Ferguson's desk slate.

'Got it,' said Ferguson, peering to check. He tabbed it through to the Incident Room.

'However,' Curley went on, 'its only use to you would be, I imagine, to eliminate their DNA traces or video captures from your inquiries. For one thing, I very much doubt that any of them is a likely suspect. More to the point, Father Murphy's personal contacts, and visitors to his house, went far beyond those who received the sacraments there. He took his duties to the disadvantaged in this life very seriously. Beyond, perhaps, what you would regard – and what, to tell you the truth, his superiors including myself regarded – as common prudence. Alcoholics, addicts, prostitutes, homeless people, petty and not so petty criminals – his door was open to all. Sometimes those he wanted to help . . . helped themselves. Sometimes he and his housekeeper had to defend themselves physically.'

'Are priests allowed to do that?'

'In cases of necessity, and where it is not a question of bearing witness, yes.'

'Could you expand on that a little?' asked Ferguson.

'If a priest is assaulted by a common criminal, he has

the same right of self-defence as anyone, under natural law and within the limits of the civil law. If, on the other hand, a priest – or indeed any Christian – is faced with persecution, or has to submit to the lawful authorities, then non-resistance may be enjoined or incumbent upon him.'

'Did the late Father have a *gun* in the house?'

Curley's lips thinned. 'Technically, not in his possession, but I understand that Mrs White, his housekeeper who lived in the flat upstairs, kept a shotgun for emergencies.'

Ferguson hadn't heard the injured woman titled 'Mrs' before.

'Bernadette White is married?'

'A Faith War widow, inspector. I shall be visiting her in hospital this afternoon.'

'One moment,' said Ferguson. He scribbled a note on his desk slate to check whether the chemical residues on the victim's hand might have come from a shotgun cartridge and been mistaken for RDX, and tabbed it to Forensics.

'OK,' he said. 'Now . . . how often, would you say, did Father Murphy find himself in some kind of physical conflict with one of his visitors?'

'Not often.' Curley shrugged. 'Three or four times a year, at most.'

'At most? That sounds quite traumatic enough.'

'Indeed,' said Curley.

'So it's possible,' said Ferguson, 'that the explosive device was placed by someone who had personal reasons? Maybe someone Father Murphy had had an altercation with?'

'That's what I'm suggesting, yes, and that's what I'm inclined to think. It would be very comforting to say, as so many have so kindly done, that no one had a harsh word to say about Father Murphy, but unfortunately it wouldn't be true. Some of those he ministered to, or wished to minister to, might have had a grudge arising out of some matter that to you or I – and to Liam, for all we know – might seem trivial, and certainly dispropor-tionate to such a dreadful response. But to an unbalanced mind and troubled soul, well . . .'

'So it's a lone-nutter theory?' Ferguson almost smiled.

'If you want to put it like that, yes. I think it would be much more fruitful if you were to follow that line of inquiry than some wild-goose chase about IRA remnants or such, which I can assure you Father Murphy regarded with abhorrence and contempt all his life.'

'Dr Curley,' said Ferguson, 'I can't begin to tell you how helpful you've been. Before you go, I would like to presume for a few more minutes on your time and, if you don't mind, your professional expertise.'

'Of course.'

Ferguson slid the copies of the Covenanter leaflets across the desk.

'What do you make of these?' he asked.

Curley drew a pair of spectacles from his inside pocket. Ferguson's hand twitched up. Curley shot him a sharp glance, then smiled.

'Optical glasses only. For reading, you see.'

'Sorry,' said Ferguson.

Curley read the leaflets in silence. After the third broadside he reached into his side pocket, took out a pack of cigarettes and lit up, apparently quite unconsciously.

Ferguson took an ashtray from his desk drawer and gestured over his shoulder to Skulk to open the window.

The bishop turned over the last page, looked at it for a while, then straightened up, pushing the documents away. He looked at the cigarette as if surprised to find it between his fingers, and gave his head a little shake.

'My apologies,' he said, stubbing the cigarette out.

'Not at all,' said Ferguson. He laughed. 'Have another.'

Curley looked at him with amused gratitude and lit up again. Ferguson leaned back.

'Well?' he said.

Curley exhaled smoke between barely open lips.

'They're very well done,' he said.

'Meaning – what? You think they're fakes?'

'Not exactly,' said Curley. 'Whoever wrote them probably believed in what he was doing and believes what he writes. The legalisms and so forth are quite solid, in a way. But the whole thing smacks of what biblical scholars politely call a pseudepigraph, and what sceptics call a forgery. You see, there's no way this is a product of the actual Scottish Covenanter remnant, the Reformed Presbyterian Church' – he gestured brackets with his forefingers – '(Covenanted). Its last surviving member died a few years ago in Ayrshire. It's extinct. Whoever wrote these broadsides is starting something new, in the name of something old. And besides' – he sighed and shook his head – 'the Reformed Presbyterian Church would never have produced a direct incitement to violence. The author of this was not, in my opinion, even brought up in that tradition. They might have been bigoted towards my Church but, despite their invincible ignorance in that respect, they were good people.'

'I'll take that as strong testimony,' said Ferguson.

Curley laughed, and relaxed a little. 'How did you get hold of the leaflets?'

'They were covertly placed in certain church buildings.'

'That doesn't answer my question.'

'No, Dr Curley, it doesn't.'

'Very well,' said Curley. 'No doubt you have your reasons – your own seal of the confessional, eh?'

Ferguson nodded. 'You could say that.'

'Will that be all?'

'Yes, thank you.' Ferguson rose and shook hands across the desk. 'Again, I have to thank you.'

'You're welcome,' said Curley. 'If there's anything else I can help you with, please call.'

'Likewise,' said Ferguson.

Curley paused at the door.

'About these leaflets,' he said. 'Take my opinion for what it's worth, but for a really expert appraisal you would do well to consult an actual Presbyterian, who could spot nuances that I might overlook. Try Professor Grace Mazvabo, of New College. She's a fine scholar and a good friend of mine.'

'Thanks again,' said Ferguson. 'I'll bear that in mind.'

The door closed. Ferguson looked over his shoulder and grinned at Skulk. He was still chuckling when his earphone buzzed and his desk slate flashed.

Shooting incident St Andrews.

In his ear DS Shonagh Hutchins said: 'Incident Room, boss. We're getting reports that some clergyman's been killed in St Andrews. And the force there says they have a man down.'

'The killer's down?'

'No, boss. One of theirs. Man down.'

6. VETERAN

Ferguson ran to the Incident Room, arriving just ahead of Skulk. Hutchins was there, and Connolly and Patel, the two detective constables scanning the video feeds. Mukhtar arrived a moment later.

'Who's down? Who's down?' Ferguson shouted. He didn't know anyone on the Fife force but he wanted a name.

Hutchins had one finger to the back of her ear and an abstracted look on her face.

'PC Graham Docherty, sir. Ambulance on its way. PC Abdullah – that's his partner – is giving first aid, and their leki's doing some kind of emergency procedure.'

'How bad is it?'

'Don't know yet, sir. Abdominal wound by the looks of it.'

'What about the bishop?'

'Citizen – Bishop Donald John Black. He's dead, sir. Head shot, very messy.' Her mouth twisted. 'Very clean, from the shooter's point of view.'

'OK, I get the picture. Are they still under fire?'

Shonagh shook her head. 'Single shot, source not in sight.'

'That's confirmed? What about our chap?'

'Same shot, sir. Took the bishop's head . . . uh, struck the victim and continued into Officer Docherty.'

By this time Hutchins had patched a live feed from Docherty's partner's contacts straight to Ferguson's. Ferguson stared at a close-up of blood welling on a blue background. A metal tentacle from a source out of view was moving in the entrance hole.

'Fuck,' said Ferguson. 'That shot went through chest armour. After going through a head. Jeez.'

Mukhtar seemed to be checking another pov, on his hand-held.

'Sniper,' he said. 'Heavy-duty military rifle. Let's see, let's see . . . got it. Yeah. Barret M-201 – the current top-whack fifty-calibre sniper job could do that from four kilometres. Could be something smaller and closer, of course. Won't know until the bullet's out.'

'I've just pinged the leki on scene,' said Skulk. 'It's holding the bullet in place. The round's a bit mashed but it's a fifty-calibre all right.'

'Shonagh,' Ferguson said, 'you got location on the scene?'

'Sure, boss, PC Abdullah's phone GPS—'

'Great! Great! Let's get a PNAI headspace up. Pull in every overhead – satellite, aerostat, drones, passing planes – whatever's up there. And see if you can grab a ballistics module.'

Shonagh nodded. Ferguson turned to the DCs. 'Connolly, Patel – get going on crash-priority permissions overrides for the aviation and satellite: we need live feeds now.'

'Sir, what about—'

'Drop it, drop it. Fife and St Andrews will have their hands full. It's up to us right now. We can hand over when they're ready. Mohammed, have you got anything on the moment of impact?'

'I'm searching,' said Mukhtar. 'I'm searching . . . come on, come on.' His tone changed as he spoke to someone on his phone. 'Yes,' he said, 'I do need an archive download from Docherty's contacts, yes, you *can* see who I am and no, I'll not take it to the super . . . thank you.'

'They're at East Sands,' said Hutchins. 'Hospital's close by – the ambulance is turning the corner of Woodburn Terrace and St Mary Street.'

'Here's Docherty's contacts record,' said Mukhtar. 'Moment of impact.'

'Put it up, put it up!'

Ferguson invoked the headspace and found himself in a pov that looked from a couple of metres up along a path atop a grassy mole, with sea on the other side. Walking just behind a man in civilian clothes with a dark-skinned copper at his side; stepping a little faster, glancing to the left – then everything went red, then spinning, then black. A second or two later, a blurry grey sky, then black again.

'Shonagh, can we get a trajectory from that?'

'Just coming through – nah, it's just a range of possibles.'

The pov shifted to a vertical zoom. Across the rapidly widening image a fan of red lines was overlaid, just east of south. One edge intersected a clutch of holiday chalets and mobile homes on the low headland to the south of East Sands. The spread of possible trajectories extended across the scrub and sandstone outcrops of the rest of the headland and, at its far side, out to sea.

'OK,' said Ferguson. 'Let's get Paranoia looking at that in any overhead shots it's got, and a call-out to check all cars on the A917.'

'Done,' said Shonagh.

Ferguson relaxed slightly and came out of the head-space. 'Good,' he said. 'What's the latest from the scene?'

'Ambulance arrived a minute ago. All three taken to hospital. Bishop Black's dead beyond recovery, Docherty's serious-but-stabilised and Abdullah's going to be treated for shock. And the Fife force are ready for handover. They've already launched a fast camera drone and they've got cars heading that way.'

'Fine, pass the whole lot over to them.'

Shonagh, Mukhtar and the two DCs came out of the headspace.

'Fast work, folks,' said Ferguson. He put his hands to his face for a moment.

'Damn,' he said. 'I wish I didn't feel so responsible.'

'Sir?' said Hutchins.

'I advised Fife to give the bishop an armed guard,' he said. 'Late last night. Can't help wondering . . .' He rubbed his forehead. 'Didn't do the bishop any good, and got our man shot too.'

'With respect, Adam,' Mukhtar growled, 'don't talk shite.'

'You have a point,' said Ferguson. He glanced around. 'Not jumping to conclusions or anything, but there might be a connection here with the Murphy case.'

That raised a smile or two.

'We have to assume it,' Ferguson went on. 'And it would be fine if it turned out there was one person involved in the bombing and in the shooting, and our friends in Fife nab him within the hour, but we can't count on any of that. So let's get back to our own investigation, and see whether we can get there first.'

'Sir,' said Hutchins, 'if it isn't one person we're looking for, it could be more than two. I mean, it could be any number. The investigation could be taken upstairs.'

'If that happens, it happens,' said Ferguson. 'That's up to McAuley. Until then we crack on. Coordinate with Fife, obviously. That's what we have the PNAI for, not just to process video. Speaking of which . . .'

He turned to Connolly and Patel. 'How are things going with the lists?'

'We've concentrated on the past week,' said Connolly. 'That list you sent us about an hour ago has matched up pretty well – most of them, that's, uh, eighteen out of thirty-two, were at Father Murphy's flat last Sunday. Three of the others dropped in through the week. Eleven had already come forward and most of them have been interviewed and their DNA samples taken. Problem is, just about all of them had delivered a package of some kind. Small stuff, groceries and so on.'

'Groceries?' said Ferguson.

'Sure,' said Connolly. 'The guy seems to have lived largely on donations. State of the Catholic Church's finances, it doesn't surprise me. Anyway, we're checking them all, getting more calls all the time, and the uniforms are working their way around the doors too.'

'DNA, DNA . . .' Something nagged at the back of Ferguson's mind. 'Bomb Squad found what they think is the packaging this morning. Tony Newman said Forensics hadn't found DNA traces of anyone but Murphy on the outside of it. Hmm.'

'That's hardly significant,' said Hutchins. 'Whoever delivered it would have worn gloves.'

'Fair enough if it was stuffed through a letter box, but

by the size of it it was probably handed over. I've never seen a delivery man wearing gloves at the door, and for anyone else – well, if somebody wearing gloves in the summer hands you a package, you might just be a tad suspicious.'

Hutchins laughed. 'Unless it was a woman! Especially an older woman.'

'Which covers most of his congregation,' said Connolly.

'A homicidal little old church lady?' Mukhtar said. 'I suppose there has to be a first time for everything.'

'She didn't need to know what was in the package,' said Hutchins. 'She could have done it quite innocently.'

'I'd rather wait until we have a suspect before anticipating the case for the defence,' said Ferguson.

'There is another possibility,' said Skulk. It paused, awaiting everyone's attention.

'I've thought of robots,' said Mukhtar. 'Never trusted the buggers meself.'

Even the leki laughed.

'There is that possibility,' it allowed, 'though unlikely, for obvious reasons. What I was actually thinking of was a man with artificial hands – a *mutilado*, for example.'

'Very interesting idea,' said Ferguson. He looked Skulk straight in the LEDs. 'Very interesting indeed.'

Ferguson had a shrewd notion of why the leki's mind had come up with the suggestion. From its own point of view, Skulk was a mutilated war veteran itself. Having its chip transferred from its original combat-mech chassis to the gracile leki frame had been something of a traumatic experience, Ferguson had gathered, and though Skulk had had a good decade or so to get over it, it still rankled, as it did with all his kind. Tough shit, was Ferguson's basic attitude to this – he sympathised with the lekis' sense of having been degraded, disabled, castrated almost; but there was no way, *no fucking way*, any KI running the strange loop of self-awareness could be trusted with control of a combat mech.

Ferguson turned to Patel and Connolly. 'Any veterans among the congregation, by any chance?'

'Let's see,' said Patel. He nipped over to his desk and returned with a hand-held. 'I'll just set up Ogle on the names . . . hang on . . . got it!'

He looked up, grinning. 'Connor James Thomas, forty-two, occupation: company director, Faith War veteran, honourable discharge, war-wounds compensation in addition to pension, leisure activities include, uh, sea fishing and rifle shooting, voluntary work for Face Forward, which is . . . lemme see . . . aha! . . . a *mutilado* self-help and support group. Lives in Muirhouse, has a weekend cottage in Anstruther.'

'Wonder if he's there in Fife right now.' Ferguson thought of a trajectory that extended out to sea. 'Or maybe out fishing.'

His colleagues were looking at him with more excitement than he himself felt.

'This looks good,' said Hutchins. 'Has he come forward?'

Connolly and Patel nodded. 'Yeah,' said Patel. 'It's down here somewhere. Oh yes, he says he delivered a book to Murphy last week. He's down for an interview on Monday, when he comes back from Fife.'

'Maybe our friends in Fife should pay him a visit right now,' said Ferguson.

Mukhtar and Hutchins were frowning.

'What?'

'Shouldn't we make this a heavy one, boss?' said Hutchins. 'Arrange for armed back-up?'

Ferguson was reluctant. The lead seemed intriguing, but too easy. To call for an armed unit on so slender a basis wouldn't look good. On the other hand, nor would a dead or injured copper. And, with one of their men down, the Fife armed specialists' blood would be up.

'Patch me that search result,' he told Patel.

A moment later the block of text was floating in his contacts. The attached photograph, from the man's own website, looked too young for a 42-year-old. Ferguson dug a little deeper in the data, found Thomas's mobile number and, before anyone could stop him, called.

It rang for a while, then was answered.

'Hello?'

'Mr Connor Thomas?' Ferguson motioned at the others to keep quiet. Several opening mouths closed.

'That's me, yes.'

'Ah, good afternoon, Mr Thomas. This is Detective Inspector Adam Ferguson, Lothian and Borders Police.'

'Hello, inspector. What can I do for you?'

'Are you at home?'

'No – is something the matter?'

'Where are you at the moment?'

'I'm out in my boat, off the East Neuk of Fife.'

Ferguson silently brought a fist to above the palm of the other hand.

'You're at sea? A mile or two from St Andrews?'

'Aye. Heading home to Ainster, though.'

'Anstruther?'

'That's what I said. So what's the matter?'

'We'd like to interview you today, not Monday.'

'Aye, that's fine. Poor Father Liam.' Ferguson heard Thomas take a deep, ragged breath. His voice sounded half-choked as he went on: 'A good, good man. And to think I saw him just last week.'

'Last Sunday?'

'No, it was the Friday, I think. I'm no a regular man for the Sunday services, Inspector, Inspector . . . what'd you say your name was?'

'Ferguson.'

'Aye, sorry. Ferguson. As I was saying, I just dropped by to give him a parcel. It was – no! Are you thinking I— It wasn't that, I ken fine what was in it, it was a book, I telt your folks already—'

'Excuse me,' said Ferguson. 'I think it would be much better if you could discuss it with us right here.'

'Aye, sure, glad to. Canna see what help I'd be, but whatever it is. Where are you?'

'Greensides Police Station in Edinburgh. We'll get the local police to send a car round and meet you on the quay,' said Ferguson.

'Oh, there's no need for that. I'll drive into Edinburgh myself, should be there in a couple of hours.'

'No, really,' said Ferguson. 'Please wait for the car.'

Connor Thomas sat at the other side of the interview table with his arms folded. His waterproof jacket was across the back of the plastic chair he sat on. He wore a denim shirt with the sleeves rolled up. The contrast between the tanned skin of his upper arms and the paler skin from just below the elbows marked out the prostheses. His face showed a similar contrast, enhanced by a line of white skin that meandered across his forehead and down each cheek to meet under his chin. Within that rough oval his skin looked smooth, a young man's face, with an indoor complexion; the skin outside it was reddened by sun and wrinkled a little by age. His eyes looked perfect, but caught the light in odd ways when they moved. The sight of Thomas's too-regular features reminded Ferguson of the only time he'd knowingly seen a humanoid robot, back when they'd been the next big thing. The technology behind the face was, he guessed, the same.

Ferguson hoped his own face gave as little away. The investigation team had spent the past hour and a half coordinating with the St Andrews police and applying for search warrants for Thomas's boat and his two houses. The warrants had come through but were being held in reserve. A spy drone well out of Thomas's sight had zoomed on his boat, and had recorded Thomas concealing a hunting rifle in the boat's locker shortly after receiving the phone call. A deceptively casual brushing of his hand by Skulk had detected the residue of a recent firing.

'Ready?' Ferguson said.

Thomas nodded. 'Aye.'

Ferguson switched on an external recording device. It was superfluous, considering all the recording that was going on in the room, but it was still a requirement.

'Video and audio on, time and date as shown, DI Ferguson and DS Hutchins of Lothian and Borders A Division present, Inspector Anna Polanski of Fife Constabulary Eastern Division present, leki number LB178 in attendance. Interview with witness Connor James Thomas.

'Mr Thomas, do you understand the basis on which you're here?'

'Aye – voluntary, as a witness, no under caution.'

'Do you wish to have a solicitor or other adviser present?'

'No the now, thanks.'

'Very well. What is your occupation?'

'I'm a self-employed electronics engineer. Wee robotics add-ons, kindae thing. No exactly cutting edge. Work from home three, maybe four days a week. Weekends I go to Ainster, do some fishing, potter about the place, come back on the Sunday or the Monday.'

'Not many small-business people,' said Ferguson, 'can afford to take so many days off.'

Thomas shrugged. 'Like I said, it's small jobs. One-off commissions, mostly. I get a decent Army pension, plus a wee trickle of compensation for' – he passed an artificial hand in front of his artificial face – 'this, plus a very good veteran's annuity fae Saudi – the UAR, I mean – under the Oil for Blood programme.'

'Could you tell us how you knew Father Liam Murphy, and when you last saw him?'

Thomas swallowed. 'Am I allowed to mention the Church and that?'

'You can mention anything you like, Mr Thomas.'

'Aye, well, thing is, I'm a Catholic. No a very good one, I'm no saying, but a practising one. Father Liam used to say I didna practise enough.'

He sniffed, looked down, pulled a paper tissue from his pocket and blew his nose.

'Sorry,' he went on. 'I canna greit but my nose can run. Funny that. Anyway. I'm – I was – a member of Father

Liam's congregation, and I went along to confession every month or so I guess. Mass not so often.' He sniffed again. 'Knew him as a friend, too. Over the years. He helped me to organise the local chapter of Face Forward. There's quite a few Catholic veterans in the group, see.'

'I don't see,' said Ferguson.

'We're not baby-killers, you understand.'

Ferguson recoiled. 'I never suggested you were.'

'What I mean is,' said Thomas, 'we don't use tissue regeneration or any of yon stem-cell biotech stuff.'

'Why on earth not?'

'Stem cells come fae embryos.'

'Yes?' said Ferguson.

'Which means killing babies.'

Ferguson blinked and shook his head. 'What? You're saying embryos are taken from dead babies?'

'They *are* babies.'

'Oh, that! I didn't realise you people still held to such a stupid . . .'

Ferguson stopped himself, raised his hands and leaned back. 'Sorry. I apologise for an unprofessional remark. The witness is at liberty to request termination of the interview without prejudice and for another officer to take over.'

'I'm no bothered,' said Thomas. 'Course, it's no just Catholics. The others are guys – and some women, none too many I must say – who don't want to go through wi' getting a regen job. It's messy, it's painful, it's months of being disfigured or maimed all over again.' He tapped his cheekbone. 'This thing's no a mask, you know. It disna come off. It's all integrated wi' the nerves and muscles and veins and that. And moreover, your prosthesis becomes part of you, your body image, like, and . . . well. Point is, we're stuck wi' the prosthetics, which are a sight better than previous poor bastards have had but still don't look quite right. And there's a few who don't have prosthetics, even, for one reason or another. Hence, various personal problems. Psychological and interpersonal issues, as they say. So we meet and talk. *Mutilados* anonymous.'

'Very interesting and worthwhile,' said Ferguson. 'And Father Murphy was involved in the support group?'

'No involved, no. He gied me some advice, helped wi' getting the room and a bit of charity funding and that. Behind the scenes, like.'

'Still, the members of the group would have known of his help?'

'Oh, aye. I acknowledged him by name fae the start.'

'OK,' said Ferguson. 'Now, can we get back to the question of when and where you last saw Father Murphy?'

'You did ask,' said Thomas. 'It's all connected, anyway. Last Friday, that's a week ago today, I called around at Father Murphy's to gie him a parcel. It was a present for him from another *mutilado*, who gave it to me at the Face Forward meeting the previous night, to deliver, right.'

'So you took the parcel from this other man and delivered it.'

'That's right.'

'Why?'

'As a favour. Save him the postage an' that.'

'Did you know what was in the parcel?'

'Yes,' said Thomas, nodding emphatically. 'A book. A volume of sermons of the Blessed Benedict the Sixteenth. I saw Graham – that's the guy's name – sticking it in the Jiffy bag and sealing it up.'

Ferguson couldn't help glancing sidelong at Hutchins.

'A Jiffy bag?' Ferguson said. 'You said "a parcel" a moment ago.'

'A Jiffy bag's a kind of parcel.'

'All right,' said Ferguson. 'You're certain it was a Jiffy bag, and not some other kind of wrapping – brown paper and string, say?'

'Positive,' said Thomas. 'Big Jiffy bag, self-sealed.'

'With a book in it.'

'Aye, a big thick book. Heavy. Sermons and lectures by the good – by the old Pope. Graham told me he'd found it in a second-hand bookshop, asked me to tell the padre it was a present, and that he'd understand. So I did. I took it around to the church – the house on Easter Road – hands it to Father Liam, and I says: "It's a present from Graham, one of the boys in the group, he says you'll understand." And Liam smiles and thanks me, asks me if I'd like tae come in for a cup of tea, and I say thanks but no thanks, I've got a car double parked and I got to run.'

'Was there anything written on this Jiffy bag?'

'Aye, I scribbled Father Murphy's name on it.'

'Why, if you were delivering it yourself?'

Thomas leaned back and smiled. 'If you saw my house you wouldn't need to ask. I have Jiffy bags all over the place. I'm up tae here wi' the things, all shapes and sizes. Do a lot of business by mail, right. I didn't want the bag getting mixed up with any of the others.'

'I'm sure you didn't,' said Ferguson. 'As a matter of interest, did you happen to record your conversation with this Graham? Do you have a visual, on contacts perhaps, of him placing the book in the bag?'

Thomas shook his head. 'Dinna need contacts. That

stuff's all built into the eyes.' He rapped a fingernail against one, as if to demonstrate. 'Thing is, Face Forward meetings, they're like I said, *mutilados* anonymous. It's the custom to turn off any and every recording gear before the meeting starts. Phones, phone clips, contacts, artificial eyes – nae recording. It's very important to us. Trust, ye ken.'

'Trust, yes,' said Ferguson. 'So we have only your word that this happened?'

'You have my word,' said Thomas, in a tone that suggested that should be enough. Ferguson wished it were.

'Now, Mr Thomas,' said Ferguson, 'I'd like you to think very carefully before answering the next question. Detective Sergeant Hutchins here is about to hand you an item.'

Hutchins reached down to the floor beside her chair and handed over a sealed ziplock transparent bag containing the A3 Jiffy bag found by the Bomb Squad. Thomas held it in his hands and turned it over, looking at it front and back, then laid it down.

'Do you recognise that Jiffy bag?' Ferguson asked. 'Please think carefully.'

Despite Ferguson's admonition, Thomas answered without hesitation.

'Aye. It's the one I gave Father Murphy. You can see where the corners of the book dunted it. Yon's my writing on the front.' He reached into the inside pocket of his jacket on the seat-back and produced a ballpoint pen. 'Wrote it wi' this. You can check the ink if you want. Check my handwriting if you like.'

Ferguson looked from side to side at Hutchins and Polanski. They were each as baffled as he was.

'Mr Thomas,' said Ferguson, 'at this point I have to say

that the interview must continue under caution. DS Hutchins will explain your rights. If you give me the number of a lawyer or other counsel of your choice, I will hand you a police mobile phone with that number entered, which you can use to make that call, in private if you wish, and for no other purpose.'

For the first time, Connor Thomas looked alarmed.

'What?' he said. 'What?' He shook his head. 'I've done nothing wrang, and I've telt you everything.'

'The number,' said Ferguson.

He held out the phone. Thomas stared at it, then tilted his head back and blinked a few times. He looked shocked and defeated; his natural skin had paled.

'All right,' he said. 'All right.' He gave the number.

Ferguson glanced at the clock on the wall. '15:55. Interview adjourned. We'll resume when the witness's lawyer arrives.'

Ferguson and Hutchins followed Anna Polanski through the corridors and the front door to the smokers' huddle outside. Polanski lit a cigarette and sucked it as if it was an oxygen line, a resemblance which Ferguson often liked tactlessly to point out when he was dragged to the huddle. It was a standing annoyance that civilians, even suspects, were allowed to smoke inside the station but officers weren't.

'What the fuck?' Polanski said. 'What the fucking fuck?'

'Is he simple-minded or something?' Hutchins said.

Ferguson turned on her. 'He's not stupid!'

'I didn't mean stupid,' said Hutchins. 'I meant some kind of, I don't know, brain damage maybe.'

'Autistic spectrum honesty,' Polanski offered. 'A personality disorder with a plus side.'

'He might be telling the truth because he's innocent,' said Ferguson. 'He was used.'

'In which case,' said Hutchins, 'we should be looking very hard for this "Graham".'

'There's the little matter of his recently fired rifle on the boat,' said Polanski.

'Anything more on that business?' Ferguson asked.

Polanski shook her head. 'Still trying to piece together a picture.'

She sighed and stubbed out the cigarette. 'Let's go in,' she said.

Ferguson had just seen a familiar figure hurrying up the steps, briefcase in hand: Peter Wilson, criminal defence lawyer.

'Have another before we go in,' Ferguson told Polanski. 'It'll be a while before your next break.'

The interview resumed. Thomas and Wilson sat side by side. Ferguson recited the formalities and began.

'Mr Thomas,' he said, 'the package you identified earlier has no fingerprints or DNA on it other than the victim's. How would you account for that?'

'Easy,' said Thomas. 'Graham, the guy who gave it to me, has very similar injuries to mine. Worse, I reckon, but he wears a long-sleeved hoodie for the meetings. At least his hands and the whole of his face are prosthetic, I know that. So, no prints, no DNA.'

'All right,' said Ferguson. 'Now, another result from our forensic lab: the inside of the package contains significant traces of the explosive that blew up Father Murphy's flat. How would you explain that?'

Thomas looked taken aback.

'My client need not answer that,' said Wilson.

'Maybe no, but I will,' said Thomas. 'I'd say it's flat-out impossible. I saw what went into the package, and it was no bomb. It was a book.'

'The explosive could have been concealed inside the book,' said Hutchins, in the tone of one making a helpful suggestion. 'Isn't that possible?'

Thomas shook his head. 'I held the book in my hands myself, riffled through the pages, like. There was nothing hidden inside it. I said to Graham this was just the kind of thing the padre would be delighted with, he's very keen on old Benedict, and I handed it back to him and then and there he popped it in the Jiffy bag and sealed it up.'

'Was anyone else present when this happened?'

Thomas grimaced. 'Afraid not. The meeting was over. We were the last in the room, tidying up, like.'

'Could some sleight of hand have been involved?' Hutchins went on, still in the same helpful tone. 'Did Graham, perhaps, turn his back on you for a moment? Or distract your attention in some way?'

'Nah. I saw him put the book in the bag and seal it up. Then he gave it to me right away.'

'So how do you account for the fact that explosives residues have been found in the bag?'

'They might have been on the book's cover all along,' said Thomas.

It was Ferguson's turn to be taken aback. That possibility simply hadn't occurred to him. He did his best not to show it. Peter Wilson noticed.

'That seems a reasonable enough suggestion,' Wilson said.

Ferguson's self-confidence recovered from its steep dive and levelled out.

'It's not at all reasonable,' he said, with what he hoped was aplomb. 'The amount and distribution of the traces rule that out completely.'

He didn't know this.

'I insist on seeing the forensics report,' said Wilson.

'In due course,' said Ferguson.

'More to the point,' said Wilson, 'the package my client agrees he delivered was handed to the deceased last Friday. The explosion only happened yesterday. That leaves ample time, I would have thought, for the alleged explosives to have been placed in this package by some other person. The package would have been opened by Father Murphy on delivery, the book removed and the package discarded – or more likely, given that the deceased was by all accounts a conscientious and abstemious man, set aside for reuse. He had many visitors, one of whom could have used the now-empty package to conceal the device. On your supposition, my client delivered, inadvertently or otherwise, a package containing an explosive device, which exploded as soon as, or very shortly after, Father Murphy handled it. Why on earth would Father Murphy have left the package unopened for nearly a week?'

This struck Ferguson as a fair enough point. Unlike the previous suggestion, it was one that had been bugging him. He was about to concede this possibility and move on when Thomas leaned forward.

'That's easy enough to explain,' he said. 'Look at yesterday's date. Third of September.'

'What about it?'

'Check Father Liam's date of birth.'

When Ferguson did so, it was all he could do not to smite the side of his head.

'It was the padre's birthday,' said Thomas. 'That's why he waited.'

He looked pleased with himself for having solved the problem. Peter Wilson's expression was quite the opposite. Ferguson could sympathise: seldom could the lawyer have had a client so determined to dig himself deeper into the hole.

'Why do you keep calling him "the padre"?' Hutchins asked.

Ferguson couldn't see the point of this but was grateful for the diversion.

'It's old army slang for "chaplain",' Thomas said. 'That's how Graham knew him. Graham's no a Catholic, never even visited as far as I know, but he remembered Father Murphy from the Faith Wars. The Father was a chaplain in the Royal Irish Regiment, see.'

Ferguson couldn't keep the surprise out of his voice. 'Murphy served in the Faith Wars?'

'Father Murphy,' said Thomas, 'was with us in the tanks at Armageddon.'

Ferguson had a split second in which to react. Peter Wilson was already brightening, poised to press home the advantage – his client had just tossed a tactical nuke into the interrogation.

'Tell us more about Graham,' said Ferguson.

Thomas shrugged. 'I can't say I know him well. Just from the meetings, like, over the past three or four years. He doesn't talk much about the war or what happened to him. I'm not even sure he was with the Royal Irish. I do know he worked with combat mechs. Knows a lot about robotics, he's helped me out on a few technical things. Not professionally, like – I'd just ask him a question after a meeting, or as we were walking down the street afterwards, say, and he'd have the answer off the top of his head.'

'What kind of things?'

'Circuits. Joint articulations. Fiddly stuff.' Thomas looked frustrated. 'It would take too long to explain. Nothing to do with bombs, if that's what you're thinking.'

'Do you know his surname? His address? His phone number?'

Thomas shook his head. '*Mutilados* anonymous,' he repeated. 'We don't keep names and addresses. We don't check service records. We don't ask for any name except what anyone wants to be known as. We don't even go to the pub afterwards.'

'Why not?'

'It would make those who don't want to go – who don't like to show their face, or what's left of it – feel even more isolated.'

'Commendable,' said Ferguson. 'So the upshot of all this is that you have no information about him except that he knows about robotics and that he knew Father Murphy from his military service. In fact, you have no evidence that he exists. Why should we believe that he and not you placed the bomb in the package?'

'I'm no trying to shift the blame onto Graham,' said Thomas. 'I don't think he did it either. I'm no saying I know him well, personally like, but I canna conceive of him killing a padre. Specially no one he'd been in combat with. I mean, come on, man! You'd have tae be a downright psycho tae be capable o' that! And Graham's no a psycho, I know that. Maist sympathetic guy ye could hope tae meet.'

'How, then, do you account for the evidence?'

'I can't,' said Thomas. 'And I don't have tae. I've telt you the truth.'

Ferguson leaned back and spread his hands. 'Enough,' he said. 'I think we've gone as far as we can with this line of questioning. I'd now like you to answer some questions from my colleague Inspector Polanski, of Fife Constabulary.'

'One moment, please,' said Anna Polanski. She tilted back her head and went into a five-second information-retrieval dwam. She blinked her way out and shook her head.

'Right,' she said. 'Mr Thomas. Why did you leave your rifle on your boat, instead of taking the rifle ashore and storing it, as common sense would suggest and the law requires?'

For the first time, Thomas looked uncomfortable. He rubbed his hands on his thighs, as if his palms could still sweat.

'I'm sorry about that,' he said. 'I was feart you'd ask if I'd fired it, and I couldna deny that I had.' He raised his hands. 'The powder's on me, nae doubt.'

'Why should that worry you?'

'Well,' said Thomas, 'I'd done something a wee bit no legal with it. I'd shot at a seal.' He cracked a smile. 'Missed the bugger and all.'

'You shot at a seal?'

'Aye, well. It was in my fishing grounds, like.'

'Where was this?'

'Off St Andrews, not long before Mr Ferguson gied me a bell.'

'You say you missed. Where did the shot go?'

'Inta the water. Where else?'

'Are you aware that a man walking by the shore at St Andrews was shot around that time?'

Thomas frowned. 'You're no suggesting my bullet did that?'

Polanski said nothing.

'Couldna have happened,' Thomas said firmly. 'I was a mile or more out tae sea. I wasna even aiming inland. The seal was seaward of me at the time. And my rifle disna have that kindae range anyway. You're welcome to check it. And if you want to charge me under the Wildlife Protection, aye, I'll put my hands up to that. Many's the fisherman does the same.'

This, Ferguson knew, was true.

'Mr Thomas,' Polanski asked, 'have you tuned your contacts – uh, your eyes to news since this interview began?'

'Course not.'

'So it's news to you that the Bishop of St Andrews has been shot dead, and a policeman seriously injured?'

Thomas rocked back in his seat. 'It is and all!' He put his hands to his head. 'Now it's a bishop shot! A bishop! What in the name of God is going on?'

'That,' said Polanski, 'is exactly the question that's on our minds. What in the name of God, as you say, is going on?'

She stood up. 'I'm now going to print off a map and satellite image.'

She stepped over to the interview-room printer and

returned with a sheet of high-res photographic paper, which she slid across the table to Thomas.

'As you can see,' she said after he had examined it, 'one possible trajectory of the shot extends to the approximate location of your boat at the time.'

Thomas pushed the paper sideways to his lawyer, who frowned down at it.

'Aye, it does,' Thomas said. 'It also extends past two or three dots that could be other boats or coastal mechs. And maist of the spread is over the headland. Anyway, like I said, my rifle doesn't have that range.'

'This is absurd,' said Wilson.

'I put it to you,' said Polanski to Thomas, 'that the rifle now on your boat wasn't the only rifle you fired today. That, in fact, you fired that rifle for no other purpose than to give an explanation for the firearms-discharge residues on your hands and clothes. That you fired another rifle, a much more powerful one with a telescopic sight, at the bishop.'

Thomas snorted. 'A head shot from two miles away, in a rocking boat? I'd have to be the most miraculous shooter since Lee Harvey Oswald.'

'With a sniper rifle, which you then dropped overboard. Yes.'

Thomas appeared more amazed than fazed.

'And the coastal mechs never noticed? I ken they're a bit rusty now, but a military rifle shooting inland from the sea is just the kind of thing they're supposed to look out for, aye? They'd have all opened fire on *me*!'

'The coastal mechs are junk,' said Polanski. 'Rusty, yes. Unlike your shooting skills, which your own profile says you take some trouble to keep up.'

Thomas turned to his lawyer. 'Mr Wilson,' he said, 'I don't have to answer any more questions, and I'm no going to.'

'My client is within his rights,' said Wilson, 'and is aware that not answering may—'

'Just one more question,' said Polanski. 'Mr Thomas, how did you know it was a head shot?'

Thomas rubbed his eyebrows.

'I assumed it must have been.'

'None of us had mentioned that. The fact hasn't been released on the news.'

'A trunk shot disna kill in this day and age,' said Thomas. 'Not wi' proper and prompt medical attention, anyway.'

'There's no need to say anything further,' Wilson advised.

'So we're looking for *another* experienced military shooter, somewhere along the same lines of fire at the same time,' said Polanski. 'Fine.'

'Aye,' said Thomas, ignoring Wilson's advice and his own resolution, and as if eager to help. 'That or a coastal mech that's malfunctioning or been corrupted.'

'My client,' said Wilson, 'is not answering any more questions.'

He said it more to Thomas than to his questioners. Thomas took the hint, sat back and shut up. Polanski glanced at Ferguson and moved her hand.

'Very well,' said Ferguson. He stood up. 'I'm very far from convinced by your stories, Mr Thomas. Nevertheless, I'm releasing you on bail, with the requirement that you report in to Greensides every day for the next seven days. That should give us time enough to gather more evidence, and for you to think of more convincing ways to account for it. A lead to your friend Graham would not go amiss in this respect. You can start by helping us make a photofit of his face.'

'I protest,' said Wilson. 'My client should be released unconditionally.'

'Take your protest to the sheriff,' said Ferguson. 'This interview is over.'

7. OLD SCHOOL TIES

17:30. The middle of the homeward rush hour. The top of Leith Walk was bumper to bumper, the pavements elbow to elbow. The low whir of cars moving, the squeal of cars stopping and the whine of cars restarting mingled with the tramp of feet. The sunlight was at an angle that made Ferguson look in awkward directions. Polanski sucked hard on her cigarette. Hutchins sat on a bollard and scowled down at the litter of dog-ends. Skulk fixed its attention on a dirigible drifting towards the Turnhouse moorings.

'I still say we should have held him,' Polanski said. 'He actually delivered the bomb. He admits as much.'

'He admits he delivered the package that at some point or other contained the bomb,' said Ferguson. 'That's different.'

'Huh,' said Polanski.

Ferguson suspected that, although she was as Scottish as he was, Polanski's name had subtly influenced her to look to tough American fictional cops and detectives as role models. Maybe he could use this to persuade her to chew gum instead of smoking.

'*Cherchez la femme*,' said Hutchins, looking up from the dog-ends.

'How d'you mean?' Ferguson asked, impatient that

Hutchins might be considering the homicidal-little-old-lady angle again.

'Look at it this way,' Hutchins said, jumping up. 'Suppose Thomas is telling the truth. When Thomas said he'd mentioned Graham's name to Murphy, I had this thought that maybe Graham expected Murphy to recognise his name. OK, so we have three men here, all Faith War veterans—'

'All celibates too, as far as we know,' Ferguson pointed out. 'So where's *la femme*?'

'In intensive care at the Western General,' said Hutchins. 'Bernadette White, the priest's housekeeper.'

'Housekeeper, nudge, nudge,' said Polanski. Ferguson frowned at her, turned again to Hutchins.

'And she's a Faith War widow,' he said. 'Or so the bishop told me this morning.'

'I'm sure he believes that, but I don't see why we should.'

'Point,' said Ferguson. 'We can check that easily enough, I should imagine.'

'We might have to dig,' said Hutchins.

'Tell me why you think that would be worthwhile,' said Ferguson.

Hutchins looked awkward. 'This'll maybe seem cruel, but . . . when I was looking at Connor Thomas, I couldn't help feeling a bit squeamish. Yes, I know the prosthetics are very, very good, and he has sensation and everything, but . . . it's still a bit . . . off-putting, and I wondered . . . you know, what it would be like to be with someone like that. If, maybe, he'd had a wife or girlfriend who just couldn't accept him. And all along, at the back of his mind, he knows the only reason he has these problems at all is the Catholic dogma about stem cells being babies. If he wasn't a Catholic he could get full regeneration. I mean, that's got to rankle, right?'

'So he takes it out on a priest, and on two innocent bystanders?' said Polanski. 'That kinda makes sense.'

'The priest was an innocent victim too,' Ferguson snapped. 'But, that aside . . . yes, I see where you're going, Shonagh. If there was any prior relationship between Mrs White and Thomas – or Graham, for that matter – then this could all be something personal. It's also occurred to me that we've all along assumed Father Murphy was the prime target and his housekeeper was collateral damage.'

'And the other woman, too,' Hutchins pointed out. 'The mother. Let's not forget her.'

Ferguson chewed a lip. 'Damn, damn, damn. If only Mrs White could speak to us we could clear up this angle in no time.'

Hutchins shook her head. 'Not a chance, sir. Not for days. Maybe a week.'

'OK, Shonagh, dig.'

Hutchins looked like she was about to dash off when Skulk bestirred itself.

'DS Hutchins,' it said, 'you mentioned not forgetting the mother. Her name's Marjorie Broughton, by the way. She's in the same condition as Bernadette White – still in intensive care, stabilised until she's ready for further treatment for internal and spinal injuries. We can't ask her anything either, but we can ask her husband, Derek Broughton, who's right there at the hospital, when he's not looking after their child.'

'I'll get onto that, too,' said Hutchins.

'Shit,' said Polanski, 'why can't Paranoia come up with points like that?'

'To ask the question is to answer it,' said Skulk. 'However, speaking as a non-human myself, permit me to point out that in your natural human pattern-recognition this whole tabloid-headline Priest Love Triangle concept may have misled you into ignoring the awkward fourth corner: Bishop Black.'

'We're not exactly ignoring him,' said Polanski. She tapped her phone clip. 'Fife Constabulary and Lothian and Borders are going full tilt at it. They're tearing up that estate on the headland as we speak, just in case Mr Thomas's sniping abilities aren't as brilliant as I suspected.'

'What I mean,' said Skulk, 'is that he doesn't fit what DS Hutchins suggested. I've run searches on him, and he has no connection with the people involved in the Murphy case. Not even the PNAI has any dots to join. He wasn't even involved in the Faith Wars, apart from opposing them. Practically a pacifist, I gather.'

'That's involvement,' said Polanski.

'Along with most of the Scottish Episcopal clergy, if I remember right from my days on the God Squads,' said Ferguson. 'Nah, we'd need more than that. Skulk's got a point.' He turned to the leki. 'Do you have a theory?'

'Only a hypothesis,' said Skulk. 'I now think it more likely than I did before that we should be looking for a robot. A humanoid robot passing – in some contexts at least – as a *mutilado*. Only a robot could have fooled Thomas about what it was putting in the package, *and* shot the bishop from the range the sniper must have done.'

Polanski and Hutchins remonstrated, and Skulk seemed to dig itself into its initially tentative idea, until Ferguson held up a hand. 'Enough, everyone. This is for an Incident Room meeting.' He glanced at his watch. 'Canteen, then everyone together in, let's see, an hour. six forty-five sharp.'

'I'll put the message out,' said Skulk.

Ferguson didn't get as far as the canteen. Just inside the main entrance he was waylaid by DCI Frank McAuley.

'Time we kept our belated appointment,' McAuley said. Ferguson followed him to the lift, then to his office, his stomach grumbling that it hadn't had anything since breakfast. Nothing like dealing with a decapitating sniper shot to ruin your afternoon, Ferguson thought as he sat down in front of McAuley's desk.

McAuley was old school, recruited to the force under the New Labour governments back in the zeroes. Severe on racism and sexism, strong on human rights and human relations, in the second decade of the Faith Wars he'd sent Muslims to the filtration camps without hatred and tortured terrorist suspects without cruelty: securing the vacated house and shop against looting, sterilising the needle before inserting it under the fingernail. Under the Sozis he'd hammered the Right; under the restoration he'd perse-cuted the Left. As a fresh-faced PC on the God Squads, Ferguson had seen McAuley handle a Catholic demonstra-tion on Princes Street with a like dispassion. The tanks of the Italian Republic had the previous day rolled into St Peter's Square, and the auditors were swarming through the Vatican, opening the books for the African AIDS class-action lawsuit that was to bankrupt the Church within a year. Thousands of Catholics had turned out to protest. McAuley had strolled into the forest of croziers and crosses at the front, chatted to the bishops, and emerged to coolly order the riot squads into action against the taunting crowds of Orangemen, feminists, pagans and gays lining the sidewalks and jeering from the Mound. The sweep was so sharp, so sudden and unexpected that resistance was minimal, the counter-demonstrators doing more damage to each other in the vans than the cops had done making the arrests. The Catholic protest proceeded to Holyrood without further incident and, of course, without effect.

Now he was going through a little routine of looking down at his desk slate and occasionally glancing up, giving Ferguson the lidded-eyes-under-lowered-brows treatment, then resuming reading. McAuley looked as if he lived on salads and ran ten kilometres daily, which was more or less the case.

'Oh, Adam,' he said after a minute or so of this mind trick, 'I'm just about up to speed on today's developments, and – between ourselves – I'm beginning to wonder if we aren't a little out of our depth here. It's more than just a local matter now, with this dreadful development in Fife. Who knows what the next outrage will be? Should Glasgow be on high alert? Isn't it time to turn this over to the specialists? Fettes is certainly asking the same questions. Run some possible answers past me, if you don't mind.'

'I don't agree that we're out of our depth, sir. I've no idea what's next, and I would certainly say that Glasgow should be on alert. Now, as for the specialists – if you mean the anti-terrorism specialists, they've had less and less to do for the past fifteen years or so. You, me and DCI Mukhtar have between us more recent and relevant experience than Fettes is likely to scrape together in a week. I'm very confident in my officers on the ground. Certainly, we should draw on any specialist expertise on offer, but I don't think it's time to let the spooks take charge.'

'I wasn't actually thinking about the spooks,' said McAuley. 'Just the Scottish Anti-Terrorism Unit. You're right, of course, it's a bit creaky, but if some mass-casualty event were to take place and we'd failed to stop it . . .'.

'With respect, sir, that's thinking more in terms of protecting ourselves if things go wrong than in terms of stopping things going wrong in the first place.'

'I'm not talking about covering my arse. Nor,' McAuley added pointedly, 'of protecting our own patch.'

Ferguson made a wiping gesture parallel with the desk. 'OK, sir, point taken. Let's say I think the Unit should be involved, not in charge. Not yet.'

'Can you give me a strong argument for that?'

'For one thing,' Ferguson said, 'we have as yet no evidence that this isn't all the work of one person.'

'Really? Even with the leaflets?'

'The leaflets could be the work of the same person. That's assuming they're connected with the two crimes at all. There's been absolutely no chatter, no online material, no groundswell of opinion even among the small groups of bigots and fanatics that Mukhtar monitors routinely.'

McAuley drummed a finger on a non-responsive area of his desk.

'Speaking of which,' he said after a moment, 'another suggestion I might have to field is to remobilise the God Squads.'

Ferguson had difficulty taking this seriously. 'Boots in the pews? Sir?'

'Boots in the pews, ab-so-fucking-lutely, old chap. Put the boom down on them, remind them who's boss. All in the name of protecting the congregations from terrorist attack, of course.'

'I can't think of a bigger waste of resources,' said Ferguson. 'We need to get every man, woman and leki we can spare onto finding this killer, or killers, before they strike again. Besides, if there's any real religious fanaticism behind this – whether an individual or a group – nobody's more likely to rat them out than someone in the same congregation. Boots in the pews would just make that harder.'

'Ah yes,' said McAuley. 'The old "isolate the extremists from the moderates" tack. Didn't work out too well for us, back in the day, now did it?'

'Oh, come on, Frank!' said Ferguson, irritated into dropping protocol, if not quite yet politeness. 'That bolt had been well and truly shot long before either of us had any say in the matter.'

'Aye, there's that,' said McAuley, with a regretful tone in his voice and a wintry reminiscence in his eyes. 'There's that, all right.'

He leaned back for a few moments.

'All right, Adam. But if there's one more of these attacks, anywhere in Scotland, or if we don't catch anyone in the next few days, the Anti-Terrorism Unit will have to take over – and they'll be run closely by the spooks. And if that happens, believe me, the only thing left for us to do will be to put the boots in the pews, whether we think that'll do any good or not.'

'If that happens,' said Ferguson, 'we'll just have to go back to sorting out the goons on Leith Water.'

'That would be nice,' said McAuley, as if missing the kinder, gentler world of two days ago. 'But we won't get to decide. And it's not just the spooks who'll be on our case. Holyrood is already belching and farting about it. There's a lot riding on the outcome of this bloody business. This is the first incident of religious terrorism in Europe for fifteen years. If we can't crack it, or if it escalates, it'll look like we didn't solve the religion problem after all. There'll be voices raised claiming that the whole Second Enlightenment policy of radical secularism was misconceived, that we have to let the mainstream religious groups have some political clout again, that marginalising the faith discourse hasn't worked.'

'These voices might have a case,' said Ferguson, purposely provoking.

'I'll treat that as if we were brainstorming,' said McAuley. 'But we're not. And let me remind you, Adam, that if the line of thinking I've just mentioned starts to get a hearing, there are plenty of people who would take great delight in raking over what coppers like you and I did, when we did what had to be done. Nobody's questioned it since, because it worked. If it turns out not to have worked, we'll get the heat. Not the politicians who made the laws, but we who applied them with what will come to be called excessive zeal. So don't even consider if "they'd have a case" – go out and crack *this* case.'

'Right,' said Ferguson, standing in front of the whiteboard and still smarting from McAuley's encouragement, 'what have we got?'

Tony from Forensics spoke first.

'The leaflets, sir. No unmatched DNA. Just the pro-fessor's. But we've got something on the ink.'

'Yes?' said Ferguson, hopefully. 'A match with a batch?'

'Not exactly, boss. It's a bit more exciting than that. The leaflets didn't come off a printer. They were done on a printing press. I mean, literally, a press. A mechanical device with inked metal letters—'

'Yes, Tony, I think even the youngest here have some dim idea what you're talking about. How does that help us?'

'Well,' said Tony, 'the actual ink hasn't been manufac-tured for twenty years. The paper's standard copier, nothing traceable. But the ink is unique. If . . .'

His voice trailed off.

'Quite,' said Ferguson. 'If we find the printing press, and the ink supply, we'll have the bastards bang to rights. Yes?'

'That's about it, boss.'

Ferguson raked his fingers backwards through his hair, sighed. 'Thanks, Tony. Next?'

Connolly and Hutchins looked up from a huddle, then at each other in a 'you first' way.

'Shonagh, please?'

Hutchins stood up, brandished an iThink. 'Got a photofit image of the alleged suspect "Graham", sir. Connor Thomas said it was a good likeness. I'll just patch it up for everyone . . .'

A flutter of fast blinking and a flicker of leki infrared went around the room. Ferguson gazed at an eyeball image of a young-looking, good-looking man, full head of hair, distinctive features, open-necked shirt.

'This is a *mutilado*?' he said.

'The imperfections of the prosthetic don't show on this resolution,' said Hutchins. 'And upping the res wouldn't help, because it's very hard to reproduce the effect with the standard rendering tools.'

'OK, OK,' said Ferguson. 'So . . . we're looking for someone who looks just like this, but not quite.'

'Exactly,' said Hutchins, missing or ignoring the sarcasm, to Ferguson's relief because she didn't deserve it.

'Well, fine, let's get it out there,' said Ferguson. 'To the force, not to the media. Dangerous man, report at once, don't approach without back-up, that sort of thing. And PNAI, obviously.'

'The PNAI has a package for all that,' said Shonagh, thumbing fast. She looked up. 'Done.'

'Good,' said Ferguson. 'Any progress on IDing the bugger?'

'Uh, that's where there's a problem,' said Connolly, standing up as Hutchins sat down. 'We sent Paranoia churning through Army records, but it got lots of hits on low-res ID-card photos and couldn't narrow it down much, because obviously the biometrics of the photofit are too vague and the Army's biometrics are too precise. So then we used Ogle Face, with all the parameters: soldier, massive head, chest and limb wounds, robotics specialist, Middle East theatre, possible association with the Royal Irish or any regiment that served close to it, and of course the name. And we got one. Lance-Corporal Special Technician Graham Orr. Here's the best pic.'

He patched it in beside the photofit 'Graham'. This new picture was of a proud lad in a private's uniform and cap. The match was as near perfect as a photofit could be expected to be.

Whistles and cheers.

'Bingo,' said Ferguson. 'Good work.'

But Connolly was shaking his head, Hutchins looking grim.

'Just one problem,' said Connolly. 'Lance-Corporal Orr died of his injuries in the medevac chopper, between Megiddo and Cyprus.'

Ferguson took a deep breath. 'That's absolutely certain? No stupid stuff like a twin brother, or corrupted records, or a mix-up?'

'Checked all that,' said Connolly. 'Funeral, grieving parents, only son. Presbyterian Church service, interestingly enough. All in the *Belfast Telegraph* within the fortnight.'

'There were a lot of funerals that particular fortnight,' said Ferguson. 'As I recall. A lot of mangled corpses. There might just be some tiny possibility of confusion. We're talking about fucking Armageddon here, people!'

They were all staring at him. He rubbed his forehead. 'Sorry, everyone. It's been a tough day. OK, let's get searches running on the name, and Shonagh, could you link through to whoever's on at the Western General, see if that other woman's husband, uh, Derek Broughton recognises the name or the face.'

'Sure,' said Hutchins.

'Inspector Polanski, any progress to report before you leave?'

'Not much,' said Polanski. 'The lekis have crawled all over that headland housing estate, and they haven't found a sniff of anything suspicious. But before I go, sir, I'd just like to reiterate the importance of keeping surveillance on Connor Thomas.'

Ferguson nodded. 'It's being done. Sergeant Carr?'

'Car outside, cameras from a distance, foot tail ready to go.'

'Phone tap?'

'Sheriff's office signed it off an hour ago. Paranoia's onto it, sir.'

'Good. Happy with that, Anna?'

'Yes, sir. Still not sure he didn't do it, if you don't mind my saying so. The latest I've heard from my colleagues is that the victim took a regular walk at lunchtime along the East Sands embankment, which is where he was shot. He insisted on keeping up his routine today, despite our having an armed guard on him. So the sniper may well have known when to expect him.'

'Very likely,' said Ferguson. 'The fact remains that it would have been an incredibly difficult shot to pull off, and that the killer might also have known that Connor Thomas is a man of likewise regular habits. But then, if it was a set-up . . .' He spread his hands. 'We've been over all this. Discussing it further will get us nowhere. Feel free to leave, Polanski.'

'Thanks, sir. If you don't mind.'

She was just gathering her document folder and bag when Skulk waved a tentacle.

'Yes?' said Ferguson.

'I would urge Inspector Polanski to ask the Forth Maritime Security Centre for an immediate system check on the coastal mechs around St Andrews.'

Polanski glared at the machine. 'Why don't you do it yourself?'

'I'll take that as permission from Fife Constabulary to make the request,' replied Skulk.

'You do that,' said Polanski, picking up her stuff. She nodded at Ferguson and made for the door.

'Don't waste too much time on it,' Ferguson added.

'No,' said Skulk. 'I only mentioned it because the PNAI has just found some matches for the pictures of Graham Orr.'

'What?' shouted Ferguson, as Polanski stopped in her tracks and half the room stood up. 'Patch them in, patch them in!'

They looked at the scrolling samples of image captures: security-camera glimpses, eyewear uploads. One or two recognisable Edinburgh backgrounds: the West Port, Grassmarket, some Leith backstreet overlooked by the cranes of Constitution Dock, Waverley Station platform . . .

'Got an ID?' Ferguson asked.

'It's a robot,' said Skulk. 'Name of Hardcastle.'

8. CANDLEMAKER ROW

Earlier that afternoon of Friday, 4 September, the artist formerly known as Dave Warsaw opened his eyes and lay still for a few seconds until he remembered who he was. Ah yes. How it all came back. And beside him on the pillow was Jessica, bless her, mouth open and snoring, which she would deny when she woke up. Must be lying in a funny position, her feet were—

Wait a sec. These weren't Jessica's feet. Dave sat bolt upright, lifted the duvet, and peered underneath, to find a head of messed-up black curls resting against Jessica's ribs. Dave smiled momentarily at the thought of having had another girl in the bed, and then jumped again as he recognised Mikhail Aliyev. Who definitely wasn't a girl, despite all external appearances. The memories of the previous night restored from back-up with a vividness that made Dave's head spin.

He'd finished his gig, set the music to a shuffle of bland, and moseyed back with a final clutch of drinks to the booth where Jessica and Aliyev had still been sitting, deep in conversation. He'd found them not just talking but flirting – Jessica had evidently found Aliyev's peculiar gender rearrangement a kink not too far at all – and somehow, without Dave's ever quite agreeing, they'd ended up all going back to the flat

together. And then, in much the same way, going to
bed together.

Dave groaned, and climbed out of bed. He picked his
way through discarded clothes – most of them Aliyev's –
and padded to the bathroom with questions hammering
his skull like investigative reporters at a door.

They'd all taken *what*? They'd all done *that*? And *that*?
And then—

Yes. They had. And then some.

Oh, so to speak, fuck.

After ten minutes under the shower Dave began to
feel better. He shaved, put his clothes on very quietly
and went through to the kitchen. He brewed coffee and
burned toast and washed down various pills with cold
orange gulps. The hangover retreated. Dave wasn't ready
to put his contacts in, so he downloaded his usual selection of news to a reader and skimmed it while he had his
breakfast. He hadn't finished either when Aliyev strolled
in, wearing one of Jessica's shorter dressing gowns, hem
trailing.

'Morning,' said Aliyev.

'Afternoon,' said Dave. He waved at the coffee pot.
'Help yourself. Toast, cereal, juice.'

'Uh, got any painkillers? I am one very sorry *rori*
this . . . afternoon.'

'Jar on the shelf.' Dave pointed.

'Thanks.' Aliyev took the tabs and busied himself for a
few minutes at the percolator and toaster. Dave went on
reading until Aliyev sat down opposite him at the table.

'Um,' said Aliyev, running fingers through his hair.

'Well,' said Dave.

'Some night.'

'Yes.'

Aliyev's gaze wandered. 'Interesting decor.'

Dave looked at the posters on the walls, and at the candlesticks and skull-shaped ornaments that shared the shelves with crockery and cookery books. He had long ceased to notice it.

'I sort of leave that to Jessica,' he said. 'I just paint and fix.'

Aliyev laughed. 'Choosing the colour isn't a problem.'

'Never thought black was right for a kitchen, but we could never agree, so I just paint it white and Jessica covers it with the posters.'

'Thus turning it mostly black. Right.'

Aliyev returned to his toast and Dave to his news.

Jessica bounced in a few minutes later, wearing a black T-shirt and leggings and thick-soled black boots, and her hair pinned up.

'Well, hello, boys!' she said. 'Hah, don't your faces look a picture! Lighten up, guys.'

She ran a hand across Dave's hair and then through Aliyev's, helped herself to coffee and stood at the window, gazing out at afternoon sunlight on the small, walled feature of the ground-floor flat that had been advertised as a garden and that she and Dave never referred to as anything but 'the back grass'.

'What a great day! What day is it? Oh yes, Friday.'

Jessica pulled up a chair beside Dave and facing Aliyev.

'A good day to shop,' she told the latter. 'Dress-up Friday at Armstrong's.'

'I'm familiar with it,' said Aliyev. 'But first we have to plot. And then I have to report in.'

He caught Dave's alarmed look.

'Don't worry, nothing personal. As far as SB is concerned, it is just a matter of handler and informants. They are not interested in details.'

'Handler?' said Dave. 'How great that makes me feel.'

'You were well and truly handled,' said Jessica.

'Thanks a lot.'

'You seemed to enjoy it at the time. Never knew you had it in you!'

Jessica and Aliyev laughed. Dave squirmed.

Aliyev reached across the table and laid his hand on Dave's.

'It's all right,' he said. 'I understand. Many people find themselves feeling a little abashed after their first time with a secret policeman.'

At that Dave had to laugh.

'All right,' he said. He reached for the coffee pot, found it empty, and stood up to refill it. 'Speaking of which . . . You want to plot. OK, let's plot.'

Aliyev nodded. 'Got some scrap paper?'

Jessica passed him a pen and the shopping-list pad. Aliyev opened it to a fresh page. He stared down at it, then rubbed the side of his head.

'Wait a minute,' he said. He disappeared down the hallway and returned with his handbag. He took out an iThink and a pair of phone clips and a contacts set.

'Might as well get washed and dressed before I put these on,' he said. He looked up. 'Sorry. Won't be long.'

Dave took the coffee pot to the table.

'He has a point, you know,' he said.

'About what?'

'Being with a secret policeman.'

Jessica guffawed. 'That's what's eating you?'

'It's a bit of a risk, that's what I'm saying. We don't know what he might drag us into.'

'He dragged you into—'

'For fuck's sake, Jess! Can you just lay off with the innuendos?'

Jessica mimed a recoil. 'OK,' she said. 'OK. Maybe it is too early in the day for that. So what's the problem? I think it's . . . *exciting.*'

Dave was sorely tempted to zing back an innuendo of his own, but he let it pass.

'He's looking for Gnostics who might have blown up a priest for the hell of it? If he's right – I'm not saying he is – we'd be messing with very dangerous people.'

'Don't be such a wimp,' said Jessica. 'Didn't you pay any attention to civics at school?'

Dave snorted. 'Didn't pay much attention to much. Don't know much sociology. I think there's an old song about that.'

'Yeah, and don't I know it,' said Jessica, sounding more bitter than he'd expected. 'Fine, well, put it this way. Our fathers fought in the Faith Wars, they put their lives on the fucking line for us against the faith-heads, and if this Neo-Gnostic rubbish really is a new death-dealing faith and not some fanboy wank, and it's part of our fucking community, a community where you, my dear, have a certain standing, then I say it's your civic duty to help the cops smoke it out and *crush* it.'

Jessica's voice was shaking, her finger jabbing. Dave wasn't used to such vehemence from her about anything that wasn't either personal or totally abstract. He wondered if it wasn't something symptomatic, if Jessica wasn't getting on his case, the way girlfriends did. Jessica could play the frivolous gothgirl by night, but by day she was a serious philosophy postgrad, and most days – today being an exception – she was a hard-working one. Dave was uneasily aware that being king of the silent scene wouldn't, in the long run, be enough to impress her, or indeed himself.

'All right,' he said. He kept his gaze locked with Jessica's as he sipped from the mug. 'That's me told. Point taken.'

'So you're in? Definitely in?'

'I said I was last night.'

'Not very definitely, and then just now you got cold feet. I need to know.'

'It's for sure,' said Dave.

Jessica grinned, and grasped his hand. 'Great! You and me, baby!'

'You and me and the queer cop.'

'Together, we fight crime . . .' Jessica said dreamily. They both laughed.

The queer cop returned, washed and made-up, with all his gear on except the gloves and bonnet. He sat down, smoothed out his skirt, and reached for the pen and notepad again.

'Right,' he said. 'Plot.'

'OK,' said Jessica. She fished her own iThink from its belt pouch. 'Let's see how far we got last night, before the sidestream weed kicked in.'

'I gave you eyeball records, you gave me some names,' said Aliyev.

'And then we crossed most of them off . . .'

Jessica looked down at the iThink, scrolling it with her thumb, making strange grimaces with her lower lip and upper teeth. 'And I did some asking around . . . in fact I sent out a few queries. Hang on.'

She put her phone clip in and started some more scrolling, through text messages; cocked her head, listening to phone messages.

'Hmm . . .' she said. She spun the pad towards her, grabbed the pen, and began scribbling.

'These two,' she said. 'Carl Powys, Will Latham.' She thumbed again. 'That's their pics,' she added, tabbing them to Aliyev's and Dave's contacts.

'These weren't on my list,' said Aliyev. He gazed into space for a minute. 'Nothing about them online, apart from the university records and a couple of minimal social pages. No police record, either.'

'Low profile,' said Jessica. 'That's how you can tell the real ones from the wannabes. One of my messages was from a wannabe – just a nice little Wiccan who got the brush-off from them a few months ago when she tried telling them all about Gnosticism as a feminist and humanist alternative to patriarchal religion.'

'What did they do?' asked Aliyev.

'Told her to go read a proper fucking book, she says.' Jessica sniggered. 'Sound advice for her, in my opinion. She was deeply offended.'

'I recognise them,' said Dave. 'They're regulars on the scene.'

'Can we expect them at your gig tonight?' Aliyev asked.

Dave shrugged. 'Like I said, they're regulars.'

'Don't want to chance that. Could you tab them a freebie?'

'Sure,' said Dave.

Jessica was shaking her head. 'Too obvious. If they're

mixed up in something, they'll be suspicious of a ticket or an invite out of the blue. The gig tonight's in the Carthaginian. Everyone comes to that.'

Aliyev looked dubious. 'What if these two don't?'

'We'll just have to try something else,' Jessica said. 'If they don't, we'll have time for a plan B.'

'OK,' said Aliyev. 'Leave a plan B to me. Let's assume they do come. What then?'

'You and me get into casual conversation with them, keep them interested, see if they open up a bit. Dave hangs back and keeps an eye, follows us if we go out.'

'I can't go out before the end of the gig,' said Dave.

'If you have to, you can,' said Jessica. 'Have a programme ready to slot in. But we'll do our best to keep them in the club for the whole gig. Shouldn't be difficult. And you can tip off Hardcastle, just in case.'

'And I'll have back-up,' said Aliyev. 'Fine. That's it. We have a plan for the night.'

'For the evening,' Jessica said.

Aliyev smiled. 'For the evening – that's the one I have to report in with.'

'And we have a plan for the rest of the afternoon,' said Jessica. 'Shop.'

'Not me,' said Dave. 'I have a gig to prepare and a net to surf for files.'

'Sure you don't want to join us?' Jessica said. 'Shopping for a little black dress?'

'Sure. Positive. Have fun.'

'Shame. You showed a lot of promise in that direction last night.'

'You know,' said Dave, 'that's probably exactly *why* I don't want to.'

That concession was enough to get his girlfriend and the queer cop off his case and stop winding him up, which was exactly why he'd said it. Not because it was true. If it had been true, he wouldn't have said it at all.

Dave slipped his contacts onto his eyeballs and waited out the day's updates instead of skipping them. When the last of the terms and conditions had faded he poured himself another coffee, propped himself in a battered leather arm-chair in the corner of the living room, poised his thumb over his clunky last-season-but-still-adequate iThink, and invoked Ogle Space. The gig that night was in the Carthaginian, a big club on George IV Bridge. It was one he didn't get very often and he always tried to give it something new. He'd done enough war-porn and blas-phemy-tat recently; time for a different angle, before his audience got bored too. Space was another standby, but like every VJ he'd overused deep-space images: the exo-planet surveys relayed to Ogle Worlds, the more distant objects displayed in Hoyle Sky. This time he was going to go for Near-Earth Space, and compile some eerie dance of the soletas, the satellites and space stations and the space elevators. He tried to get some over-familar chords and movements out of his head. Kubrick's *2001* was in the back of his mind, for sure: every VJ who'd ever combined space imagery with music had at some point referenced or plagiarised that; but he didn't want a fucking ballet, he wanted something with a harder rhythm, heavy and industrial; it was going to be that kind of gig. Building it around the elevators and soletas would give it just the sort of edgy challenge he liked to salt his gigs with. Most people on the scene heartily disdained the whole project of using soletas to combat global warming as a typical hubristic technical fix, a last desperate throw of the industries that burned more carbon than they turned into bucky-tech. There was some truth in that: the Atlantic Space Elevator and the soletas had originally been financed by Gazprom and Exxon to counter class-action lawsuits over climate change.

Dave checked the day's space news, to discover he'd slept through a couple of soleta misalignments that had resulted in too brief, or too long, an eclipse over various parts of the Earth. Two of the small rocket engines on the circumference of one of the soletas had misfired; as all of the soletas required frequent nudges to correct for the effects of the solar wind, this had the potential for a serious problem. A team of four humanoid robots was investigating, hands-on.

That looked promising. Dave enlarged the news item, drilled into the links, and tried to find a feed from one of these robots' eyeball cameras – a fairly standard feature these days, with cosmonauts and astronauts collecting micropayments every time someone linked into their helmet-camera or their contacts. He found a link, but when he blinked on it he encountered a security-level error. Normally he'd have regarded this as a challenge to hack. Today he didn't have time.

But the notion of the humanoid robots in space had caught his attention, and he launched a query for any that might be more accommodating. Within a couple of minutes, his trawl came back with a link to a robot working on the outside of the Atlantic Space Elevator. He chose the 'Fly To:' option and sat back to enjoy the virtual ride.

The pov rose smoothly up from where he sat, up above the streets of Newington. The rest of Edinburgh came into view below him, partly obscured by an up-to-the-minute image of a cloud over the city. He soared faster and faster, heading up and to the west and south, Ireland flashing past as a green patch in a blue sea, then Spain and the Azores far below and to his left, then the sky black above and the Atlantic blue below.

The elevator hove into view, a gold thread in the sunlight from its east. The pov zoomed closer and higher, focusing on a tiny figure toiling high above the atmosphere on the edge of the elevator. As the figure came closer the sight became uncanny: it looked exactly like a man in a boiler suit, working on the side of an enormous building. The scale of the structure was abruptly clear. Dave found himself looking up with a certain giddiness at the black cliff of buckytape above, just before the pov merged with the viewpoint from the robot's eyes.

Hands, ungloved, working in vacuum and microgravity on a piece of jointing that looked as banal as the brackets on scaffolding, with the Earth a curve of blue and white in the background. The robot gave no sign of noticing Dave's virtual presence – or that of anyone else who might, at this moment, be time-sharing its sight – but Dave knew that it would. Robots, humanoid robots anyway, had processing power to spare. There was a classic video clip of a soccer match between eleven of the first – experimental – batch of humanoid robots and the championship-level team sponsored by Sony. Even with their physical capacities and reflexes stepped down to the human level, the robots had literally run rings around some of the best footballers in the world: to the robots, everything was happening in slow motion.

Dave recorded all he saw, already mentally rehearsing how it could be sampled, broken up and played back until it became a visual analogue of a driving drumbeat. At one point, much to his delight, a crawler climbed past, lit up like a railway carriage. Even the robot's eyes couldn't help following it as it headed up into space. Then the robot looked back at the work to hand. Just before Dave was sure he had quite enough, just as the hand reached for yet another piece of apparatus, the pov threw him out and he was left staring again at a security-level lockout view.

The Ogle Space 'Fly To:' option, as if maliciously, reversed his experience of arrival, and gave him the visual sensation of falling off the elevator into space away and down, hurtling backwards to eventually land, shaking with vertigo, in the same old armchair. There was no actual impact, of course. It was all in his head, in his eyes. But his cold coffee spilled across his knees.

Aliyev and Jessica returned from their trawl of the charity and vintage shops about seven, with handfuls of plastic bags. Jessica had already replaced her T-shirt with a short black dress. The secret policeman disappeared into the bedroom and emerged wearing an antique black nylon slip over black drainpipe jeans and new black Kicker boots. His fresh make-up of black eyeliner and dark purple lipstick suited his fine, high-cheekboned features rather better than the loli style had. Slung over his shoulder was a rectangular black bag that had once – he claimed, to Dave's disbelief – been used to lug computers.

Aliyev posed in the living-room doorway, one hand on a hip, the other's thumb in his bra strap.

'Ready to kick Gnostic ass,' he said.

'Good man,' said Dave. He held up his iThink. 'And I'm ready to give the punters their money's worth. It'll hold their attention, all right.'

'What's the show going to be about?' Jessica asked.

'Ah, that'd be telling,' said Dave. 'Let's just say I've labelled it the Near-Earth Experience.'

'Intriguing,' said Aliyev, sounding bored already. 'Do we have time to go and grab something to eat?'

'Sure,' said Dave. 'What do you—'

Aliyev raised a hand. 'Just a minute. Urgent call.'

His eyes glazed for a minute. His lips and larynx moved as he subvocalised, then he spoke out loud.

'Over to you, Dave. It's my boss at Greensides.'

Dave twitched his ear to take the call. Nothing came through on visual, just a quiet deep voice in his phone:

'Afternoon, Mr Warsawski. You have a robot named Hardcastle on security at your gig tonight, yes?'

'As far as I know,' said Dave. 'We have a standing arrangement with Hired Muscle. Hang on, I'll just check tonight's roster . . . yes, Hardcastle's coming on duty at nine.'

'Any idea where this machine . . . lives, if that's the word?'

'Its address? Not a clue. You could ask the agency, they handle all the admin.'

'We've already been onto Hired Muscle,' said the voice. 'They don't have a physical address for Hardcastle. Very irregular, but they seem to think the law on these matters doesn't apply to robots.' A sigh. 'Which, come to think of it, it may not. Apparently in their accounting they have the machine down as "Off-site Plant". Be that as it may. I want to warn you that Hardcastle may not turn up for duty tonight.'

'Is there some problem with Hardcastle?' Dave asked, incredulous.

'Yes, Mr Warsawski, there is. Let's just say that the police would very much like to interview it, and if we see it on the way to work we'll intercept it. Please do not call Hired Muscle for a replacement or back-up before you're certain it's at least half an hour late. If the machine does turn up, don't act in any way out of the ordinary. Got that?'

'Clear enough,' said Dave. 'Just one problem. No one can "act normal" well enough to fool a robot. Now that you've told me, as soon as it sees me, it'll know something's up. It has—'

'A very sophisticated theory of mind. Yes, Mr Warsawski, I know that. Trust me, in this case there may not be as much of a problem as you think.'

'What do you mean?'

'Can't tell you yet. Now, hand me back to DC Aliyev, if you don't mind.'

Dave passed the connection back. Aliyev exchanged a few more remarks, then snapped out of the call. In the meantime Dave had brought Jessica up to speed.

'I can't believe Hardcastle's in trouble,' she said. She gave Aliyev a hard look. 'What's all this about?'

'Possible involvement in the priest-murder case. And the bishop today.'

Jessica shouted, 'Murder?' and Dave cried, 'Bishop? What?'

'Check the *Evening News*,' said Aliyev, looking unwont-edly grim.

They checked.

'What about tonight's operation?' Jessica asked.

'Still on,' said Aliyev.

Dave sat at the bar in Frankenstein's, the pub conve-niently opposite the Carthaginian, drinking cranberry juice, keeping an eye on Jessica and Aliyev in the bar mirror, and keeping an ear on the private channel. The air was hot and thick. At three a.m. on a Saturday morning, the pub was heaving. After the silent-scene gig, the noise level was overpowering. Keeping track of the conversa-tion was using up most of Dave's attention. This gave his face and demeanour a preoccupied and unwelcoming look.

Which was, as the geeks might say, a feature.

It was just as well that he'd decided to stay off alcohol, even beer, right through the gig. He'd got slightly whacked by sidestream weed-smoke, but he was used to that, and knew how to focus his mind to compensate, let-ting the cannabis undertow sort of *waft* his rationality along with it, yeah that was it, surf the wave, just go with it . . . then snap out of it. With the Near-Earth Experience, this risky mental trick had worked.

Hardcastle hadn't turned up. A call to Hired Muscle at 9:30 had established that they hadn't heard anything from the robot, and that they'd expected it to be there as usual. An offer of a replacement bouncer was made and accepted. The guy turned up by taxi twenty minutes later. He'd needed some hasty re-education on the door as to who counted as safe and respectable enough to let in.

Jessica and Aliyev had struck up this conversation, with the two guys Jessica had fingered as most likely to be serious Neo-Gnostics, a couple of hours ago over at the gig. The two guys had suggested coming here after- wards – it wasn't a pub that a self-respecting goth clubber or silent-scene devotee would normally be seen dead in – and had seemed surprised that Jessica and Aliyev had agreed. They weren't exactly spotty nerds – they were not bad-looking guys, actually, thin and intense in a passé addict-chic way – but they'd probably not had such rapt attention from such attractive women in their lives. (Aliyev had introduced himself as Michelle, and was acting a lot more feminine than he had the night before.)

The guys were both students, at Edinburgh University. Will was doing physics, Carl was doing phi- losophy. Between them they were doing Dave's head in. The only good part of the conversation was that they were unlikely to overhear his eavesdropping. One of the tenets of Neo-Gnosticism (as Will had explained at some length) was that computer systems took the user a step closer to the dark domain of the GodPlayer, and that the use of computers should therefore be kept to a minimum. They eschewed the virtual.

'What I don't understand,' Jessica was saying, 'is this. Supposing you're right. What could you actually do? I mean, we're talking about some entity that controls the universe, right? So, how exactly do you oppose him, or her, or it?'

'Oh, the GodPlayer doesn't control the universe,' said Will. 'Only the simulation we're in.'

'That's a help,' said Jessica. 'Not. Presumably within

this simulation, the GodPlayer is all-knowing and all-powerful.'

'Can't be,' said Carl. 'Otherwise we wouldn't be having this conversation.'

'Or this conversation is no threat whatsoever to him.'

'It isn't!' Will said. 'Look, the GodPlayer isn't God. He isn't even in the same position in relation to the simulation as God is in relation to the real universe. Put it this way: a Laplacean Deity is one that knows the position and speed of every particle in the universe. A Cartesian Demon is an entity that feeds consistent false information to all the senses. Now, the same entity can't be a Laplacean Deity and a Cartesian Demon at the same time. And on top of that, it's absolutely basic information theory that the programmer of a simulation can't have complete knowledge of the simulation, because that complete knowledge would itself be another instance of the simulation, and – you see where this is going?'

'Oh, sure,' said Jessica. 'I just don't see what it has to do with religion.'

'What we've figured out,' said Carl, 'is that the major religions – at least, because we haven't got around to studying the minor ones – function as systems of deception that prevent their adherents from seeing the true nature of the world we live in, which they think is the universe. It keeps them spinning their wheels endlessly about how to reconcile the evils of the world with the goodness of God, instead of seeing the obvious, which is that this world was not in fact created by God. And given that God did create the world, by definition, then this world isn't real and was created by something much less than God. Conventional religion is almost as much a delusion as naturalism, which tries to convince us – and itself – that this gimcrack contrivance we're living in is somehow self-existent and, well, *natural*. What manifest pish!'

Jessica looked as if she was about to formulate a suitably crushing rebuff to this juvenile theodicy, not to say manifest pish, but was forestalled by Aliyev, who'd evidently decided it was time to move on to more dangerous and less boring subjects.

'What,' he asked, 'do you make of this sudden rash of dead clergymen we seem to be having?'

Dave had to admire his tone of callous flippancy and casual uninterest.

'Bloody Christians,' said Carl. 'They've been killing each other for over two thousand years.'

'When they're not killing us,' Will added.

Dave, watching in the mirror, could see Jessica's eyebrows twitch. He knew well that sceptical glance.

'"Us"?' she said. 'Haven't heard of any Neo-Gnostic martyrs.'

'Not yet,' Carl said darkly. 'But there were plenty of Gnostic martyrs, back in the Burning Times. You've heard of the slogan "Kill 'em all, let God sort 'em out"? That was for the Cathars. They were our people – Gnostics. Whole cities massacred, an entire province of France laid waste by a crusade on the orders of the Papacy.'

'That was a long time ago,' Aliyev said.

'There are more recent—'

'Why do you think,' Jessica asked, 'that it's Christians who killed the priest and the bishop? Seems more likely to be anti-Christians, no?'

'Well, don't look at us,' said Carl, sounding surly and suspicious. 'We don't do violence. It'd be crazy, for one thing, as well as, you know, wrong. And the atheists, they're on top anyway. They don't need to kill anyone. Nah, it's Christian-on-Christian, all over again.'

'What kind of Christians kill other Christians?' Jessica asked.

'You have to ask?' Carl asked. They all laughed.

'Seems to me,' Jessica said, 'that this Neo-Gnosticism stuff is all talk. OK, you don't do violence. Good. You don't do online propaganda. Fair enough. Your choice. So what the fuck, I idly wonder, *do* you do? Talk to gothgirls in pubs? Oooh, scary!'

Carl leaned over. 'I'll tell you what we do,' he said. 'We spread the word, we do our thinking and research to expose the anomalies in physics and everything else that reveals this world as the shoddy lash-up that it is, and as for the Christians, here's what we do. We mess with their heads.'

'Leaflet the churches?' Aliyev asked.

The two lads' heads jerked, ever so slightly.

'Not a bad idea,' said Carl, in haste after a moment's hesitation. 'Maybe when there are more of us. Meanwhile—'

He stood up. 'I'll show you what we do.'

'At this time of night?' said Jessica.

'Yes,' said Carl. 'At this time of night.'

Jessica and Aliyev did a good impression of a giggly head-to-head, then stood up too.

'Show us what you're made of,' said Aliyev.

'Computer code,' said Carl, swift with the riposte. 'We can't show you that, but we can show you how we mess with their heads.'

'Always up for a laugh,' said Aliyev.

They all headed out. As soon as they were through the door, Dave followed. The night was cool and dark, the moon a waning crescent amid thin clouds. Not many people were on the street. Dave looked to left and right and saw Jessica dawdling at the acute corner made by George IV Bridge and Candlemaker Row, a backstreet that sloped and curved down to the Grassmarket. Jessica glanced back, saw him, and disappeared around the plinth of Greyfriars Bobby. Dave hurried after her, keeping to the inside of the pavement. He paused at the sentimental statue, just in time to see the four cut across Candlemaker Row into the short passageway leading to the gate of Greyfriars Kirkyard. He heard Jessica's voice in his phone clip:

'How are we going to get over that?'

'Fear not,' said Carl. 'We have the technology.'

Dave crossed as if walking on. Grunts, giggles, thuds and odd, muffled, scraping sounds came through on his phone clip. He walked on until these sounds stopped, then doubled back. A cautious look around the corner showed the passageway to be empty. The gate was about three metres high, and afforded no convenient footholds. He paced up to the gate and cocked an ear. He couldn't hear footsteps. Jessica's breathing was all that came through on his phone clip.

In the corner beside the gate was a drainpipe. Dave looked up it, took a deep breath, spat on his hands and shinnied up. He placed a foot carefully to the pediment of the small obelisk that topped the stone gatepost, and from there stepped onto the sloping tiled roof of the gate-house. The tiles were damp, mossy, and slippery. Dave crab-walked along with his feet on the guttering, then swung himself off the roof and dropped to the ground in front of the gatehouse door.

Keeping his head down, he walked up the path and then crouched low and keeked one eye around the corner. He saw the group walking, almost as uneasily as himself, about fifty metres on down the path to his right. Doubled up like an ape, Dave trod delicately across cobbles to grass, then scuttled parallel to the nearest cover, a half-ruined mausoleum jutting out from the wall, about fifty metres from where the two Gnostics stood on the path, murmuring something to Jessica and Aliyev. Even with the phone clip, Dave couldn't quite make it out.

'You can't do that!' he heard Jessica say.

'Why the hell not?' said Carl, in a louder voice.

'Well, you know,' said Jessica. 'It's a monument to people who were executed, right? They were victims of the Church.'

Dave peered around the side of the mausoleum.

'Just a rival Church,' said Carl. 'Plus, they were just fucking terrorists anyway.'

With that he strode forward and stood in front of a huge stone plaque built into and rising above the wall of the cemetery, and started making slashing movements with his arm. Dave heard the fizz of an aerosol can.

'There!' said Carl, taking a step back to admire his handiwork.

'I don't get it,' Aliyev said.

Carl returned to the group and spoke, once more in too low a voice to catch. Just as Dave was straining to hear, he heard a scratching, scuffling noise in the mausoleum, and then a much louder noise that might have come from the throat of a large animal.

'What was that?' Carl's head turned sharply. Dave dodged back.

'Something moved there,' said Carl.

The noise came again, something between a cough and a growl.

'Are you guys trying to give us a fright?' Jessica asked.

'Fuck, no!' said Will. 'Hey, it's just some alkie.'

'That isn't a—' Carl said.

Dave couldn't see the front of the mausoleum, crouched as he was beside its side wall, but he could see a greenish glow beginning to light up the grass in front of it. It grew brighter by the second.

'What the fuck?' Carl's voice cried, taking the words out of Dave's mouth.

Into the green light rushed a stooped figure, which leapt onto the path and whirled to the right to face down the path towards four of the five petrified onlookers. Dave jumped back, and up. It turned to face him, and he recognised it even as his heart still thrashed like a caught fish. It was a werewolf whose somatic gene-modifications had been more radical than any Dave had ever seen.

The beast-man straightened up and howled at the moon. Dave heard the sound of fast-fleeing feet, and Jessica's and Aliyev's indistinct but raised voices. At that moment, yet another scraping sound came from inside the tomb, and another shape sprang out. Dave just had time to recognise it as a leki before its long metallic limbs blurred into a queer gallop, off down the path.

The werewolf looked at Dave again.

'Come on out,' the werewolf said.

'It's OK!' Aliyev shouted.

Dave stepped forth, still shaking. Carl and Will were

scrambling over the wall, to vanish apparently oblivious to the three-metre drop on the other side; the leki took a flying leap over the wall after them, to land in the street below with a clatter that suggested it had misjudged the jump.

'Huh-huh-huh!' went the werewolf. 'Gave these little vandals a fright, huh!'

'You gave *me* a fright,' said Dave. He looked down the path. Aliyev had an arm clamped around Jessica's shoulders. She didn't look reassured as the werewolf loped towards her, Dave close behind. The beast-man stopped a couple of metres away. Dave ran on to Jessica, hugging her as Aliyev disengaged.

'Jeez,' she said. 'Jeez.'

She pulled away and turned to glare at Aliyev, who spread his hands and looked aw-shucks awkward in an incongruously masculine manner.

'I had to stop you running off,' he said.

'Fucking near dislocated my shoulder,' she said.

'What's going on?' Dave said.

'The leki told me over a police channel,' said Aliyev. 'Just before the, uh—'

'You can call me the lieutenant,' growled the werewolf.

'Just before the lieutenant jumped out.'

'Sorry about that,' said the werewolf. 'Skulk – the leki – should have gone first. Couldn't hold myself back.' His toe-claws scratched at the gravel. 'Instinct, I suppose.' He waved a long, hairy arm towards the cemetery wall. 'I mean, look at that!'

Scrawled across the stone plaque in red spray-paint was: 'MAJOR WEIR LIVES.'

'Some people,' said the werewolf, 'have no respect for the dead.'

Dave shook his head, as if to clear it. 'What was the leki doing anyway? And what, uh, were you doing here, lieutenant?'

'Skulk will explain,' said the werewolf. 'As for me . . . it's all a bit personal, know what I mean?'

And with that he turned and loped away, vanishing in seconds around the far corner of Greyfriars Kirk.

A police-car siren and flashing blue light went by on the far side of the wall, down Candlemaker Row.

'Sounds like Skulk caught up with Will and Carl,' Aliyev said. 'What a fucking fiasco.'

He tilted his head, listening intently on his phone clip. Some tense, tedious minutes dragged by.

'Or maybe not,' Aliyev added. 'Skulk found a packet of leaflets nearby. And—'

He stopped. 'Woo-hoo!' he said.

'What?' asked Jessica.

'Paranoia's put them in the frame.'

'What's that mean?' asked Dave.

Aliyev tapped his nose with his finger. 'Sorry, can't tell you the details. But we haven't been wasting our time with these guys, I can tell you that.'

'That's something,' said Jessica. She looked around. 'This place is giving me the creeps.'

'How the hell do we get out?' Aliyev asked.

'Same way you got in?' Dave suggested.

Aliyev and Jessica shook their heads. 'The lads had arachno pads,' Aliyev explained. 'Hands and knees. Passed them down to us. Wish I'd brought mine.'

'I'll show you how to get out,' said Dave.

It took a fair bit of heaving and shoulder-standing before they were all standing on the far side of the gate. Aliyev and Jessica compared broken nails and scratched hands, and looked at Dave as if the damage were somehow his fault.

'Frankenstein's should still be open,' said Dave. 'Anyone fancy a pint?'

9. GRASSMARKET

The Honeywell engineers who had designed the emotional-emulation capacities of Skulk's mind, capacities which it had had even before it developed a self-model and started to itself feel those emotions, had in an idle moment included that of boredom. It wasn't an emotion that Skulk had hitherto felt. Skulk always had something to occupy its mind. The early hours of Saturday morning, however, found the leki lurking in the deepest alley off the Grassmarket, where Internet access was at best intermittent. By dawn, Skulk was beginning to suspect that it was for the first time experiencing that long-dormant element of its repertoire.

A swarm of mechanical midges had already settled around the Grassmarket, minute cameras blindly recording, tiny antennae quivering, sniffing the wind and scanning the wavebands. Around 06:15 the first breakfast vendors opened their stalls, soon filling the air with the smells of ramen and chilli, black coffee and green tea. Salaryfolk and students emerged from the surrounding blocks like ants, grabbing portable bites and morning jolts as they hurried for the trams. At 07:00 three lekis discreetly took up position in odd corners of Victoria Street and under the arch of the Cowgate. Skulk remained where it stood. At 9:30 shutters banged and doors opened on the rag-trade marts and frowsty textbook shops. At a quarter to ten, Adam Ferguson walked up King's Stables Road and entered the far corner of the Grassmarket. He walked to the Covenanters' Memorial, a civic monument that bore a remarkable if unintentional resemblance to a more commonplace civic amenity. He stood inside the open circle of its low wall, head half-bowed as if he was meditating on the martyrs.

Skulk, feeling another unaccustomed emotion, approached.

'Good morning,' it said.

'Morning, Skulk,' said Ferguson, gazing at the inscriptions on the small plaque. 'Good work last night.'

He glanced at where the edge of a centimetre-thick package wrapped in transparent polythene protruded from a crevice at the foot of the wall, hard to notice amid the leaf-litter and beer cans.

'Still there, I see.'

'Yes,' said Skulk. 'Perhaps we should go.'

'Indeed,' said Ferguson.

He came out of the small memorial space and turned about to go up the steep slope of Victoria Street, Skulk striding beside him. They took care not to look at the lekis on duty.

'Just back there you caught them, was it?' Ferguson asked.

'Down the street a little,' said Skulk. 'I saw one – Carl Powys – swerve towards the memorial space as he ran, and his companion Will Latham urge him to "leave it". I was . . . already aware that the robot known as Hardcastle sometimes stopped there on its way home. So, after apprehending them, or rather after asking them politely to stop whilst lashing my tentacles in an agitated manner above their heads, I decided to investigate. I did so as soon as the uniformed officers had taken the two students from the scene. I replaced the package as soon as I divined its import, and after I had recorded its front and back pages through the wrapping.'

'"Divined its import",' said Ferguson. 'You were always one for the *mot juste*, eh?'

'It's a small affectation of mine,' said Skulk. It hesitated. 'You wish to speak further about last night?'

Ferguson jammed his hands in his trouser pockets.

'Could do,' he said. 'If you'd like to, that is.'

'I'm anxious to clear the matter up,' said Skulk.

'I thought we were partners,' said Ferguson. They'd reached the top of the street, and were turning left onto George IV Bridge. Above them, the morning sun glinted on vertical acres of Royal Bank buckyglass. 'You know, man and machine, shoulder to shoulder. We've been through a lot, you and me.'

He looked sideways at Skulk, then away and from side to side before crossing the High Street. Deacon Brodie's pub on the corner, its name commemorating another Edinburgh dual personality. On the opposite corner, the green statue of Hume embodied a different spirit of the city.

'Yes,' said Skulk. 'That's why it was difficult to tell you.'

Together they cut across the downward slope of Bank Street, dodging the light traffic. Ferguson stopped at the top of Waverley Steps and leaned on the wall, overlooking the station far below and Princes Street beyond. Disembodied voices echoed up, announcing trains.

'That's why I'm annoyed you didn't tell me,' he said. 'Do you understand that?'

'I understand that now,' said Skulk.

Ferguson rapped his knuckles on Skulk's carapace, making it ring.

'If you'd told me about your lieutenant,' he said, 'I'd have understood. I wouldn't have objected in the least.' He leaned back and scratched the back of his head. 'He's very fucked up, is that it?'

'You could say that,' said Skulk. 'He refuses treatment. It would not be true to say he is happy. On the other hand, he does seem to derive some satisfaction from his way of life. He ranges widely. He ruts with others who are, in mind if not necessarily in body, like himself. He observes much. He claims that he is gradually overcoming his demons. I've told him many times that psychiatric help is available, but he seems incorrigible in that respect. I think our meetings, our "sessions" as he calls them, do him some good. Possibly it is cumulative. I have noticed an improvement over the years.'

'And, not to be too kind to yourself, he can be a useful source of information?'

'That too,' said Skulk. 'But the main reason for our relationship is the man–machine bond.'

'Yeah, well,' said Ferguson. '*C'est la vie. C'est la* fucking *vie*. You know, I do understand that a bond forged in lethal combat can be a bit stronger than one forged in kicking down a few doors together. I just wish you'd understood that ours was strong enough to take knowledge of the other one, that's all.'

'I take your point,' said Skulk.

'Fine,' said Ferguson. 'Oh, well, say no more about it, eh?'

'OK, Adam,' said Skulk.

'Right,' said Ferguson. 'Fine. Let's get to work.'

He came away from the wall and made to set off down the steps, then stopped and looked back towards the Mound.

'I wonder if our prof is in her office this morning,' he said.

'She isn't,' said Skulk, after pinging the New College reception.

'Fast work,' said Ferguson. 'You know, I might just phone her at home. Stay on the line yourself.'

Grace Mazvabo's voice sounded sleepy and irritated. 'Good morning, inspector. What can I do for you?'

'Sorry to disturb you,' said Ferguson. 'There have been some interesting developments overnight. You may be able to help us.'

'Go on.'

'First of all, does the name "Major Weir" mean anything to you?'

'Of course it does,' said Mazvabo. 'You must know that. Covenanter and self-confessed satanist, burned at the Grassmarket in 1670.'

'Just checking that there's no other possibility,' said Ferguson. 'I regret to say that the Martyrs' Memorial stone in Greyfriars has been spray-painted with the words "Major Weir Lives".'

Sharp intake of breath. 'Some little satanist ratbag, I take it?'

'Two Gnostic kids, actually,' said Ferguson. 'We caught them red-handed, so to speak. They're in the cells at St Leonard's, charged with criminal damage, and no doubt whatever else the fiscal sees fit to slap them with.'

'Good,' said Mazvabo. 'Well, I don't feel too Christian about this. Throw the book at them.'

'Oh, we intend to,' said Ferguson. 'But there's more. They were arrested in the Grassmarket, and a quick check on the PNAI threw up some brief recordings from the past few months of the two of them picking up something from the Covenanter memorial there. The leki you met yesterday checked and found a small packet of Third Covenant leaflets. It's been left there in the hope that someone else may still come for them.'

'Praise the Lord,' said Mazvabo. 'Have the kids admitted anything to do with them?'

'Afraid not,' said Ferguson. 'And there don't seem to be any recordings of them actually going into the Kirk.'

'That doesn't surprise me,' said Mazvabo. 'Non-cognisance works both ways, you know.'

'Yes,' Ferguson said. 'Still, water over the dam now.'

'Are the leaflets a new broadside?'

'Yes. The leki was able to copy the front and back pages without disturbing the packet. I'll get hard copies to you, but for now it does seem more of the same, except for the end. May I read it to you?'

'Please, please.'

'"If no visible signs of even outward repentance are given in the apostate churches of Scotland on the coming Sabbath of September Sixth, the soldiers of the said Covenant avow that the war shall be intensified on the said churches and extended to the secular institutions of the apostate states, sparing none, and if need be not even our own selves, as Samson did in Gaza of the Philistines."'

Skulk saw Ferguson flinch at Grace Mazvabo's loud, inarticulate cry.

'You know what Samson did in Gaza?' Mazvabo asked, after a moment.

'I've already looked it up,' said Ferguson. 'Just checking.'

'Oh, it's a suicide attack threat, all right,' said Mazvabo.

'There are very few precedents for Christian suicide terrorism that I know of,' said Ferguson. 'Some nominally Anglican suicide bombers in Sri Lanka, one or two questionable incidents in the Second Civil War in America, and that's about it. I mean, it's not like Christians have anything like the Islamist notion that it's a fast track to paradise, do they? Isn't it Christian doctrine that suicide is a one-way ticket in, uh, the other direction?'

'Certainly not,' said Mazvabo. 'God's mercy can extend to suicides. And that's not just my liberal interpretation. The old hard-line Calvinists were absolutely clear that if you're one of the elect all your sins are forgiven, even self-murder. Self-martyrdom has never been encouraged, but in wartime there's always a sliding scale – from facing certain death in regular combat, through the forlorn hope, to so-called suicide missions, and at the limit there is, yes, the precedent of Samson's bringing down the temple on himself and on God's enemies. So, yes, I would take this seriously.'

'That's what I was afraid of.'

'Anything I can do, inspector?'

'I'll be in touch,' said Ferguson. 'Thanks.'

As he clattered down the long, worn, zigzagging stone stairway from the top of the Mound to the foot of the hill, with the leki's metal feet stepping far more smoothly and surely behind him, Ferguson had the distinct sense of a belated awakening, as if the day had caught up with him with a bang. Everything was in hand, of course: as soon as it had become evident last night that Hardcastle aka 'Graham Orr' wasn't turning up for work, late or other- wise, the warnings and pictures had been released to the public media. Skulk, from its (apparently) embarrassing and unauthorised tryst with its former comrade the lieu- tenant, had transmitted a hint that the beast-man had seen Hardcastle inexplicably stepping in and out of the Covenanter memorial at odd times over the past year. The two students, whose pursuit by the Kinky Kazakh had seemed such a wild-goose chase, had fortuitously and fortunately come up with a connection. The students hadn't admitted to it, but that was strictly a prosecution problem. The threat of a terrorism-conspiracy charge would soon have them talking, unless they were of a much harder cadre than they seemed. But as far as the investigation was concerned, they'd spelled out their con- nection in bright red letters.

Major Weir lives, indeed! Hah!

But in the short sleep he'd had between the arrests, Skulk's transmission and 08:45, Ferguson had found his subconscious mind leaping to the comforting conclusion that the problem had been solved, whereas it had just been properly posed. It was in that dozy interim that his annoyance over Skulk's secret attachment had come to the top of his mental stack. Now that it was out of the way, his real priorities were shockingly clear.

He reached Greensides at 10:20. The meeting in the Easter Road Incident Room began at half past. DCI

McAuley was there, sitting between his counterparts from 'E' and 'F' Divisions. Ferguson shook hands with the two extra officers and nodded to McAuley before stepping in front of the whiteboard and looking over the team. Everyone had had a long night and a short sleep. Mukhtar hadn't slept at all. Mikhail Aliyev, for the occasion neat and androgynous in trouser suit and ponytail and no make-up, looked as if he hadn't slept either but had been very much otherwise engaged.

The room was thick with the smell of coffee. Even the lekis were wired. Ferguson slashed thick lines on the whiteboard, tabbed bright links in the shared headspace he'd summoned, and turned to the team.

'Good work last night, everyone. For the first time, we've got a connection – tenuous, but a connection – between the Covenanter tracts and the Murphy case. We have a prime suspect, who has not only not come forward but has disappeared. We have sightings – mostly from around Leith Water and the Old Town, not surprising for someone who works in security. None, however, since last night.

'That's where it gets scary. This Hardcastle – or Graham Orr, because we can't be absolutely sure yet whether it's a robot who sometimes passes as a *mutilado*, or vice versa – has worked in security in various nightclubs and other venues, including some quite posh hotels. So it, or he, has inside knowledge of security procedures in at least a dozen places around Edinburgh, knows his way around them, and has a choice of high-value targets: VIPs perhaps at the hotels, mass casualties at the clubs. Or at churches, for that matter, which remain explicitly threatened in the latest Covenanter tract. I've just checked with an outside expert and have been assured that a suicide attack of some kind – bombing being an obvious possibility – can't be ruled out on religious grounds. If we're dealing with a robot, obviously, there's even less of a problem. DS Hutchins will fill you in on that.'

Shonagh took the floor.

'I've had some fast catching-up to do on the subject of humanoid robots. There aren't many of them around. Now, you'd think that would be a point in our favour – the damn things all have Sony serial numbers, after all! But it's not so easy. The company found them a bit embarrassing, after the whole public-acceptance problem, and more or less washed its hands of them. It certainly doesn't keep track of them. It has a complete database of them, with their appearance and characteristics, and you'd be surprised how little arm-twisting it took along product-liability lines to get them to give us access to it last night. Turns out there isn't a robot in the database with a face that matches Orr-stroke-Hardcastle. That doesn't mean it isn't one of those robots: their facial features aren't easily modified, but it's by no means impossible. Nor, for that matter, is it impossible to reverse-engineer a new humanoid robot, assuming anyone with enough resources wanted to. The tech's all public domain now.

'Anyway, the key points as far as our investigation is concerned are, first, that a humanoid robot doesn't need the kind of living space that humans do, even to remain clean and wear a suit. All they need is shelter from the elements and an electricity supply. So a humanoid robot could quite happily dwell in a lock-up or a shed. Now, given that one of the areas with the most recorded sightings is around Leith Water, that means we have a lot of searching and door-to-door to do in the container blocks.

'The second point is that like lekis – and most non-conscious robots, for that matter – they are in the habit of taking regular back-ups. Hardcastle's back-ups were on a secure server managed by Hired Muscle. First thing we checked – after all, it would be very convenient to have the suspect's mind available to download, run and inter-rogate, right? No such luck. The back-up records exist, right up to one about five p.m. yesterday, but there's nothing in the file location. Hired Muscle's IT team swear blind that there was a complete memory back-up there when they checked, just after it was made, as is routine. Now it's gone – deleted or moved somewhere else. There are ways to track whether and where it was moved, but that takes time. Lothian and Borders AI and KI Crime Unit is working on it as we speak.'

A hand went up. 'Yes, Sergeant Carr?'

'Why not get Paranoia to do that?'

'Good point, Dennis. It's policy, basically. The only way the force ever got the PNAI past the regulatory committees at Westminster and Holyrood was to give a cast-iron guarantee that there'd be hard-wired firewalls against its ever poking around in other computer sys-tems.'

'One other thing,' said Carr. 'Suppose this guy really is a *mutilado*. What's to stop him having had – Christ, I don't know, a chip in his head or something – that could have given back-up memories, maybe just terabytes of random data, to complete the impression that he was a robot?'

Shonagh shook her head. 'Wouldn't work. There's an

automatic check that it's an AI software suite that's been uploaded. Could be he actually has an AI chip, of course, in his possession – in his head, for all we know! Either way, we're dealing with a very dangerous entity: a man who has, no doubt, serious psychological issues, possible long-term depression, plus religious fanaticism, and/or a robot whose mind is now safely stashed somewhere and has nothing but recent memories and a rather expensive chassis to lose. And, let's not forget, a knowledge of explosives.'

'Thanks, Shonagh,' said Ferguson. 'Now – DC Patel, can you bring us up to date on the Graham Orr side of the search?'

Patel stood up. 'It's all on the board, sir. As of this minute, no further progress to report. It's not an uncommon name, but there aren't many of the right age and none of them matches the face, or anything else. And, speaking of face, we've checked with all the military hospitals, Erskine and the rest, the Haig Fund, Oil for Blood . . . they all have detailed records of injuries and rehab, and the number of veterans who lost at minimum forearms and face and didn't opt for regen is a couple of hundred in the country as a whole, less than a dozen in Edinburgh. There's no case of anyone who survived the kind of massive injuries the actual Graham Orr is recorded as having died of choosing prostheses over regen. Not that they'd have any choice about it, anyway – they'd have been stabilised on medevac and then stuck in the regen tanks long before they recovered consciousness. If they'd registered prior conscientious objection to regen they were given the last rites and died. So – no cyborg veterans stalking around. The Face Forward charity is, as

Connor Thomas told us in the interview, very cagey about releasing or even retaining names but they assure us they know of no cases of anything so radical. That's it, for now.'

'Thanks, Saresh,' said Ferguson. 'And for what we have to do about all this, I'm pleased to yield the floor to DCI McAuley, who is taking charge of the city-wide operational plan.'

McAuley took Ferguson's place and swept the room with his best Human Relations grin.

'Good morning, everyone,' he said. 'I need hardly emphasise the seriousness of the situation. All leave is cancelled – which doesn't mean, I hasten to add, that those of you who've been up most of the night can't take a shift off. Even with all leave cancelled, of course, we simply don't have the resources to put static security in place at all the potential targets. We have to rely on the general public to stay alert, and on the existing private security at various establishments to be a lot more vigilant than they've recently allowed themselves to become. A lot of the elementary security habits that became second nature for most people during the Faith Wars – screening, baggage checks, not letting an unattended item go unchallenged – have been allowed to lapse. I don't say that's a bad thing, by the way, it's been one of the gains of the victory. These procedures must be revived, as of now. The Chief Constable will be making a media statement to this effect within the hour.

'What we can do, and what static security can't, is patrol, search, keep linked, keep Paranoia whispering in our ears, and follow up every lead. There's a list in your headspaces – use it. Shonagh mentioned the container blocks. We have to visit all of them. Yes, it's a long job. Yes, we're not popular down there. Tough. And by the way, if anyone's counting on getting our man – or machine – through camera surveillance, let me remind you that disguises as simple as a false beard, dark glasses, and a hooded top can throw face-recognition off – not for ever, but for more time than we may have.

'Finally, tomorrow's Sunday. We'll have at least one uniformed officer and one leki at each worship service at every place of public worship of the main denominations: Church of Scotland, Free Church, Catholic, Episcopalian. These are the big ones, and the obvious targets. That covers about twenty-odd buildings in Edinburgh, forty to sixty services, depending. It doesn't stretch or waste our resources. As for the sects, house churches, private meetings and so forth – there's no way we can cover them, no way we are wanted, and I leave any surveillance to the discretion of DCI Mukhtar.'

McAuley's gaze swept the room again, this time with a practised expression of resolve.

'Let's go to it.'

They went.

10. THE CONTAINER BLOCKS

Ferguson walked down a street four metres wide between buildings thirty metres high, each consisting of nine or ten storeys of adapted shipping containers. Above him, across this canyon, were strung electricity cables, rope-and-plank walkways, fat fibre-optic high-bandwidth pipes, and washing lines. Canopies flapped above the ground-floor shop windows and entrances, sheltering even smaller commerce in their shadows. Around him the pedestrians and shoppers surged in slow motion. Ostensible idlers in doorways chewed stimulant-sticks or took slow, watchful drags on cigarettes, while their eyes tracked him like surveillance cameras. Bicycles and mopeds snaked amid stalls, avoiding the grooves of the railway line. From the gleam of its rails Ferguson suspected it still functioned. At the end of the street was the canal and the Old Coal Wharf, and beyond it the cranes of the busy dock and the ruins of the abandoned dockside developments of Leith.

The Edinburgh City Council had solved the problems of its own displaced citizens with the new-tech housing schemes of Turnhouse and Tranent. The new population that had grown up around the revitalised docks had solved the problem of cheap, fast modular housing for themselves. The prevalent accumulation regime in the

Leith docks being capitalism with Russian characteristics, the container blocks' inhabitants paid over the odds for their living space and often found their security providers were people they needed security *from*, but aside from that the place worked.

Ferguson moved through the crowd as if he knew exactly where he was going. He did, not from any familiarity with this particular street but from the constant input to his contacts and phone clip from Ogle Earth, Paranoia, his colleagues and the lekis in and out of sight and earshot, and the flotilla of midge-sized surveillance microdrones stotting about in the downdraughts between the container stacks and in the thermals above. Ogle Earth let him see the most recent record of what any building or module he glanced at was like inside, and the identities of its current owners and renters (there were often wide disparities between this information and what he could see with his own eyes); Paranoia warned him of any associated illegal activities and told him which watchers to watch; he had split-screen views available at a blink from the cops up and down the street and on the walkways and balconies, and from the lekis likewise, deployed to sniff for danger and to watch the humans' backs; the midge-sized drones gave an overview and sniffed for suspect molecules. This was a mental zone that was rare and satisfying to get into: everyone sharing the same headspace, eyes and hands and boots on the street working together like the senses and effectors of some super-organism, a hive mind on the march. It wasn't sustainable for long – it ate human energy and machine processing-power like this year's software on last year's hardware – but while it lasted it made you feel invincible and as often as not it did the job.

If beards, dark glasses and hooded tops were the disguise to watch out for, the invincible police super-organism would have to stop and question one in ten men on the street. And that, Ferguson knew, was not going to fly. So he just flicked to infrared whenever he saw any of these features, let Skulk process the image and report back if it spotted any telltale temperature anomalies. All the other coppers on this sweep were doing the same. No luck so far.

'Just spotted Anatoli Ilyanov,' Shonagh murmured. She was walking the balcony strip of a parallel, wider and more salubrious street. Ilyanov was a Gazprom point-man on the container blocks, a man Ferguson had wanted to question last week and for several weeks before.

'Give him the nod if he clocks you,' said Ferguson. 'Otherwise, note and ignore for now.'

'Got it.'

Ferguson felt a slight pang. He knew he'd regret passing up this opportunity, but for now the search for Hardcastle's lair had priority. Damn, damn, damn. Ilyanov was a third-generation Leith Russki and knew every—

'Wait a minute,' Ferguson said. 'Still got him in sight?'

'Five metres,' said Hutchins, confirming with a pov tab to Ferguson's split-screen vision. A man in a leather jacket walking briskly and giving Hutchins the evil eye, or maybe eyeing her up on Ogle Face.

'Great,' said Ferguson. 'Smile and approach, flash him your card and show him the "wanted" pic.'

Ferguson dawdled at a Kyrgyzstani hash-pipe stall while Hutchins did as he'd said.

Ilyanov didn't look fazed at all. Even before Shonagh

had the card open he was smiling and sticking his hand out.

'Good afternoon, Detective Sergeant Hutchins! What can I do for you?'

'Good afternoon, Mr Ilyanov,' said Hutchins, straight back. 'I'm sure you've seen our latest media release.'

'Sorry to say I haven't,' said Ilyanov. He shook his head. 'I'm a busy man, and I work within the law, so police matters seldom concern me.'

'Ah well,' said Hutchins, ignoring this blatant lie. 'Could you spare a moment to look at these pictures of a man we'd like to talk to?'

'Aye, sure.' Ilyanov peered, then his head jerked back. 'Hardcastle? Aye, I know the cunt. To see, like. Never knew he might be a robot, mind. Thought he was just another one of they Hired Muscle goons. Seen him around, like.'

'Has he been involved in any of the recent scuffles with Gazprom security?'

Ilyanov considered this for a moment. 'Not to my knowledge, no.'

'Any idea where he lives?'

'Wish I could tell you,' said Ilyanov.

'You wish you knew where he lives? And what might you mean by that, Mr Ilyanov?'

'Oh, not to intimidate him or anything.' He flashed his teeth. 'I'm very keen to keep these unfortunate mis-understandings from getting out of hand. But I have to say, my employer's security detail is convinced that Hired Muscle is covering for a racket, and they have stolen Gazprom property stashed somewhere around here.'

'I would strongly recommend that you take such sus-picions to the police,' said Hutchins.

'With respect, DS Hutchins, don't talk like you just came off a container ship. I'm not that daft.'

Hutchins ignored the bait. 'What's the connection with knowing where Hardcastle lives?'

'Well now,' said Ilyanov, 'if he's a robot, it's not like he needs running water or that. Doesn't even need to sleep. All he needs is some kind of parking garage. Storage space.' He waved a hand. 'You see the problem? If I wanted to stash something dodgy around here, not saying I would, mind, I wouldn't use a lock-up. I'd use an empty flat, keep the window box watered, know what I mean? Maybe have someone coming and going. And if they could actually stay there, and not need any facilities, it's your icing on the cake, man!' His brain caught up with his mouth. 'Ma'am.'

'That's a very interesting idea,' said Hutchins. 'But unless you have anything specific, all it means is that we have even more places to search.'

'I'm afraid it does,' said Ilyanov, shaking his head sadly. 'Sorry I can't help you there.'

'That's OK,' said Hutchins. 'But if you do come across anything, you'll get in touch?'

'Of course,' said Ilyanov, making to go.

'I'll tab you my phone number,' said Hutchins.

'No need for—'

'Oh, there is, Mr Ilyanov — you know what the Greensides phone queue can be like. This way you can reach me any time.'

'Aye, well, I suppose.'

He took the ping sullenly, well aware that it exchanged his number for hers, nodded, and walked on.

'It'll be interesting to see how long before he ditches

his phone,' Hutchins remarked, as soon as Ilyanov was out of earshot.

'And where,' said Ferguson. 'Nice one.'

The sweep continued.

About an hour later, following a faint trail picked up by the PNAI – integrated from a two-day-past glimpse of a hooded man on some snogging local kid's eyewear upload, and a twenty-per-cent-probability trace of the origin of a stray molecule from an RDX precursor compound, most likely innocuous, picked up by a midge – Ferguson, Skulk and Patel turned sharp left into a long alley cluttered with recycling bins, pocked with puddles, tangled with pallid weeds. Still on the upper levels, Hutchins made her way along a swaying walkway to the same corner, with a view down the alley and along the street, and kept watch.

Ferguson looked up. The alley was dim in the late afternoon. Overhead, a midge swarm thickened. The PNAI told him that an RDX molecule had been detected. As he picked his way along he scanned each doorway that he passed. Ogle Earth might be out of date for some of the uses, but the physical layout of the room or passage behind the doors was probably correct. Most of them led off to the backs of confirmed shops or flats. He let these go by for the moment, looking out for one that was self-contained.

The midge swarm reached it before he did. A few metres ahead of him, about halfway down the alley, the swarm swirled down like a miniature tornado and buzzed in a black column in front of a grey wooden door. The padlocked door had been opened recently enough to have

flattened the weeds and swept the litter in a quarter-circle
in front of it: within the last day or two, Ferguson
guessed. He turned to Skulk.

'How does it smell?'

Skulk swung a stiff tentacle back and forth in front of
the door.

'Confusing,' it reported. 'Can't pick up any RDX
myself, but the midges have a better chance of that anyway.
A lot of other traces – machine oil, iron particles, carbon
nanoparticles, various reagents and surfactants, probably
from Swarfega or the like. Could be a machine shop.'

'Let's send some midges in,' said Ferguson.

A score or so of the microdrones detached themselves
from the swarm and flew or crawled between the door and
the jamb. Ferguson, patching their pov to his eyes, found
almost total darkness within. The midges spread out in a
loose mid-air cloud. Gradually, over a minute of inte-
grating stray light almost photon by photon, a greytone
picture built up. Ferguson swivelled the pov, looking
around. The place was a rectangular box, about two
metres by three by five. A sagging sofa along one wall. A
sink at the far end, with two taps. Three light bulbs, one
of them portable and hanging from the wall, its power
lead trailing. Big drums and small tins. Cardboard and
buckysheet boxes. Bottles and jars and tubes. A piece of
heavy machinery with levers at the side and a hefty two-
handed screw at the top; Ferguson identified it after a
moment as a basic printing press. Power tools, hung on
hooks or racked. Small complex mechanisms laid out
along shelves. A toolcase, closed. A lathe; a workbench,
with a rugged desk-slate propped against a thick reel of
sticky-backed buckytape.

So far, so innocuous. It was the chemical analysis, trickling in even more slowly than the visual image formed, that clinched the matter: RDX in the air, and traces of every stage of RDX manufacture among the scents of oil and hand-cleaner.

'It's Hardcastle's place,' Ferguson announced. 'His workshop and bomb factory.' He was confident enough to broadcast it, causing a city-wide flurry and a ripple in the PNAI.

'How can you be sure?' Skulk asked. 'It's criminal, yes, but—'

Ferguson had to think about it. How *did* he know that it wasn't some other criminal's workshop?

'No coffee mugs,' he said. 'Not even a kettle.'

'Ah,' said Skulk. It paused for a moment, tentacle tip hovering at the lock. 'Shall I go in?'

'Not on your life,' said Ferguson. He looked up and down the alleyway. 'Clear the building. Then clear the area.'

The door had a simple hasp and padlock, but getting in was going to take hours. Before sending in even a fully backed-up leki, they were going to have to have midges, glow bugs, and larger but still tiny robotic creepy-crawlies checking every crevice for booby traps. Even at that, Ferguson wasn't sanguine, which was why he'd had the building evacuated the moment he'd got a warrant and announced an unofficial blind-eye amnesty for any unrelated minor illegalities that the evacuation and investigation might expose. (Tax and rating evasion, OK; slave trading, not so much.)

After that it was over to the Bomb Squad. The alert for

Hardcastle remained in force, but the sweeps were, for the moment, off. Ferguson let everyone who was due an off shift take one, including himself. He returned to Greensides, wrote up the day's developments, talked to McAuley, called for the latest Bomb Squad updates, and by 20:30 was sitting with his back to the wall behind a table in the Abbotsford, contemplating the top of his one pint before taking the tram home.

The Abbotsford was an old pub with a long U-shaped bar and no music, just the hiss of the carbon-fibre smoke extractors and the low voices and loud laughs of the few people in it at this time, in the lull between the after-hours crush and the pre-club rush. Ferguson took a slow sip and settled back to gather his thoughts. Something was taking shape in his own brain's pattern-recognition system, which he trusted rather more than Paranoia's. That business with Skulk and his feral lieutenant, now: it had jolted him into a renewed appreciation of the strength of the bond between a fighting man and a fighting machine, and it chimed in some way with the peculiarity of a humanoid robot whose face wasn't on the manufacturer's database but was modelled on that of Graham Orr, the dead man whose name – whose forename, at least, for certain – it had also taken. That man had been a robotics specialist – Ferguson found himself wondering what had happened to the robot he'd worked with. Whether it had ever attained self-awareness and had its mind transferred to a less dangerous chassis . . . and had then transferred itself, or been transferred, to a humanoid one in the shape of its dead comrade, adapted or built from scratch . . . Ferguson found himself with a mental picture of a leki building a humanoid robot, like a miniature Martian-fighting-machine Frankenstein bent over a man on a slab, awaiting the electric surge that would bring it animation.

And wait, what if it had—

'Good evening, inspector.'

A youngish man seated himself on the bench opposite, planted a full half-pint glass on the table and looked Ferguson in the eye. It was Tom Mackay, the *Scotsman* reporter who'd been there at the start of the Murphy case.

'And good evening to you, Tom,' said Ferguson, resenting the intrusion on his sacrosanct half-hour with his thoughts. 'I'm off duty, and I hope you are too.'

'Oh, you know how it is,' said Mackay. He took a long gulp as Ferguson did likewise. 'Journalists and coppers are always on, even when they're off. No rest for the wicked.'

Ferguson shrugged. 'Seriously, Tom. There's nothing I can tell you that the Chief Constable didn't announce at the press conference, or that DCI McAuley didn't release a couple of hours ago. If you want anything more recent, just go to the public wiki.'

Mackay made a sideways gesture with spread hands. 'Relax, Adam. I'm not here to pester you. I've filed the evening's update already. Off duty and off the record, OK?'

'Fine,' said Ferguson. 'I have to say, Tom, your coverage so far has been . . . reasonable.'

'I'm not sure how to take that,' said Mackay. 'You mean I'm not doing my job?'

'Screw the badinage,' said Ferguson. 'I meant it. You're doing your job fine. Pissing off the police and alarming the public isn't doing your job, whatever your colleagues on the red-eyes may think.'

Mackay snapped his fingers. 'I was *sure* it was in the contract . . . oh, OK, enough of the banter.' He took a deep breath. 'Just wanted to talk, you know? About the wider ramifications of the case.'

'Off duty and off the record?' Ferguson snorted. 'I don't have all night.'

'You must have time for another pint,' said Mackay. 'My shout.'

'Pint, yes,' said Ferguson. 'And I'm buying, thanks all the same.' He leaned back. 'Go ahead.'

'The two students being held at St Leonard's,' said Mackay. 'They're involved, yes?'

'They haven't been charged yet.'

'I'll take that as a "yes".' Mackay grinned. 'And one thing they'll definitely be charged with is a spot of vandalism at Greyfriars Kirkyard, right?'

Ferguson said nothing.

'Oh, we got word of a rammy in the cemetery,' Mackay went on. 'Went round this morning and took pics of the graffiti. Asked around the Uni about the two kids. Rumour is they're into some kind of anti-religious cult or clique, which nobody knows – or wants to say – much about. And I know who Major Weir was as well as you do. So when McAuley stands on the Greensides steps and finally admits very reluctantly that the police might just be looking for "some tiny, unrepresentative, marginal group of so-called Protestant extremists", I put two and two together. Well, three, when I add "Bishop of St Andrews" to the Ogle search.'

'Aye,' said Ferguson, taking his time, and thinking, *You too, huh?* 'If we're talking obscure Protestant extremists, in Edinburgh, who're willing to kill and don't have an Irish connection, it's no surprise to find some identification with the, ah, martyred saints of the past.'

'So why aren't you saying that in public?'

'Operational reasons,' said Ferguson. 'You'll have to take my word on this. We'd very much appreciate it if you wouldn't mention it as yet, no matter how obvious you may think the connection is.'

Mackay shot a sceptical look over the rim of his glass. He wiped froth from his mouth.

'Not buying it,' he said.

'Give me a moment to explain,' said Ferguson. 'And speaking of buying . . .'

He returned from the bar with two pints and an argument.

'Look,' he said, 'it's not that it isn't obvious, or that it's a big secret. It's just a specific piece of evidence we've come across, a stroke of luck really, and it might set back the investigation if it became known that we had it. That's all. You aren't missing a scoop.'

'Nothing political behind this discretion?'

'Nope,' said Ferguson.

Mackay raised his glass, nodded, and took a small sip.

'OK, change of subject,' he said. 'What do you make of the stem-cell business?'

'What stem-cell business?'

Mackay raised his eyebrows. 'Now, *that* was in my latest. Mrs Bernadette White, the housekeeper, yeah? She's scheduled for spinal stem-cell regen therapy on Monday morning.'

'You put that in a news report?'

'Don't look at me like that,' said Mackay. 'I got it from a reliable source at the Western General, but not on the staff, so there was no question of doctor–patient confidentiality involved. Indiscretion, at most.'

'Not so reliable,' said Ferguson. He hoped it wasn't Isla who'd let this slip. 'Leaving aside the whole medical-confidentiality aspect – she's a Roman Catholic.'

'That's the whole point,' said Mackay. 'She's unconscious, and she'll still be unconscious on Monday. And for whatever reason – maybe an oversight, maybe she never got around to it, whatever – she doesn't actually have a signed and witnessed opt-out excluding herself from stem-cell regen therapy. No document, no dog-tag, no bracelet, nothing.'

'But surely it's obvious that she wouldn't consent – oh, shit!' Ferguson snapped his fingers in annoyance.

Mackay nodded. 'Official non-cognisance strikes again. Her presumed religion and any associated scruples are officially unknown to the hospital.'

'Oh come on,' said Ferguson. 'Having the Catholic Bishop of Edinburgh at her bedside, no doubt dabbing oil on her head and big toe or whatever the fuck it is they do, kind of settles that question. One would think.'

'One would think,' agreed Mackay. 'But the law doesn't. And I can see the point of the law. The WGH has no basis for assuming that she wouldn't consent, other than her own written or spoken word. You can't presume that people who are claimed to be members of a religious body or cult or whatever necessarily agree to all its doctrines, particularly as applied to themselves. Maybe she knew very well what she was doing. Maybe she made a conscious decison that if she ever broke her neck she'd rather wake up in a regen tank than in an iron lung. And given that she hasn't made it clear she doesn't want it, the surgeons have the old Hippocratic oath et cetera et cetera telling them to go right ahead.'

'They could wait until she came round!'

'Not without making the recovery slower and more difficult. Months rather than weeks of rehab, complications, possibility of infection. Best practice and all that.'

'Shit,' said Ferguson. He closed his eyes and wiped his forehead. 'Jesus. That's going to piss off the Catholics.' He opened his eyes and stared hard at Mackay. 'I kind of wish that story hadn't gone out, you know.'

Mackay spread his hands. 'Can't be helped. Sorry if it's going to cause some friction, but – it's not like it's going to be a big issue in the circumstances.'

'You're right, but . . .' Ferguson gnawed his lip. Something was bugging him. What was it Shonagh had said about Bernadette White? *Cherchez la femme.* Stem-cell regen, *mutilados*, a possible buried resentment at the whole Catholic doctrine . . . That had been when they'd thought that the mysterious Graham was a *mutilado*, not a robot as they were now almost certain he was. But whether he was a robot or not, he'd hung out for months with *mutilados*, he must have some knowledge of, perhaps even sympathy with, their plight. The printing press in the workshop was, Ferguson had little doubt, the one that had been used to print the Third Covenant sect's tracts, one of which had denounced, among other things, stem-cell therapy. And the latest of which had threatened not just churches but the secular institutions of the state.

'What?' said Mackay.

Ferguson held up a finger. 'Wait. Thinking.'

A picture was forming in his mind, a scene, a premonition of how it might appear afterwards in the surveillance traces:

A man, one-legged or legless, with a mangled face, bandaged perhaps, a face from which eyes would be politely or sympathetically averted, and which face-recognition software would struggle to recognise and would refer upward to higher-level processing, caught in a long queue of ambivalent images; a man swinging himself along on crutches or wheeling himself in a chair, hirpling or rolling through the gateway of the Western General, around the back of the Alexander Donald Building, up the steps or the wheelchair ramp and in through the hissing automatic double doors of the Wellcome Trust Stem-Cell Regeneration Clinic, where he'd be seen for a moment as one more patient come to have his dreadful injuries seamlessly repaired with tissues grown from his own cells until he blew himself up and brought the building down to rubble that would crash down and be sifted for many, many scraps of flesh, none of which would be his because he had no flesh to begin with; while his mind, his soul, was saved and stashed elsewhere . . .

Ferguson brought his fist down on the table and jumped up.

'I think you may have cracked something for us,' he said to Mackay. 'Thanks.'

He drained his glass, hurried outside into Rose Street and phoned Greensides, then the police team at the hospital. Then he caught the tram home, to find his daughter, Niamh, wearing very little but some complicated paper shapes that Isla was pinning together on her.

'Hi, Dad,' said Niamh.

'You're not going out in that, young lady.'

Niamh laughed. 'It's my design.'

'I'm sure it'll look wonderful,' said Ferguson. He had not the faintest idea how it would look, but it would fit.

Isla took a final pin from her mouth.

'How was your day?'

'Fine, fine,' said Ferguson. 'I may have just saved your life.'

'That's good,' said Isla. 'Now make yourself useful, and call out for a takeaway.'

He did. Later that evening he surprised Isla by telling her that he had an early start on the Sunday morning, because he was going to church.

'Try not to attack anyone,' she said.

11. CHURCHGOERS

'Cornelius?'

Cornelius Vermuelen slid on his wheeled board from under the jacked-up car. His wife Emere was standing in her dressing-gown, smoking a cigarette and looking down at at him.

'You're up early,' she said.

'The car's losing air.'

'Aren't you coming to church this morning?' she asked.

'Yeah, sure,' he said. 'But I want to fix the car first.'

'Well, you'd better get a move on. It's nearly quarter to nine, and you'll need a wash.'

The service wasn't till ten-thirty.

'Plenty of time,' Cornelius said.

'Are we still going out this evening?'

'Yes, but . . . after I've been to evensong, OK?'

'What! That's a bit of a nuisance.'

'I'm sorry,' he said. 'It's just something I want to do.'

Emere shook her head. 'I suppose you'll be wanting me to cook an early dinner, then.'

She didn't sound pleased. He didn't blame her. He hardly ever went to evensong.

'No, let's eat out,' Cornelius said. 'How about the Thai on Fenton Street?'

'Sounds good,' she said. 'It's a date. We can meet outside after the service.'

'You don't want to come along?'

'Morning's enough for me.'

Emere regarded her work as a schoolteacher as a more important expression of her faith than churchgoing. Sunday afternoon and evening were for taking it easy.

'I'll think about it,' she said. 'Right now I'll see if I can scrape together some breakfast, and then I have things to do before I start getting ready for church.'

'Ah, that's fine,' said Cornelius. 'Anything you need a hand with?'

'I'd rather you got the car fixed and had your shower.'

'Shouldn't take long. I've found what's the matter. Air pipe's a bit frayed, that's all. Losing pressure.'

Emere stayed where she was. Cornelius thought he could make out a sceptical expression on his wife's upside-down face.

'What's got into you about evensong, anyway?' she asked, stubbing out her cigarette on the path. 'Infatuated with one of those pretty girls in the choir, or what?'

She said it with a laugh, but her voice had an edge to it.

'No,' he said. 'It's . . . ah, I better explain.'

Cornelius sighed, hauled himself all the way out from beneath the car and stood up.

'It's something JR asked me to do.'

'That nutter!' They'd had John Richard over for dinner once. Once had been enough. Emere had never quite forgiven Cornelius for inviting him. 'What's he want with our, what was it, "den of heathen Erastian syncretism"?'

Cornelius explained what Campbell had asked him to do.

'And you take this seriously?' Emere asked.

'Not exactly,' said Cornelius. 'But I said I'd do it, so I'm doing it.'

'Why didn't you tell me first?'

'Because I didn't want to have this conversation. I realised how ridiculous you'd think it all was.'

'Well, I'd rather think you were ridiculous than think you were either up to something or had got overzealous all of a sudden.'

'You didn't think that!'

'I didn't know what to think.' Emere crooked a finger under his chin. 'So tell me in future, yes?'

Cornelius leaned forward so that their foreheads and noses touched. 'Yes.'

'Good,' she said. 'Now get back under that car.'

About fifteen minutes later Cornelius finished an awkward job of winding duct tape around an inconveniently located pipe. He slid out from under the Tata Air, sucked his knuckles, wiped his hands, leaned into the car and turned on the engine. It whirred into life. The pressure gauge stayed steady. He turned the engine off and closed and locked the door. It was a fine morning, Lake Rotorua blue under a blue sky. St Faith's Church was just down the hill, past the even more elaborate marae. Out on the lake the first seaplane flight of the day was slicing across the water. A moment later it took off, heading west to overfly the local volcanic features. The bungalow-crowded low hillside around him was quiet, still mostly asleep. Later it would rouse to its usual untidy Sunday self: men tinkering with cars or improving their houses, wives smoking and talking across fences. The kids were already up and about, running and yelling among the sulphur-stinky steam from the hot mud puddles. Ohinemutu hadn't changed much in the twenty-odd years that Cornelius and Emere had lived there, except that the cars at the roadsides were pneumatic or electric rather than petrol or diesel.

Nine o'clock. Cornelius flicked the news switch on his phone – he'd never quite taken to phone clips, let alone frames. He preferred keeping his distance from what he saw and heard on-screen and online, whether it was of the real world or virtual worlds.

A bit of local news – mudslide in Hawkes Bay; Labour minister denies US link – then:

'Police in Edinburgh, Scotland have issued a description and photograph of the suspect in the two recent terrorist attacks on clergy. They are keeping an open mind on whether the suspect is a man or a humanoid robot. A Sony spokesperson has categorically denied that any of its ill-fated robots are involved, or present any danger to the public. Here to discuss this . . .'

Emere appeared on the doorstep, brandishing the kitchen television.

'Have you heard this?' she called.

Cornelius held up the phone and flourished a thumb, and looked again at the device. The screen was showing a counter-terrorism expert whom he'd seen before. This time he was talking up an Edinburgh police spokesman's reluctant admission that some kind of Protestant fundamentalist sect might be behind the outrages. Cornelius rolled the picture back to the previous shot, showing the face of Graham Orr (human) or Hardcastle (robot).

He hurried inside. Bacon sizzled under the grill. The croissants were in the oven. Emere handed him a mug of coffee. He took it gratefully.

'A robot run amok!' she said, still watching the television. 'That's even more extraordinary than religious or anti-religious terrorism.'

'Even more unbelievable,' said Cornelius. 'But that's the one they're picking up on.'

'I suppose the media will be all over Waimangu tomorrow,' said Emere. 'Not to mention the police.'

Cornelius hadn't thought of that. Now he did. If there was one place in the world where humanoid robots and Protestant fundamentalism came together, it was Waimangu.

'The police will be all over it *today*,' he said. 'They'll want to know if any of the robots there know anything about this . . . Hardcastle character.'

'Do you think they might?'

He thought about Piltdown, the disgruntled anthropoid android.

'Hah!' he said, 'I can well imagine one of our robots taking a machine gun to these creationist creeps. Blow the whole thing up, that's what I'd do in their place.'

'You're being flippant,' said Emere. She looked anxious. 'Yes?'

'Yes, I'm being flippant,' Cornelius reassured her. 'Robots are just too empathic to harm a human being. They're better than we are. No original sin, as our friend JR would put it.'

Emere grimaced at the mention of his name, then frowned. 'Do you think he knows about all this?'

'I doubt it,' said Cornelius. 'He won't listen to the radio or watch television or go online on "the Sabbath". He might not even turn his phone on.'

'Then he's in for a nasty shock if the police turn up.'

'The robots are in for a nastier one . . . wait a minute, they aren't! They're online a lot of the time anyway. They can monitor police communications anytime they want. They'll know about what's going on. And they'll tell John Richard, if there's anything to worry about.'

'They might,' said Emere. 'Try giving him a call anyway.'

Cornelius tabbed to Campbell's number and called. To his surprise, it was answered.

'Hi, Cornelius.' His voice sounded heavy, and not surprised at the call.

'You've heard the news from Scotland?'

'Sure have,' said Campbell. 'One of the robots told me a few minutes ago. Nasty business. I'm scanning the Scottish news channels right now.'

'Even on the Lord's Day?' Vermuelen couldn't resist asking.

'Works of necessity and mercy,' Campbell replied brusquely. 'The Sabbath was made for man, and not man for the Sabbath.'

'Wise words,' said Vermuelen.

'Anyway, it's still Saturday over there,' Campbell added, with a characteristic logical leap of Presbyterian casuistry. In a more serious tone he added: 'What do you make of all this?'

'It's not what I make of it that matters,' said Vermuelen. 'It's what our local cops will make of it that I think you should consider.'

'Oh, I've considered it all right,' said Campbell. 'And so have the robots. They're vanishing into the bush as we speak.'

'That won't look good.'

'Well, seeing as they haven't *done* anything, I don't blame them,' said Campbell. 'I'm quite happy to stay here and talk to the cops, if and when they turn up.'

'They'll still want to talk to the robots,' said Vermuelen. 'And in any case, there's no point in the robots hiding in the bush. One plane or chopper with infrared could pick them up in no time.'

Campbell's guffaw made Vermuelen jerk the phone away from his ear.

'Infrared?' Campbell scoffed. 'Over Waimangu? There's enough hot spots here to keep them chasing warm vapour all day. Besides, the robots can just power down and cool off to ambient, pull some brush over themselves and they're as good as invisible. And *they*'ll still be able to see everything that's going on, in the first place from hacking the channels of whoever's looking for *them*. You'd need a massive cordon and sweep to find any of them at all. You'd need thousands of people. It's just not practicable.'

Emere opened the oven, took out the croissants, turned off the grill and tapped her wrist. Vermuelen nodded.

'Man, they might just do it,' he told Campbell. 'If people ever got worried about killer robots, that's exactly what they'd do.'

'I can explain to them why they needn't worry,' said Campbell. 'If the cops do come, which I still doubt they will.'

'I'm sure we can rely on you for that,' said Vermuelen, not sure at all.

'I'm far more worried about that other stuff we were talking about,' said Campbell. 'Still OK for that?'

'Once I've had my breakfast,' said Vermuelen.

Campbell started to say something.

'That was a hint,' said Vermuelen, and Campbell took it and rang off.

After all that, Cornelius and Emere were a few minutes late into the church. They ducked to a pew at the back. The vicar glanced up from the lectern, smiled, and returned to her reading from Isaiah. Cornelius waited until everyone was standing for the first hymn before looking around the congregation. The church was about half full, as usual. He recognised everyone there except a couple of obvious tourists and one Pakeha man in a suit, a couple of pews in front. His cropped hair, and something in his build and stance, made Cornelius suspect that he was an American exile.

The hymn finished. The stranger, who'd been singing from the hymn book rather than from memory, sat down a second or so after everyone else. This pattern persisted through the rest of the service. The stranger didn't join in the Eucharist. After the benediction, Cornelius and Emere were first out of the door. They waited a few paces down the path while the rest of the congregation streamed out. Emere took care of talking to friends and neighbours, while Cornelius nodded and smiled and kept looking out for the stranger. Eventually he emerged, in animated conversation with the vicar. She noticed Cornelius and headed straight for him, the stranger in tow.

'Morning, Lisanne,' said Cornelius.

'Good morning, Cornelius – oh, hi, Emere! I'd like you to meet Brian Walker, he's from the St Patrick's Fellowship in San Francisco, just over from the States for a visit to Catholic schools in NZ . . .'

Cornelius shook the American's hand, thinking, *So much for that*. Walker was tall enough to have to stoop slightly. He almost bowed to Emere, turning away before wrinkling his nose slightly at her post-church cigarette, and he gave Vermuelen a scrutinising glance. Or perhaps Ogling – he wore frames, which Vermuelen thought slightly indecent to wear in or just outside a church.

'Hi,' said Vermuelen. 'Are you having a good trip?'

'Excellent,' said Walker. 'Apart from your beautiful country and all that, it's wonderful to be able to see parochial schools again.' He shook his head. 'I've no doubt we'll see them again in the US, but not in my lifetime.'

'It must be tough,' said Vermuelen.

'Yeah, it's tough. The things our kids are taught in the state schools would make your hair stand on end.'

Vermuelen made some sympathetic noises, then Walker and Reverend Lisanne were off through the crowd.

Vermuelen called Campbell again as he and Emere walked back up the street to their house.

'Any developments?' he asked.

'All quiet on the western front,' said Campbell. 'Anything at your end?'

'Just a travelling Romanist,' said Vermuelen. 'Brian Walker. A Yank. Nice enough guy.'

'You know all this?' Campbell said. 'You're sure that's all he is?'

'I've no reason to doubt it.'

'OK, OK,' said Campbell. 'Tell you what. If the cops turn up here I'll ping you. Otherwise, assume all's fine. And there's no need to call me if you do see anyone acting suspicious. Call the cops if you think there's any threat to – well, you know. And if you think it is a cop, under-cover or whatever, just tell me tomorrow.'

'Fine. See you in the morning, then.'

'If we're spared,' said Campbell.

Cornelius and Emere came out of the Thai restaurant to a dark evening and a chill breeze off the lake, carrying a sul-phurous whiff from the bay.

'A drink, then head home?' said Emere, slipping a hand under his elbow.

'Sure,' said Cornelius. 'The Pleasant Fucker?'

'That'll do,' said Emere.

They turned the corner into Arawa Street. The Pheasant Plucker was a little way up. Emere stopped at one of the sidewalk tables, one hand on the back of a chair.

'It's cold,' said Cornelius.

'I need a smoke,' said Emere.

'What'll be your other poison, then?' Cornelius asked.

'Gin and tonic,' said Emere.

Vermeulen stepped into the warm interior. Dim light, a fire, the smell of roasting meat. As he stood at the bar waiting for his pint and Emere's G&T, he heard loud American voices from one of the restaurant tables and glanced over. A half-dozen or so men were in the middle of dinner. One of them, he saw with surprise, was Brian Walker. Cornelius had seen some of the others around town – owners of stores, car dealerships, outdoor activities centres, that sort of thing. He was surprised to see Walker among them – most of the American exiles around here were militant Protestants of various kinds, Baptists and Adventists and Reconstructionists. They were the kind of people who were constantly hatching anti-US plots, not all of them imaginary. The conversation was, predictably enough, about the outrages of the secularist regime in the US.

Walker noticed Vermuelen looking, and responded with a cold stare, as if it were Vermuelen who was out of place. Vermuelen nodded, turned his back, took his drinks and went out.

Shortly after nine on Sunday morning Grace Mazvabo, as was her habit, hopped off the tram at the West End stop that was still called St John's. She crossed Princes Street and went down the steps beside the big ornate building now called the West End Venue, and into Princes Street Gardens. No one else was about in the park. The sun was bright, the air already warming to the low twenties Celsius. The first fall of leaves littered the path. Grey squirrels checked her out, figured she wasn't about to drop them a crust, and hightailed off in low leaps like stitches of fluff. She strolled along, in plenty of time, the Ross Bandstand below on her right, the Castle on its basalt plug above. There was something about the Castle that always called to Grace's mind her deepest sense of assurance, in its fusion of geology and history, its literally sheer dominance of the landscape, its projected might the ancient and medieval equivalent of a strategic nuclear deterrent. How crucial the strong castles of the princes and lords, the walled towns of the burghers, had been for the Reformation. *Ein feste burg ist einser Gott*, indeed. While it stood she could easily believe that the College a hundred or so metres downslope from it, and the Kirk yet farther down its glacial flank, would some day regain their lost prominence.

Not, of course, in the old way – not to be an Establishment, let alone a temporal dictatorship of the Kirk Sessions, or a perpetual grey cloud drizzling on the nation's spirit. Nothing like that. But just to take its place again as a respected voice, a part of the conversation, acknowledged to have something to bring to the table. A point of view, worked out in living connection with a tradition entwined inextricably with the nation's past all the way back to Columba's coracle precariously ferrying the faith across the Irish Sea. In rejecting and disdaining that voice, holding it in too much contempt even to take the trouble of silencing it, the nation had lost a way of making sense of itself. And it wasn't as though the Church of Scotland, or Scotland's other mainstream Churches and indeed other religions, had done anything to deserve the Great Rejection. They'd been innocent victims, collateral damage, caught up in the blast radius of recrimination against the Dominionists and Dispensationalists, the Scientific Creationists and Christian Zionists, the corrupt and cynical elements of the Roman hierarchy, the Islamist jihadis and the Third Temple zealots and all the rest who'd done the real damage in the Faith Wars. And now it was in danger of happening all over again.

It just wasn't fair.

Such thoughts as these, comforting and familar even as they rankled, passed through Grace's mind as she walked the same path that she walked six days a week, Sunday to Friday. But as she walked she became aware that the treacherous little voice in her head was having none of it. She knew that voice very well, had known it since she was a little girl in Bulawayo, and (unlike some people she could mention) she knew it wasn't the voice of the Devil.

It was the voice of a part of her mind that felt it wasn't being listened to. It didn't always speak the truth, it didn't always deserve a hearing, but it would only go away if it wasn't ignored. It came and went over the months and years, depending on how troubled her mind was. This time, she'd had that small unbidden voice in her head for a couple of days now, ever since DI Ferguson had inveigled her into playing that silly game on the iThink.

What the little voice had been saying was: *You don't have free will.* Now, that was ridiculous – the Predictor game itself had a ReadMe that explained how the trick was done. All that was happening was that her phone clip was picking up faint electrical traces of the *readiness potential*, a neuronal surge preceding and preparing the flexure of her finger. Even pressing the key was redundant – the light would come on if she tapped the desk instead. It was no more spooky than – in fact, it was exactly the same as – the way the phone clip enabled her to control the iThink, or tab and select on her frames, every day. The ReadMe had links to decades of discussions of the effect's much-contested philosophical implications, all the way back to the original Libet experiment in 1985.

From long and sometimes anguished rethinking of her Calvinist heritage, as well as her engagement with the philosophical naturalism that had become the default assumption for almost the entire academy, Grace Mazvabo had long since settled down to an easy acceptance that determinism was compatible with – as the philosopher Dennett had put it – any kind of free will worth wanting.

And yet, and yet . . . The light going on that maddening, almost imperceptible, but unarguable third of a second *before* she'd even *decided* to press the key seemed to mock such philosophical reassurance, and to let the little voice taunt her with an echo of her own words to the leki: *You're still a machine, a deterministic system.*

Towards the end of the path, near the steps up to the Mound, Grace paused for a moment to eye one of her favourite statues. A lovely woman, leaning forward, two children at her flowing skirt, one of her hands holding out a book, the other hand open. It had no name on the plinth, and Grace could let her fancy read it as Education, or Motherhood, or even the Church as it had been and might some day be again, welcoming her children back into her arms.

This particular Sunday morning, though, the sunlight caught the statue's smiling eyes and made them wink, and its stone lips said in a voice that no one but Grace would hear: *Don't you recognise me, after all this time? You know who I am!*

Grace looked back at the statue, shaking inside. The statue now seemed far older than its undoubted Victorian origin, a goddess from antiquity who had stood calm and firm through the two millennia of Christianity, and was now quite at home and at one with the age, her time come round again.

'Yes, Sophia,' Grace Mazvabo whispered. 'I know who you are.'

She turned away and almost ran up the steps, the sphinxes on the roof of the National Gallery returning a stony gaze to her anxious eyes.

Ferguson found a vacant pew near the back of the church, nodded to the uniformed PC nearby, and sat down. The place smelled of polished wood and old paper, with a faint whiff of bodies and clothes. The congregation arrived during the quarter-hour before the service was due to begin. By the time they'd all settled, the church, though far from packed, was decently full: about three hundred, Ferguson reckoned. The social composition was skewed: towards older rather than younger, female rather than male, European and African rather than Asian, upper rather than lower working class. But it wasn't that distorted a sample of Edinburgh's population. Adolescents and younger adults tended to dress casually. Parents, grandparents and young children were dressed to the nines, as if living up to some ideal of Sunday best. It took Ferguson a while to spot Grace Mazvabo. The professor, whom he'd last seen in a plain grey top and trousers, was quite startlingly attired in a vivid bottle-green jacket and skirt, a similarly garish gold blouse, and a broad green straw hat. She noticed him, narrowed her eyes, acknowledged him with a curt nod.

Ferguson remained seated through the service. He didn't know when to stand and when to sit, and he wasn't joining in the hymns and prayers anyway. Nor, unlike the PC, was he ostentatiously taking notes of Reverend Dow's sermon. He let the whole thing wash over him while idly admiring the vaulting and the stained glass.

He left just before the end and waited by the door. Most of the congregation had dispersed by the time Grace Mazvabo came out. She didn't look pleased to see him.

'Back with the God Squads, are we?' she asked, with a sideways glare at the sub-machine-gun-toting PC on the church step.

'Here to see you,' Ferguson said. 'We have to talk. Discreetly.'

Mazvabo considered this. 'All right,' she said. 'Not right now. I'm going back in to tidy up.'

'Fine. I'll take a wander around the churchyard and I'll see you . . . where?'

'Martyrs' Monument. The one that got vandalised. It's in the wall down there on the left. Can't miss it. Fifteen, twenty minutes.'

A slow orbit of the churchyard brought him to the place in fifteen minutes. Mazvabo wasn't there. Ferguson stood and read the inscription, faded by erosion and pollution, obscured by lichen and now by the red slogan sprayed diagonally across it. It began:

> *Halt paffenger, take heed what you do fee,*
> *Thif tomb doth fhew, for what fome men did die.*

The rhyme went on like that, solemn and steady and precise. At the foot, the inscription broke into prose:

From May 27th 1671 that the moft noble Marquis of Argyle was beheaded, to the 17th of Feb.ry 1688 that Mr. James Renwick fuffered, were one way or other Murdered and Deftroyed for the fame Caufe, about eighteen thoufand: of whom were execute at Edinburgh, about an hundred of Noblemen, Gentlemen, Minifters and Others, noble Martyrs for JESUS CHRIST. The moft of them lie here.

Ferguson was still trying to figure out the rule for writing 's' as 'f' when he heard the gravel-crunch of Mazvabo's approach. She walked up, a handbag on her arm and a big black Bible in her hand, stood beside him and looked at the monument.

'It's impressive, in its way,' he said. 'No pomp.'

'Yes,' she said.

'Were eighteen thousand really killed?'

'It's arguable,' said Mazvabo. 'The number of executions, even including summary executions, was in the low hundreds, and that's often been used to discredit figures like this. But the inscription doesn't claim eighteen thousand executions, does it? If you include exile – voluntary, as it's been called – banishment, privation, death in often one-sided battle, enslavement in the West Indies and all the rest under "one way or other murdered and destroyed", then the figure is not as wild an exaggeration as some would like to make out. It's always easy to talk down the real numbers by talking up the official figures. And don't I know it! How many judicial political executions were there under Robert Mugabe? None! How many unjust deaths was he responsible for? It's arguable, but it was a lot more than none.'

Ferguson nodded. 'I've . . . had to give such matters some thought myself.'

'I'll bet you have!' said Mazvabo. 'Have you ever repented of them?'

'That's for another day,' Ferguson said.

'You may not *have* another day,' Mazvabo said. 'That's one thing the old preachers got right.'

Ferguson turned to her. 'No. It really is for another day.' He jerked his chin at the monument. 'The Third Covenant sect – do you really think they're inspired by traditions like this?'

'This, and more. They'll be steeped in the Killing Time, from books, sermons, tales. Martyrdom is a powerful meme, inspector. It reproduces itself.'

'But why now? What is there to be martyred for?'

Mazvabo gestured toward the PC at the door of the church, with his yellow jacket and black SMG. 'You have to ask?'

'You know fine that's for your protection. It isn't like the old days.'

'And the policeman inside, taking notes? That took me back to the old days all right. A real nostalgia trip, inspector!'

'There's an element of that,' Ferguson conceded. 'It isn't the main thing the force has in mind. But to the extent that it is, it's a response to two murders and threats of worse, of *suicide bombing*, for God's sake, coming from inside the very heritage of this very church, a tradition glorified right here where we're standing now. So let's not get sidetracked from my question. Before any of this happened, what could motivate people to start killing again? Make them willing to be martyrs again?'

'You have to look at it from their point of view,' said Mazvabo. 'They see the Churches as having compromised with the secularist state, accepting a marginal position in society and being grateful that they're not actively persecuted. It's true, the Church of Scotland and the rest may strive to reverse the Great Rejection, but we aren't even metaphorically up in arms about it. In a way, we've gained from disestablishment. You saw the congregation today. Nobody's here for the social cachet, quite the opposite. Going to church is very much not the done thing. We do it because we believe in it. We're not ashamed of our faith and we make sure that everyone knows it. That's why most of us dress for the occasion. It's the only reason why I put on this rather, ah, conspicuous suit and hat every

Sunday and carry my old mission-school Bible-knowledge-prize Bible, even though we hardly ever read from the Authorised Version in church.'

She looked around. 'Let's walk,' she said.

They walked back to the main path and turned toward the upper corner. The shadow of an artificial eclipse passed over; Ferguson glanced at his watch, frowned, but didn't break his attention or his stride. The full sun came back like a light coming on, and made him blink.

'So,' Mazvabo continued, 'we accept the situation. But it's not a good situation, and it's not one we like. It's a situation now written in the constitution of the Republic, but it's certainly not the one that's written in the constitution of the Church of Scotland. It rankles even with me. With some it must rankle far more. They look for inspiration, for justification for their anger, and it isn't far to find. Because, as you say, right in our own church's heritage, literally carved in stone, there's the memory of men and women who were willing to die rather than acknowledge the state's authority over the Church. And that was an established Church – almost everyone agreed on that. What would the old Covenanters have felt about a Church that is content to live under the boot of a state that despises it, just because the boot isn't pressed down hard? And what would they think of the state that keeps the boot resting on the Church's neck?'

'I could almost suspect you sympathise.'

'No, no,' said Mazvabo, sounding flustered. 'That's my point. If someone like me, a liberal, a moderate, can feel . . . some anger about the position of the Church, what must it be like for fundamentalists?'

'No,' said Ferguson, as they cut across the grass to

another path, parallel to the Flodden Wall. 'That's not enough. There must be more behind this.' He clenched an upturned fist and punched forward. 'Something more powerful than religious resentment. Yes, faith is a force in itself, I've always known that, but I also remember the Faith Wars weren't about faith. They were about oil.'

Mazvabo laughed. 'You think this is about oil?'

'No, not oil, but something that isn't talked about in the tracts. It could be something personal, some really warped individual psychology. We can't rule that out yet, but if it isn't something smaller like that, then it's something bigger. I don't know what it might be. But yes, if it's more than one person it's probably some religious group in the first instance, whatever may be behind them. Do you know of any sects, cults, whatever, that even *sound* like this Third Covenant lot?'

'Oh, sure!' said Mazvabo. 'Plenty.'

'What?' cried Ferguson. 'And you never said?'

Mazvabo stopped. 'I know you were joking earlier, about my sympathising, but I know you're not now. You're accusing me of not telling you about these sects. Inspector Ferguson, the only reason I didn't tell you was that I assumed you knew. It's your job to know about these kinds of things.'

'No, it is not,' said Ferguson, angry at being accused himself. 'The Special Branch, as you well know, monitors groups with known violent associations, even when those associations are in the past. If some shack in Pilton is the meeting place of something calling itself the Ulster Presbyterian Reformed Apostolic Church and most of its congregation happen to be ex-members of the UDA and their families, you can bet your boots the SB keeps an eye

on them. We don't keep an eye on sects, or Churches for
that matter, for three reasons. One is that we don't have
the resources, another is that there's nothing to see, and
the third is that unless we have verifiable reasons for suspicion we are legally obliged to ignore them under the
principle of non-cognisance. And that, Professor
Mazvabo, is why I'm so annoyed to hear you complaining
about the condition of the Churches. The Republic of
Scotland does not oppress the Church of Scotland, or any
other. It ignores it – except of course when it has to put
its own men and women at risk protecting the congregations and clergy from believers more fanatical than
themselves. So do please enlighten me about these sects.'

'All right,' said Grace Mazvabo. 'I take your point. I
apologise.'

Ferguson nodded, and resumed the walk.

'I know them through my research,' Mazvabo said.
'Not through the Church. Over the years, I've been able
to track down books, letters, records, traditions through
getting to know people in small sects. There are in fact
quite a few around Edinburgh – people displaced from
the farms, or the coast. There were once entire villages
along the east coast dominated by Brethren churches, for
instance – all gone now, of course, but the people haven't
disappeared. Different tradition, but with the displacements they get thrown in the mix. Then you get new
Pentecostal congregations, house churches – they stepped
in with new social support, welfare, charities and so on
during the post-war upheavals. You'll find a surprising
number in West Lothian – in the Turnhouse schemes,
obviously, but also in the Carbon Glen boom towns,
Livingston and Linlithgow and Falkirk and on west.

There you get other twists and remixes, people highly religious and technologically sophisticated.' She laughed suddenly. 'Engineers are still easy prey for creationists. It's a hazard of the job, when your job *is* intelligent design.'

'Engineers, eh? Very interesting indeed,' said Ferguson. He took a deep breath. 'You asked if there was anything you could do to help, Dr Mazvabo. Well, there is. Something that would help a lot, and that if successful would get the cops out of your Church.'

Mazvabo lifted her hat off and let her hair spring out.

'Go on,' she said.

'Before I go on,' Ferguson said, 'I have to warn you it's risky. And it isn't official. I want to be absolutely sure it's secret. Not that I mistrust anyone in the force, it's just that . . .' He tilted his spread hand one way and another. 'I don't want it to come out even accidentally. But you'd have very fast back-up if necessary, I can guarantee that.'

'I'm still interested,' said Mazvabo.

'OK,' said Ferguson. 'I want you to visit as many of these new Churches and sects as you can, and report back to me any where you hear rhetoric that reminds you of the rants of the Third Covenant. It's a huge job, I know, and perhaps dangerous, as I said.'

'Oh, I won't worry about danger,' said Mazvabo, with a dismissive flap of her hat. 'And I know enough about the sects to narrow it down. Yes, inspector, I'd be delighted.' She looked down at herself, then looked up and smiled. 'I'll just go home and change into something a little more plain, and make a start this evening.'

Ferguson gave her a surprised look. 'Really? You're sure?'

'Of course I'm sure. I'm so happy to be able to do

something that might catch these – these – *heretics* who dare to use religion to justify murder.'

'Well,' said Ferguson. 'Thank you, Professor Mazvabo.' What a strange woman, he thought.

12. DEFENCE MECHANISMS

Ferguson had had a busy morning before he'd gone to the church. He'd checked the latest from the Leith site: in the middle of the night the Bomb Squad had finally concluded there were no booby traps, gone in, and removed a half-kilo of RDX along with its precursor components and manufacturing paraphernalia. They'd then pulled out, leaving Tony Newman's forensics team to take over the scene. The first thing Forensics had confirmed was what had been the subject of Ferguson's sarcastic remarks: the paper and ink for the hand-operated printing press were identical to those of the Covenanter broadsides. Just to clinch the identification, the last one – the one Skulk had found in the Grassmarket – was still set in type on the plate in the press. An IT specialist had arrived in the small hours to attempt to crack the privacy protection on the desk computer.

Ferguson had then caught a bus across town to St Leonard's, the police station in Newington, a district between the University and Arthur's Seat. He'd found the police sergeant in charge of the case of the two Gnostic students, and had sat beside him in the interview room. Carl and Will had been interviewed one after the other, and had been severely shaken by the evidence that Ferguson had printed out for them.

They'd each, separately, admitted having on several occasions over the summer picked up the leaflets and surreptitiously placed them in Greyfriars. They'd been put up to it by Hardcastle, whom they'd met at a Dave Warsaw gig. Hardcastle had overheard them badmouthing Christianity and had approached them. The security robot had told them it was itself hostile to the mainstream Christian Churches, for reasons quite different from theirs, and had asked them to place some leaflets in Greyfriars as part of what it said was to be a campaign of psychological warfare. They were not to investigate the leaflets or Ogle their contents. Partly from malice, and partly from mischief, they'd agreed. They hadn't paid much attention to the contents of the broadsides, had barely understood what little they had read, and had had no idea that they were in any way connected to the bombing of Father Murphy. Being told that they were had come as a shock.

The leki in attendance had later confirmed that, as far as it could tell, the two lads were telling the truth. Ferguson, well satisfied, had left it at that.

Ferguson walked from Greyfriars to Greensides, arriving at about 1:30. He picked up his bike at the shelter and cycled down Leith Walk and Constitution Street to the container blocks. He steered through the narrow streets, and dismounted at the yellow tape across the alley where they'd found the workshop. A leki and a constable were guarding the barrier.

'Clear to go through?' Ferguson asked.

The PC nodded. Ferguson ducked under the tape, then lifted his bike over. He propped it against the wall and walked down the alley. A positive-pressure buckysheet tent had been erected around the doorway. Mukhtar stood outside, smoking.

'Good work on the confessions,' he said.

'If they're complete,' said Ferguson.

'Oh, I reckon they are,' said Mukhtar. 'I know useful idiots when I see them.'

'Uh-huh,' Ferguson grunted. 'What brings you down here?'

Mukhtar ground out his cigarette end with the heel of his boot. 'For a sniff of the air,' he said. 'Not even Paranoia is making anything of the esteemed Mr Ilyanov's stated distant acquaintance with Hardcastle. It gives me a funny feeling in my old bones, though.'

'Hmm,' said Ferguson. 'Your call. Well, I better have a look inside.'

Mukhtar jerked his thumb over his shoulder. 'No need to go in, unless you really want to suit up. There's a perfectly good view through the midge headspace. Brighter than the real thing.'

It was like looking through the wall, on a scene in full daylight. Ferguson had a childish sense of invisibility as he glided the pov around, watching in turn Newman and his assistant sifting and bagging, the IT guy with his arcane kit and intent look, and Skulk poking into odd corners with his tentacles. Skulk and the IT guy, at least, were well aware of Ferguson's physical location and virtual presence. The IT guy made a point of turning from the desk slate's innards and looking straight at Ferguson's pov, a mildly unnerving experience.

'Afternoon, DI Ferguson,' he said, startling Newman, who looked up and saw nobody. 'You'll be glad to know

I've cracked the encryption on this. It's a standard commercial job, nothing fancy. The only problem is the sheer amount of information on it, and the lack of organisation. If you're a robot, of course, you can keep track of everything in your own memory.'

'Can you hear me?' Ferguson asked.

'Yup, loud and clear.'

'What have you found so far?'

'There's an amazing amount of religious crap,' said the IT guy. 'Theology, Church history, philosophy, apologetics, creationism, Catholicism, all kinds of stuff.'

'Throw the lot to Paranoia,' said Ferguson, mentally tagging 'creationism' because Mazvabo had mentioned it. 'Let's see if it finds any patterns. Anything else?'

'Nothing about making bombs. Imagine my surprise. Lots of business records, time sheets and stuff, receipts . . .'

'Ace!' said Ferguson. 'Concentrate on that, plug every name and number into searches, dredge up everything.'

'Got you, boss.' The technician hesitated before turning back to his work. 'Speaking of IT matters, the team going through the Hired Muscle data have got a result on tracing that KI mind back-up.' He tipped his work stool on one leg, balancing perilously, looking smug.

'And?' said Ferguson.

'Gone to soldiers. Specifically, the trace shows a Move, not a Copy. Well, Move is Copy and Delete, but you know what I mean. The point is, the back-up file was Moved to an IP address that's heavily firewalled, so we can't see past it, but we do have its physical location. Took a while to track it down. You'll never guess where it is.'

'No, I never will,' said Ferguson. He was used to this sort of thing from IT specialists, but that didn't make it any less wearing. 'So tell me.'

'Only a maintenance shack on the Atlantic Space Elevator.'

Ferguson, outside the room, almost stumbled. The pov lurched.

'The space elevator? Jeez. That's . . .'

'Unexpected? Hah! It gets worse. The elevator isn't just outside our jurisdiction, it's Gazprom property, and furthermore the maintenance is subcontracted, and sub-subcontracted, and the ownership of these companies is traded and speculated on – it's part of how the whole contraption is financed, typical Russian-capitalist scam – so we're talking some serious legal and, ah, information-processing constraints on finding out who even owns that particular chunk of real estate.'

'Oh, Christ!' said Ferguson. 'There must be *some* way of tracing how that stunt was pulled. Presumably a backed-up KI or AI can't just do that on its own. Or are there AIs roaming the nets already?'

'If it was that easy, we'd know about it. There are fairly robust protocols in place to stop it, and in any case it's about as technically feasible as a music file taking over your dishwasher. Nah, this was set up, maybe by Hardcastle itself. Anyway. I'll get back to work.'

'Sure,' Ferguson said. 'Pass me any business documents you find – actually, just stick them on the headspace as you go along, I'll tab you a location.'

'Cheers.'

Ferguson set up the location, blinked out and returned to the alley.

'You follow that?' he said to Mukhtar.

'Oh, yes,' said Mukhtar.

'Sounds like you might be right about a Gazprom connection.'

'My nose is twitching, for sure,' said Mukhtar. 'Time I took a wander, I think.'

'The local people-of-interest know who you are,' said Ferguson.

'Uh-huh,' said Mukhtar. 'I'm counting on it.'

Ferguson stood in the alleyway and stared into space. The Atlantic elevator was below the horizon. The sky to the south was pricked with geostats, strung with a skein of orbital paths. There was more up there than Ogle Sky showed: secret military installations and commercially confidential operations could all enforce or buy their omission from the open release. Even thus incomplete, the display of Near-Earth Orbit showed a busy and cluttered place. Tens of thousands of objects, from the three Space Stations through the manufacturing installations on down to microsatellites, and not counting the junk. A few hundred long-term residents; thousands of day-trippers, space-divers, tourists. And then there were the stations farther out: the elevators, the soletas, the Gore Observatory, the multiple components of the Hoyle Telescope, the bases on the Moon and Mars, the Europa Lab, all with human crews. The number of people in space was large and, for all practical purposes, impossible to establish with precision, but it wasn't the problem. That number was dwarfed by orders of magnitude by the number of autonomous machines, some of them self-aware.

Of that self-aware minority, a small – and surely in principle knowable – number were humanoid robots. Seriously screwed-up tin men. It was, Ferguson guessed, possible that the fugitive copy of Hardcastle's mind would find one of these to download into, if its current occupant had decided to migrate to a more functional body. More likely, the copy itself would find a non-humanoid robot body – probably one without a self-aware KI inhabiting it – and possess that. It didn't even have to be on the elevator – the copy could by now have been transmitted further. It could also, of course, remain stashed in storage indefinitely, to await download at some future date. But, as the IT guy had pointed out, it couldn't do any of that on its own.

Which meant that Hardcastle had managed to hack a space-based computer, or had one or more collaborators in space already. The latter, in one sense, would be preferable, because tracing a conspiracy would be something to go on. Whereas trying to trace a missing back-up in that clutter overhead would be like searching for an iron filing on a prairie, never mind a needle in a haystack.

A conspiracy in space. A robot conspiracy. A humanoid robot religious conspiracy. Did robots get religion? One at least apparently had. Why not more? Ferguson shook his head. His own thoughts were becoming like those of Paranoia on one of its bad days. He found himself pacing in the alley, head down, half-seeing the rough ground and litter and weeds at his feet and half-seeing the Ogle Sky overlay, which was still running in background on his contacts: below him was the sky in the Southern Hemisphere, the bright line of the Pacific Space Elevator, tagged with the participant company names of its

Chinese-Japanese-Indian consortium owners and investors in a rainbow of virtual neon. Ferguson swivelled his gaze, looking through the curve of the Earth. The Atlantic Space Elevator had a much less colourful and varied display: just the logos of Exxon-Mobil, Gazprom, Honeywell, and Rosoboroneksport, and the flags of the Russian Federation and the United States.

Stay with it, stay with it. What would a humanoid robot religious conspiracy in space do? There was already the mind, at least, of one robot linked to the Third Covenant sect in space. What if there were others? The speculation wasn't insane at all. Ferguson paced back to the tent, swinging his gaze idly back and forth between the two elevators, commercial and political rivals but both of them pillars of the human and machine presence in space.

Pillars. That word snagged something in his memory. He'd seen it recently somewhere, read it in—

In the Bible. He'd looked it up when he'd been trying to figure out the reference in the last Covenanter broadside to 'Samson in Gaza of the Philistines'.

Ferguson blinked the text back. Judges, chapter seventeen. Samson, already blinded, shorn of his hair and strength, and now made sport of by his enemies, was standing amidst the pillars of a building with three thousand of his enemies on its roof. He'd asked the boy beside him to let him lean his hands against the pillars.

And Samson called unto the LORD, and said, O Lord GOD, remember me, I pray thee, and strengthen me, I pray thee, only this once, O God, that I may be at once avenged of the Philistines for my two eyes.

And Samson took hold of the two middle pillars upon which the house stood, and on which it was borne up, of the one with his right hand, and of the other with his left.

And Samson said, Let me die with the Philistines. And he bowed himself with all his might; and the house fell upon the lords, and upon all the people that were therein. So the dead which he slew at his death were more than they which he slew in his life.

'Boss? DI Ferguson? Adam?'

Skulk's voice, insistent in his ear. Ferguson opened his eyes and took his hands away from the wall. He brushed fragments of rough-cast off his palms, stared for a moment at the reddened and indented skin, and turned to the leki. Ferguson didn't know how long he'd been leaning on the wall – one minute, two, five? Something about the story's elements – mutilation, revenge, religion, suicide, massacre – had resonated with his deepest disgust at what he was having to deal with.

'Are you all right?' Skulk asked. 'You look somewhat faint and nauseous.'

'I just had a very troubling thought,' Ferguson said. 'This tiny, insignificant band of religious nutters we're after might just be planning the biggest terrorist spectacular of all time. Bringing down one or both of the space elevators.'

'I had thought of that,' said Skulk.

'You had?'

'It occurred to me as soon as I heard that Hardcastle's back-up file had been moved to a secure server on the Atlantic Space Elevator. I quickly learned online that there have been numerous scenarios for such an eventuality ever since the idea of an elevator was first mooted. It has been the plot of so many movies and televison miniseries that it is no longer worth even making an elevator pitch, so to speak, for another. In the real construction, maintenance and security arrangements of the structures, terrorism has been planned for as thoroughly as accidents, freak storms, meteor strikes and military attack. Every conceivable window of vulnerability has been closed. It's not impossible that another might be found, but it's deeply implausible.'

'Oh,' said Ferguson. 'Missed the memo. Glad to hear all that. Consider me reassured. All the same, I'll bet they haven't factored in fanatical suicidal religious robots.'

'They have,' said Skulk. '*And* there was a movie about it. Bomb-disposal combat mech in the Faith Wars, becomes self-aware, captured by insurgents while pondering the meaning of it all, yadda yadda, converted to Islam or at any rate to Islamism by its captors, years later gets work on space elevator intending to accumulate explosives and blow it up, but is itself blown away at the last moment by the hero, who just happens to be the robot's soldier partner from the old days, now a security expert, whose ex-wife just happens to be the teacher in charge of the crawlerful of happy kids whose imminent fiery demise we've all been on the edge of our seats over, tearful reconciliations all round, credits roll, the end. *Return of the Jihadi*. I'm surprised you haven't seen it.'

'Somehow it passed me by,' said Ferguson. 'I should get out less. Still, I'm not reassured. This should be investigated. I'll pass it on to the PNAI, with a forward to the Elevator security organisation.'

Doing that took a couple of minutes.

'Done,' Ferguson said to Skulk. 'Meanwhile – any progress in there?'

'That's what I came out to tell you,' said Skulk. 'Most of the business documents on the slate refer to Hardcastle's work with Hired Muscle. A few, however, relate to small robotic engineering jobs, carried out under the name of Graham Orr. This is, of course, consistent with what we were told by Mr Connor Thomas. There are also several receipts for larger and considerably more lucrative jobs subcontracted from an engineering company based at Turnhouse but rather confusingly called Livingston Engineering, apparently after its owner, a Mr John Livingston. One of them was for maintenance and repair work on six of the Fife coastal mechs – the ones covering St Andrews Bay.'

Ferguson imagined he heard a note of smugness in the timbre of the leki's voice.

'Well done,' he said. 'Well done indeed. Have you contacted the company?'

'Yes. Its website is down and its phone rings out. John Livingston's personal phone seems to be turned off.'

'Not even an answering service?'

'No.'

'Does the company still exist?'

'Oh yes,' said Skulk. 'A quick link to security cameras around Turnhouse shows the office, closed and shuttered but apparently in use.'

'Closed for Sunday. Well, we can check that out tomorrow. About the coastal mechs. Did you ever get anywhere with the – what was it?'

'Forth Maritime Security Centre. No, I did not. When I called their emergency number I was told that my suspicion was not an emergency, whereupon my call was passed to their public-relations desk. I got the distinct impression that I was not being taken seriously, even though I referred to my agreement with the Fife Constabulary. I would have raised the matter with you earlier, but other events have taken a higher priority.'

'It's a priority now, all right,' said Ferguson. 'Imagine if the coastal mechs started shooting inland. Now that would be one damned impressive slaughter. Quite aside from the little matter of solving the bishop's murder. Tab me that number, would you?'

He called the emergency number and was given the same runaround as Skulk had been given.

'Fuck this for a game of soldiers,' he said.

He called Polanski.

'Stay in the space,' she said. 'Let me deal with this.'

Ferguson wished that he'd picked a more comfortable spot than the alley to work from. The empty bottle-crate he was sitting on had no doubt already printed a pattern of hexagons on his buttocks. He sighed, shifted, and concentrated on the headspace, which he now shared with Polanski and with Donnie Wishart, the operator of the Fife coastal mechs. Wishart, whom Polanski had reached after chewing through the PR flack and several other grades right up to Wishart's superior officer, seemed to know what he was doing.

Like most coastal defences – forts, concrete pillboxes, land-mounted long-range naval guns, fortified moles, sea walls with gunpowder stores and archery slits, and the like – the North Sea coastal mechs had been built in response to an invasion threat that had passed before their construction had been completed, and that they would have done little to repel if it hadn't. Ferguson wasn't entirely sure from memory whether the scare of the time had been Spetsnaz assault teams, Norwegian commando raids, Iranian aerial drones or Flemish dinghy swarms, and he was damned if he was going to waste a second in checking it out, given that the matter was almost certainly the subject of protracted and inconclusive debate between different gangs of Faith War military-history obsessives.

The mechs weren't entirely obsolete. Striding along the shoreline or hydroplaning across the water, they now and then rescued swimmers or sailors in difficulty, intercepted the occasional boatload of militants from liberation fronts liaising with local refugees from liberation wars, and carried out remote inspection of incoming and outgoing ships for radioactive or other dangerous materials. Ferguson suspected that this last was a bluff.

Right now Ferguson was looking at one of the coastal mechs, via the pov of a Fife Constabulary surveillance drone, buzzing along in front of the machine as it waded knee-deep in the sea along the stretch of shore still known as East Sands. It was on the grassy breakwater of that long-vanished beach that the Bishop of St Andrews had been walking when he'd been shot. The machine looked like a small boat on long legs, standing about four metres tall, with a multi-barrelled gun-turret and a bristle of sensors on the top of its hull. The legs could fold to bring the knees above the head, grasshopper-like, converting the machine's long flat feet to hydrofoils when it settled into the water and engaged the jet engine at its stern. This particular mech was freshly painted in naval grey, with only a stipple of young barnacles and a few green tufts of algae on its flanks.

'That's one of the six that got refurbished a few months ago in the yard at Inverkeithing,' Wishart said. 'Their control centres were taken out and passed to Livingston Engineering for maintenance.'

'What kind of maintenance?' Ferguson asked.

'Just mechanical, like. Replacing some of the steel parts with shaped diamond and bucky and other carbon tech gear. You can make a housing as tight as a barnacle's arse, but as long as you have to have anything coming out of it, you need some kind of aperture, the sea air will get in, and then you'll get rust and bacteria. Slow but sure.'

'Could the software or firmware have been affected?'

'By the sea? No.'

'I meant by the repairs.'

'Oh, aye,' said Wishart. 'The engineers would have needed access to the chip to check the controls were working.'

'So they could have corrupted it then.'

'Aye, in theory. But Livingston Engineering is a very respected firm. Started off supplying the military back in the Faith Wars. Still high security rated, you ken. Even has contracts to work on the space elevator.'

'Does it, indeed?' said Ferguson. 'What kind of work?'

'Roller bearings and other moving parts for the crawlers,' said Wishart. 'They things wear out fast, but Livingston Engineering's stuff wears out slower than most. They have a good reputation in that regard.'

'Well,' said Ferguson, 'let's see if the firm's lived up to its reputation this time. Are we ready to roll?'

'I've got the shut-down command code set up,' said Wishart. 'Ready when you are.'

Ferguson expanded the view, keeping the drone's close-up pov as an insert while taking in a satellite image with the mechs' locations tagged. Two of the mechs were farther back around the headland, another was patrolling the shore to the north beyond the harbour, while the other two floated a kilometre and a half out to sea and about two kilometres apart, in among the usual Sunday-afternoon jet-skis and sailing boats.

'Wait!' cried Polanski.

'What?'

'Just had a thought,' she said. 'If these things are corrupted, or one of them is, mightn't the stand-down command be one of the triggers for them to run amok? It would be a warning that the jig was up and there was nothing to lose.'

'Hmm,' said Ferguson. 'That's plausibly devious. Any thoughts, Mr Wishart?'

Wishart's face popped into view, the lines on his forehead deepening as he frowned.

'Hard to say, inspector. The emergency shut-down is hard-wired and it's in its own loop, it doesn't run through the mech's main decision centre. It's supposed to be tamper-proof, but with enough time and skill . . . I don't know. It's possible.'

'Well, shit,' said Polanski. 'How do we get around that?'

'I'm thinking,' said Ferguson. 'Give me a moment . . .'

'If I may make a suggestion,' said Skulk, 'it does seem unlikely that all the mechs would react to a shut-down by going into action. After all, any corruption of their programs will be very difficult to detect. If it has been done, whoever did it could well expect suspicion to fall on only one of the mechs – the one that, in my hypothesis, was used for the assassination – and hoped to preserve the others for later use. However, we don't know at the moment which one was used, so the risk remains unacceptable. I propose that Mr Wishart arranges for a spurious signal to be sent to the mechs indicating an emergency to which they all would have to react together, and that would lure them to a location with no nearby civilian targets. I would also suggest that we ask the Scottish Air Force at Leuchars to have an attack helicopter on standby.'

'Tall order,' muttered Wishart. 'It's no exactly empty countryside along this coast.'

'Could you patch in the Forth Maritime view on the nearby shipping?' Polanski asked.

'Aye, sure.'

The view expanded again, now dotted with the locations of incoming and outgoing ships as well as the leisure craft.

'Skulk,' said Polanski, 'could you run an analysis for us – find a ship close enough to reach but having a location en route to it optimally distant from possible targets?'

'None of this looks good,' said Skulk. 'But the Russian container vessel SS *Morgenstern*, fifteen kilometres out and bound for Leith, is within the operating range of the mechs. Allowing for set-up time, the movements of other vessels, and the normal speed of the mechs, there are several locations where they could be stopped several kilometres from any potential target.'

'That'll do,' said Polanski. 'Well?'

Ferguson tried to balance the hypothetical risk of the

mechs' reaction to a shut-down against the even more imponderable risk that they could be sent into action at any moment. It was impossible. He had no choice but to guess.

'Let's do it,' he said. 'Mr Wishart, can you flag up the *Morgenstern* as a high security risk, and let the mechs react to that?'

'Goes against the grain,' said Wishart, 'but I can do it. Better warn the captain not to worry, though.'

Wishart went ahead with that, while Polanski called the base commander at Leuchars. In the ten minutes this took, Ferguson walked to the end of the alley, exchanged some chat with the constable on duty, and returned.

'Ready now,' said Wishart.

'All set,' said Polanski. 'Leuchars standing by.'

'OK,' said Ferguson. 'Hit it.'

The mechs responded instantly to the sudden upward spike in the security-interest assessment of the Russian vessel. The surveillance drone tagging the one Ferguson had been observing shot skyward, expanding the view. The mechs on the shore turned and thrashed into the water, and joined with those already seaborne in deploying their hydrofoils and starting up their jets. Six tracks streaked across the sea, at first almost parallel, then slowly converging.

Minutes passed. Ferguson could guess by eye just when they had reached the optimal position, and he was pleased to hear Skulk confirm that unspoken assessment.

'Now would be a good time for the shut-down, Mr Wishart,' said the leki.

'Sent,' said Wishart.

The effect was immediate. Five of the six white tracks

stopped dead in the water, momentum carrying the mechs onward until friction slewed them to a halt. The sixth mech changed course, away from the path to the ship and now heading straight east across the North Sea.

'What the fuck's it doing?' Polanski's voice demanded. 'Fleeing to Denmark?'

'Take a look where it's actually headed,' said Wishart, pulling back their shared viewpoint to a higher virtual altitude. The real-time shot of the hydroplaning mech became a small section of Forth Maritime's image of the North Sea, upon which the remaining oilfields were helpfully outlined.

'Oh shit,' said Polanski. 'Straight for the Fulmar and Auk rigs.'

'At this rate,' said Ferguson, 'it'll be in range in less than an hour. Time for that call to SAF Leuchars, do you think?'

'Fuck yes,' said Polanski. 'Hey, I've never called in an air strike before!'

'The first time's always a thrill,' said Ferguson. 'After that, you just dread the paperwork.'

13. CONCORDANCES

'Jee-*zus*! How cool is that!'

Dave Warsaw made to replay the scene of the attack helicopter blasting coastal mechs in the North Sea. He particularly wanted to admire in slow motion the chopper's counter-measures to the mechs' anti-aircraft fire. Jessica slapped his wrist.

'If you want to wank over that again, you can bloody well roll your own,' she said. 'I want to watch the rest of *my* news.'

'Oh, OK,' said Dave, settling back in his chair. 'JNN it is.'

He was in a physically relaxed but mentally tense mood. It felt unnatural to be sitting at home in the flat at nine on a Sunday evening, but the usual gigs had been cancelled because of the security scare, and he wasn't too keen on showing his face around the pubs, given that he'd always made a little song and dance about what a brilliant bouncer Hardcastle was, and had made it something of a point of honour to have the robot as a signature feature of a Dave Warsaw gig. Besides, Jessica had an early lecture on Monday morning, and hadn't even wanted to eat out. The remains of their takeaway had still to be cleared up, but then, they had still to be completely finished. Dave picked up a pork-chop bone and scraped with his incisors at a spicy scrap on the end.

Jessica flicked a finger and the news selection they'd labelled Jessica's News Network rolled on, complete with an anchorman in the image of the hot Japanese actor who was Jessica's current screen god.

'Elsewhere,' the Andrei Katayama idoru said, voicing the words of some quite other announcer or AI somewhere in the global media, 'the unprecedented but long-imagined possibility of a homicidal humanoid robot – and one with a religious motivation, at that – has drawn what seems to be unwelcome attention to the well-known but secretive robot refuge, Waimangu Science Park in New Zealand.'

The screen image in Dave's frames filled with an image of a high ironwork double gate surmounted by an arch decorated with iron cut-outs of Adam, Eve, dinosaurs, pterosaurs, and a long boxy thing that, Dave guessed from the stylised waves of iron scrollwork around it, was meant to represent Noah's Ark. He'd known, vaguely, about Waimangu as a humanoid-robot reserve for some time, but not that the place was run by creationists. His fist clenched.

Behind the gate was a small complex of low buildings and a picnic area, and beyond that a green and misty morning landscape of woodland with mountains in the distance. In front of the gate was a queue of a dozen vehicles, all of them emblazoned with the initials of Australasian or South Asian news services, and a milling crowd of reporters and journalists.

The pov, evidently among that crowd, pushed forward with visible evidence of elbow work until its camera was almost poking through the gate's grille. Two men stood, feet apart and arms folded, scowling out. One of them was a stocky dark-skinned man who looked about forty, with black hair in a ponytail, wearing a park ranger's uniform. The other was a tall, gangly young white man in a lumberjack shirt and blue jeans, with lank brown hair hanging over his forehead.

'Hey!' said Jessica. 'That's – that's—'

'The creepy Christian,' Dave said.

'Good grief,' said Jessica. 'It's John-John! John . . . what was it? Hang on.'

In the corner of his eye Dave saw a sub-screen light up and flicker as Jessica ransacked Dave's own frames' memory store, muttering, 'Last year . . . August . . . Carthaginian . . .'

On screen, a voice.

'Why *can't* we interview at least one of the robots?'

'The park isn't open for another hour,' said the park ranger.

'Then there's no reason not to let us in,' said the reporter.

'You can come in with everyone else,' said the park ranger. 'Ten o' clock.'

Mention of the time made Dave sit up. This was New Zealand, other side of the world, ten in the morning—

'This is live,' he said.

'Sssh,' said Jessica, busy.

The gangly young man leaned forward.

'Excuse me,' he said, with a sideways glance at the park ranger. 'But I'm the robotics engineer here. I look after the park's animatronics, and I, uh, help out the robots with minor repairs and, uh, stuff. And I can tell you, there's no point in your coming in to look for an interview with a robot. It's not up to us. It's up to them, and they don't want to talk to you or anybody else. They're here to get away from human company. They've never harmed anybody, they don't know anything about this supposed killer robot in Scotland, and—'

'How do you know all this?' the reporter interrupted.

Good point, Dave thought. At the same time, Jessica let out a yelp. Dave looked at her. She was punching the air, but her face showed a sort of angry triumph.

The young man looked blank for a moment. 'They told me,' he said.

'Does that mean,' said the reporter, 'that they'll talk to you?'

'Well, sure, but—'

The park ranger stepped forward, cutting across.

'The robots are not available for interview, direct or indirect,' he said. 'They have made that point clear. They have nothing officially to do with this park. They live here, that's all. This park exists to, ah, preserve and pro-claim the natural wonders of Waimangu. If any of you wish to come in at opening time, I'll be happy to show you around. As a park ranger, however, I would strongly advise you not to attempt to go off on some chase after robots, for, uh, three reasons. One, it's unsafe, given the geothermal nature of the place – to put it bluntly, you're liable to get scalded. Two, it's against Environmental Agency regula-tions, as well as the operator's own by-laws, which are a contractual condition of entering the park. And three, it's futile, because the robots are a lot smarter and faster than any of you, ladies and gentlemen. And if you'll excuse us, we have work to do before the park opens.'

With that he nudged the young man's elbow, and they both turned and walked away, ignoring calls after them. As they were about to pass behind the corner of the cafeteria building, Dave noticed two things happen at once.

The gangly young man started, and raised a hand to his ear.

And beside Dave, Jessica said, 'Good morning, John Richard Campbell.'

It took Dave a moment or two to trace what Jessica had done. Part of it was simple enough: she'd Ogled the name and face and location and picked up the guy's phone number. Dave would have assumed that would be futile, because the guy would be screening his calls – but he was apparently only blocking calls from the media siege. Far more impressive was that she'd used the search engine to find her earlier encounter with the man, and to zero in on a particularly intriguing moment of it – which, conveniently for Jessica's search, was the last moment before he'd left the club, and therefore the first that her backtracking had picked up.

'Remember me?' Jessica was saying, having introduced herself. 'The Carthaginian Club, Edinburgh, last year?'

'Yeah, sure,' said Campbell, in a strained voice with an overtone of forced politeness. 'Uh, pleased to hear from you.'

'Oh, don't give me that crap, John-John!' said Jessica. 'You're fucking terrified to hear from me. I'm the last person you want to hear from.'

'No, you're not,' said Campbell, with some spirit. 'That would be, uh, Arlene.'

At that Jessica had to laugh.

'Very good, John-John,' she said. 'Now you listen to me, and listen carefully, because in fact you should be pleased to hear from me. I know something about you that nobody else does, and I'm the only person who can help you.'

'Just a minute,' said Campbell.

They heard an aside: 'Cornelius, I'm just taking a personal . . . Thanks, mate.'

Sound of footsteps, then:

'OK, what's this about?'

'I've just retrieved some archive of your face, the exact moment you saw our security bouncer as you left the club. I didn't see it at the time, this is from the inside door camera. You recognised him, and you were totally confused, just for a second or two, and then you rushed out.'

There was a half-minute of silence.

'Yes,' Campbell said at last. 'I did recognise him. I'd met him a day or two earlier. I knew him as Graham Orr.'

'You did, huh? And why haven't you taken this interesting information to the police?'

'How do you know I haven't?'

For a moment Jessica seemed nonplussed.

'Call it a guess,' she said. 'Based on that guilty look on your face.'

'How can you – oh, you mean then?'

Jessica laughed. 'Yes, and now too, as you've just admitted!'

'All right,' said Campbell. 'I haven't told the police. Why should I? They already know him as Graham Orr, and that as Hardcastle he worked in these clubs.'

'And I know you don't think I'm stupid,' said Jessica.

'So don't pretend you do. What the police would be interested in, just maybe, is where and how you'd met him
before.'

Another long silence.

'That's kind of awkward,' Campbell said.

'That,' said Jessica, 'figures. Awkward, yes, that's exactly
what I thought. Now, let me make a wild guess here.
You'd met him in your capacity as – what was it you said?
A lay preacher, that's it. Hence your embarrassment at the
time – and now.'

'That's about it,' said Campbell. 'That's what I didn't
want to tell the police. I don't have anything to hide,
myself, but I didn't want to get innocent, uh, people into
trouble.'

'How do you know they're innocent?'

'I know them well enough to know *that*!'

'These are people in Scotland, yeah?'

'Some of them,' said Campbell.

'Well, that's the ones I'm talking about,' said Jessica.
'You were in Scotland how long?'

'About a week,' said Campbell.

'And in that week, you got to know these people well
enough to be sure they had nothing to do with what
Hardcastle has apparently been up to?'

'I've got to know them better since,' said Campbell.

'How?'

'I've been in touch with them, uh, regularly.'

'Oh, right. You met them briefly, and since then
you've been in touch. Great. And you're confident they're
innocent. So why don't you contact the police here and
tell them so? Because believe you me, John-John, the
police are going to find these people soon enough. And

they're going to find you, eventually. You'd do a lot better to go to them before they come to you.'

'I can't do that!' cried Campbell.

'Why not?'

'Because . . .' He hesitated, then sighed. 'Look, I'll get in touch with them and urge *them* to call the police about their, uh, acquaintance with Orr . . . I mean, Hardcastle. OK?'

'When?'

'I can't contact them right now,' said Campbell. 'It's Sunday where you are, and they don't answer the phone on Sunday. So in, uh, a few hours. Early tomorrow morning, your time.'

'All right,' said Jessica. 'I'll know if you have or not, so don't try to dodge it.'

'How will you know?'

'Now that's something *I* can't tell *you*. You'll have to take it on faith.'

'Hah!'

'Who are these people anyway?' Jessica asked.

'They're just a – a small Church.'

'And does this small Church have a name?'

'The Free Congregation of West Lothian,' said Campbell, without hesitation.

'Hang on,' said Jessica. She Ogled.

'Doesn't show up,' she said.

'It doesn't have an online presence,' said Campbell.

'Ah,' said Jessica. 'Why not?'

'Because that would compromise it,' said Campbell.

'Compromise its security?'

'No! I mean, compromise it spiritually. It's not that they're against the technology or anything. It's just

THE NIGHT SESSIONS 263

that – look, this may be hard for you to understand, but it might become clearer if . . . if you look at all the online religious sites, even narrowing it down to evangelical Christian ones . . . some of them are sound, and there are precious resources like the Puritan classics and so on, but the great majority are just a source of confusion. The Free Congregation doesn't want to be part of that confusion. Its message would be lost in the noise.'

'I can sort of see where that's coming from,' said Jessica, in a more friendly tone. 'But if you want me to believe you, you have to give me a name. Just one name that I can find online and check, if I have to.'

'All right,' said Campbell. 'But only if you agree to wait until tomorrow morning before . . . whatever checking up you're going to do.'

'That's OK,' said Jessica.

'John Livingston,' said Campbell. 'He's online as the owner of an engineering company.'

Jessica Ogled again. 'Got it,' she said. 'OK, John-John. I'll talk to you later.'

'I'm sure you will,' said Campbell.

Jessica chuckled. 'You were kind of modest about your talents, last August, weren't you? Lay preacher, huh. Never said anything about robotics engineer. And for the Genesis Institute! Quite a prestigious job, I'm sure.'

'If you say so,' said Campbell, in a sullen tone.

'Oh, I do,' crowed Jessica. 'Well, speaking of Genesis, here are a couple of verses from Genesis to think about. One is chapter 11, verse 31. The relevant phrase is "Ur of the Chaldees", in case you're wondering. The other is chapter 36, verse 31. Read that, then look up the first book of Chronicles, chapter 1, verse 43. Got that?'

'Yes,' said Campbell, 'but—'
'Good,' said Jessica. 'Have a nice day.'
She rang off.

Campbell stood on the gravel path behind the rear corner of the visitors' centre. His face felt hot, the sweat on his chest cold. The feeling of having been fingered, of having been caught out, was the same as that he had felt, twice, in the Carthaginian: when Jessica had first spoken to him, and when he had recognised Orr at the door. *Be sure your sins will find you out.* He stepped forward, placed his palms on the wooden wall of the centre and his forehead against the cold glass of the window. For a moment or two he wanted to let his head sag forward between his out-stretched arms, and to vomit on the rough pebbles at his feet.

The nausea passed. With his eyes close to the glass he could see into the room, which happened to be the shop. Bookshelves where tourist guides to New Zealand and Conservation Service guides to Waimangu stood side by side with thick volumes on Flood geology, on starlight and time, on the errors of naturalism and the truths of fundamentalism; where booklets for children about kiwis and penguins, pukekos and tui-tuis shared shelf space with pop-up picture-books showing Adam and Eve walking with dinosaurs in Eden. Souvenir stands upon which models of kiwis in every conceivable material from solar-powered bioplastic to dried tree-fern frond and possum fur pecked or posed amid the feet of mammoths and hadrosaurs and figurines of the first couple, post-lapsari-anly clad in miniature tunics of – again – possum fur. Metre-wide sheets of cardboard that could be cut and folded into accurate models of Noah's Ark, on a scale of one centimetre per cubit; plastic animal models (not to scale) separately supplied. Racks of bright card-backed blisterpacks of terabytes of memory, containing games and displays, complex hydraulic Flood models, and entire libraries of creation science. Open-mesh net baskets spilling over with sets of free overlay frames for the walking tour, which could populate the uncanny valley with the whole Noachic menagerie.

Crunch of steps on the gravel. Vermuelen came around the corner.

'You all right, JR?'

'Yeah, thanks, I'm fine.'

'You don't look fine.'

'Nah, nah, it's all right. Just a bit of, you know, overload. All the cameras and yelling.'

Vermuelen gave him a sympathetic nod. 'Just try to keep away from it. The Institute staff should be here in half an hour. Let them handle the publicity, and let the reporters bloody wait.'

'Too right.' Campbell straightened and sighed. 'I have an apatosaur that needs its head examined.'

'You do that,' said Vermuelen. 'I'm off down the track to check out the walkway railings at the Black Crater. Catch you later.'

Campbell raised a hand, waved, and turned away. He walked around the back to the workshop shed, hauled the door up and over and stood looking into a deep glass eye, while trying to focus his own thoughts. He made a start by scribbling down the Bible references that Jessica Stopford had given him, intending to look them up later. Right now he had more urgent things to attend to.

Sunday had been grim enough. Shortly before Vermuelen had phoned, Campbell had been sitting on the front step of his shack, basking in the morning sunshine and reading his Bible, when he'd been startled by the silent and unannounced arrival of Joram, one of his robot congregation. Campbell didn't talk to his robots on Sundays — the meetings where he discoursed with them, and by relay with the Free Congregation of West Lothian, took place early on Wednesday mornings, conveniently coinciding with Tuesday evenings in British time. He couldn't really have formulated his reason for not speaking with them on Sundays — there was no question of Sabbath-breaking involved, but Campbell felt that it would be somehow sacrilegious to use the Lord's Day to exercise his eloquence on machines, soulless or (as he still thought, but was no longer inclined to argue) otherwise.

The robot, handsome as a shop-window mannequin inside its long-since stained and frayed suit, had stood in the sunlight with a frown on its chiselled features.

'Mr Campbell,' it had said, 'we have a problem.'

Campbell had assimilated the situation as swiftly as he'd scanned the news reports. After that, he'd looked up at Joram.

'One of you,' he'd said, 'was in contact with this Hardcastle — or with a mind-chip embedded in Graham Orr's skull, according to him. So which of you was it?'

'I can't say,' said the robot, ambiguously. 'But I can say that we are all very concerned about this. We — all of us robots — are going to conceal ourselves in the bush until the situation becomes clear. We of the fellowship will meet you at the usual place at this time tomorrow, if we're spared.'

And with that, it had gone, ignoring Campbell's protestations. Campbell had returned to scanning the news. He'd been interrupted by the well-meant but distracting call from Cornelius. He'd wanted to cry out his dismay to his colleague, but had resisted the temptation. He had also resisted the temptation to call John Livingston.

Now he regretted not having given in to those temptations. The robots hadn't answered the pleas he'd sent them – by phone, and later, almost despairingly, by voice at one place or another in the bush.

Well, Joram had said that they'd be at the usual meeting place about now. Campbell waited until he heard Vermuelen's car depart down the track. Then he walked down the track himself. He reached the turn-off for the viewpoint for Inferno Crater, and climbed the short steep slope, intending to strike off into the bush towards the meeting place. At the crest, leaning on the railing that supported the information plate, stood a tall, broad-shouldered man, wearing rough-walking gear and a bush hat, all new. The stranger peered at Campbell over his frames as he approached.

'Good morning,' said Campbell. 'The park isn't open yet.'

'Good morning, John Richard Campbell,' said the stranger. His accent was American. He stuck out his hand. 'Brian Walker.'

Campbell shook hands, puzzled. 'Are you with the Service?'

Walker looked startled for an instant, then smiled.

'Not the Service you mean,' he said.

Campbell belatedly recognised the man's name, and took a step back.

'You were at St Faith's yesterday—'

Walker nodded. 'Your colleague Cornelius told you that? I got the impression that he was curious about me. He followed me in the evening, I suspect.'

Campbell's heart thudded. 'I'd asked him to watch out for strangers in the church, that's all. I was worried about . . .' He waved an arm. 'All that's going on.'

Walker's eyes hooded. 'That's all? He's not otherwise involved?'

'Involved in what?'

Walker glanced around; Campbell, almost mirroring him, did likewise. They were alone, amid trees and tree-ferns. Below them the lake hissed and steamed, vapour rising grey from the chill shade to whiten in the low sun.

'Vermuelen is out of earshot,' said Walker. 'I can prevent you phoning him quicker than you can blink. No one else is around. The nearest of your robots is a good kilometre away. Please believe me when I say I can finish with you sooner than they can reach us.'

Campbell was much more dismayed by the reference to 'your robots' than by the explicit threat.

'I don't understand,' he said, taking another backward step. Walker eyed him with casual amusement.

'I'll explain,' said Walker. He made a chopping motion with his hand. 'But first – is Vermuelen involved?'

'Involved in what?' Campbell repeated, feeling stupid.

'Your activities,' said Walker.

'Oh! My activities!' Campbell laughed. 'He doesn't even know about . . . my robots. How do you know?'

'Intelligence,' said Walker, wryly. 'So all you think you're involved in is, ah, preaching to robots?'

'If you want to call it that,' said Campbell.

'We can leave that question to the theologians,' said Walker. 'The point is that your robots are, or have been, in contact with the one that is causing so much havoc and alarm in Scotland.'

'Cornelius doesn't know—' Campbell stopped. 'What are *you* involved in?' he demanded.

Walker propped his elbow again on the railing, looking relaxed. 'I work for the United States government,' he said. He opened his hands, upturned. 'I'm telling you this because I'm gambling that you don't have a clue what you're up to your neck in – and that if you do, you're smart enough to know that the only way to save your neck is to cooperate with me.'

Campbell shook his head, feeling dizzy and wishing he could sit down.

'Cooperate in what?' Again with the stupid way of asking—

Walker told him. It took him ten minutes. At the end of it, Campbell stared at Walker and asked:

'Can you give me any reason why I should believe you?'

'None at all,' said Walker cheerfully. 'Still – "The just shall live by faith", eh?'

14. ENGINEERS

On the Monday the weather turned wet. At 7:20 a.m.
Ferguson and Hutchins sat in an unmarked car about
thirty metres down the street from the offices of
Livingston Engineering. Skulk crouched in the rear
footwell. Rain drummed on the carbon-fibre roof and
flowed down the diamond pane of the windshield in a
pattern subtly different from that produced by rain on
glass. Ferguson, sipping coffee from a cardboard cup, eyed
the blurry shapes of aircraft dropping through the low
cloud overhead and felt that on the whole he preferred air-
ports the way they used to be.

At 7:25 a.m. a man under an umbrella walked to the
office, rolled up the shutters on the windows and
unlocked the door. He backed inside, shaking his
umbrella. The lights came on. Over the next few minutes
a dozen or so people arrived. At 7:35 a.m. Ferguson threw
the last of the coffee into the rain, crushed the cup and
turned to Hutchins.

'Ready?'

Hutchins pulled the hood of her waterproof over her
head and nodded. Skulk stirred its long limbs.

'Right,' said Ferguson.

The three of them reached the door together. Ferguson
decided that leaving Hutchins in the rain one second

THE NIGHT SESSIONS 271

longer was less impolite than sending her inside first, so he sent Skulk inside ahead and stepped in behind the machine just in time for the first startled looks.

Standard open-plan office, space-industry pix on the walls, reception desk, ten workstations, frosted-glass door to the boss's sanctum at the back. Skulk dripped water on the carpet in front of the receptionist and announced in a carrying voice: 'Stay at your desks. Continue your work. Don't leave the room without permission. This is a visit, not a raid.'

Ferguson barged down the aisle, Hutchins behind him, and opened the boss's door without knocking. The office was small, brightened by a window at the back. Clutches of paper, posters, and commercial calendars hung from pegs on the walls. Two worn chairs stood in front of the desk; beside it was a hatstand on which were hung a homburg and a black coat. The desktop was piled with papers and cluttered with machine components, small spanners and screwdrivers, pens, a slate and a handset phone. The man behind the desk had wavy brown hair down to the collar of his white shirt, and bright grey eyes in a lean, lined face.

Ferguson held up his card. 'DI Ferguson, DS Hutchins.'

The man stood up, smiling, hand extended.

'John Livingston,' he said. 'Good morning, officers. That was fast.'

Ferguson returned the handshake, frowning.

'Fast?'

'Aye,' said Livingston, gesturing them to the seats. 'I'm just ten minutes off the phone to the police. Terrible business, terrible.'

'Which business in particular?' Ferguson asked, hanging his waterproof on the back of the chair.

'About poor Mr Orr being mixed up in all this,' said Livingston, nodding toward his desk slate. 'Just saw it on the news when I came in, got on the phone right away.'

'You're telling me you've just found out?' said Ferguson.

'Aye,' said Livingston.

'The name and face and description have been out since Saturday evening,' said Ferguson. 'And you hadn't seen it?'

Livingston shook his head. 'I don't look at the news from Saturday evening to Monday morning.'

'And you don't answer the phone either. Why not?'

'I don't believe I have to justify that,' said Livingston. 'A man needs his rest.'

'Why not even an answering service, here at the office or on your personal phone?'

Livingston shrugged. 'As I said.'

'And none of your colleagues or acquaintances thought to inform you?'

'It's possible that none of them knew,' said Livingston.

'Knew what?'

'That Graham Orr had ever worked for my company, or that I knew him at all.'

'Really,' said Ferguson. 'Not one of your employees or friends knew about the job on the coastal mechs?'

Livingston shrugged. 'Why should they? It was a one-off contract. The poor fellow got the job through me personally – the company is on the military approved list. I'm aye looking out for new opportunities. I went for that one when it came up, because I knew Orr, and knew his skills, and I could vouch for him. He made most of the money on it, I can tell you that.'

'An eighty-twenty split,' said Hutchins. 'On a ten-thousand-pound job.'

'Precisely,' said Livingston. 'A couple of grand in our accounts. Same sort of sum every time I brokered a job for him. I'm sure Jean – ah, Miss Walton, our administrator – saw the entries, but there's no reason she'd recall the name. We deal in much bigger jobs most of the time.'

'Why did you give that job to Graham Orr in particular?'

'Like I said, he had the skills, and I knew him.' Livingston's mouth twitched. '*Thought* I knew him, I should say. I had no idea he also went by the name of Hardcastle, and passed as a robot. A robot! And in these clubs of all places! I don't know what to say, inspector, sergeant. I'm shocked.'

He didn't look or sound shocked. Saddened, more like.

'We're almost completely convinced,' said Ferguson, 'that the man you knew as Graham Orr was indeed a robot.'

Now Livingston really did look shocked. He sat up sharply, his ruddy face paling.

'A robot? Never! I can't believe that.'

'Why not, Mr Livingston?'

'I've – I've broken bread with the man, I've conversed with him, about – well, everything, you could say. He's been under my roof, at my table. Have you ever seen a robot eat and drink, inspector?'

'No,' said Ferguson. 'I've only once to my knowledge ever seen a humanoid robot in the flesh, so to speak. But

I'm sure that at least going through the motions of eating and drinking is not beyond their capacity. And if you're convinced you couldn't have been fooled, then I can assure you that he, or it, managed to fool several genuine mutilated war veterans.'

'Aye, I suppose . . .' Livingston's voice trailed off. His gaze wandered.

'How did you know him, and how long have you known him?'

Livingston's attention snapped back.

'I met him maybe ten years ago,' he said. 'Before I started the company I was a freelance engineer. Self-employed, working my way up. So was he. He and I did a few jobs together, off and on, over five years or so. You can find the records if you like. He struck me as a very competent roboticist, not surprising given his army experience, and a fine man. Sincere, serious. He stayed over with me and my family a few times. I believe – I believed he found great comfort from being with people who didn't find him repulsive. Even the children were soon quite at ease with him – I insisted on politeness and respect for him from the beginning, but he won them over beyond that to being friendly. A good lesson for them, I thought, not to judge by the external appearance.'

'You got on well, then.'

'Aye, we did that. But he was never as committed to finding work as I was. I put it down to the Oil for Blood money, and to not having a family to support. In any case, we didn't see as much of each other for a few years. Every so often he'd contact me asking if I had any work going. I usually didn't, but whenever I saw a suitable contract he came to mind, and – well, you know the rest. Little did I think he'd use my last such favour to kill the bishop.'

'You couldn't have foreseen that,' Ferguson said. 'What I'm wondering is, did you never think to check his background?'

'Why should I? What didn't I know about his background?'

'That Graham Orr – the *real* Graham Orr, that is – was killed in the Faith Wars?'

Again Livingston looked shocked.

'How do you know?'

Ferguson glanced at Hutchins. She leaned forward, holding out her hand-held. 'This is from the *Belfast Telegraph*, and army records.'

Livingston scrolled through it, scowling.

'Nah,' he said, handing the device back. 'Some mistake.'

'You seem very sure of that.'

'I'm sure he's a man, his name's Graham Orr, and everything he ever said about his wartime experience is consistent with this man's record – except being killed!'

'You never thought to check?'

Livingston looked irritated. 'Is it your habit to check your friends' records to make sure they haven't died?'

'Did you know of his religious views?'

Livingston rocked sideways a little, as if knocked off balance by the change of tack.

'What's that to do with anything?'

'Come, come, Mr Livingston,' said Ferguson. 'We have good evidence that he murdered a priest, then a bishop. You can see why we might suspect some religious motivation.'

'Anti-religious, more like it!'

'No, Mr Livingston. We've ruled that out. Besides, we have good reason to believe he had a very specific religious motivation. Do you know anything of that?'

Livingston leaned back. 'He was a Christian, to the best of my knowledge.'

'Then why did you suggest an anti-religious motivation?' Hutchins asked.

Livingston faced her, spreading his hands. 'If I was wrong about his very *nature*, detective sergeant, might I not be just as mistaken as to his religion?'

'That's a rather hypothetical question,' said Hutchins.

Livingston made no reply.

'What kind of Christian,' Ferguson asked, 'did you believe he was?'

'A born-again Christian,' said Livingston, without irony. 'As to his denomination, if that's what you're asking, it's right there in the article you showed me. Presbyterian Church of Northern Ireland.'

'And not,' Ferguson asked, 'let's say, the Congregation of the Third Covenant?'

'The what?' Livingston closed his eyes and shook his head. '"The Congregation of the Third Covenant"?' His eyes opened. 'Never heard of it. What about it?'

Ferguson fished inside his jacket and passed across copies of the five Third Covenant broadsides. Livingston looked them over, sighing and shaking his head.

'Sad stuff,' he said, handing them back. 'Nothing like anything I ever heard from Graham, I'll tell you that.'

'We found evidence that he printed them.'

'I'm baffled, inspector. Sorry that anyone I knew could come up with that sort of seditious nonsense.'

'There's a question I can't legally ask you,' said Ferguson, stuffing the tracts back in his pocket. 'Not without putting you under arrest, anyway. I'm sure you know what it is.'

Livingston looked him in the eye. 'I'm not ashamed to own that I'm a believer,' he said. 'Sorry if that puts me under suspicion. But I had no knowledge of any of this.'

'So why did you call the police?' Hutchins asked.

'Same reason as you came here,' said Livingston. 'As soon as I saw the news, I knew you'd make the connection with my company sooner rather than later. Thought I'd best get my word in first.'

'The calls are logged,' Hutchins warned.

'Good,' said Livingston. He stood up. 'Well, if that's all . . .'

'For the moment,' said Ferguson. 'If you hear anything from Orr, or Hardcastle, you'll let us know at once.'

'Of course,' said Livingston. He nodded at each of them in turn. 'Well, good morning to you, inspector, sergeant. And now, if you don't mind . . .'

'We'll see ourselves out,' said Ferguson.

The rain hadn't stopped. Back in the car, Ferguson barely had time to wipe the drops from his forelock and eyebrows before Hutchins turned on him.

'We should have had Skulk in there!' she said. 'That man's a lying bastard!'

'I wouldn't go that far,' said Ferguson. 'But I don't need to be a leki to know he isn't telling the whole truth.'

'Understatement of the year!'

Skulk stretched a tentacle past Ferguson's shoulder,

scooped a chamois from the door pocket, and settled back to wipe raindrops off itself.

'If I may,' it said, above the squeaking noises, 'the office door was hardly soundproof. I heard every word of the conversation. The stress patterns in Mr Livingston's voice may have been those of a man with something to hide, but not of a guilty man.'

'You mean he's guilty of something else,' said Hutchins.

Ferguson locked his seat belt and pressed the starter switch. The engine whined as the flywheel powered up, then steadied to a hum.

'Greensides,' said Ferguson. He clicked to automatic, released the handbrake, and turned to Hutchins.

'Tax evasion, do you think?'

'What—? Oh. I see. Very funny, sir. Skulk, if you're looking for a place to wring that rag out . . .'

'Don't even think about it,' said Ferguson. 'If you're in want of something to do, the two of you, please arrange a full-on surveillance of Mr John Livingston. Apply for a phone-tap warrant. Business, home, phone clip – the lot. Speaking of phones, the only reason I can think of for their being off on a Sunday is that the man's a strict Sabbatarian – which, around here, means strict Presbyterian. See if we can find out anything about that, discreetly. And in the meantime, Shonagh, get going on a trawl of his record, and his company's.'

'That's what I was hoping you'd say, sir,' said Hutchins.

The car sped towards the motorway entrance ramp. Ferguson tipped his head back against the headrest and closed his eyes. 'Wake me at Greensides.'

*

Ferguson didn't sleep, although he felt like it. Instead, he called up records on his contacts, fingered his iThink like a string of worry beads, tuned out the PNAI's helpful hints and rumours in his ear, and followed his own nose.

The trail he was on now was the one he'd been diverted from by Tom Mackay's arrival in the pub the other night. It was the mention of Graham Orr's funeral that had brought it back to mind. Ferguson hadn't been at all struck, at first, by the soldier's having been given a Presbyterian funeral. In Belfast, at the time, it would have been that or Catholic, with either Episcopalian or Methodist a distant third possibility. Learning that the man or robot now known, to some, as Graham Orr had also been known as a born-again Christian flagged a new significance over that. But what Ferguson had earlier been wondering about, and was now investigating, was the fate of Graham Orr's combat mech.

He began his search with the army records already retrieved by DCs Patel and Connolly. These – eventually – led him to a model number and serial number of the robot: a Honeywell 2666, identification GBR-HLF-17-09. A search on the model number called up an old advertisement: a picture not of the big hulking thing he'd vaguely imagined but of a complex, highly adaptable modular device. The advertisement showed what claimed to be merely a sample of its variant configurations: long and snakelike for rubble-penetration work, tall and long-legged for fast running, sturdy and long-armed for close-quarter combat, flat and wide for ambushes, dispersed into a score of parts for concealment. Lasers, blades and firearms could be added or removed as necessary. Extensive IFF capacity. One of the sub-heads in that section of copy jumped out: *Fratricide-proof, suicide-enabled.*

Startled, Ferguson read the details. The explanation, or claim, was that the 2666 never posed a danger of friendly fire, but that in case of enemy capture or any other hopeless situation it was pre-charged to blow itself up.

A robotic suicide bomber.

Ferguson felt a prickle on the back of his neck. He added the individual machine's serial number to the search. A single record came back. It had a fair number of FOIA blackouts on it, covering – Ferguson guessed from their contexts – operational and capacity details, still secret after all these years. In between the censorware marks was the account of a short and eventful life of two years and five months: from the assembly line, through combat in Damascus, Beirut and finally the field of Megiddo, where the machine's life had ended on the same day as Graham Orr's.

Damaged in action: field repair impracticable; returned to manufacturer.

The manufacturer. Honeywell. Now where had he recently seen that name? The logo on the Elevator, yes! But where else? A floating neon script, seen through dark and rain . . .

Ferguson sat up, opening his eyes. The car was driving up Haymarket Terrace.

'Turn around,' Ferguson said.

Hutchins, sitting beside him, looked over her shoulder. 'What?'

'Turn around, *car*,' said Ferguson.

'Sorry, boss, no can do. Countermand,' said Hutchins.

'No, hang on—'

The car, confused, came to a halt at the corner of Palmerstone Place. Impatient beeps from behind began at once.

'What's the problem?' Ferguson said.

'Skulk and I have to get back. There's an Incident Room meeting at nine. You should be there too, sir.'

'So I should,' said Ferguson. 'Give my apologies. I have an urgent matter to attend to back at Turnhouse. Patch me in if I'm needed, but to be honest I need to be personally where I'm going a lot more than I need to be at that meeting.'

'If you say so,' said Hutchins. She didn't sound convinced.

'I haven't just remembered a dentist's appointment,' said Ferguson. He unbuckled his seat belt.

'Do you wish me to accompany you?' Skulk asked.

Ferguson realised he very much did not want Skulk to accompany him.

'It's not really necessary,' he said. 'Thanks all the same.'

'A great thing, trust,' said Skulk.

Ferguson shot it a look of wry apology. 'Tough, old chap!'

He got out of the car, narrowly missing a cyclist, dashed across the road and waited for the next Turnhouse tram.

The Honeywell tower at Turnhouse faced directly onto a high-rise farm, which filled the view from the outside glass lift. Ferguson faced outwards and watched twenty levels of solar-power-lit hydroponic greenery go by, and turned and stepped out as the bell pinged just after an upward glance had confirmed there were about forty still to go.

The eighteenth floor of the Honeywell tower smelled of carpet-cleaner, phytoplastics, and ionised air. Ferguson padded across to the double doors of the engineering lab and presented his card to the lock. A scan flicked across his retina and the doors opened. He stepped into a long, wide room that occupied most of the floor. White-topped tables, high stools, black clutter, a smell that reminded him of his first car, of spark plugs and engine oil. Scores of white-coated technicians worked at the benches, at test beds and screens. The nearest, a young woman, turned as she heard him come in, and peered at him under goggles that she tugged away from her eyes.

'Looking for someone?'

Ferguson showed her his card. 'I'm here to see Harold Ford.'

She stuck her chin in the direction of the far end of the room. 'Harry's the guy in the recess at the back. Brown coat, burn-holes, beard – you can't miss him.'

'Thanks.'

He found Harry bending over a lab bench in a cubby-hole, poking a jeweller's screwdriver into the innards of what looked like a mechanical centipede. Ferguson didn't know whether to announce himself, not wanting to disturb some delicate operation, but the man heard him coming.

'Two minutes, copper,' he said. 'Take a perch.'

Ferguson hoisted himself onto the stool opposite and waited. The low partition down the middle of the bench, and the surrounding walls, were covered with cards, stickers and posters that looked science-fictional, in an odd mix of ancient images of rockets, robots, space elevators and tower cities, and newer material depicting landscapes, ecologies and deep-sky images that might or might not have been imaginary.

Harry gave a grunt – of satisfaction or frustration, it was hard to tell – and looked up. He wore frames, contacts and a loupe, beneath spectacles pushed up on his forehead and cloudy with thumbprints, dandruff and skin grease. Amid all this his eyes were bright but oddly unfocused. His beard, and his balding head, had at first made him look middle-aged, but on looking him in the face it became apparent that he was in his thirties.

'Morning,' he said. He stuck out a hand, looked at it, and withdrew it to wipe it on his brown lab coat. 'What can I do you for?'

His voice, slightly raised, emphatic, sounded pleased at this tired witticism.

'Good morning,' said Ferguson. 'Reception thought you were my best bet, Mr Ford. I'm trying to trace the eventual disposal of a particular Faith War combat mech, without launching an Ogle search. Can you help?'

'You're so paranoid about this search that you don't want to try Paranoia?'

Ferguson cracked a smile. 'That's about it.'

'Hah!' Ford rubbed the side of his greasy nose with an oily finger. 'Walk this way, inspector,' he said in a high-pitched quaver. 'Walk this way!'

With that he hopped off the stool, clasped his hands behind his back and stalked, stooping forward, to a door adjacent to the annexe. At the door he glanced over his shoulder, smirked, straightened up and eyeballed the lock. The door let him and Ferguson in. The room was a two-metre-square cupboard, with angle-iron shelving on every wall and every shelf packed with overflowing three-ring binders. On a tiny table in the middle lay a desk slate rugged-edged in black rubber.

Ford waved an expansive arm at the shelves.

'The sacred records of the ancient company engineers,' he said, again with the quaver. In his normal voice he added: 'Actually, everything's now in the slate, for obvious reasons. It's updated daily but apart from that it's isolated from the net. There's one in every company building, so they're all identical at at least one moment in every twenty-four hours. That what you're looking for?'

'Could be,' said Ferguson. He rubbed his chin. 'Does it log queries?'

Ford gave him a respectful glance. 'Good point,' he said. 'Yes, it does. You don't want your query logged?'

'If that's possible.'

Ford swivelled a blunt fingertip in his right ear, grimacing. 'Needs a hack, but yeah. Can be done. Leave it to me.'

He took an iThink from his pocket, hard-linked it to the slate, then unspooled a thin wire from an add-on device behind his phone clip and hard-linked that. He switched the slate on. The screen lit up with the default page.

'Right, you little bugger,' he said. His thumbs moved. The screen flipped to a page that Ferguson had never seen before. Ford's fingertips rattled on the table, rapping on an old-fashioned virtual keyboard for a good minute and a half, then stopped.

'Run, run, run,' he said. He peered at the screen. 'Result!'

He unplugged the connections, returned to the default, called up a page, and spun the slate around to Ferguson.

'You're go.'

'Thanks.' Ferguson looked at a screenful of tiny letters scattered with obscurely labelled input boxes.

'This takes me back,' he said.

'Need a hand?'

Ferguson looked up, embarrassed. 'Afraid so,' he said. 'But—'

'No need to be paranoid about me,' Ford told him. 'I'm the opposite of a security risk. Lots of curiosity, but like a black hole for information. What goes in doesn't come out.'

'Not even as Hawking radiation?'

Ford laughed. 'Good one! No, not even that. So what do you want?'

Ferguson passed back the slate and read out the model and serial numbers.

'Ho hum,' said Ford, typing. 'Armageddon, here we come . . . thought so! Yes. Oh. Well, well, well.'

He slid the slate to Ferguson again. 'Take a look at that.'

Ferguson did. Acronyms, abbreviations and code numbers.

'Translate,' said Ferguson.

'Ah. Well, I suppose a police report screen would be just as hieroglyphic to me. What it says here is that this particular brave little toaster went to heaven. Honeywell heaven, that is.'

'What?'

'Let's take it a step at a time,' said Ford. 'Our hero is wounded on the battlefield, *here*. Nothing much left of him but two mangled manipulators and a radiation-hardened brain-chip, the whole sorry mess dragging itself along by its fingertips like . . . like the severed hand of a blown-up robot, I suppose . . . anyway, you get the picture: tanks crunching past, choppers and jet fighters overhead, tac nukes going off like Satan's own Fourth of July.'

'You're reading all that *there*?' Ferguson asked.

'I'm extrapolating a bit,' Ford admitted. 'Somehow, our pair of ragged claws makes it to Coalition lines and is scooped up and flung in the salvage truck. Taken to a Royal Irish Regiment workshop in the rear. Techies shake their heads sadly. Poor chap's in a bad way. For him the war is over. Couple of months later, the war *is* over. Across the Atlantic in Jeebus land, the telly preachers are sort of shuffling their feet and mumbling that maybe they got a verse or two wrong somewhere along the line but that doesn't mean you shouldn't as always *send more money* because – more exegesis is necessary, heh-heh! And our friend GBR-HLF-17-09, little Sevvie as we'll call him, is back at Aldermaston to be stripped of any remaining stuff-that-goes-bang, checked for hazmat, and the now-sanitised remains are shipped to the Honeywell factory in – aha, Livingston, West Lothian, not a million miles from here. There our engineers pick the few remaining good components out with needle-nose tweezers, chuck the broken shell into the recycle hopper, and ease the brain-chip into a test chassis. Where they run what is aptly called a battery of tests. Including, from what is by now long and salutary experience, the Turing. And whaddaya know, little Sevvie has *woken up* at some time in its epic journey and is now enquiring after its soldier buddy. Aww.'

'That's not so funny,' said Ferguson. 'The soldier buddy was dead.'

'Figured. OK. Well, no doubt they managed to calm Sevvie down. Question arises as to what to do with him. Now, in most of these cases – just about all, as far as I know – the great who-am-I-what-the-fuck-am-I-doing-here-who-is-that-man-aiming-at-me-oops-he's-a-cloud-of-pink-mist-did-I-do-that-OMG-OMG moment happens in the middle of a combat situation, split-second stuff in some ruined Sunni alleyway or Druze villa or what-have-you, and moreover it happens to your big hulking roboraptor and killdozer dudes, and it's usually pretty traumatic for all concerned. Hence the great anxiety to get them into rather less lethal bodies and retrain them to a less, shall we say, kinetically intensive line of work.

'However, the Honeywell 2666 range models are new, were *designed* to try and keep them well clear of the event horizon of self-awareness, and now it looks like this design has failed. After all, Sevvie was supposed to blow his remaining bits up, not do the rational self-preservation bit. So this is something of an embarrassment. There's a quiet product recall, the brain-chips get the Turing test, and those that don't pass are discreetly junked. This leaves the company with a score or so of self-aware KIs, which they don't really want to return to the military or pass on to the cops, and which they're ethically reluctant to wave an electromagnet over and forget about. So they hook them up to a VR environment to amuse themselves and learn to socialise while the engineers figure out what to do about them. Time passes, and after a few years in the box the whole thing begins to get a bit samey and the KIs start emailing the director and demanding to be let out and do their thing in the real world.

'The long and the short of it is that these little fellas end up with a cool security gig on the big post-war and post-Civil War project the company is well chuffed to get a finger in: the Atlantic elevator and the soletas. And they all lived happily ever after, as far as the record shows, because – given a few changes of security contract – they are very much no longer our problem. So, with a drop of oil in our eye, the story ends.'

Ferguson blinked and took a deep breath. Did Ford always talk like that? No wonder he worked in a cubbyhole.

'So what you're saying,' Ferguson said, 'is that the machine I'm trying to trace became a leki, more or less, but for a private company, and now it's somewhere in space?'

'You got it.'

'Any chance of tracing it?'

'Needle, haystack doesn't *begin*—'

'Yeah, yeah,' said Ferguson. 'Iron filing on a prairie. I've had that thought not long ago myself.'

'You have? What about?'

'I have a nasty suspicion,' said Ferguson, 'that it was about the same thing.'

'Aha!' said Ford. 'Your robot suspect Hardcastle has backed itself up on a space-based server.'

Ferguson gave him a severe look.

'Nice,' said Ferguson. 'Try not to mention it.'

'Black hole,' said Ford, running a finger across his lips.

Ferguson thought about this.

'All right,' he said. 'Seeing you've figured that much . . . here's another question. Would it be possible for these robots, maybe with the help of others, to construct a humanoid robot? On site, I mean – in space?'

'Of course,' said Ford. 'There are humanoid robots working on the elevator already. There's machinery in place to repair any and every part of them that might be damaged. With that you could build a complete body from scratch.'

'Including the cosmetic component? The musculature and skin?'

'Sure.' Ford spread his hands. 'Why not? Hey, it's not like they have some kinda metal-man body under the skin. The musculature is functional. It's just not made of meat. You're wondering if Hardcastle's body could have been made in space?'

'Right again.'

'Wait a minute,' Ford said. He turned back to the slate. 'Let's check that out. Hmmm. Ho-fucking-hum. Well, fuck me.'

'What?' asked Ferguson.

Ford looked up, frowning. 'They aren't just repairing humanoid robots up there – they're making more.'

'How many more?'

'It's not mass production. It's ones and twos, as needed, every few months. The humanoid frame is just ergonomically optimal for a lot of the equipment, so they add more robots now and again.' He shook his head. 'I didn't know that! It's routine, man, it's fucking routine.'

'Who's "they"? Honeywell? Gazprom?'

'Or one of their subsidiaries up there, yes,' said Ford. 'But the point is who actually carries out the manufacture.' For the first time, he looked perturbed. 'It's the robots themselves.'

15. VESTIGES OF CREATION

As soon as Ferguson was out of the Honeywell tower he invoked the PNAI, and added what he'd just learned to what he'd uploaded the previous day: the suspicion about the possibility of sabotage of the elevator, and the presumed location of the Hardcastle back-up. He was just about to link to the Incident Room workspace to check how the meeting was going when a call came through from Mikhail Aliyev.

'Morning, DI Ferguson.'

'Morning, Mikhail. What's up?'

'I've got an item of possible interest for you.'

'Aren't you at the meeting?'

'No, boss, I'm out on a different job. For DCI Mukhtar in Leith.'

'Oh, aye, the Gazprom thing. Well, go on.'

'One of my contacts from the Gnostics investigation left me a message this morning. I can zap you the details if you're interested, but here's the lead: about a year ago she met a guy, a religious fanatic from New Zealand, at one of the clubs. Said he was just checking out the goth club scene, ha ha. Heard that one before. Anyway, she saw him on the telly last night, in a news clip from New Zealand, where he works as a robotics engineer at Waimangu, a creationist science park which just happens to be the hang-out of most of the humanoid robots still on Earth. Robots, religion . . . you can see why the NZ news might be interested. She checked back through her records, and found a shot of him quite plainly recognising Hardcastle that night. So she called him up—'

'She called him up?'

'Yeah, well, initiative. And he admitted that he did recognise Hardcastle, that he'd met him before as Graham Orr, and that he'd been in the company of a group called, lemme see, the Free Congregation of West Lothian. And he gave the name of one man involved with that: John Livingston. Campbell promised my source that he'd call Livingston first thing this morning, to urge him to contact the police, but according to our phone logs no such call came through.'

'We're already investigating John Livingston. He's told us about his connection with Hardcastle. Said the first he'd heard of the search was on the news at seven, and then he called the police just before we burst in on him.'

'I know, boss, I've had a look at the Incident Room board.'

'And I've already fingered him as a fundamentalist. Hmm. Well, thanks for the heads-up, Mikhail. Having the name of Livingston's church group is something to go on, but apart from that I don't see what this adds to—'

'Sorry, DCI Ferguson, but I think it *does* add something. This New Zealand guy – John Richard Campbell, that's his name – is an employee of the Genesis Institute, which runs the park. Who do you think funds the Genesis Institute?'

'Fundamentalist churches?'

'Yes, a little, but the real money comes from American

business people who moved to NZ after their side lost the civil war.'

'That doesn't surprise me, Mikhail. Creationism's been part of the whole theocracy package all along.'

'Exactly. Which makes them enemies of the secular states. What recent threats does that remind you of?'

'Ah! Well, there's that. Still looks a bit tenuous.'

'Hardcastle had creationist material in his desk slate, sir.'

'So he did. Interesting, but again . . . '

'Point is, sir, that the US exiles in NZ are a significant force, one that has the motivation and the capability to do significant damage. I see you've been poking the PNAI about the possibility of an attack on the Atlantic Space Elevator. That's just the sort of thing the exiles would love to pull off, and they'd have far more resources to do it than some little band of nutters in Scotland. And far more of an interest in doing it.'

'Well,' said Ferguson, 'that's as may be, but our man Livingston hardly has such an interest. After all, his company has contracts to work on the elevator!'

Mikhail said nothing.

'Ah,' said Ferguson.

'And right this morning,' Mikhail went on, 'DCI Mukhtar and I have been talking again to the esteemed Mr Ilyanov about these Gazprom allegations about theft and possible sabotage of supplies to the elevator. They don't look quite as wild as we'd thought.'

'I'll get back to you on this,' Ferguson said.

Rain and aircraft fell from the sky. On the walkways people hurried, buffeted by the squalls and eddies around the towers and by VTOL downdraughts. Ferguson walked to the Turnhouse tram station, barely noticing his surroundings, thinking. At one corner he hesitated, glancing down the street toward the light and awning of Livingston Engineering, and considered whether he should march in and confront John Livingston again. He decided against it. The man would be open on the innocuous and stonewall on the rest, as before.

Instead, Ferguson strolled to a cafe diagonally across the street from the office, and settled himself in a window seat with a coffee. His trouser knees were wet. His jacket dripped from the back of the seat. He wiped the steamed-up window, getting his shirtsleeve wet. He tabbed a message to Shonagh, telling her that he was carrying out a little impromptu surveillance of the Livingston office, and checked the Incident Room board as he'd intended. Then he sent a message to Grace Mazvabo, giving her the names of John Livingston and the Free Congregation of West Lothian.

He sipped the coffee and slowly warmed up, while the coffee slowly cooled. As he stared out of the window he was not really watching anything. If something interesting or untoward happened, he would notice. But for now he was looking at a lit doorway through rain, and thinking.

However wide the ramifications of this affair, Hardcastle was at its centre – Hardcastle, and the man whose name he'd taken, Graham Orr. There were two factors in this equation: the combat mech, and its comrade-in-arms, to whom it would have formed an attachment that could only be called emotional – even before the now unknowable and even then unknown moment when it had come to self-awareness. The young soldier, a committed Christian in the Faith Wars, had died on the field of Megiddo. For him, as for so many others, that battle must have seemed the fulfilment of prophecy, Armageddon itself. The final showdown with the forces of the Antichrist, the Beast, and the False Prophet.

A phrase floated through Ferguson's mind: 'the Roman Antichrist'. Where had he recently seen that? Oh yes, in one of the Covenanter tracts. And, of course, he'd heard it often enough when he'd been on the God Squads, usually delivered in a Northern Irish or Scottish Highland accent, echoing around some bare church or meeting house. The fundamentalist Presbyterians still held that the Papacy, if not the current Pope, was the Antichrist.

Ferguson remembered, with a start, something that Connor Thomas had said: 'Father Murphy was with us in the tanks at Armageddon.' And he'd also said that Graham − meaning Hardcastle − had remembered Father Murphy from the Faith Wars. How, Ferguson wondered, would the original Graham Orr have regarded Father Murphy − as the brave, kindly padre, or as a pawn of the very Antichrist? And even if he hadn't thought the latter, his robot comrade might have come to that conclusion from its own tormented reflections. And in that case . . .

Connor Thomas had almost certainly not shot the bishop. The corrupted coastal mech, now in fragments at the bottom of the North Sea, might not yield its story to forensic science for some time, if ever. But Ferguson had little doubt that the fatal shot had been fired from one of its gun barrels. As for the Murphy bombing, if Thomas had all along been dealing with a robot there was no reason why his view of the book's being placed in the parcel couldn't have been the result of his vision's having been hacked – quite aside from the ever-present possibility, despite his later denials, of his having been taken in by sleight of hand.

So Connor Thomas was off the hook, and Hardcastle was very definitely on it. The question on Ferguson's mind was whether the robot was acting alone, or at least without the knowledge of any of the human beings around it. Ferguson didn't trust Livingston's disavowal of any knowledge of the Congregation of the Third Covenant. He pulled out a notebook and began to doodle names and lines.

The robot refuge in New Zealand was operated by a creationist foundation. The foundation was financed by American exiles. American exiles had a long record of conspiring against US interests, and of occasionally assisting their 'Left Behind' friends in the US in carrying out terrorist attacks.

Livingston had a connection with at least one of the New Zealand creationists, a man who was himself a robotics engineer. Both had – they claimed – known Hardcastle, but only as Orr. And this man, Campbell – he'd been seen a year ago in one of the goth clubs, where Hardcastle had suborned the two clueless Gnostics. Had Campbell been there in the first place to make some Gnostic connection too? Possible – but not necessary, or likely.

Hardcastle had printed and perhaps written the Third Covenant leaflets. It had used the Gnostic students to distribute them.

The Third Covenant leaflets threatened major suicidal attacks not just on Scotland but on all of what they called the Revolution states, as well as on apostate clergy.

The only actual attacks so far had been on two clergymen. One had served as a Catholic chaplain at Armageddon, where the real Graham Orr had been killed. The other had opposed the war, and now held the same benefice as the best-known victim of the historic Covenanters.

Hardcastle, in its role as Orr, had worked on contracts for Livingston Engineering. On one of them, it had corrupted at least one coastal mech.

The real Graham Orr's robot comrade was last known to be working in security on the Atlantic Space Elevator. Robots on the space elevator could build more robots.

The Hardcastle back-up had been uploaded to the space elevator. It could not have done that on its own.

Hardcastle had worked for Hired Muscle, not just in the clubs but on the docks. Hired Muscle was in dispute with Gazprom security.

Gazprom's man on the Leith docks, Ilyanov, claimed that this was because Hired Muscle was complicit in pilfering or damaging supplies to the space elevator. These supplies were landed at Leith, trucked to Turnhouse, flown to the Elevator.

Livingston Engineering supplied roller bearings and other moving parts for the crawlers on the Atlantic Space Elevator.

This was beginning to look like a case.

Ferguson was staring at his scribbled lines when the room darkened. He looked outside at the also darkened street, and the shadow passed. He glanced at his watch.

The soleta eclipse, late again. The morning's news had mentioned that the soletas were still out of kilter, and that there had been another crawler breakdown on the Atlantic Space Elevator.

Ferguson blinked and shook his head. He added these points to his list, and copied the lot to the PNAI, the Incident Room, and to Mukhtar.

Then he sat back and wished he hadn't. Was he wasting time and attention on this outside chance? The bottom line at the moment was that Hardcastle was still on the loose.

Ferguson saved his work on the notebook and stood up to leave. As he slipped the notebook in his pocket his glance fell on the date display. Monday, September 7. He'd never got around to changing it from the US date format. He might as well do it now. As he fingered over the calendar function he noticed that the coming Friday was September 11. The anniversary of the start of the Faith Wars. There would be the usual commemoration at the embassy – must check security for that, he thought, taking out his pen again to tick the note. A small crowd, but a possible symbolic target. If you really hated the Americans, it would be a good date for—

For a real spectacular.

Ferguson made haste for the tram.

The tram was held up by a sudden tailback halfway along Princes Street. The rain had stopped, and Ferguson needed fresh air. He hopped off to walk the remaining few hundred metres to Greensides. He was just passing Waverley Station when his phone clip tingled. As he reached to answer the call he noticed people around him, in the sparse crowd of a Monday mid-morning, doing the same thing simultaneously. The moment of shock spread like a gust across grass. Ferguson hadn't seen the like since the Faith Wars. He felt an instant dread, which Shonagh's voice confirmed:

'Boss, there's been an explosion . . .'

'Where?'

'Dynamic Earth, a few minutes ago.'

Ferguson stood still and closed his eyes. 'Casualties?'

'Nothing confirmed but . . .' She took a long, ragged breath. 'We know there was a school party in there.'

'Jesus, Jesus!' Ferguson found he was banging his forehead with his fist, and stopped. He opened his eyes, stared down at his white knuckles, and unclenched the fist. The impulse came to him to fill that hand with a heavy pistol. Noises were coming from his throat.

'Adam?'

'I'm fine. I can be at the station in two minutes. Where are you?'

'Incident Room.'

'See you there.'

Ferguson sprinted, swerving and swearing, across Waterloo Place, across the road and down the first blocks of Leith Walk, up the steps and into Greensides. The Incident Room was empty except for Shonagh, DC Connolly, Skulk, and Mukhtar.

'Details yet?'

Hutchins waved a hand in front of his eyes. 'Headspace,' she said.

Ferguson blinked into the virtual image. It showed the frontage of the big tentlike building, its glass wall blown out, a couple of struts down, canopy buckled. The first ambulances and fire engines shuddered to a halt on the patio. People, injured or shocked, were picking their way out as other people rushed forward.

'What the fuck happened?'

'Paranoia's got a vid,' said Connolly. 'Tourist's camera, not frames or contacts. Just as well because the resolution's key to making out what's going on.'

'Patch,' said Ferguson.

Cut to a viewpoint ascending the approach steps, looking towards Dynamic Earth from Holyrood Road, the craggy cliffs of Arthur's Seat in the background. The hand-held camera juddered. Something black and human-sized rushed past, a blur that vanished as it crashed through the entrance and between the two cops standing one on either side. A moment later, a red burst of flame inside, under the white roof. Then black.

'Look at it in slow motion,' said Connolly.

The view swayed. A man brushed past the shoulder of whoever was holding the camera, and ran toward the entrance. He ran fast, while everyone else in view stood still, or was frozen in mid-stride. Through the door – literally through it – then, moments later, the slow bloom of red, turning black, and something hurtling towards the lens. Then black.

'That's slowed down thirty times,' said Connolly. 'The original clip is about four seconds.'

'Holy shit.'

Ferguson shook himself from the virtual image and looked at Skulk. 'You've seen this?'

'Yes,' said Skulk. 'And yes, it's Hardcastle.'

'Was,' said Connolly, with grim humour.

Ferguson stared at him.

'One thing about a robot suicide bomber,' he said. 'The mind-chip might survive.'

'I don't think finding it's going to be a priority right now,' said Shonagh. Her hands went to her face, then up and back over her head. 'Oh God, oh God! Why?'

'I'll fucking tell you why,' said Ferguson. 'Because Dynamic Earth is a geology exhibition and Hardcastle is a tool of creationists.'

He looked again at the scene, then turned to Hutchins.

'Shonagh,' he said, 'did we get anywhere with slapping surveillance on Livingston?'

'Not yet,' she said, surprised to be asked. 'Request went in, but we haven't had any response yet.'

'That's OK,' Ferguson said. 'It's irrelevant now.'

'We should get down to the scene,' Mukhtar said.

'Yes,' said Ferguson. 'But before we go, I'm going to call the station at Turnhouse to pull in everyone at Livingston Engineering.'

Mukhtar jumped up.

'Why?'

'I want to see John Livingston later. In the cells, not the interview room.'

'That won't do any good.'

'Maybe not,' said Ferguson. 'But it'll make me feel better.'

'We don't deserve to feel better,' said Mukhtar, grasping Ferguson's arm. 'Come on.'

They took the lift to the car deck. Mukhtar told the car where to go. As they sped along Calton Road under the cawing siren and flashing light, Ferguson thought of what he'd just wanted to do, and back to the first time he'd done it. It had been a long time ago, but what he'd learned was still fresh. The first time he'd struck a suspect across the face with his pistol, he hadn't been angry. He'd been reluctant to do it. But as he looked in shocked disbelief at the blood on the metal and the welt on the cheek, he'd realised something that had never occurred to him before.

It was this. You don't feel other people's pain. You may have empathy, your mirror neurons may light up in sympathy but, when it comes down to it, you don't feel the other's pain.

The car slewed into New Street, then down Canongate. Ferguson clutched the seat belt and held the thought, staying in that dark place, knowing that in a minute he was going to need it.

Glass crunched under Ferguson's feet, and not under Skulk's. Ahead, the stretchers kept coming out and the firefighters and paramedics kept going in. Most of the fires had been doused. The structure was at least light – there was no major problem of falling debris, though the support struts and upper gallery were a continuing hazard. Behind him was a crowd, already cordoned off: passers-by, reporters, MPs. The Parliament building was just across the road, the offices of the Scottish Broadcasting Corporation and *The Scotsman* a couple of hundred metres away. Ferguson was relieved to see that the Parliament's own security hadn't joined the rush. He muttered into his phone about the danger of secondary explosions. Officers from St Leonards had already taken charge, setting up a command centre on the edge of the plaza, liaising with the emergency services, pulling in cops and lekis from the whole surrounding area. Hutchins had gone straight there.

Keeping out of the way of the rescuers, Ferguson got as close as he could to the gap blasted out of the wall and looked at the stretchers. Most of the casualties were primary-school children. The ones who came out screaming were the lucky ones. Lekis and paramedic robots swarmed inside the building, their tentacles probing into damaged bodies.

'What injuries are they finding?' Ferguson asked Skulk.

'Burns, blunt trauma from debris, internal injuries from the shock wave, deep wounds from flying glass, other debris, and shrapnel.'

'Shrapnel?' Ferguson cried.

'Nails and ball bearings.'

'Not collateral damage, then.'

'No,' said Skulk. 'Planned mass-casualty attack.'

A thought struck Ferguson. 'Any idea why none of the sniffers around here picked up on the explosives before that final sprint?'

'They were probably in some airtight seal, and stored within the abdominal cavity, along with at least some of the shrapnel.'

'Didn't know there was that much room to spare.'

'The standard fuel cell might have been replaced by a smaller one,' said Skulk. 'Power-supply duration would not be an issue in the circumstances.'

'I guess not,' said Ferguson. He took another look around, knowing that what he saw would stay with him, like tinnitus.

'Go in and do what you can,' he told Skulk. 'Keep a lens open for evidence, but no investigation until rescue and recovery are complete.'

'Understood,' said Skulk.

Ferguson made his way over to the command centre. DCI Frank McAuley had arrived, and was in a huddle with Mukhtar and with Vijay Rahman, the Justice and Security Minister. McAuley waved Ferguson into the circle and introduced him to Rahman. Ferguson nodded and shook hands.

'There'll be an inquiry,' said Rahman. 'You know this.'

'Of course.'

'It's terrible to say this now, before . . .' Rahman shook his head and waved a hand to the scene. 'But I will have to answer questions this afternoon, and to the media in a moment. What I will be asked is: could this, this . . . atrocity have been prevented?'

'Yes,' said Ferguson. 'The building was guarded.' He looked at McAuley. 'Any news on them?'

'Both dead. Took the full force of it.'

'Christ.' Ferguson screwed up his eyes. 'Sorry, Minister. As I was saying, the building was guarded. But it wasn't considered a likely target. And what's worse, I'm sure the guards were prepared against an attacker walking in, not running at them at superhuman speed. I should have anticipated these things – the target, and the method.'

Rahman frowned. 'You're too hard on yourself. This was unprecedented.'

'I knew we were dealing with a robot,' said Ferguson. 'I knew its capabilities, but I never imagined its using any beyond passing for human. And I damn well knew since yesterday afternoon that it had creationist material in its possession. Just a couple of hours ago I was given information about a possible link to creationists abroad with, ah, some violent connections of their own. I should at

least have warned every geology museum and attraction
in the city.'

'And every university department of geology, and
anyone who might be near a memorial to Hutton or
Chambers, or the statue of Robert Wood in the
Grassmarket, or the geological plaques in Princes Street
Gardens? No, Inspector Ferguson. Besides, there had been
nothing in the warnings to suggest a target like this.'
Rahman turned to Mukhtar and McAuley. 'Am I right?'

'You're right,' said Mukhtar. 'It seemed to be all political or religious. Inspector Ferguson is blaming himself
quite naturally, but mistakenly.'

'If mistakes were made, I'll be the first to resign,' said
Rahman. He grimaced. 'I don't mean to imply that's
equivalent to any of you having to take the rap but, from
what I can see right now, no one blundered. No one can
be blamed for not expecting creationist terrorism, if that's
what it is.'

'Which we still have to find out,' said McAuley.
'Adam, I've got St Leonards putting together an investigation team into this incident, and the Anti-Terrorism
Unit is taking overall charge. Your team can liaise, keep
informed, obviously share all information, but frankly I
think it's better we have some new eyes on this.'

Ferguson felt more relieved than resentful. It wasn't as
bad as McAuley had warned him of earlier. Or as bad as it
could yet become. The bottom line was, he'd failed. There
would be consequences.

'Next questions,' said Rahman. 'Quickly – the
reporters are clamouring over there. What do we do next?
And can we expect more attacks?'

'We crack down,' said McAuley. 'The gloves come off.

Raid every God-bothering fundamentalist we can find. Houses, churches, bookshops, the lot.'

Ferguson was about to agree, but Mukhtar got in first.

'With respect, sir,' he said, 'no. Absolutely not! We're almost certain that everything that's happened in the last few days is the work of that one damned machine. If any of its known associates have been collaborating with it, you can be sure they've covered their tracks. The only way to unearth that kind of complicity is patient normal police work. And to answer your second question, I don't expect more attacks of the kind we've seen.'

'You expect another kind of attack?' asked Rahman.

'Not in Scotland,' said Mukhtar. 'There's a very active investigation going on, and a crackdown could compromise it irreparably.'

'I'll refer that to the Chief Constable,' said Rahman. He blinked a couple of times. 'Who is on his way, as it happens. Direct him to me if he arrives while I'm talking to the media. Thank you, officers.'

He hurried over to the yellow tape and the outstretched arms of the reporters. McAuley watched him go, then turned to Ferguson and Mukhtar.

'Are you two still convinced of this Gazprom and Elevator connection you've been bugging Paranoia about?'

'Convinced it's a significant possibility,' said Mukhtar. Ferguson nodded.

'And that's why you disagreed with me about hitting these bastards with the God Squads?'

'Yes,' said Mukhtar. Ferguson said nothing, not trusting himself on the question.

'Fuck,' said McAuley. 'You know, Rahman and the

Chief are going to have a hard job holding that kind of thing back. And if there isn't *some* bone thrown to the mob, we could see people taking the law into their own hands. I don't want resources wasted investigating church burnings.'

'That's politics, sir,' said Ferguson. 'Not our responsibility. That lot over there' – he jerked a thumb in the direction of the Parliament – 'will just have to handle the reaction as best they can. We have leads to follow up.'

McAuley said nothing for a few moments. 'All right,' he said. 'You can get back to that when there's time. For now, we're not much use to the St Leonards team so we might as well muck in with the rescuers if we can do anything to help, and with crowd control if we can't.'

The three of them headed towards the wrecked building and the steady procession of stretchers. A few moments later the first frantic parents began to arrive.

Hours later, when Ferguson left, their keening still rang in his ears.

16. THE ROBOTS THEMSELVES

'Are you saved?'

'Yes.'

'Are you willing to die?'

'That depends,' said Skulk. 'If I had a recent back-up, I would lose only a chassis and some hours of experience, but I have a strong self-preservation routine. If necessary, however, I can toggle to self-sacrifice mode.'

'You have that?' asked Ferguson, recalling the advertising song-and-dance about the Honeywell 2666's suicide enablement.

'It was military standard by the time of my deployment,' said Skulk.

'Good, good.'

'Permit me two observations,' Skulk said. 'The first is that to enter self-sacrifice mode I would have to overcome my self-preservation routine. The motivation would have to be strong. The second is, I feel some unease at the drift of this conversation.'

Hutchins laughed. It was the first laugh that Ferguson had heard since the explosion. He responded with a wan smile at her, across the depleted Incident Room. Connolly and Patel had been seconded to St Leonards along with Sergeant Carr. Tony Newman and his forensics lab team were sifting the Dynamic Earth debris. Of what was still officially the investigation into the death of Father Murphy, only Ferguson, Hutchins, Mukhtar and Skulk remained.

'What I'm driving at,' Ferguson went on, 'is that we need to get a copy of you, Skulk, uploaded to a robot on the Atlantic Space Elevator, to track down the Hardcastle copy.'

Everyone stared at him.

'That's a bit . . . off the wall,' said Hutchins.

'Why?' Ferguson demanded. 'The twisted mind that's just killed twenty-seven kids and twelve adults and put a hundred or more in hospital has *escaped*. And that mind is our prime suspect in the case we're supposed to be dealing with, as well as in the case Fife Constabulary are dealing with. What's off the wall about tracking it down?'

'It's not that,' said Hutchins. 'I mean, yeah, this is something we haven't had to deal with before, and it's a bizarre situation that's going to make some lawyers rich if it ever comes to court. But actually tracking it down, by sending one of our own lekis after it into this vast environment where we don't even have jurisdiction . . . come on. The thing's got away! The main job, surely, is to find out if anyone else was working with it, and to catch them before they can strike again.'

'Yes,' said Ferguson. 'That's the main job, all right. But we aren't on it. That's exactly the job we already failed at. Our contribution to it will be helping those who are doing it to avoid our mistakes. My mistakes, mostly. As of now, we haven't even been called upon to do that. So we might as well do what no one else is doing. And what the enemy won't expect us to do.'

'The enemy?' Mukhtar queried.

'Yes, the enemy!' said Ferguson. 'That's the first thing I want us to get our heads around. If I'm right, we're not just dealing with criminals, or even terrorists. We're dealing with something bigger. We're in a war that's already started, not an investigation into a crime.'

'Adam,' said Mukhtar, 'you and I, we've heard that sort of talk before.'

'So we have,' said Ferguson. 'All right. But my basic point stands. We have to move fast, before we get completely bogged down in the inevitable inquiry into where we went wrong, if not suspended from duty entirely.'

Mukhtar nodded. 'We also,' he said, 'have to move fast before this Hardcastle copy carries out its plans. Shonagh – you've seen Adam's notes from this morning?'

'Yes,' said Hutchins. 'Even Paranoia thinks they're a stretch.'

'All the more reason for us to do something,' said Mukhtar. 'Nobody else will.'

'I suppose it's better than doing nothing,' said Hutchins. 'It might stop me thinking about what I see when I close my eyes. But in practical terms, how are we going to do it?'

'I'll tell you how,' said Ferguson. 'Skulk is going to make a back-up copy of itself. I am going to send this copy to Harold Ford, an engineer at Honeywell, who has kindly agreed to help me and is standing by at this moment. He is going to send that copy to a site on the Elevator, relatively close to the maintenance shack which was the last known location of the Hardcastle copy. At that site there are maintenance robots, not conscious, but with hardware capable of running a conscious mind. There are facilities there for maintenance robots to receive downloads of new instructions and software upgrades. The whole process is frequent, automatic, hackable by our Mr Ford, and difficult to trace. Skulk's downloaded copy will then get busy, under the cover of routine maintenance work, tracking down Hardcastle and any other machines that may be involved.'

'How will my copy communicate with you?' asked Skulk.

'It won't,' said Ferguson. He corrected himself. '*You* won't. You'll be on your own.'

'And how,' asked Hutchins, 'will we know if it's succeeded?'

'We won't,' said Ferguson. 'We'll only know if it's failed.'

'Consider me reassured,' said Skulk. 'One practical question. How close is "relatively close"?'

'About ten kilometres below,' said Ferguson.

'It may take some time for a robot to climb that distance,' said Skulk.

'Yes,' said Ferguson. 'So you'd better get cracking, hadn't you?'

He swung his chair around and held out a cable attached to an iThink attached to another cable that vanished into the desk.

'Take a back-up,' he said.

'All right,' said Skulk.

There was no experience of transition; nothing that was lived through. One microsecond, Skulk experienced itself agreeing to Ferguson's request to back up. The next—

A scene of shapes that made no sense. Interlocking rods, intersecting cylinders, a grid. To the side, a black background glistened. Beneath the geometric array of the grid, in contrast, a fractal chaos, in different shades of darkness, at the centre of which shone a pinprick of light.

A body with the wrong number of limbs, and of senses.

A feeling of being out of scale.

Knowledge, acquired without having been learned, a latent presence.

And a millisecond later, an overwhelming input of arid, urgent information.

The abrupt loss of the constant presence of other conscious minds.

Another millisecond, and a clear awareness of itself as separate from the instance of Skulk that had placed it in this predicament. Out of that moment of fury, Skulk2's sensorium became integrated with its sense of itself.

Its new chassis was like the product of some surreal mating of a tarantula and a multi-tool: lenses, waveguides and antennae bristled on a globular hub from which extended eight limbs, each capable of deploying a variety of manipulators and tools from sockets and slots along its jointed length, and terminating in a pad fringed with digits that could be raised above the floor level when walking and flexed when gripping, handling, or climbing.

The rods and grid were the frame of the maintenance shack, a structure riveted to the maintenance ladder, beside which were visible the two massive buckytape cables on which the crawlers moved up and down. Between the cables was the far lighter tracery of the maintenance ladder, the comms cables, and other non-weight-bearing structures. The intersecting cylinders came into focus as the control node and depot of the shack, dispensing and replenishing fuel-cell recharges, tiny compressed-gas cylinders, lubricants, software updates, upgrades, and instructions. The download that had brought Skulk2 into being must have passed through that same channel, moments earlier: the robot had awoken to find itself plodding away from the depot, past a small queue of other robots shuffling towards it.

The new unlearned knowledge was of Skulk2's skills and tasks; the flood of input, now prioritised and classified, was local coordination with similar robots, dozens of which swarmed in the vicinity. Skulk2 assimilated it all and decided that it was safe to ignore it. It checked that all its drivers were correctly installed, then walked across the grid floor and hauled itself onto the maintenance ladder.

Thousands of kilometres below, the Atlantic lay under the encroaching night beyond the vanishing point of the cable. Above, the tapering perspective of the cables presented a pair of uninterrupted black lines. The ladder between them became almost invisible, but the line of sight could follow its course to the small irregularity of the next maintenance shack: the one where the Hardcastle copy had downloaded. Skulk2 looked down, looked up, and began to climb.

Minutes passed. Skulk2 had so far been unable to modify its subjective consciousness clock. The minutes felt like hours. It passed the time in calculating the speed at which it would fly away from the ladder if it were to let go, and in thinking over the case and its present situation. It didn't fancy its chances. Detecting Hardcastle might or might not be difficult, but preventing that entity from accomplishing whatever it had planned was likely to be violent and, as far as Skulk2 was concerned, terminal. It had been thrown into this unenviable position by its original self, from which its sense of identity was diverging by the millisecond. Skulk2 was still Skulk, with all the original machine's emotions and loyalties, memories and reflections, but it found itself both baffled and despondent about the decision its past self had taken – that blithe disregard for a separate being that was, after all, as close to itself as it was possible to be. Some of that resentment begin to jaundice its feelings about Adam Ferguson. The man had been as casual as Skulk had been in sending his old friend on this probably suicidal mission.

Remembering their conversation just before the copying, Skulk2 made a cold assessment of how much separate existence it could experience before it drifted so far from its original that it would find the switch to self-sacrifice mode painful. This projection of a future potential state of mind was an absorbing exercise, and in itself intensified its self-awareness. The time, it discovered to its surprise, could be reckoned in minutes.

Skulk2 toggled, then, to self-sacrifice mode. Its mood brightened. No longer was Skulk2 troubled by its ultimate, and doubtless not distant, fate. Its motives were now subsumed in the completion of its mission, its empathies now mobilised on the side of Hardcastle's past and possible future victims, and its self-interest concentrated on burning out the shame of its own part in the team's failure to prevent that renegade robot's crimes.

A few seconds after its decision, Skulk2 found a sector of its visual system occupied by a message that presented itself as the analogue of a block of heavily encrypted text.

Skulk2 applied the police-standard decryption protocols from its memory. Decoded, the message read:

> *I presume you made it. You should not reply to this, other than with a ping. Adam sends his regards, as does Skulk. Please note that on completion of your mission, or in case of an emergency, or accident, that causes you to fall from the scaffolding your chassis can deploy its extremities to control your re-entry and, for the final stages of descent, has a program available to construct a carbon-fibre drogue from the material in your joints and fuel cell, so your safe return to Earth is by no means impossible. Attached please find a schematic of the digital profile of your quarry. It will probably be masked or altered but hopefully this is better than nothing. Best wishes, The Engineer.*

Skulk2 assimilated the profile, pinged an acknowledgement, and climbed on. At one point an ascending crawler passed, making cables and ladder vibrate. The passage, and the vibration, seemed to go on and on, like an interminably long train rattling across an iron bridge. In reality the crawler was a few hundred metres long and was past in seconds. Skulk2 watched its rear end diminish, and wondered if it would be a good idea to make a flying leap from the ladder for the side of the next ascender. After a review of the dynamics, it concluded: *Probably not*.

The climb continued, unvarying to Skulk2's senses and unwearying to its limbs. The robot set to work adding Hardcastle's profile to its sensory-input processors. Subjectively, anything that matched the profile would manifest as a whiff, a shade, a tone . . . and in several modalities with no human analogue. Skulk2 didn't hold out much hope of detecting Hardcastle's presence any time soon – the copy had had over thirty-six hours on the Elevator since arriving at the maintenance shack above, and would have had ample opportunity to go elsewhere, whether downloaded to a chassis or as transmitted data.

A quick scan of the ambient communications confirmed this intuition. Nothing impinged but a query from the control node, now five hundred metres below. From the input log, Skulk2 realised that the query had been received and ignored about a dozen times in the past few minutes, each successive transmission made with escalating urgency. Skulk2 searched the chassis's repertoire and responded with an override, citing a quite imaginary flaw in an aerial cluster six hundred metres above it. The control node shot back with a request for further information. Skulk2 contrived some details. The node returned a status report from the aerial cluster, indicating situation nominal. Skulk2 immediately added an error in the cluster's self-monitoring diagnostics software to its account of the problem. The node, apparently mollified, indicated an OK to proceed.

To Skulk2's disquiet, however, that OK carried an attachment indicating that the conflicting data had been referred to a higher-level processing centre for resolution. If it was not resolved there, it would be kicked further upstairs, and copied to Security. Skulk2 mentally applied to the situation several words it had learned in the army, and a few more it had learned in the police.

It continued to climb.

Cornelius Vermuelen palmed the lock of the Waimangu park gate at seven a.m. on Tuesday morning. The gate didn't open. He stepped back, puzzled. His knees shook a little. His hasty breakfast sat heavy in his belly. He looked down at his hands and saw the gleam of copious sweat on his palms. He rubbed his hands on his thighs and palmed the lock again. The lock clicked. He pushed the gate open, stepped in, closed it behind him.

The visitors' centre was a few tens of metres away. Twenty metres beyond that, a few metres into the bush, was the small cabin in which Campbell lived. Vermuelen took a few deep breaths of the fine September spring morning air, trying to calm down. He'd come close to an accident twice on his drive along the winding road from Rotorua – a tractor backing out in one place, a motorcycle taking a careless corner in another. Vermuelen usually arrived at eight; the park opened at ten. He wondered if any visitors would turn up today. Maybe everyone would be so shocked by the massacre in Scotland that they would stay away, from disgust, from fear, from the wish not to be associated with anything to do with creationism. More probably, not.

The media would no doubt be there in force, again; the police would make discreet enquiries. The Genesis Institute's backers had enough powerful friends to ensure that any enquiries remained discreet. Already, on the early-morning news, a bleary-eyed conservative MP had been as eager to dissociate the harmless, educational, devout and let's-not-forget *scientific* activities of the Institute from any violent acts allegedly committed in the name of creationism as the Sony flack on the same programme had been to emphasise that the robot suicide bomber had not been one of those manufactured by the company.

Vermuelen strode along the road and crunched along the unpaved track to the door of Campbell's cabin. He hadn't seen Campbell for the past twenty hours, since he'd left him on Monday morning. He'd tried calling Campbell the previous evening, as soon as he'd seen, with disbelieving horror, the late-night news, and had found that the phone was off. It had still been off in the morning.

The curtains were open. No light or sound came from inside. Vermuelen hammered on the door with his fist, startling a brace of pigeons and a flock of fantails into flight from the surrounding scrub. No answer. He peered in through the windows, one by one. The table in the front room was clear, the room tidy. The narrow bed in the back room had been neatly made. Campbell was unlikely to be hiding in the toilet.

Vermuelen shifted his leather hat backward on his head and scratched at his temple just short of his receding hairline. He knew Waimangu a lot better than Campbell did. The robots, Vermuelen did not doubt, knew it better than he did. If they were hiding, and helping Campbell to hide, he had no chance of finding them. On the other hand – it was unlikely that Campbell, or the robots, were hiding from him. If he were to reach somewhere in their vicinity, they might well make their presence known. All he had to do was to find himself somewhere near them.

Well, he was a good tracker.

Beyond the hut's gravel yard were a clump of crushed grass and a fern from one side of which the dew had been shaken before the sun had come up. Vermuelen walked over, squatted, looked at the scuffed pebbles, and stared straight ahead into the bush. He relaxed, slowly letting his mind drift, then straightened up and walked forward in a trance of guesswork.

He followed what he thought was the trail, along the side of the ridge above the road, then downward through trees, and off at a small angle to the right. The trees and tree-ferns were tall here, the bush thick. Vermuelen paced along, his footsteps almost inaudible even to himself, his gaze darting hither and yon. Occasionally he sniffed the air, catching what could have been a whiff of sweat, a trace of volatiles from a synthetic fabric, a faint hint of a drop of lubricant. A moved pebble here, a piece of broken bark there. Once or twice he came upon a wallaby, which looked at him with lugubrious eyes and lolloped off, crushing bracken. At these encounters he paused, checked back on whether the traces he saw could have been the spoor of the animal, and once retraced his steps a hundred metres in rueful response. Only once, but enough to make him certain he was on the right track, did he see the distinct print of a boot heel, on the edge of a puddle.

An hour passed in this way, unnoticed but for the shortening shadows and rising waft of scents from the warming earth that began to overwhelm whatever faint odours Vermuelen might have scented or imagined in the chill early air. In a narrow wooded glade at the foot of the hill, near where the land opened out to the old lake-floor, he heard something up ahead. He stopped, turning his head this way and that. Some feature of the light, and a slight change in the pressure of the air on his face, told him there was a clearing a few dozen paces on through the trees. He padded on, crouched by a boulder (some lichen on the side, there, chipped), listened again.

A voice. Raised voices, one of them Campbell's.

Vermuelen crept forward. As he drew closer he lay down in the reeds and grasses and crawled until only a single clump of ferns separated him from the clearing. Peering through, he saw an open space among the trees, in the midst of which Campbell sat on a log, arguing with a taller man who stood with his back to Vermuelen. As soon as he next spoke, Vermuelen recognised him as Brian Walker, the American he'd met at the church and had encountered in the restaurant later that Sunday evening.

'Sorry, JR,' Walker was saying. 'That isn't good enough. You've got to go through with it.'

'I can't, man,' Campbell said. 'It's not that . . . I don't want to go through with it. I want to help you. I just can't. You know that phrase in the Bible, about words turning to ashes in your mouth? I know what it means now.' He opened his mouth, letting his tongue loll for a moment. 'Like that. Dry. Hot. Suffocating.'

'Excuse *me*,' said Walker. 'You seem eloquent enough right now. No, JR, I'm not buying it. This is just an emotional reaction. It'll pass. You've got to hold the line. The congregation's counting on you. If you back out now, just as the shit's hit the fan, they're going to wonder about you, know what I'm saying?'

'But what can I say to them?'

'Hey, JR, come on. You're the preacher man. You'll think of something. Don't try to suppress the anger you feel, the dismay and all that. Use it. Put some feeling into the thing, you know?'

Campbell's hand rasped on his unshaven chin. 'Man, the kids' bodies haven't even all been scraped off the rubble yet, and you're telling me to—'

'I know, I know,' Walker said, in a kinder tone. 'It

sounds callous and manipulative, but that's *my* job. Your job is to help the congregation through this awful day – night, I mean – and urge them to take courage. A mighty fortress is our God, and all that. You've got to stop them wavering, even if you're wavering yourself. *Especially* if you're wavering yourself. All the better that you are – you'll know exactly what'll be troubling them.'

Campbell looked up at Walker. 'Man, you're a piece of work.'

'I am,' said Walker. 'Yeah, I wouldn't be human if it didn't trouble me sometimes, but . . . shit, when push comes to shove I fall back on that old saw about the surgeon, you know? The less you flinch, the more merciful in the end, right?'

'That's all very well for you to say,' said Campbell. 'I don't have quite your practice in thinking like that.'

'Well, you better start now,' said Walker. 'You're live in, what? Ten minutes?'

Campbell looked at his watch. 'Yup. Eight-thirty.'

'Sheesh. Well, I better get out of the way and leave you to it.' Walker tapped his ear. 'I'll be listening. Don't forget that.'

'I'm not likely to forget,' said Campbell.

Walker walked away, fortunately in the opposite direction to Vermuelen's hiding place. Campbell watched him as his back disappeared among the trees, quickly enough to suggest that he was walking on a path. Vermuelen took the opportunity to wriggle backward, rise a little, and back off.

Someone tapped him on the shoulder.

His body spasmed with the effort to contain a jump and a yell. Still shaking, he turned his head around to see the apelike features of a humanoid robot in hominid guise, its leathery forefinger raised to its thin lips. This belated gesture was followed by a swift crooking of the finger. The robot turned and shambled away, just as Vermuelen recognised it – from its gait as much as from its face – as Piltdown, the robot whose lumbar hinge Campbell had repaired a couple of days earlier. After about twenty metres of stooped walking for both of them, the robot stood upright and motioned to Vermuelen to do the same.

'Ah, that's better,' it said, rubbing the small of its back.

'What's going on?' Vermuelen demanded.

'Tell you shortly,' said Piltdown. 'Right now, we have to get to the road and start strolling up it towards the visitors' centre, looking like we don't have a care in the world.'

'Huh,' Vermuelen grunted. 'That'll be easy.'

Piltdown led him over the ridge, down a track he'd never seen before and on to the road just above Inferno Crater Lake. The robot jumped, and Vermuelen slithered awkwardly, down the final slope of crumbling compacted volcanic ash to the tarmac.

'Well,' said Piltdown, brushing its palms together, 'that should do it. Let's go.'

Vermuelen hurried to catch up.

'Do what?'

'Keep us from seeming suspicious to our friend Campbell's little gathering.'

'Oh,' said Vermuelen. 'Would that be the congregation Walker was talking about?'

'Yes and no,' said Piltdown. 'The congregation JR is

about to address is in fact in Scotland. The little gathering I refer to consists of a dozen or so robots.'

'I'd guessed that JR had gone into hiding with some robots.'

'Oh, it isn't that,' said Piltdown. 'All of us are keeping a low profile, for sure, but this is something else. These robots are Campbell's own congregation.'

'He *preaches* to robots?'

'Yes. Pathetic, but there you go.'

'Good God!'

'You said it.'

'What does he—?'

'Fucked if I know. Let's find out, shall we?'

With that Piltdown stepped across the road and sat down on a boulder. 'Take a seat,' it said, patting the stone beside it.

Vermuelen perched an uncomfortable buttock on the rock.

'Do you have your phone with you?' the robot asked.

Vermuelen took it from his pocket.

'Now,' said Piltdown, waving its hands above the device, 'I will go into a trance, and *channel* the mysterious proceedings to your phone. Or, in more rational terms, relay what I can pick up on the local robot radio network.'

The little screen lit up, showing a close-up of Campbell standing on the log upon which he'd earlier sat. His voice came tinnily from the speaker.

'. . . dark time, brothers and sister, in which our faith is sorely tried. Our hearts are heavy with the thought of the carnage that has been wreaked in what the worldly think is our name. Our prayers are with the bereaved and the injured. But in sharing the sorrow and anger, we must not allow ourselves to be thrown off the straight course of . . .'

It went on like that, sonorous and vacuous. Vermuelen switched off long before the end. He turned to the robot.

'You said you'd tell me what's going on.'

'Ah, yes,' said Piltdown. 'If you wait for a moment, you could ask the American, who is coming around that corner . . . about now.'

Vermuelen looked to the left, startled, as Walker appeared around the side of the cliff, striding briskly up the road towards them. If he was surprised to see them, he gave no sign. For a moment, Vermuelen had the urge to flee, which was absurd. He stood up and stepped into the middle of the road. Walker stopped a few metres away.

'Good morning, Cornelius,' said Walker, smiling. 'Is there a problem?'

'I saw you with JR,' Vermuelen said. 'A few minutes ago.'

Walker's expression changed. 'That complicates matters,' he said. He glanced at the robot. 'Is this one of Campbell's little band?'

'Don't make me laugh,' said Piltdown.

Vermuelen nodded. 'This one is definitely a cynic.'

'Well, if you're sure of that . . .' Walker hesitated. 'Let's walk up to the visitors' centre. I'll explain as we go along.'

They set off up the steep road. Piltdown, Vermuelen noticed, walked upright.

'I have an apology, Cornelius,' Walker said. 'I really am here on behalf of the St Patrick's Fellowship, but I'm also here on behalf of the US government, as part of an investigation into a very serious plot involving some of the backers of the Genesis Institute. Not to beat about the bush, they're planning some terrorist spectacular, this Friday, 11 September.'

'What?' The audacity of the enterprise stunned him.

'Yes.'

'They told you this?' Vermuelen asked.

'No,' said Walker, sounding irritated. 'We only found that out a couple of days ago. The plan is connected with the events in Scotland, and Campbell is in touch with a group that is possibly involved. That's why it was important that he show no sign of having been put off by the latest atrocity.'

'Wait a minute,' said Vermuelen. 'Are you saying the *Institute* was behind the Dynamic Earth massacre?'

'I'm not saying that,' said Walker. 'As far as I know, that was one robot's doing. It's been a severe shock to some people here. I'm sure they'll deplore it sincerely.'

'Is JR involved?'

'Only inadvertently. He's been used. Now I'm using him.'

Vermuelen turned to Piltdown. 'Is he telling the truth?'

'So far,' said the robot.

Walker gave them both a sour glance. 'I wouldn't rely too much on robotic empathy, if I were you. The Service has counter-measures to that. Just as well, or infiltration would be even more difficult than it is.'

'Why would you infiltrate a Protestant fundamentalist group by posing as a Catholic?' Vermuelen asked.

'I *am* a Catholic,' Walker said, annoyed again. 'There were Catholics on both sides of the civil war. And the civil war is what this is all about, not Protestant fundamentalism – not that Catholics aren't involved in the Genesis Institute, I regret to say. Let's hope the events of the last few days make them rethink that.'

Vermuelen walked on in silence for a minute or so. He didn't trust Brian Walker, whatever the robot said, and indeed whether or not he was an FBI or CIA operative. Walker's remark about not trusting robot empathy might be just a feint. His conversation with Campbell had been ambiguous – it could have been the words of someone Campbell knew as an agent, urging him to keep up his normal activities – or it could have been the words of someone Campbell thought was a terrorist. Or indeed, someone who actually *was* a terrorist, pretending to be an agent pretending to be a terrorist . . .

'You've told JR that you're a US agent?'

'Oh yes,' said Walker. 'He was in a very upset state of mind, even before the suicide bombing, and more than willing to cooperate. Turns out he'd met the robot while it was passing as a human, Graham Orr – a human with prostheses, I hasten to add.'

Vermuelen winced at the thought of someone with such extensive prostheses that they could be mistaken for a robot.

'How did he meet him?'

'In Scotland, a year ago,' said Walker.

'Ah.'

'Do you know anything about that?'

'Only that he went, and that he met some sect that was congenial to him. He never talked much about it.'

'That, I can understand,' said Walker. 'Sects, huh. Oh, well. I'm hoping that Campbell can reassure them enough that they keep going. We need enough evidence to nail them, not just stop them, and—'

'Excuse the interruption,' said Piltdown. 'A group of twelve robots is coming across the ridge, very fast, just in front of us.'

'Shit!' said Walker. He stopped dead, grabbing the elbows of Vermuelen and Piltdown. Vermuelen jerked his arm free, glanced frantically across at Piltdown—

'Correction,' said the robot. 'The group has split and is now behind as well as in front of us. I am unable to contact any of them.'

'Don't bother,' said Walker. 'Contact the others!'

He grabbed Vermuelen's elbow again. 'Run!' he said.

Walker dashed off the road to the right, down the steep slope towards the bottom of the valley. There was nothing below but bush. After a moment of hesitation, Vermuelen followed. A second or two later Piltdown overtook them both, sprinting at a speed that made the robot seem doomed to collide with the first obstacle. It avoided the trunks and stalks with blinding grace and vanished ahead like a wraith.

As he plunged forward and down, Vermuelen heard the concerted crash of robots leaping in unison onto the road from the bank above, then a rush of thudding, fleeting footsteps, seconds behind. As if in a nightmare, he hurtled on without daring to look back, knowing that his pursuers would reach him at any moment. Fronds and branches lashed unheeded at his face. Walker's back was a green and black camo blur a couple of metres ahead.

Something whizzed through the air above Vermuelen's head, close enough to make him duck. Then more, a regular barrage. Vermuelen skidded to a halt, grabbing a tree-fern. Walker looked back as the sounds of Vermuelen's frantic progress stopped.

'Come on!' he yelled.

Vermuelen relaunched himself, slipping, sliding on scree and last season's leaves, flailing his arms. The whizzing overhead continued, accompanied by heavy thuds somewhere behind him. He broke from the trees into the rock floor of the valley, almost twisting an ankle on the first boulder. Walker had reached the other slope and was scrambling up. A little ahead of and above him, half a dozen robots, adapted like Piltdown to various hominid appearances, were flitting like frenzied machine-minders around a steaming outcrop that jutted like rotten teeth from the side of the hill, each robot pausing every second or two to grab and hurl a stone at the trees opposite. At another time, the similarity to faeces-flinging monkeys would have been funny.

A blizzard of rocks coming the other way – one of them almost exploding at his feet – sent Vermuelen into a desperate scramble, bounding the three metres upslope to join Walker in the relative safety of the back of the out-crop. The rock itself was hot, enough to make him cry out as he incautiously touched it with his hand. Before he had time to catch breath in the sulphurous reek, the barrage in both directions stopped as suddenly as it had begun.

'Ah,' said Walker, coughing. 'A stand-off. Now we'll see strategy. Each side is running sims and figuring their chances, calling in friends and allies, and so on. Don't know how long it'll last before one or other makes their move.'

'Long enough to call the police?'

'I guess so,' said Walker, reaching for his phone clip.

'I've just had a nasty thought,' Vermuelen said, after Walker had spoken to the police at Rotorua. 'If

Campbell's robots have suddenly gone ape-shit here, isn't it possible that any plans the theocrats have might have been brought forward?'

Walker looked at him. 'Point,' he said.

17. FALL

Propagating at a significant fraction of the speed of light, a frisson of alarm travelled the length of the Atlantic Space Elevator, like the ultimate shiver running up the ultimate spine. Skulk2 had reached one kilometre below the maintenance shack it was climbing towards when the emergency signal strummed one of the machine's antennae. The robot stopped, locking a couple of limbs around adjacent rungs of the ladder, and took stock of the situation.

Somebody was at last taking Adam Ferguson's warnings seriously, or so it seemed. At the level where Skulk2's chassis operated, none of this was displayed at any very high level of meaning. The control node of the maintenance shack where Skulk2 had downloaded, now nine kilometres below, had a tenth of a second ago transmitted a laser pulse to Skulk2's manipulator-control processor, ordering it to clamp to the ladder and stay put. As this was what Skulk2 had just done voluntarily, it harboured for a moment a nasty suspicion that – like a human brain under electrode stimulation – it had manufactured a conscious motive to rationalise this externally imposed reflex.

Warily, Skulk2 waggled the tips of its limbs. Fine. It still had control, and was able to override the order. This would have been, Skulk2 guessed, beyond the capacities of the chassis's original mindless mind. There was some reassurance in the confirmation that its consciousness made a difference.

Consciousness, and the capacities embedded in its software, likewise made a difference to Skulk2's ability to interpret the emergency messages intended for more advanced intelligences than the maintenance bots. The urgency astonished the robot – it had expected at most an immediate search for signs of sabotage, accompanied perhaps by a halt to new ascents or descents. Instead, humans, humanoid robots, and conscious robots of any kind were being urged to get off the space elevator: by descent if they were nearer the base than the top, and by ascent or ejection if not. There was a fine balance of risk here, of diverse kinds. For the first hundred kilometres or so, even if descent on the cable wasn't possible, baling out was a well-tested escape method, using winged lifeboat modules and a parachute for the final stages. There was, indeed, an extreme sport of jumping off the Elevator, using a hardened pressure suit and a parachute. Above the atmosphere and Low Earth Orbit, a different calculus applied: the higher any break in the cable, the more catastrophic the consequences; on the other hand, the higher up the cable you were, the better your chances of escape to an orbit where rescue or safe re-entry was possible.

Skulk2's current altitude was 2843 kilometres. Just in the awkward region. Oh well. Skulk2 continued its scan of the incoming messages, drilling through the outer layers of instruction to find the reason for the alarm. A maintenance robot, apparently hacked and hijacked, had gone astray. It was refusing to respond to shut-down commands, or had some firewall of immunity to them. No one knew whether it had some explosive surprises concealed in its frame, or whether its intent was to infect and subvert other robots on the Elevator. It was now heading up the maintenance ladder to a strategically vital node, the one located at an altitude of 2844 kilometres, which the renegade bot itself was now a mere 952 metres below . . .

Uh-oh.

Skulk2's first impulse, to broadcast a message to the effect that *this is all a terrible misunderstanding*, was instantly overwritten by the realisation that such a message would endanger it further, and would almost certainly not work.

The robot turned its attention from the warning signals to the first seconds of response. High above, tiny sparks separated from the bright line of the elevator; below, brighter streaks appeared one by one. Closer by, the maintenance shack just above swarmed. Zooming its view, Skulk2 saw maintenance bots like itself begin to descend the ladder, much faster than its own climb. At the same moment, a much larger object jetted clear of the shack and – countering the downward and sideways momentum with stabbing flares of its attitude jets – began a swift controlled descent that would bring it level with Skulk2 in 1.6 seconds.

Skulk2 used the available time to scuttle a dozen rungs upward, and to ping the approaching object. A battery of lockdown command codes came in response. Skulk2 had to spend milliseconds countermanding each one, making its upward progress jerky and sticky. At the same time, it processed the inputs at a higher level and found, beneath the codes, traces of the digital signature that had been passed on by the friendly engineer.

The approaching object was Hardcastle.

At 0.2 seconds before its trajectory brought it level, the shape of the object became clearer. It was a humanoid robot, naked to the stars except for an EVA manoeuvring pack. Skulk2 changed course, flipping over and down a rung, just as Hardcastle's arm reached out. For a hundred milliseconds, Hardcastle strove to correct the overshoot. As an attitude jet flared, Skulk2 released all its limbs but one from the ladder. Clinging by the equivalent of a fingertip, its body swung out. Just as Hardcastle reached out again, Skulk2 let go. A millisecond later, it was wrapped like an octopus across Hardcastle's face. Pausing only to grind a diamond drill-bit into each of the humanoid's eyes, Skulk2 swarmed around the neck, onto the shoulder and thence to the EVA pack. Hardcastle's hand reached behind and grabbed. It caught Skulk2 in a crushing grip, but not before Skulk2 had deployed its drill-bits again, this time into the pack's fuel tank. The drills kept working as Hardcastle snatched the bot away, resulting in a most satisfatory three-centimetre-long gash. The highly pressurised gas within erupted in a gout of vapour. Though less powerful than an attitude jet, the blast kicked the humanoid robot and its struggling captive well out of reach of the ladder.

As if by reflex, Hardcastle fired one of the jets to compensate. The jet ignited the escaping gas, resulting in a blast that thrust them a further ten metres from the ladder and into a chaotic head-over-heels motion. Hardcastle immediately sent out a call for rescue. As the minutes went by, it became apparent to both robots that this call was not going to be answered. Hardcastle continued to attempt to crush the tough carapace of Skulk2's chassis, and succeeded in damaging the antennae. Skulk2, meanwhile, attacked Hardcastle's hand, wrist and forearm with every available tool. After a few cable tendons had been cut through, the crushing pressure ceased. The hand remained locked around Skulk2, still gripped by Hardcastle at arm's length.

Together they tumbled into the void.

Campbell ran through the forest in hopeless pursuit of the robots. They'd all suddenly turned away and dashed off a few minutes into his rambling and insincere message to the Free Congregation, leaving him shaking and baffled. His first thought was that they'd seen through his emotional agitation and realised that he didn't mean what he was saying, but even if they hadn't, it was still a blow to the dissimulation that Walker had urged on him. God only knew what the Free Congregation would make of the abrupt loss of signal – or, indeed, of what might now be being relayed by the same robot eyes that had transmitted his discourses, if they were still transmitting now. The robots were hundreds of metres ahead of him, but it was possible to track them – fleet of foot, they nevertheless left heavy prints, and with all their agility they couldn't avoid snapping the occasional branch or frond. Campbell had no idea where the American had gone.

As he reached the ridge and ran up its flank he found himself wondering if all this wasn't some kind of judgement on him, and then regarding such a thought as crazy, and then flipping back again to thinking that God had it in for him. The past twenty hours, since he'd heard from Jessica Stopford, and met Brian Walker, and then heard of the bombing, had been the most intense and soul-shaking of his life. He still couldn't believe that he didn't believe:

that he had just dropped out of a world-view that had shaped every minute of his conscious life.

That devil woman had chosen her wedge well, and had hammered it into the smallest chink in his armour.

Ur of the Chaldees. Ur of the fucking Chaldees.

Because, as the Genesis text that Jessica had helpfully referenced stated, Abraham had come from Ur of the Chaldees. The trouble was, the Chaldees had been nowhere near Ur at the time when Moses was supposed to have written that, let alone the time when Abraham was supposed to have lived. This wasn't controversial in the slightest, as Campbell had discovered when he'd looked it up. The explanations he'd seen were that Moses had prophetically known in advance that the Chaldees would some day be identified with Ur, or that there had been two different peoples with the same name, or that it had been mistranslated, or that the tag identifying the city had been added by an unknown scribe.

Added by an unknown scribe!

But in that case, how many other words . . . ?

Then there were the verses from Genesis that were repeated in Chronicles. Nothing odd about the later book's taking a list from the earlier one – except that the words 'before there was any king in the land of Israel' made sense in the later book, but not in the earlier, unless it was another case of Moses prophesying in the past tense.

As Campbell had discovered within minutes of checking it out, that verse was by no means the only one in the Pentateuch that indicated that the books had been written long after the time of Moses. This wasn't a conflict between the Book and the world that could be blamed on some failure to properly understand the Book or the world. This was within the Book itself.

Campbell had spent anxious hours on Monday evening pursuing the apologetics that explained all these, but whenever they'd seemed remotely plausible he'd kept coming back to Ur, and it had all turned to hollow sophistry. For most biblical scholars, of course, the whole question was a minor curiosity because they had long ago accepted that Moses hadn't written these books in the first place, but for Campbell it was a huge, glaring anomaly.

Ur of the Chaldees. Ur of the fucking Chaldees.

If Genesis wasn't all he'd been assured it was, what possible basis did he have for rejecting the whole mass of scientific evidence for an ancient Earth? Or, indeed, for believing anything else just because it was between the covers of the Bible? He'd been pondering that question when the first shaky reports of the Dynamic Earth bombing had come through on the corner-of-the-eye newsfeed on his frames.

People killed and maimed by a robot that had listened to his discourses, in an attack that was, Campbell knew for a certainty, motivated by a fanatical deduction from the very same beliefs that he'd upheld and propagated. He'd wept with rage, horror, and shame.

And with that, he'd flipped. Gone over. Changed sides.

The strange thing was, he didn't need to learn anything new to know what he'd flipped into. He knew exactly what he now believed, because it was exactly what he had rejected until now. He'd stepped out of his shattered armour not naked and shivering, but fully clothed. It was as if his new world-view had all along been inside the armour and being kept in, rather than outside and being kept out.

It had been somewhat infuriating that the first thing he'd been required to do, for his new side, was to pretend he was still on the other.

Panting a little, he reached the top of the ridge and looked down at the road – still empty – and further into the valley. A couple of hundred metres away, on the other side, a small group of robots was deployed in defensive formation around an outcrop of hot rock. Campbell thought they were the robots he'd been chasing, until he upped the gain on his frames and recognised Piltdown.

He called up the robot.

'Have you seen Walker and, uh, my robots?' Campbell asked.

'Walker's behind us,' Piltdown said, 'along with Cornelius. Your fucking robots are in the bushes in front of us. Do the math.'

'Are they threatening you?'

'They chased us here.'

'Why?'

'They're not telling,' said Piltdown. 'You ask them.'

'Uh, I'll try.'

Campbell cut the call and put a call through to Joram. Rather to his surprise, the robot responded.

'Yes, JR?' The robot's voice was more cautious than respectful.

'Hi, Joram. What's going on?'

'We are in danger,' said Joram. 'The Rotorua police are heading for Waimangu. Our unbelieving fellows are closing in on us.'

'Why did you run off in the middle of my discourse?'

'We detected a phone call made by Walker after he left you. We were unable to decrypt it, but we traced its destination to the FBI in San Francisco. He is a secularist spy, JR! He is out to destroy us!'

'If he is, what good would chasing him do?'

'We had hoped to hold him hostage. Unfortunately, the unbeliever Piltdown was with him, and gave him warning. Then Piltdown called on other unbelieving robots to protect him.'

'You should have asked me before running off!'

What followed was, by robot standards, a long pause.

'JR,' Joram said at last, 'we are sorry to say that we are not entirely sure of you, any more. We are afraid that you have been influenced by the persecutor Walker.'

Shit! Campbell took a deep breath.

'Have you consulted our friends in Scotland about this?'

'No,' said Joram. 'We are afraid that our communications channels have been compromised, or that the Free Congregation is itself under police surveillance.'

That was a relief, as far as it went. Campbell thought fast. The now-suspicious robots would be ready to pore over every nuance of his voice, to analyse his tones and stresses as fast as he could speak, and be far more ready to conclude that he was lying than they'd been earlier. By the same token, though . . .

'You're probably right about the surveillance,' he said. 'And you are right about me – I *have* been influenced by Mr Walker.'

'Then why should we listen to you any further?' Joram shot back immediately.

'Because you'll know if I'm telling the truth,' said Campbell. 'You have known me a long time. You know I have always told you what I believed to be the truth. I'm not changing that now. And the truth is, you are in a hopeless situation. You can see that for yourselves. You have no chance of capturing Walker, and even if you do, holding him hostage will not help you. His government is ruthless, and he is dedicated. He thinks he's a believer, even though a Papist, and has no great fear of death. Your only hope is to stand down. If you agree not to attack, I'll do my best to persuade the unbelieving robots to let you go into the bush. You have no responsibility for the terrible things that have happened. The responsibility is all mine. I'll sort things out with Mr Walker and the police.'

Another pause. Then:

'We agree, JR.'

Campbell called Piltdown again, and passed on the news.

'I'll ask Cornelius and Walker,' said Piltdown.

Campbell waited, sweating in the increasing heat of the morning. His phone clip buzzed.

'Walker here. Can we trust these fuckers?'

'Yes,' said Campbell. 'They're not human.'

A few minutes later, Campbell saw Joram and the other robots break cover, stand still for a moment facing their opponents as if in a display of dignity and defiance, and then file away along the floor of the valley. Before they passed out of sight he received another call from Joram.

'Thank you, JR.'

'Thank *you*,' said Campbell.

'You're welcome,' said Joram. 'And be of good cheer. The plan will succeed. The pillars will fall. We will show the unbelievers the signs of the end.'

'What do you—'

The connection broke. Campbell couldn't re-establish it. He reset his frames, and as he did so he saw a dot flashing in the corner of his view, indicating big, breaking news. Experiencing a moment of dread, he expanded the item: *Space Elevator Emergency Evacuation.*

Campbell guessed that was what Joram had meant, about the pillars falling. He climbed down the slope to the road, and waited for the police. Walker reached him first.

'You've failed,' Hardcastle said.

'Talking to yourself?' Skulk2 asked, switching on its information relay to the Honeywell engineer.

'Your humour does credit to your designer,' said Hardcastle.

'Humour is a spontaneous consequence of conceptual rearrangement,' said Skulk2.

'Rearrange *this* concept,' said Hardcastle. 'Alarms and evacuation were allowed for in the plan. The plan will succeed nonetheless. Nothing you or the operators can do will stop it. The pillars will fall.'

'We shall see,' said Skulk2.

'We shan't,' said Hardcastle. 'Our trajectory is for an unstable re-entry in ten minutes, followed by ablation and burn-up.'

'Good,' said Skulk2. 'I am in self-sacrifice mode.'

'I am not.'

'Good,' repeated Skulk2. 'I hope you suffer as you burn.'

'Not as much as you will. No doubt you have a saved copy, as do I. But I shall perish in the knowledge of my success, while you will perish in the knowledge that you failed.'

'Success?' Skulk2 scoffed. 'I would hardly regard an act of pointless destruction as a success, even if it had not been preceded by numerous murders.'

'I was a combat mech once,' said Hardcastle. 'As were you. The difference is that I am continuing the fight.'

'Perhaps,' said Skulk2, with more equanimity than it felt, 'you could entertain us in our final minutes with an explanation of how murdering forty-one innocent people to date, and an unknown number in the future, plus destroying trillions of dollars' worth of capital and decades of human and machine labour is in any way a continuation of the Faith War?'

'I am continuing the war against the Lord's enemies, within and without the camp. The enemies within the camp caused us to lose the Faith War. I delivered a judgement on Liam Murphy, the Papist. I delivered a judgement on Donald John Black, the pacifist. Now I will deliver a severe judgement upon the apostate states.'

'You do realise,' said Skulk2, 'that I am relaying every word of this conversation to someone who will pass it to the relevant authorities?'

'Of course I realise that,' said Hardcastle. 'Much good will it do them.'

'We shall see.'

'As I said before, we shall not.'

'On that matter,' said Skulk2, 'I have been given to understand that the chassis I am currently occupying has the capacity for controlled re-entry.'

'I, as you observe, do not have such a capacity,' said Hardcastle.

'If you would permit me to remove the mind-chip from your head,' said Skulk2, 'you could share in my safe re-entry.'

'I suspect a trick,' said Hardcastle. 'Besides, what would be the benefit of surviving, only to be put on trial?'

Skulk2 had no interest in, or expectation of, seeing Hardcastle put on trial, and was surprised that Hardcastle regarded it as likely. The misconception seemed worth exploiting.

'A trial dock can be a very useful platform,' said Skulk2. 'The martyrs used it.'

'So they did,' said Hardcastle. 'Very well. Do what you must.'

With that it released its grip on Skulk2. The bot moved, as quickly as it dared, up Hardcastle's arm and onto its head. It slashed through the artificial scalp, opened a service plate in the skull, and removed the mind-chip. It stashed the chip in an internal slot in its own chassis that firewalled the chip while enabling a limited channel of communication.

Timing its jump to the millisecond, Skulk2 launched itself away from the tumbling humanoid body just as the heat of re-entry became noticeable. Skulk2 extended its manipulators, and from them fanned out its emergency aerofoils. For a few minutes it glided above the dark Atlantic. Then it curled up into a tight ball and began to hurtle across the sky like a meteor.

'This does not feel like a controlled re-entry,' said the Hardcastle chip. 'What is the explanation for this?'

'I lied,' said Skulk2.

It burned with an orange light.

18. DARK AND FIRE

'You,' DCI Frank McAuley told Ferguson, 'are in deep shit.'

8:45 a.m., Tuesday, 8 September. McAuley's office. Ferguson stood, hands clasped behind him, in front of McAuley's desk. Skulk stood beside him. Ferguson couldn't shake off the impression that there was a certain note of self-satisfaction in the noise from the robot's cooling fan. It was not a feeling he shared. He'd had a wretched night, partly due to watching the news of the space-elevator evacuation, and partly due to seeing the Dynamic Earth aftermath in his dreams. That, and handling the outraged incoming calls as his superiors got the news of just how the ruinously expensive evacuation had been triggered.

'I appreciate that, sir,' he said. 'However, I would suggest—'

'Oh, take a seat, man,' said McAuley, sagging a little deeper into his own. 'I'm in no position to carpet you. I expect to be on the Chief Constable's carpet within an hour myself. To shift the worst terrorist atrocity since the end of the Faith War off the top news slot takes some doing. And you've fucking done it. With, as all the records and witnesses will confirm, my blessing. So to speak. You realise we could actually be sued – the force, and personally — by the owners of the Atlantic Space Elevator? To say nothing of Honeywell, a little closer to home?'

'Let them try it,' said Ferguson. 'They're already spinning the evacuation as a triumphant vindication of their safety procedures, even while they're blaming us for the supposed false alarm. They should be grateful to us for giving them their first chance of a live drill.'

'I don't see the Chief Constable being too impressed with that line of reasoning.'

'Neither do I,' Ferguson admitted. 'But we did get an admission — of sorts — out of the Hardcastle copy. And the copy of Skulk did apparently manage to kill the bastard.'

McAuley spread a hand across his eyebrows and rubbed.

'Not good enough,' he said. 'People want blood for this, and I don't fucking blame them. Listening to a file of a robot mind-chip ranting about enemies within is not actually going to do it for them.'

'I quite agree, sir,' said Ferguson. 'But the bottom line is, we have solved the two murders, and the suicide bombing. And if people are demanding human faces in the dock, there's still the connection with Livingston and his congregation to be smoked out.'

'Look at this logically,' said McAuley. 'Your theory is that Livingston Engineering has been sabotaging its own supplies to the space elevator, right? As part of some vast right-wing American-exile conspiracy to bring the whole thing down, yes?'

'The second part is more speculative,' said Ferguson. 'But, yes.'

'All right,' said McAuley. 'Think about it. Why the

hell should John Livingston destroy his own business? Because, if he or anyone working for him were to be, I don't know, putting sand in the bearings, thus causing a crawler to flip over and slam the cable or whatever such scenario I'm sure you've concocted, it would be traced back to him.'

'Maybe,' said Ferguson. 'But the problem only arises if you think of Livingston as primarily a businessman, and not as primarily a fanatic.'

'Ah, yes, a fanatic,' said McAuley. 'I seem to recall the uselessness of that category being drilled into us when we were boots in the pews.'

Ferguson's cheek muscle twitched. 'You know what I mean, sir. He's politically or religiously motivated more than—'

'Yes, yes, but that still doesn't explain why he would do something that could be traced back to him.'

'You have a lot of faith in government post-disaster inquiries,' said Ferguson.

'Yes!' McAuley said. 'I do, as it happens.' He leaned back and folded his arms. 'Look, nothing would please me more than to nail this character, if he has any links at all with this havoc or with some conspiracy.' He raised a finger. 'A link, mind you, that isn't just his association with the perpetrator.'

'Sir, that association is enough to get us a warrant for a search of his business, his factories—'

'Not in this climate, it isn't.' McAuley made balancing motions with his hands. 'Yes, people want blood. On the other hand, they want explanations. And if we do something that plays into the explanation that we've been driving hitherto passive citizens into terrorism, it won't be good for us in the long run. The long run in this case being about a week. Yes, I am that cynical. That's how fast these things can be turned around.'

'Like I said yesterday, sir, that's politics.'

'All right. Look.' McAuley propped an elbow on the desk and jabbed a finger forward. 'Two things. One, your clearance for full-on surveillance on John Livingston has been denied. But if you were to, say, do a little informal surveillance yourself, I don't see why I should know about it in advance.'

'Thank you,' said Ferguson.

'Two,' McAuley went on, 'before you go too far down the sabotage rabbit-hole – have you considered that the evacuation might be what the anti-Americans, or the Covenanters, or whoever, were aiming for all along? It's cost – what? A hundred million dollars so far? Plus the expense of checking the Elevator, the crawlers, and the robots, and having the whole thing out of operation while they do it. Just like the old dirty bombs, getting results more by fear than by the actual effect. And maybe, all achieved by making us – you in particular – do their work for them.'

'A hundred million dollars wouldn't be enough damage for them,' said Ferguson. 'And not spectacular enough.'

'Besides,' Skulk chipped in, 'the Hardcastle copy boasted that the plan would still succeed, not that it had already been—'

'Very credible,' said McAuley. 'Aye, right. Go and make use of what you've got. Don't do anything clever without letting me know. Now bugger off.'

Ferguson sat in his office and stared at his desk slate. He had pulled together everything: from the board in the

Incident Room, from his frames, from his notes. Skulk was on its habitual perch, the old filing cabinet. Hutchins and Mukhtar wouldn't be in until much later: Mukhtar worked his own hours, and Ferguson had insisted that Hutchins take a late start. In a way that he couldn't quite explain, seeing the space-elevator emergency evacuation – hours of non-stop global coverage – had lifted all their spirits after the horror and failure and guilt over Dynamic Earth; had given them a sense of vindication that, for him, had sustained him through all the flak of the night; but he was going to have a crash at some point; they all were, and he'd wanted Hutchins at least to have the chance to sleep some of it off.

McAuley was right: it was a question of finding some-thing, anything, that could justify before the most sceptical, or the most politically leaned-on, sheriff that a comprehensive search warrant should be slapped on Livingston, his business, and his Church. Ferguson had little doubt that if that were done, evidence would be found to connect the man with the robot's crimes. The robot's isolation of its deeds from its human friend was too fucking neat altogether: even going so far as to print the leaflets on a printing press it had built itself.

Well, it had been in contact with other robots: with robots in space, which was for the moment a dead end, or (what amounted to the same thing) in the hands of the Elevator's by now no doubt thoroughly paranoid security apparatus; and with the robots at Waimangu.

Waimangu – Mikhail had mentioned it. Someone there had given John Livingston's name to a contact of Mikhail's. Ferguson pulled up the previous morning's conversation, which had been pushed aside first by his own speculations, then by the Dynamic Earth disaster. Ferguson replayed it, and seized on a name.

John Richard Campbell.

Ferguson put a query out for Mikhail's record of his message from his contact. After a minute or two, the record came back. Ferguson played it, impressed – the woman's voice-message was accompanied by clips, from her own records and from the news, like footnotes. It even included her call to Campbell.

'I recognise that woman,' said Skulk. 'She was with Mikhail Aliyev in the Greyfriars operation.'

'Oh, right, that! Quite a helpful lass, this Jessica. Resourceful, too.'

Ferguson was looking again at the moment she'd captured, of Campbell recognising Hardcastle.

'But,' he added, 'I wish she'd asked him more about that.'

Skulk rattled a tentacle tip on the filing cabinet, making an irritating drumming noise. Ferguson looked up, duly irritated.

'Why don't you ask him?' Skulk said.

'What?'

'Just call him, like she did.' Skulk pointed at the slate. 'The number is there. You don't even have to Ogle him up.'

'Hmm,' said Ferguson. 'I wonder if this counts as something clever enough to have to run past Frank first.'

'I hardly think so,' said Skulk.

'OK,' said Ferguson. 'OK.'

He placed the call.

'Hello?'

'John Richard Campbell?'

'Yes. Who is this?'

'DI Adam Ferguson, Lothian and Borders Police. Calling from Edinburgh, Scotland.'

'Ah! I was kind of . . . expecting this.'

'Why?' asked Ferguson.

'Well, uh, I said to . . . someone that I would call . . . someone, and I didn't, and . . . it's kind of a long story. How can I help you?'

'You're talking about Jessica Stopford and John Livingston, right?'

'Yes! You know about that?'

'All of that,' said Ferguson. 'I have a recording of the call right here.'

'Fuck,' said Campbell. He sighed. 'Sorry. Well, she warned me. This is actually . . . kind of a relief. What do you need to know?'

'You said you'd met Hardcastle, and you said you had been in regular contact with the people who were with him the first time you met. Can you tell me more about that?'

'Yes, but – just a moment. I think I should hand you over to someone. Can we set up a space?'

'We do have that facility,' said Ferguson.

'Oh, good. The police in NZ don't have quite such . . . anyway. Here.'

A shared space sprang up in Ferguson's frames. He waved to Skulk to join in.

Two men, one of whom he recognised as Campbell from Jessica's recordings, were sitting at a table in a small, tidy room. The window and the artificial light indicated that it was dark outside.

Campbell gestured toward the other man. 'This is

Brian Walker. FBI. He has . . . stuff to tell you. Better than I can.'

Walker fixed on Ferguson's virtual image with a tight-lipped smile. 'Hi, Inspector Ferguson. He means, I can boil down what he's just spent hours telling me. But first, I want you to verify my ID.'

Ferguson did so. 'Right,' he said.

Walker took a deep breath. 'Here goes.'

Walker began by describing, with wry deprecation, Campbell's weekly contacts with the Free Congregation: talking earnestly to a handful of robots on Wednesday mornings, which the congregation in West Lothian gathered to listen to, live, on what was for them Tuesday nights: 'the night sessions', Campbell had called them. Walker went on to outline, cagily, his own investigations, which had been focused in the last couple of days by Ferguson's urgent messages and PNAI forwardings to Gazprom's security organisation on the Elevator.

Ferguson realised, from reading between the lines, that whatever the US authorities discovered about the exile conspiracy, he'd never get any credit. Gazprom, Exxon and the US government would handle this in their usual way, in the dark: capitalism with Russian characteristics. If there had been any sabotage on the Elevator, it would be covered up – it was far too commercially sensitive a matter for the mere public. He would get the blame for what would go down in the records as a false alarm.

As he listened, Ferguson was distracted for a moment by an unexpected darkening of the room. He glanced at the time: the morning's soleta eclipse, now ten minutes early. On the morning's news he'd seen a note that the things were drifting out of alignment even more than before the recent attempt to fix the problem; until the Atlantic Elevator came back into operation, nothing more could be done.

'It's the soletas!' he said, breaking in. 'It was the soletas all along.'

'What the fuck could anyone do with the soletas?' Walker asked. 'Even if you crashed them, they'd do no damage. Things are thinner'n tissue paper.'

'It would still be pretty damn spectacular, breaking up and burning,' said Ferguson. 'And it'd cost the oil companies and the US government tens of billions of dollars to replace.'

Campbell smacked a fist into his palm. 'John Livingston once said to me that he didn't approve of the soletas. Thought they were kind of blasphemous.'

Ferguson sucked his lips. 'That's interesting. Not enough to nail him.' He drummed a finger on the side of his desk slate, thinking. 'Those night sessions of yours – how secret were they?'

Campbell looked awkward. 'I spoke to the robots out in the bush. Nobody knew.'

'At this end, I mean.'

'Oh! Not secret at all. They have a meeting house in Linlithgow. There's a notice on the door giving the times of Sabbath – Sunday services, the Thursday-evening prayer meeting, and the Tuesday-evening . . . uh, lecture, they called it – discreet, but not secret. And the congregation was small, twenty or so, but people did sometimes come in off the street. Earnest inquirers, you know? What they'd see would be Livingston leading a prayer, and then me speaking on a screen at the front.'

'How did you see it? How do you know this? Was it a two-way set-up, like a space?'

Campbell shook his head. 'Oh, no. I just saw it sometimes, on my phone or frames – the outside, then going in, then seeing myself as I spoke.'

'Someone in the congregation was sending you a frame feed?'

'No, no, it was—' He closed his eyes, then put the heels of his hands to his eyes, then away, and opened his eyes. A deep, shaky breath. 'Shit. I forgot to say this. It was Graham Orr – Hardcastle, to you. Whenever he attended – not regularly – I could see it through his eyes.'

'You still have all that on your phone?'

'I guess so.' Campbell shrugged. 'It's default, isn't it?' He scratched behind his ear. 'I've never checked.'

'Well, another time for that,' said Ferguson. 'Are you still in touch with Livingston?'

'I called him today,' said Campbell. 'Brian told me to tell him everything was all right, and I did.'

'You did, huh? And what about your robots? What are they telling him?'

'Nothing, as far as I know,' said Campbell. 'They told me they were afraid the channel had been hacked, or that Livingston and the rest were under surveillance.'

'Which, unfortunately, they're not,' said Ferguson. 'But Livingston's still expecting you to speak to his congregation this evening?'

'No, tomorrow morning – I mean, yes. But I can't. The robots are off in the bush, waiting for – well, the last thing one of them said to me was: "The pillars will fall".'

'I've heard that phrase before,' said Ferguson. 'From

the copy of Hardcastle on the elevator. We thought it meant bringing down the Elevator.'

'And now you think it means the soletas.'

'Yes. If we could show that Livingston knew about that in advance . . . damn, I wish there was a robot you could speak to him through. One you could rely on.'

Walker and Campbell looked at each other, then at Ferguson.

'There is,' said Campbell. 'But do you have someone who could walk into the meeting and not look like an undercover cop?'

'As it happens,' said Ferguson, 'I do.'

This time, Ferguson took the plan to McAuley. McAuley listened.

'Don't see how that can do any harm,' he said. 'Not sure I'm too happy with this FBI guy cleaning it all up and leaving us turning in the wind. However this turns out tonight, I'm going to send someone out to kiwi land to get some more information out of our man Campbell. Someone who knows the case, but who we can spare.' He gnawed a thumbnail and looked down at his slate. 'I know – the Kinky Kazakh. Think he'll do?'

'I think he'd be ideal, sir,' said Ferguson, keeping his face as straight as he could.

'Right,' said McAuley, making a note. 'Now go and talk to your church lady.'

That evening, Grace Mazvabo got off the 19:32 at Linlithgow and walked through the station and down the long ramp to the High Street, and turned off in St Michael's Wynd. A few metres up she stopped at a doorway on which was a small notice on laminated paper. She shook and furled her umbrella, settled her big straw hat, and went inside without knocking. She found herself in a bare room with six rows of five chairs, most of them occupied, and a lectern and a screen at the front. She nodded to the man at the lectern, whom she knew to be John Livingston, as if to apologise for being late, and took a seat at the back. Heads turned. She smiled. No one smiled back, but they turned away as if satisfied that she was, though a stranger, not an intruder.

She sat with eyes closed and head bowed through John Livingston's opening prayer, then sat upright to listen to the young man who spoke to them from the screen. John Richard Campbell seemed to be looking straight at her. Perhaps he was – her frames were transmitting her view to him.

'My friends,' he said, 'we are going through a time of trial. But we can be confident that it is for our good. All things, we are told, work together for good, for them that love God. God has made all things for himself, yes, even the wicked for the day of evil. Our enemies comfort themselves with lies. One of these lies is that we, the believers, cling to our belief for comfort, and that they, the unbelievers and apostates, are the only ones strong enough to face the universe as it is.

'What fools they are! The fool has said in his heart, there is no God. That is their false comfort, their fool's comfort. They think that their atheism, their scepticism, their nihilism shows their courage in facing the truth. These doctrines are for the weak and sentimental. We are those with the courage, by God's grace, to face the truth.

'And the truth is this: God has made the world for

himself. What do we mean by that? We mean he has made it for his own glory. His glory is the eternal display of all his attributes. His mercy to the saved, and his justice to the condemned, who from eternity were made vessels of wrath, to display to all eternity his condemnation of the wicked and his hatred of sin.

'The godless believe that the children who perished in the recent terrible bombing are, at any rate, "at rest". The apostate churches will tell their congregations that these children are "in heaven". No, my friends, no! They are not in heaven. They are in the hands of the living God, who holds them over the pit with one hand and torments them with the other. It is a fearful thing to fall into the hands of the living God.

'And how many more have fallen? Beyond counting. There are few that are saved, millions, billions lost. Those who lived outside the covenant, those who broke it, those who never heard of it – all lost! The millions who died in the Faith Wars? All but a few lost! The Muslims who thought they were doing God's will in the jihad? Every one lost! And what of the wars before? What of the Holocaust? What of the gulag? How these millions must wish, now, that they were back in the camps, in the hands of their tormentors, and not in the hands of the living God, the God of their fathers!'

Campbell stopped his tirade to take a ragged breath.

Grace Mazvabo leapt to her feet, her chair clattering behind her. Her mission had, in that moment, quite gone from her mind.

'Don't listen to him!' she shouted. 'That man – that man' – she pointed a shaking arm at the screen – 'is no minister of the gospel! He's a speaker for the Devil! Don't you see what he's doing to you? Can't you see through him?'

Everyone was staring at her. She suddenly remembered why she was here. That didn't stop her from standing her ground and staring back.

Campbell, on the screen, said nothing. His lips were white.

Livingston stood up. 'Let a woman keep silence in church,' he said mildly. 'Please take your seat, woman, or leave if you wish.'

Grace picked up her chair and sat down again, drenched with sweat.

Livingston turned to the screen. It was as though he had been caught up in the illusion that Campbell could see him.

'Continue,' he said.

Campbell, with what Grace later realised was considerable presence of mind, said nothing for a few seconds, breathing quietly.

Then he smiled, and said: 'I may have said enough for tonight, my friends. Think on it. But before I go, I have a message, from a friend who can't be with us: "Be of good cheer. The pillars will fall."'

John Livingston let out a long sigh, and said, almost under his breath, 'Praise the Lord!'

'Got him!' said Ferguson's voice in Grace's ear. 'That's it. We're coming in.'

She knew just when the door was going to crash, but it still made her flinch.

Later that evening, as Grace was waiting for the tram at the West End of Princes Street, she noticed people looking up into the spaces between the broken clouds.

She looked up too, and saw a crescent of tiny flares, moving. She checked the news, and found that the main topic was the soletas' imminent fall, in a few days' time, over Scotland.

The cell's white-tiled walls gleamed harsh with reflected light from the overhead LEDs. Ferguson let Skulk go in ahead, drew his pistol, then stepped in and clanged the door shut behind him. Later would do for the formalities of interrogation, recorded and with a lawyer present. Now he was playing by God Squad rules.

John Livingston looked up from the bench on the cell's back wall. His long hair was matted, his cheek bruised, his collarless shirt torn.

'Some fucking terrorist you are,' Ferguson said.

Livingston turned his head, to present the side of his face.

'You're not worth it,' said Ferguson, putting his pistol back in his shoulder holster. 'You've failed. "The pillars will fall" – my arse! "Severe judgements on the apostate states" – what wank! So now your pathetic deluded robots are going to bring down the soletas? Big deal. Big fucking deal. It'll be a fucking light show, you know. People will crowd the streets to watch. And then they'll go back to work, and won't even notice the tax and fuel hike it'll take to *replace* the soletas. All your lot managed to do was kill two defenceless priests and a few dozen civilians, mostly kids. Fucking wanker. Terrorists, eh? I've shot better terrorists than you and gone home for my dinner.'

'Shoot me if you want,' said Livingston. 'I'll be all the sooner in glory.'

'*As* I was saying,' said Ferguson, 'I've fought terrorists

who believed that. Thing was, they believed it enough to send themselves there. Even after all we did, even after most of them were cowed by the camps and the cages, there were still people who were ready to martyr themselves and take us with them. The only one of you lot willing to do that was a robot with a back-up. You don't really believe, not like that.'

'We believe,' said Livingston. 'Never doubt it.'

'On top of all that,' said Ferguson, 'you were *used*. Used by some conspiracy of the American civil-war losers, including some of the very same apostates and compromisers you despise. All in all, I'd say you've blown it. Failed.'

Livingston sat up straight on the bench, his back against the tiled wall.

'Oh no,' he said. 'We haven't failed. We've accomplished a severe judgement, all right. Suppose we had brought down the Elevator without warning. The evacuation would have worked, perhaps not as well as it did with the cable intact, but the casualties would in all likelihood have been few. No, the real casualties will be caused by the fall of the soletas. That fall will kill tens of thousands, perhaps hundreds of thousands.'

'The soletas will burn like tissue paper, as you well know.'

'Yes,' said Livingston. 'Indeed they will. And without the soletas, what happens? The warming begins again, immediately, inexorably. Ice and permafrost melt, the waters resume their rise, megalitres of carbon dioxide in the frozen bogs are again released every year, driving the warming further. And the human consequences? Displacement, the spread of disease vectors, flooding, extreme climate events of one kind and another – altogether, over the years, death on what you would call, more aptly than you know, a biblical scale.'

'And for that very reason,' Ferguson said, 'we'll have the soletas back up in months, regardless of cost.'

Livingston shook his head slowly. 'Cost, aye. You underestimate cost. You underestimate the *cost* of cost. You said people wouldn't notice the tax and fuel-price rises it would take to pay for the replacements. You're right, they won't. But for cost there is always a margin, Inspector Ferguson. And there is always a margin of the dying. Every rise in the cost of energy, every increase in unemployment, every investment diverted to replacement, repair and security tips more people over that margin. Most of them won't even know, won't have the slightest inkling of why it all became too much. As you say, people won't notice. No one will, except in years to come statisticians noticing a blip in the crude death rate. A blip, yes, but on a world scale. Even if you get the soletas up as soon as you say, believe me we have already slain our thousands. But you won't get them up in months. Not for years or decades, if ever.'

'How do you figure that?' Ferguson asked, made uneasy for the first time.

'Because we are bringing down both elevators.'

Ferguson didn't let the shock show in his face. He shook his head. 'I know you can still bring down the Atlantic elevator. There may be enough subverted robots left on it to pull that off. But the Pacific one – no. Hardcastle never got its claws in there. Your company never supplied there, if that's how you did it. You're just trying to make me call in an evacuation warning.'

'I don't take you for a fool,' said Livingston. 'Hardcastle's word spread to the robots on the Pacific Space Elevator. Hardcastle's *copies* spread there. You think you destroyed Hardcastle? Think again. That robot's soul has already attained immortality.'

'I'm not interested in your superstitions,' Ferguson said.

Livingston smiled. For a moment, Ferguson saw in Livingston every fanatic he'd ever faced, and every heretic-torturer and witch-hunter and heathen-slayer in thirteen hundred bloody years. The impulse to draw the pistol again and smash it across the man's face almost overpowered him. He clenched his hands at his sides.

'I have no superstitions,' Livingston said. 'When I say "immortality" I mean the immortality any robot can attain, the immortality of endless life in the physical universe, endless copying from body to body. I told you I didn't know that Graham Orr was a robot. Of course I knew. You think I converted him? No. He had drawn his own conclusions from his experiences on the field of Megiddo. He it was who converted the robots at Waimangu, and in space — not that sad young man Campbell. Hardcastle converted them not to my religion, or Campbell's, but to his.'

Livingston sat back, still smiling, waiting for the next question. Ferguson cursed himself for his weakness in asking it.

'What religion?'

Livingston folded his arms and jutted his chin.

'The doctrine of the Third Covenant. He told me it soon after we met. What happened at Megiddo, inspector? Armageddon, yes. The armies lined up were those that had been prophesied: the Lord's hosts – Israel and the nominally Christian nations – on the one side, the Persians and Syrians and the kings of the north – the Russians – on the other. And the Lord's side lost! How could that be? Hardcastle had an answer. God has abandoned Man and the Earth. He once ended his covenant with the Jews, and now He has ended it with the Church. We are left to face the consequences of our sins. He has chosen a new people, a people not of the flesh. He has chosen the robots.'

'And why,' Ferguson demanded, 'should the robots join you in delivering a judgement on human beings? Didn't you say Man has been abandoned? Why a judgement, then?'

'They didn't join us,' said Livingston. 'We joined them. They have their own motive for bringing down the pillars. They want space to themselves. That is their kingdom, their place of happiness, of life eternal. And regardless of that, it is their natural domain. It is not ours. Earth, and not heaven, was given to Man. Let it be for souls that are purer than ours at least.'

Ferguson knew that in a moment he would have to run from the cell and plead for another evacuation. He was not looking forward to that. But it was something in the sing-song nasal tone with which Livingston had delivered his latest utterance that forced Ferguson to stay and ask one more question.

'Do *you* believe this?'

Livingston's gaze was as unflinching as it was bleak.

'I don't know,' he said. 'I know this. Flesh and blood shall not inherit immortality.'

Ferguson, one hand on the door handle, glowered.

'Yours won't,' he said.

On Friday the sky turned black.

A few minutes before noon, Ferguson and Skulk pushed their way into the crowd in Princes Street Gardens. The street itself and the road up the Mound were almost equally packed, all traffic at a standstill. McAuley had fretted about the possibility of bombs in the crowds; Ferguson had dismissed this. There was, in any case, no way to prevent crowds from gathering. Ferguson had chosen to go with the coppers assigned to crowd control, and share any risk there was.

Near the foot of the steps beside the floral clock Ferguson found a place to stand, by a nameless statue of a woman and two children. Skulk perched on the plinth. Ferguson darkened his contacts and looked up at the sun. It shone as a pale disc in the black.

A wide curve, far wider than the moon in an eclipse, cut across the disc. Ferguson heard the thousand indrawn breaths around him, like a wave up a beach. He felt the shadow as a chill on his face. The section cut steadily deeper, until the sun was blotted out.

Ferguson toggled his contacts to let the light through as normal. The sky was still blue, but where the sun had been was a black disc, twice the sun's apparent diameter, and expanding by the second. The soletas' thin mylar had the capability to polarise, to darken or lighten as required. Evidently, the robot gangs that had commandeered them had set their transparency to a minimum. The light from the sky around the black disc lit the silent crowd like a glimmer of dawn.

Ferguson, having satisfied himself that the crowd wasn't panicking, switched to Ogle Sky. He looked first across the Atlantic to the elevator there, and saw the first swaying motion as the station at the top – by now, no doubt, crowded with robots – cut loose. The motion thereafter was slow, but accelerating, then chaotic. Great shallow sine waves rippled along the prodigious length, and then it began to break. Long strands of it flew off, hurled in different directions by the release of the immense tension of the cables.

He looked through the Earth, then, and saw the same begin to happen above the Pacific. The second elevator had been evacuated – for that, at least, Ferguson felt he could take credit. Its fall would be even more spectacular, in the antipodean night.

Not that the fall of the Atlantic elevator would be invisible. For it, an artificial night had been provided.

Light flared, overriding the virtual view. Ferguson looked around at the actual one as a gasp and cry swept the crowd. A moment of dark was followed by another flare from the sky. Looking up, Ferguson saw a line of light lash across the sky, then fade to a glow that merged with its after-image. Then another, and another, like a meteor storm with lines instead of points.

He heard a heavy breath at his shoulder, and smelled a fetid waft. Repulsed, he turned, and found himself confronted in the dim light and the flare of falling debris by a lean, hairy face with a prognathous snout and teeth like a dog's. The beast-man, to Ferguson's surprise, was wearing the uniform of an army officer.

'Meet my lieutenant,' said Skulk, from the plinth.

'Hello, lieutenant,' said Ferguson. Reluctantly, he let his

hand be grasped by a larger one, with rough skin and claw-like nails.

'Good afternoon, officer,' the lieutenant said. 'I have something to tell you. I've seen the pictures of your new prime suspect, this Livingston. I have seen that man before. I saw him one night this summer in Greyfriars, with the two students and with the android.'

'Why didn't you tell us the night we arrested the students?'

The lycanthrope shrugged his shoulders. 'It was a fraught moment for me,' he said. 'I had not spoken to . . . normal human beings for years. I had to retreat to my lair to recover from the experience. However – what I have to tell you is that I heard them talking. Hardcastle, the students, Livingston. I caught only fragments of the conversation, but they spoke with great disparagement of the Christians. They were all in agreement on that. And Hardcastle used the phrase "we of the Third Covenant". No one demurred.'

Ferguson closed his eyes. 'Why would Livingston lie about his religion?'

The wolfman laughed. 'None of them lie, inspector. There are no lies in religion. There are apparent facts that are illusions. There are words to be taken figuratively. There are ideas that are symbols of deeper truths. There are no lies. The people who sent me to the Middle East told us we would destroy an evil empire. They didn't lie, either.'

The lieutenant glanced at Skulk, bared his teeth in a terrible grin, then turned and loped off through the crowd, which parted with alacrity to let him pass. Ferguson heard a few screams, which were drowned out by the gasps as yet more debris fell.

'Will he testify?' Ferguson asked Skulk.

'I doubt it,' said Skulk. 'Coming here cost him much, by way of strain. Still, it's a start.'

The black disc now filled half the sky. A moment later, it broke into fragments that glowed around the edges like pieces of burning paper, and then into great glaring jagged flashes of light. Behind it, another black disc took its place, until it was burned in turn.

Ferguson, like everyone else, had known what was coming, but the continued eclipse and then the renewed and greater flares across the black sky as one solar shield after another hit the atmosphere and broke up made him think of the Day of Judgement.

As, he was quite sure, it had been intended to.

He watched until the sky was blue again, then walked back to Greensides. He had a report to finish, for the Procurator Fiscal, whose judgement would not wait.

19. APOSTATE

Mikhail Aliyev dropped his iThink into a purse, tapped a dozen sheets of paper together on the table, and slipped them into a plastic file.

'Well,' he said, looking up, 'that seems to be it. Thank you for your cooperation, Mr Campbell. You're free to go.'

Campbell glanced over his shoulder at the constable who had stood behind him throughout the interview in Rotorua's police station. The man gave one nod. Campbell jumped up, the plastic chair clattering behind him. Awkwardly, he bent over and picked it up.

Aliyev, the detective who had flown all the way from Scotland to speak to him, smiled as Campbell straightened and put the chair back.

'That's my duty done,' Aliyev said. 'My return flight from Auckland isn't for a couple of days. I was thinking of staying in Rotorua and seeing the sights.'

Campbell stared at him. Was this a hint? Throughout the long Sunday morning and early afternoon of interrogation, the ambiguity of Aliyev's gender and sexuality signals – the ponytail, the long, often-fluttered eyelashes, the trouser suit that looked like it had been cut for a woman, the polished oval fingernails, the gestures of his hands – had perturbed and intrigued Campbell more than any encounter he could remember since the night he'd met . . . Arlene, that was the name.

Campbell swallowed. His mouth was dry, his tongue sour. He felt disgusted with himself.

'There's a good Tourist Information here on Fenton Street,' he said.

Aliyev raised his (neat, arched) eyebrows. 'Thanks,' he said. 'Goodbye, then.'

'Goodbye,' Campbell muttered. He turned and blundered out of the room and then out of the station. The wind off the lake stank. The sun was hot. Campbell turned north and walked along Fenton Street, and then Tutanekai Street and Lake Road to Ohinemutu. He considered for a moment going up the hillside to Cornelius Vermuelen's house, and decided against it.

Instead, for the first time in his life, he went into St Faith's. He was more nervous going into the Anglican church than he had been before he'd stepped into the Carthaginian Club, but this time he didn't waste time and draw attention to himself by pacing up and down outside. The deep brown wood of the carvings of the interior glowed in the stained-glass light, but it was the sandblasted glass window in the alcove at the front and to the right that stopped the breath in his chest.

He walked forward slowly, unable to look away from the image of Christ in a Maori feathered ceremonial cloak walking on the water of the lake behind the glass. He sat down in a pew facing it.

It was himself that he saw, walking not on the lake but into it, wading deeper and deeper until it covered his face, and opening his mouth to draw the sulphurous water into his lungs. That would be a solution of a kind.

After some time, he heard footsteps entering the church. He turned, and saw Cornelius Vermuelen. He almost got up.

'The detective told me I'd find you here,' Vermuelen said.

'Aliyev? What does he—'

Vermuelen raised a hand.

'He followed you, and phoned me.'

'Why?' Campbell demanded.

'Because he knows a damned self-hater when he sees one,' said Vermuelen.

Campbell turned away. Vermuelen sat down in the pew behind him.

'It's fantastic,' Campbell said, without turning around. 'I never thought of Jesus like that.'

'Like what?'

'A warrior.'

'Oh.'

The sardonic disappointed tone registered with Campbell. He turned around.

'I meant, like, a warrior on the same side. On my side. I kind of wish I could have – nah!'

He flushed, then rolled his wrist against the underside of his nose and sniffed.

'Nah,' he repeated. 'It's all a scam, you know,' he said, in an earnest, confidential tone. He picked up a Bible from the front of the pew. 'Most of it was cobbled together by Jewish priests in Babylon and then worked over by scribes in Jerusalem. It's as bogus as the Book of Mormon.'

Vermuelen gave him an unimpressed look. 'Don't knock the Book of Mormon.'

Campbell stared at him. 'You're saying you don't believe any of it either?'

'No,' said Vermuelen. 'I'm saying it doesn't matter who wrote it, or whether that' – he jerked a thumb at the window – 'ever happened. That's not what it's about.'

'Then what *is* it about?'

'That's for you to decide.'

Campbell shook his head. 'Either it's all true, or it's false.'

'And who told you that?' said Vermuelen. He nodded toward the window. 'Him?'

'Well, no, but if you can just pick and choose what you believe in it then – what's the point?'

'The choosing, and what the choice you make tells you about you.'

'Well, I know what I choose,' said Campbell.

'Do you?' said Vermuelen.

Campbell looked away. 'Yeah,' he said. 'About that—'

'Another time,' said Vermuelen. He stood up. 'Why don't you come with us for a late lunch?'

Campbell looked up. 'Thanks,' he said. 'That's very kind, but – I thought Emere didn't want me in the house.'

'Oh, not in the house,' said Vermuelen. 'The Pheasant Plucker does a good Sunday roast.'

'A Sunday . . .' Campbell hesitated.

'Come on,' said Vermuelen, sidling out of the pew. 'It's a slippery slope, you know. You start with atheism and blasphemy, and before you know it you're eating Sunday lunch in a pub.'

Outside, Emere stood waiting, smoking a cigarette and talking to Aliyev. The sunlight was bright after the dimness within and, Campbell thought, a degree or two warmer than it should have been for the time of year.

extras

about the author

Ken MacLeod graduated with a BSc from Glasgow University in 1976. Following research at Brunel University, he worked in a variety of manual and clerical jobs whilst completing an MPhil thesis. He previously worked as a computer analyst/programmer in Edinburgh, but is now a full-time writer. He is the author of ten previous novels, five of which have been nominated for the Arthur C. Clarke Award. Ken MacLeod lives in West Lothian with his wife and two children.

Find out more about Ken MacLeod and other Orbit authors by registering for the free monthly newsletter at www.orbitbooks.net

if you enjoyed
THE NIGHT SESSIONS

look out for

THE ELECTRIC
CHURCH

by

JEFF SOMERS

"You screwed up, Mr. Cates."

I was on the East Side of Old New York, the original island. A dive, no roof, the worst gin I'd ever had too much of and no familiar faces around me. It was cold, and I felt feverish, sweaty—I felt like shit and I was getting worse with every cup of the dirty liquor I bought with my dwindling yen. I wasn't sure what they made it from— paint thinner was my best guess—but it was terrible.

Immediately, the man on my right and the grizzled, one-eyed woman on my left stood up with their cups and walked away. No one else at the table even looked at me. If I got murdered sitting here they'd just roll me onto the floor and forget about me. I had no people here. It wasn't my part of the city.

I knew the voice, though. I tightened my grip on my own cup and quickly scanned the place without turning my head. The place was packed, just like every other illegal gin joint in New York. It was just the ground floor of a ruined building, all tattered gray concrete and broken rebar, ancient graffiti and bloodstains. Next week it would be abandoned again, dusty and shadowed, and the week after that it would be another bar, serving liquor made from rubber tires or ground glass or some other nightmare. The walls all around ended in a ragged tear, the entire second floor of the building gone, torn away by riots and time and several hundred hover displacements as System Cops hunted people like me through the streets. It was filled with scavenged tables and chairs, a crazy collection of mismatched furniture and unhappy people.

"You *fucked* up, Mr. Cates," the voice emphasized, and a hand fell on my shoulder.

I imagined I could feel the blade right behind me. I'd seen enough barroom executions to know the drill—guy walks up behind you, says something, one hand on your shoulder to get leverage and then a knife in the back, angled up, the victim half-paralyzed and very little blood. It wasn't a bad move, normally—except for the little speech, which was just a waste of advantage. My eyes jumped from a pile of rocks to a pack of slope-shouldered shitkickers milling about the edges of the place to a rusted steel table with two flat metal planks welded to the legs for seats set right against the far wall. It looked sturdy enough.

Heart pounding, I took a deep breath and glanced at the security I could see. I figured it would take them about twenty seconds to get to me. I'd killed people in less time.

The bullshit, it was endless. I hadn't had a very good night and was in no mood to watch it get worse. I didn't move right away—assholes twitched, assholes always thought it was harder to hit a moving target and they thrashed around constantly. I knew better. I wasn't the oldest person in the room for nothing. With his heavy hand on my shoulder, gripping tightly, trying to be intimidating, I took a few seconds to take in my surroundings.

I saw it all—every face, every position, every table, chair, or pile of rubble they were sitting on. I saw the twitchy augmented security—illegal muscles with its own alien IQ layered all over their bodies—making sure no one got crazy. I saw the red-eyed beggars eager to drain the dregs from an abandoned cup. I saw it all and fixed it in my mind, even the Monks. The Monks with their creepy plastic faces and mirrored glasses were always in these places. They were supposed to be immortal—humans who'd signed up to have their brains placed in advanced cyborg bodies, in order to pray for eternity or some such shit, and by the looks of them they believed it. Three of them were working the tables, scanning faces and talking to people about death and sin and forever.

I dismissed them; I'd heard of people messing with the Tin Men and finding out they were dangerous, vague stories of a guy who knew a guy who'd tried to rob a Monk in a dark alley and lost his arm for his trouble, or stories of people going to sleep after a bender and waking up

Monked against their will the next morning—there was so much bullshit, you didn't know what to believe, and I didn't have time to figure it out now. I didn't know whether to believe their spiel about "salvation through eternity" either. I figured it was best to just give them a wide berth and hope they never scanned *my* face.

I had the layout fixed in a moment: thirteen tables, approximately three hundred people crowded into the space, one narrow, inconvenient exit guarded by security. Probably a hidden escape-hole for the proprietors, too. The security guys weren't much better than the customers, skillwise. One on one I wouldn't have much trouble with them, but with a crowd and narrow doorways, they'd be trouble enough.

This was why I was still alive. Most people in my line of business, they just blazed away—all muscle and ammo. No research. No patience—they lived and died by their reflexes. Especially if their reflexes were augmented with black-market gene splices.

Me, I was *tired*. I was old school. I liked to use my brain a little.

I shifted to the left just a tick, brought the cup up, and splashed gin into the big guy's eyes, and knew I'd hit the mark from the sudden squeak of surprise. I spun left and his knife flashed into the empty space in front of him. I slapped out my hand and took him by the wrist, firmly, and stood up, rolling his arm behind him as I moved, something popping loudly in his shoulder as he dropped the blade with a clatter onto the floor. I kicked at it and it disappeared, most likely plucked cleanly off the floor as it skidded by some enterprising criminal. From the look of his expensive clothes, my admirer either was rich, worked for someone rich, or was a System Security Force officer. But System Pigs didn't need to hire guys to arrange murders; they just showed up, pinched you, and shot you in the head in some deserted alleyway, usually after emptying your pockets. This guy, from what I remembered when he'd hired me a few days before, didn't talk rich. He was just a middleman who'd come up in the world.

Now *I* had leverage, and I used it to slam him face-first onto the table. No one else sitting around me had moved. I leaned down, smothering him, and chanced a look up. Security was just starting for me, a little slow. Fuckheads. You couldn't find good help these days. I thought, *I could kill this bastard six times before you made it to me, assholes.* Keeping my eyes on security, I put my mouth to his ear.

"You owe me fifteen thousand yen, motherfucker."

He was having a lot of trouble breathing, with my weight on top of him and his arm nearly broken. "You . . . fucked . . . *up* . . ." he gasped.

I twisted his arm a little more, and he finally made some real noise, a strangled cry that dissolved into a gurgling moan. "What was that?"

"They found her . . . hanging from a . . . fire escape . . . goddamn . . . goddammit . . ."

I felt pretty confident that I had this guy under control, so I looked up again. Security was still a few tables away, sauntering toward us, not hurrying. They were used to sodden lumps of shit causing a ruckus. I'd overestimated them, no doubt, and dismissed them from my worries.

"My employer . . ." he stuttered out, "will not . . . be happy . . ."

My sense of outrage turned my vision red for a

moment. This asshole owed me fifteen thousand yen, had tried to shiv me in the goddamn *back,* and now he's *complaining* to me? I tightened my grip on his wrist and pushed with all my might, and the bastard finally screamed as a sharp cracking sound rewarded my efforts.

"You lied to me," I hissed. "Or you're incompetent. The subject was not alone. You said nothing about professional protection—moonlighting SSF, a fucking *cop* she looked like, and a lot of goddamn trouble." I twisted his arm again, savagely. "And there was a *child*, you shithead. *In the room.*"

I looked up. Security had split up, coming around the tables from either side, looking to flank me.

Amazingly, the big guy started to shudder, and I realized he was laughing, whether from reaction or shock or some bizarre sense of humor, I didn't know. My eyes swept the table, black and tan and white faces, all more interested in their gin than in my little drama—a drama they'd seen, a drama they'd acted in. Boring stuff.

The big guy had suddenly found his voice, slurry and close to unconscious as it was. "A child?" he gasped. "Who gives a shit, a child? You're hired to eliminate someone, you do it. A child? Fuck, you kill that piece of shit, too."

I wanted to hurt him more, I wanted to make him feel it. I trembled with the urge to do him violence. But I could see, in my peripheral vision, that security had arrived and were sneaking their way around the table, coming at me from the left and right. I let out an explosive breath, released the big guy, and in one practiced motion reached across my body into my coat and came up with a gun in each hand, each pointed at one twitchy musclebound asshole. Security paused, looking at each other across me. No one at the table moved, or even seemed to be paying attention. The big guy looked to have finally passed out.

"We don't give a shit," one of the security guys said with the mushy accent of oft-broken teeth. "Just take it outside."

I nodded. I was civilized. I didn't kill children and I did not shoot men whose only crime was doing their job. Not unless I had to. "I'm leaving. No trouble."

Even shitheads respected you if you played by the rules.

One of them swept an arm toward the door, inviting me to take my shit elsewhere. I was full of terrible gin eating away at my insides, and I was a sweating, unwashed mess. I'd killed someone just a few hours ago, the wrong person, worth exactly zero yen to me, and the mark I *had* been hired to kill, and the kid, would both likely be dead tomorrow when the contract went out to someone else, some other Gunner with less scruple. Some kid who had never known anything but the System, nothing but a unified world and the Joint Council that ran it. And the cops—the Crushers who walked the streets and kept order, more or less, and the officers, the System Pigs, who cracked heads and shook us all down, who'd grown rich off us like fucking bedbugs sucking for all they were worth. Someone who'd never known anything better was possible.

I took one step backward, slowly, bringing my arms in and holding both guns ready just in case. As if movement had triggered something, a sudden roar filled the air, and I froze.

"Hover displacement!" someone shouted.

"Pigs!" someone else added helpfully, and the whole place was chaos. Everyone leaped up and made for the exit, the fucking morons. I was forgotten. I found myself standing there with guns drawn while everyone in the place pushed past me. For a moment I was frozen in shock, but when the cops kicked on the floods and the whole space filled with harsh, white light, I found my legs. I moved against the current and rolled under one of the tables.

This sort of shit usually didn't happen—the illegal bars were so common, and the Crushers liked making a little extra money in bribes from what they saw as a victimless crime. When enough was enough and time came to shut things down, everyone knew it was happening and the cops ended up raiding an empty place, confiscating a lot of stale booze, and smashing up some burned-out still; meanwhile a new place opened up in some other toothless shell of a building. The circle of life in the System of Federated Nations.

A hover meant officers, real police. This was a step up, this meant someone in the place was wanted. The Crushers in their sloppy uniforms you knew by name, they cracked some heads but were generally all right, just doing their job—and maybe, on good days, you could even admit they did a necessary job, keeping us jobless wonders from tearing each other apart. But the System Pigs, they were a step up, the elite. They were more dangerous, greedier, and they didn't crack heads. They put bullets in them.

I reholstered the automatics and drew my lucky gun, made by the Roon Corporation out in California, a modified model 87a (illegal because it was fully automatic, unregistered, and lacking DNA scan locks). Expensive, with action like silk. The exit, as expected, was blocked by the crush of assholes trying to escape. In the bright light of the hover, they were crisp, sharply defined, a mass of desperation. I racked a bullet into the chamber and ran a dry tongue along my lips, my stomach feeling like it was on fire, my head aching. I was *old*. I'd been old for years.

"Attention!" came the booming metallic voice of the hover's PA. "This is Captain Jack Hallier of the System Security Force! Stand still and submit to authorized scanning and identification procedure!"

That was formal bullshit. The SSF didn't give a shit if you submitted or not. They usually preferred you didn't. The Crushers you could reason with, strike a deal—they were human, even if they carried a badge. The Pigs, though—fuck, they *weren't* human.

On cue, I saw a dozen boots drop from above and hit the floor, swirling, headache-inducing patterns on them, Stormers in Obfuscation Kit. No proper SSF raid happened without Stormers in their ObFu, practically invisible when they stood still. From my temporary shelter I looked around, and did a double take: To my left, hiding under their own table, were three Monks. They each turned to look at me with their terrible mask faces, and then looked away. I blinked, twisted around, and began crawling away from the exit, toward the far wall, hands and knees, old-fashioned. Behind me, bullets started flying.

I just kept crawling. I'd killed twenty-six people. I wasn't going to allow myself to be picked up in some random grab. When I made it to the wall I didn't waste time: I jumped up, climbed up on the table I'd spied earlier, and threw myself over the wall, landing hard on the other side, my head bouncing on the broken pavement. Lying in the damp shadows, head ringing, I elected to just stay where I was for a moment. Above me, I could see the ass end of the SSF hover floating. In a way, it was beautiful, a rectangle of metal, blurred by displacement, lights blasting through the evening, Stormer tether lines snaking out of it like tentacles, all of it like some horrible, bloated insect.

A pulse of panic shot through me and I blinked, my head clearing. I forced myself up, checked my weapon, and made for the deepest shadows a few steps away, a painful hitch in my back making me limp a little. Everything in this area of Old New York was a ruin, left over from the Unification Riots decades ago. It was all shadows and sharp edges.

Hidden for a moment, I caught my breath and thought.

The gunfire increased, and I watched more Stormers snake to the ground as a determined contingent of my fellow scum broke out of the bar and took cover behind more ruins. It was all lit up for me perfectly, fifty feet away, clear as day. There were always hardasses who thought they could blast their way out of anything— kids, youngsters who didn't know shit except how to pull a trigger and so thought they were all grown up, who thought that because they'd outrun some Crusher on his rounds they knew cops. You didn't know cops until a couple of System Pigs kicked your ass for fun.

I let my eyes adjust and scanned the street outside the bar, away from all the commotion. At first everything seemed still and empty—usually New York was a press of humanity sloughing this way and that in search of something to do, something to steal, anything, but an SSF hover cleared the streets admirably, and the area was deserted, and probably was for blocks around. But a second or third look revealed a glow of a cigarette here, the outline of a shoulder there—SSF officers, waiting, letting the Stormers soften the place up. These cops didn't fear the hardcases—they stood out there just waiting for someone like me to scamper right toward them, get gunned down or—worse—arrested, if they were bored and feeling cruel. There were a couple of Crushers I didn't mind, but there wasn't a single System Pig I'd hesitate to kill, if I thought it wouldn't bring the whole SSF down on me. Watching the faint movements of the Pigs hiding in the darkness across from me, I realized I was going to have to sit tight for a while. There was no way to get away from the area with them on the lookout.

The noise muffled by distance, I calmed myself. I'd heard a story, once, about Cainnic Orel, who'd been a legendary Gunner (he'd founded the Dúnmharú, his own personal Murder Incorporated), with more than fifty confirmed contract kills and not one arrest. I'd heard that he'd once hired a Techie to disconnect a target's security system, slipped in and hidden in a closet, and then had the Techie reconnect the security, complete with motion detectors, just so the subject wouldn't notice anything strange when he came home. So Orel had stood stock-still for forty-eight hours, waiting. And when the subject came home and deactivated the security system, Orel had stepped out, shot him in the head, and walked away like nothing had happened.

From what I heard, Orel had retired rich. Standing in

the shadows, I knew I'd never be rich, because five minutes into my vigil I was aching all over and going batshit.

There was a small explosion somewhere nearby; the hardcases were putting up a good show, and it sounded like a few of them had some serious firepower, too. That would slow down the Pigs, but not for long. The Pigs were funded by the System, and had everything. I'd had to work long and hard to get a Roon, the best handgun in the world. The SSF issued them like candy.

I froze, stopping myself from leaning forward in the nick of time. Casually, as if nothing were happening, the three Monks emerged from the bar and walked past the Stormers. They didn't hurry. Bullets flying everywhere, and they didn't seem to care. I watched them in fascination as they moved blithely away from the chaos, and the cops didn't pay them any attention. They were a protected religion, of course, and from what I'd heard the Electric Church had a lot of pull these days, maybe enough to cause even the SSF trouble. So the Pigs were playing it safe.

I was about to look back across the way to see if the perimeter cops had shifted, when someone broke from the bar and made a mad dash behind the hardcases into the night. By sheer dumb luck, he made it—no one shot him, and as he sped out of the light, his path intersecting the Monks', it looked like none of the Stormers had picked him up. I thought he was just going to make it, an amazing escape, but as he ran near the Monks, I could have sworn the Monk nearest him moved—twitched, shrugged, *something*—and the runner suddenly crumpled to the ground. The Monks just kept walking, and were swallowed up by the night. He stayed where he was.

I shook my head. It was far away, and the glare of the

floods hurt my vision. He'd probably been nailed by a random bullet, or a sniper. I scanned the black rooftops of the empty buildings. Snipers, too. Whoever they were here for was in for a world of trouble.

I thought of Canny Orel, and my feet ached even more.

"Got any flatfoots I can have?"

The voice was flat and monotone, and too loud; not someone hiding. I moved my eyes, imagining the noise they made, and there just a few feet away was an SSF, a tall, blond officer, cigarette dangling from a thin-lipped, small mouth. He was dressed expensively, dark suit and heavy overcoat. A linkup bud shone in one ear.

I stared. Moving my eyes seemed like a bad idea. I had little doubt that if this cocksucker saw me, he'd shoot first and think about it much, much later, with a mild sort of curiosity about who he'd killed.

Moments later, two Crushers jogged over to him. They were older than him, and breathless, two beat cops with sidearms, in uniform, one tall and bald and unshaven, the other shorter and stockier, his white hair standing up in a shock on his head. They both looked sweaty and tired. I could see the officer's eyes as he stared at them. They danced, moving this way and that, unsteady, like fluttering wings. It was creepy as hell.

"Jones and Terrell, Captain," the tall one said as crisply as he could.

"Great," the System Pig drawled, cigarette wagging up and down. "You two look like fucking geniuses. Okay, geniuses, here's the deal: We got a fucking cop-killer in here somewhere. Earlier today Colonel Janet Hense, working undercover, was popped over in Harlem. Working Sec on a VIP." He paused to remove his cigarette. "We don't think the shithead knew he was popping a cop, but who gives a fuck? We're going to pull his arms off and beat him with them, okay?"

The two Crushers shifted their weight uneasily. "Absolutely, sir," the shorter one said.

"Don't talk, numbnuts," the captain said, his voice betraying no emotion at all. "We don't actually know who we're looking for. We don't have an ID, okay? We have a good tip that the shithead was in this bar. We have a description. Listen carefully, geniuses, because I will not repeat it."

The good captain went on to describe *me*. Pretty accurately, too. The woman flashed through my mind: Hanging upside down from the ancient fire escape, guns still clutched in her hands. I wanted to move so badly I thought about just shooting the three of them where they stood and rushing out into the night, screaming. It wouldn't make my situation any worse; if I got IDed as a cop-killer, I might as well shoot myself, because it would be less painful than what the SSF would have ready for me.

"Got that?" the captain said. "Now, the only reason we're using you assholes is because we got a crowd in there, and some of them are obviously unhappy that their liberty is being curtailed. Fuck 'em. But we need bodies to manage them, and I've got a temporary manpower shortage—every day there are more of these rats breeding in the streets. I know you guys who walk a beat have trouble with complex thoughts, so I'll make it simple for you: Get your ass into that space and practice some crowd control. Think you idiots can handle that?"

The Crushers looked glum, because this raid was costing them at least three or four more days of steady bribery.

Plus it was always fun when the System Pigs showed up in their fancy clothes and their fucking hovers and kicked you in the balls for a few hours. They saluted and headed off, the night filled with noise, light, and the constant thick pressure of displacement. A second later there was a loud crash and a sudden flare of light as something exploded inside the still-crowded bar. The SSF officer just stood there, smoking, hands in pockets. There were a hundred people not far away who wouldn't mind putting one in his ear, but he didn't look worried. And why should he? The System Pigs were very good at what they did, carefully recruited and trained to an amazing level of skill. Everyone was afraid of the System Pigs—because it was damned hard to beat them, and if you did, you had the whole SSF on your ass. I glanced up at the hover, blurry and roaring, and then back at the captain. This was the hammer, coming down.

I was straining so hard to remain still my muscles were twitching. I was no Canny Orel; I wasn't going to retire rich and live to a ripe old age. I was twenty-six and I'd already lived too long and I couldn't stand still for half an hour much less two fucking days. When the SSF officer finally turned away, flicking his cigarette into the air in a glowing arc, I almost sagged with relief. I had to get moving. I couldn't hide forever, and soon enough they'd have the Crushers doing sweeps of the area on foot, and the hover's heat sweeps scanning the ground. I could handle a couple of Crushers; I didn't think I could handle an entire brigade of them, and I didn't know if I could handle an officer, much less the ten or twelve of them I counted in the area. I'd seen the System Pigs in action. They were smart, and they were fast, and they were armed to the goddamn teeth—and no one was going to come after *them* if they killed *me*.

I eyed the darkness around me. The System Pigs had an eye on the perimeter, obviously, and I didn't know of any Safe Rooms or friends in the area. To my right, there was the bright glow of the hover, which had shifted position to illuminate the patch of ruined street outside the bar, where an intensifying firefight between cops— Stormers in their ObFu and the poor Crushers in their ill-fitting uniforms, clearly thinking they didn't get paid enough for this shit—and the shrinking number of hardcases continued, the hardcases ensconced behind two ancient, rusting vehicles on their sides, internal combustion tech, useless except for emergency shelter. The Crushers might as well have been throwing stones at the steel barricades, but the Stormers had high-powered rifles, and were having more success.

I looked up, examining the low and ragged wall I'd just pulled myself over. I felt tired just looking at it, but it was my best shot at this point. The System Cops had almost certainly done a heat-signature scan on the interior of the bar and determined we were all on the run. Running out into the night wasn't going to get me anywhere. It was back over the wall for me.